THE COAL TOWER

TONY GENTRY

NExTExT
books

A NExTExT book

Copyright 2018 by Tony Gentry

Printed in the United States of America

Cover illustration: Sally Hemings sculpture by Todd Murphy as it looked on installation June 2000 on the old coal tower, downtown Charlottesville, Virginia.

Cover photograph: Tony Gentry.

Cover design: Stephen Gentry

Typesetting: Katy Munger

ISBN: 978-1-7327608-0-6

❀ Created with Vellum

DEDICATION

For Christine

ACKNOWLEDGMENTS

Thank you to my longtime friends Katy Munger and Paul Witcover, whose examples of artistic brilliance and fortitude have long inspired and shamed me, and whose encouragement has kept me typing.

DISCLAIMER:

This story is a work of fiction, and if you know anything about Charlottesville you'll immediately grasp that none of the characters represent any of its real citizens. There is a coal tower, of course, and enough unfortunate things have happened there that it now sits surrounded by chain link and barbed wire. But the events in this story didn't happen. I made these things up.

PROLOGUE

Every town has a place like this. In Charlottesville, Virginia, it's the coal tower. A squat, concrete bunker roughly the shape of an enormous thermos bottle, it stands shaggy with kudzu on six ponderous concrete legs next to the train tracks that run east and west through downtown. A few coal and gas trains still run along these tracks, rumbling between mines up in the mountains and power plants dotted around the Virginia Piedmont, but now that all the revamped warehouses have gone electric or solar, the tower serves no purpose. Its steel-reinforced walls are too sturdy to dynamite, and so far no developer has imagined a way to turn it into condos. At one point, years ago, a sculptor built a 20-foot tall dress frame atop the tower, then draped a giant's white cotton dress on it, naming the work in honor of Thomas Jefferson's slave mistress Sally Hemings. He meant it to be a thought-provoking, lovely memorial and provocation, and it did serve – if nothing else – as a middle finger aimed at Monticello, the Founding Father's hilltop home.

The artist was surprised, however, to learn that the dress would not stay on. He'd get a call at his studio in Staunton and drive over the mountain to find the yards of fabric that made up the sculpture's dress stretched across the honeysuckle thickets, torn and dirty, as if blown off by the wind. He'd unstitch it into washable sections, have it laundered and resewn, then spend a whole day with ladders, tools and a couple university students precariously fitting the dress back onto the frame. Two days later, he'd get the call again. This happened three times. After that, he bought a thermos of coffee and parked his pickup behind some scrap lumber by the tracks and waited. Woke up with a start to find the dress gone again, but this time it was nowhere to be found. He looked everywhere it could have blown, then noticed something, a crack in the coal chute door. The door was carved into the face of the tower ten feet off the ground, but he was able to straddle a rail siding in his pickup and hoist himself up from the cabtop. To his surprise, the door was not sealed at all, just blocked by a flap of plywood that he easily pushed aside. You couldn't see much in there, but his flashlight revealed that someone had found a use for the coal tower after all. A rusty ladder bolted onto the interior wall stretched down to a circular room littered with squatter's treasure: blankets, pans, an old mattress and piles of other debris. Crumpled in one corner, like a deflated hot air balloon, lay the torn and coal-streaked dress.

The artist climbed down inside the tower and retrieved the dress. He then notified the police and personally sealed the coal chute door with an old oaken tabletop that he bolted into the concrete. But he gave up on the dress, leaving the skeletal frame atop the tower, having convinced himself that the sculpture was more interesting that way. But really, it would have been such a hassle to dismantle it, and nobody cared anyway. When he left, as far as anybody knew, the kudzu took over. The sturdy monstrosity squatted ugly and forgotten along the tracks.

Except not really. It had taken all of five minutes to pop the door bolts with a crowbar. The squatter's camp was back in business in a week. A seasonal refuge, largely abandoned in the summer and winter, but cozy during the rains of spring and fall, it serves a transient population that the proud, go-getter town does not even imagine.

And in the summer, when the squatters are gone, local kids make it their own private club, the last place to go on the first pub crawl of their lives, a townie's holdout from the University's all-grasping frat boys and sorority sisters, who can overrun a pizza stand in a second. There it sits at the foot of downtown, a lump of gray concrete topped by a rusting skeleton, an eyesore, and beacon to the lost and yearning.

ONE

DAWN AT THE MALL

"WHAT THE?"

Startled awake, Officer Mosby pulls himself upright in the driver's seat of his Dodge Challenger cruiser, torn from a drooling swoon. He blinks off a hot flush of shame, licks copper-tasting lips, then rubs his grizzled face and gradually begins to register the squawk-box and all the familiar panorama beyond his windshield, the long stretch of bricks that pave the Downtown Mall welling to pink and gold at dawn. Relief, no soul in sight. No selfies, he prays, with the sleeping cop. Grabbing the wheel with both fists, he shakes his head alert, allowing himself one belly deep suck of the cruiser's stale air. It was just a catnap, maybe an hour, no more. In the dream, already fading off to nothing, he'd been a hound chasing foxes, urgent and driven, actually flying inches above a swath of wet leaves down a holler livid with autumn color and the baying of the pack. Then a handclap, a pop, a firecracker, from the dream?

His bleary eyes lurch to a waking scene maybe stranger than all that, a hundred yards away at the top of the store-lined stretch of pedestrian mall a herd of deer skitter and slip to a halt on the uneven brick walk. Coiled within the kind of red light alert and in-the-body vitality only wild things know, their every nerve poised for instant flight, they pose in silhouette like a fancy Christmas card. The buck takes a tentative step on a ridiculously tiny cloven hoof, calculates the challenge of the hard, uneven and slippery bricked path, balances risk and opportunity in this narrow, foreign canyon, then having somehow signaled the herd, waits for the others to move forward. They flow around him like water down the Mall.

At this distance, Mosby cannot count points, but the buck's rack crowns his head like a ridiculous tree afire with the first glow of sunrise. Those antlers sit weightless on his bull neck, the way a skater lifts his partner as they twirl. Mosby turns down his two-way, lifts the door latch and eases out to crouch behind the door, fretting at his all-too-human clumsiness. Up the Mall, the deer do not seem to have noticed, having discovered the potted plants arranged in barrels around antique lampposts. They graze hungrily on the blossoms, no more graceful in their chomping than cows at a trough.

Mosby eases the door closed without shutting it completely and dares to take a step away from the cruiser, angling for the cover of an oak. His eyes sharpen on the buck, the leader of the pack. That wary prince has not yet joined the flower feast, much as he wants to. His image ripples strangely back at him in store windows; harsh streetlight and angled shadows offer irregular cover; the rising sun rapidly narrows their window of opportunity. It's a long way to any reasonable thicket. But the six doe and two fawns take to the flowers like candy, twisting their narrow noses and long tongues within the foliage to extract and chew the velvety blossoms with simple, bovine relish.

Stock still behind the tree, Mosby watches, his jaw trembling, readily grasping the anxiety, the desperate care, of this sleek patriarch. The policeman stands gone in the hunt's great thrill, that instant identification with the wild. Ten miles from here, two months from now, 30.06 in hand, this would end in obliteration, a gunshot like coming to wipe away that girly instant of inner knowing. But it is a delicious thing, with its own acrid taste, and the one best moment he has ever known. What would some early morning jogger think, happening onto the Mall and this face off?

The deer come on, knock-kneed, heads dipping, their satellite dish ears scanning left and right, their eyes black domes like the surveillance cameras in *Kmarts*. Their cartoonish black-bulb noses and swishing flayed tails. On past the gelato shop, *Chap's Ice Cream* and the *Paramount Theatre's* glittering marquee. They round the news kiosk and skirt the fountain, nosing briefly at its chlorined splash. Their images repeating in the windows of bookstores, bars and antique shops, they miss no opportunity to strip the flowers from every Garden Club barrel they pass. Now even the old buck has surrendered to their shopping spree. It is the strangest thing, the sort of gift reserved for cabbies, bakers, late shift cops, these weird apparitions of dawn. What brought them here, out of the safety of the lowgrounds by the river? Who knows if they may make these rounds every night? If some late-to-bed bartender is not watching them now from a window above the stores, welcoming them with a raised hair of the dog, just a part of his bedtime routine?

Come on now Mosby, get back in the game. If a mall cam sees you allowing the destruction of public property, if the chief sees that, she will have your ass. Do something. But to spook them would send them off in a half dozen directions, in skittering flight down city streets, and who knows what would happen then? Dogs barking, cars crashing, hooves entangled in fences. Let them come, let them come on, and they do, until at last just yards away, his scent no longer tolerable, they jerk alert, all noses targeting the policeman beneath the tree. Close enough now to hear their shallow breaths, to count the spots fading on the fawns, to clock their pelts' fallow scent.

The buck snorts, startling Mosby, so he pulls back behind the tree, and with that the deer bolt. Amazingly, they don't scatter, leaping as a squad down a side street leading to cover. Mosby creeps up to the corner to watch them go. Already, they have regained their composure, slowing as they tip up the hill past the soup shop, pausing at the peak of Market Street, where they look both ways like good children. Blessedly, no car or bus appears to spook them. A siren down by the old Martha Jefferson Hospital whines, but they pay no attention. Flanking their king, the herd meanders on out of sight past a parking deck into the rest of their almost imaginable lives.

TWO

DAWN, THE DAY BEFORE, HEADED NORTH

COAL TRAIN HOPPER, black as ink, coal train bed don't sleep a wink. Lucas taps out the lyric on his cell, saves it as a note, then snaps the phone off to conserve its precious juice. He tries to stand up in the angled hopper bay, with one foot on either side of the chute, then bends to stow the phone in his backpack before slinging it on. The train lurches then, pitching him down hard on one elbow in the absolute dark. "Man, that was close, never would have found that phone in here." He stays on his knees to work the pack through his arms, then leans back against it, the only soft thing in this crazily-angled compartment, rubbing his elbow and gazing up at the most spectacular show on earth, the end of the night occurring everywhere, but most especially in the blast of open air directly above his head. This is where the galaxy comes out to play, sprayed like cum across the heavens. After awhile, staring up at it, the night seems as various as day, though it's all a splash of swimming white, pin-holes blown wild through a black sheet of paper. Even splayed and braced to hold the view, it can keep you occupied.

A thousand times already tonight Lucas has traced the outstretched wings and long craning neck of the Swan

9

traversing the Milky Way, with the winged horse Pegasus galloping alongside. The Little Dipper has swung on its star nail as the rattling hours expired, while occasional startling blasts of shooting stars – one green, another vivid orange – criss-crossed so brazenly that they seemed to sizzle. *Coal train bed don't sleep a wink, your lullaby's a clack and clink.* This train is long, empty and uniform, laboring for hours up an incremental grade around pinwheel cliffs. With his head down between the wheels, it's all rumble and screech, with no flat place to stretch out between the steeply angled walls, except the lips of the chute itself, and Lucas is terrified – though he suspects it's a ridiculous fear – that the chute's steel jaws might spring open while he sleeps to spit him like chaw between the rails.

The tunnels come up without warning so that wham the stars blink out, the metallic clang explodes, and for a whole minute or more sometimes he's trapped in a black kettle drum. In the night's very first tunnel, somewhere down in Carolina, a flock of bats had whipped in through the cartop. Crouched small in the bay, ducked behind upraised forearms, Lucas imagined hundreds of them – swooping, clicking and popping – desperately radar-shaping the exact size of this cage, working to stay abreast of it in flight as it shooed them through the tunnel. They seemed right in his ears, all a leathery flutter, then the sky peeled open and they were gone, chaff blown back in the wind.

A lot more tunnels, but luckily no more bats. Eventually, he grows brave or bored enough to scramble up the wall and hang at the hopper's lip, irises wide open to dim shapes in the dark, taking the snap of insects on his cheeks, as the whole line of identical coal cars goes gargling down a gap-toothed mouth cut in the face of a mountain. He thrills almost to peeing himself at that immediate dank black, the rough ceiling close enough to touch, then pow the multitudinous sky. At one point, the train runs half a dozen tunnels in an hour. Those old hard nuts had carved this track straight up the Appalachians, blasting through the heart of the oldest rock on earth. How could you sleep or even rest athwart such a history? Excitement grows and ebbs across the hours inside the honor of it all -- the illicit danger and privilege -- that churns along with yet more of the same. Sometimes he hangs by his fingers in tears, right at the edge of an exultant mistake. Then slumps to the tilted floor, praying to doze a few.

But even then, trying to sop his sputtering nerves, Lucas knows as well as he knows his name that he rides a swell, a life marker, taking a path that diverges well off the beaten way. He will remember that this night is where it began, where his real life – the one he owns – kicked off. And have the stars all his days to prove it. If he could only see Chloe now, if he could just text her at least, but no way here in the deep mountains with not a bar on his cell, and she's probably asleep anyway. *Her breath like chocolate, her sighs like songs. Her lips like summer flowers.* True but corny lines, not worth digging for his phone to add them to his song diary. Lucas squirms against his backpack, sandaled feet braking his slide into the chute, and tries to sidle into a corner, conjuring that girl clanking closer by the mile.

When his eyes next open, the contours of the hopper lie sketched before him in colorless outline, the way he imagines it seemed for the bats. The Milky Way long gone, other stars and galaxies washed out by the millions in the tide of bruised light before sunrise. He stares dreamily up at the shoebox of sky. You can't get that almost dawn color anywhere else, he thinks, and you can't stop its sneaky changes. Indigo. Indigone. Hey, a new color! A hoot to try to pin it down – when is it best, when does it start to go bland? Bent into a pretzel shape in a low corner, drily licking the coal dust from his lips, he shakes himself awake to the situation. If he's getting off, it has to be now, and not a second too soon, sick as he is of this loony bin. Scrambling up top, he peers over the lip of the car, glimpsing the lights of a town ahead past a dimly glistening trestle. As the train edges out over the river, the trestle disappears beneath it, so the whole slinking snake of it seems to tip on air. He hangs high above rock and rapids that sprawl tickled by wisps of fog. If he can just make out a sign, try to pin down where this place may lie on a map, come back to stinking human reason for one minute.

The train moves at a dirge pace off the trestle, snuffling and moaning like a zombie. Two dozen hoppers ahead, the locomotive's whistle blows for the first time all night, its mournful howl startling over the rattle and shimmy of the wheels. Lucas makes out a couple of brick storefronts and a few wooden houses lining a narrow street hung lopsided between a mountain wall and the river. All of them dark, no streetlights, just the clang-clang-clang and blinking yellow flash of the crossing sign. Maybe it's a ghost town, he thinks, making out the word *Collierville* painted in peeling black on the clapboard of a shuttered old depot. He's been out in the deep mountains all night, alone in a coal car in the middle of a long and empty train, but this sign is the loneliest thing he's seen, pinging his empty stomach with misgiving. Somewhere a hound or it could be a coyote howls in answer to the locomotive; a second dog barks viciously very close, and Lucas pulls his head down fast. He's got a name for this town, all he needs to know. He scrabbles in the backpack for his cell, swipes to the GPS map and waits as its electronic wand sweeps back and forth, searching the steely heavens for a clue.

When the triangulation locks in, Lucas' grimy finger drags the onscreen map north along the rail line thread, past Collierville – it's actually on the map! – across whole screens of empty green to a dot labeled Gardner crossed by a thin blue thread of road, then more green screen and Swords Creek, then a 3-way fork at a place called Richlands, and who knows which of those forks the train will take? On the GPS rail overlay, the map turns into spaghetti there, the one wiggly strand running up from South Carolina getting tangled and dotted with forlorn names like Grundy, Pineville, Marrowbone. And one strand only of all that knot spreading out in all directions continues on east to yet more tangles in the railyard at a place called Roanoke.

He taps the phone off, its battery down to a sliver, and sinks back into a slanted corner, beaten. This is the destination Lucas has hoped for, since plotting it out on the computer at the library in Columbia a week ago. Empty coal train north to the mountain, then loaded train east to Chloe. In the library, sneaking Skittles and scanning a map on the computer screen, that had seemed like the hard part. How to switch rides to a train headed in the right direction, instead of north to the Ohio power plants or back south again the way he's come. Then, if headed east across Virginia, the train has to take a northward fork to get anywhere near Charlottesville, Chloe's town. The south fork, where most trains out of Roanoke go, runs arrow straight down the flatlands along the Virginia-North Carolina border rolling right on to the ocean far out of his way.

Two states south, stealing time in front of a computer at the town library, it had seemed a challenge, yes, but not a deal breaker. Something to figure out when he got there, and what better choice did he have? Well, there were other choices, and as the train slows towards the rail fork at dawn they grow in their attraction as they recede in possibility. He has almost a bus fare folded tight in the secret pocket he's made at the crotch of his sawn-off jeans. Jobie'd taught him that his first hitch. Even if they conk you, they're not likely to look there. That had been a pleasure cruise, the empty grain gondola long and flat-floored, with a wide open top, and Jobie'd pointed him back the way they'd come on an actual old-fashioned box car before lighting out for Nashville or its general direction. Then he'd tried one on his own, headed wherever, but the train never stopped, never even seemed to slow, a dry wind whirling chaff inside the open-topped bin, and he was wrung-out, numb and famished when it did finally come to light long enough to clamor off, daypack and guitar across his back. That had been a cartoon small town, with an outdoor mall, and young people in new sneaks everywhere. Just laid out his pack, and before he could strum half of *Dooky* had the cash for lunch.

And then another busker'd offered him a place to crash for a few, and then Chloe, and why did he ever leave? His sister could do it, kids or not. She just sits out there on the base all day firing off texts across a half dozen time zones to Afghanistan anyway. But she wouldn't. He'd seen her bail before, would let her own mother choke on her own spit if he wasn't around. Called these weekends *respites*, like she was doing him a favor to sit and suction her own mom. *I'm just a yoyo, yearning to go, hooked on the curve of your finger. Out I fling to the end of your string, and pray that you'll let me linger.* What you call a beeyotch, sister or no.

This time he'd thought it through, the computer map in the library warning him that the straight shot route he'd taken before had gone dead since a derailment shut down the line. So this dogleg route made sense. In the library. But here he stands, peering up from the middle stretch of a long coal train that's about to slot itself onto a siding amidst a thousand other hoppers and gondola cars. Somewhere on that red blotch on his phone other trains sit fat and burdened with tons of coal, waiting for an order to start their mostly downhill roll off the mine-seamed mountains in half a dozen directions – to Baltimore, to Cleveland, to Norfolk or Charleston or Atlanta or any of the power plants in between -- and this notion of picking the right one has multiplied in its complications.

For courage, Lucas wolfs down his last half of a protein bar, swiped at a railside service station a lifetime ago yesterday. One last time, he crouches down in the bin, nervously arranging his backpack, tucking his cellphone away in a zippered side pocket, grateful he's left the old guitar at home. As Jobie'd advised, he then rubs his hands along the steel wall before smudging his face all over with coal dust. This whole transfer has to happen before daybreak. The train has to come in and park without incident or delay. He has to cross the Yard on foot, somehow avoiding the bulls and their dogs, pick a loaded train on an east-west track, and not just headed east but taking the less-traveled north fork through Charlottesville out in the middle of Virginia to DC or to the coal plant near there in some place called Bremo. Total crap shoot, but any other train and the game's up. He chuckles ruefully. Likes the sound and tries again. Probably get killed before I even find a ride, so fuggit.

All the night's exhilaration has drained through his jelly-like legs, as he hangs by his elbows on the hopper's lip, aching, dog-tired, and parch-tongued. Trapped like a rat – nothing to do but go through with it. The train has squeaked and whined its way past the forlorn rows of mobile homes and rusting cars at Gardner and Sword's Creek. More barking dogs, pickups with their headlights on at the crossings. For all he knows, he's been spotted. Maybe the train's got a camera. Some do. Since Columbia, they've been calling ahead, waiting to pounce. To drag him off, break his ribs and teeth, smash his fingers, crack his skull, and toss him to the grading. It was just an insane idea.

The dregs of one magnificent night drain fast, sky lightening in the hillside gaps to rose. His grimy hands now plainly visible before his face. Not good. Lucas drops back down into the hold again to tighten his sandals and backpack, then pulls himself up and swings a leg over the leading edge of the car, finding a foothold on a rusty outboard ladder. If there is a camera, he's made. Waves a hand in mock resignation towards the distant locomotive. Then, climbing down the ladder, he pitches onto a narrow steel grate attached to the front of the hopper. Straddling beams wide open to steel wheels that spin just inches from his feet, he startles at the cross-ties repeating in the gap between the cars. But things are still silvery here, and the wheels roll hypnotically on, relentless and deliciously tempting. This is how close you can get, right up to the maw of the dragon. Look how you can even hold it there, your only shield that hunk of meat between your ears.

If he doesn't slip, if his strength holds out, he's secure here, even hidden, until full daylight. But pulling into Richlands, the whole town seems wide awake and waiting for him. A gas station bright as a supernova, then a busy diner, people scratching themselves on porch stoops, the street full of trucks. Everybody up and at 'em already for a working Saturday in a company town. Lucas sucks back against the steel wall, in plain view if anybody actually looked. The train's not even really creeping now, moving forward in the tiniest fits and starts, as if trying to make up its mind about which of three tracks to take. Eeny-meeny-miney-mo. A drum roll of brakes moves up the line car-by-car right to his feet, causing the linked cars to seize and nearly pitching him onto the grading, before passing on to the hoppers behind. Then all over again with more slamming, convulsive lurches. Like the dragon is folding its monstrous wings after an all-night flight.

How far to the fork? The train can't just sit here with its ass hung out in the middle of town, blocking traffic all day, can it? Frozen there, helpless, he stares directly down into the rear window of somebody's kitchen, sees bare feet crossing on the board floor, almost close enough to touch. Lucas presses hard against his backpack and the wall, making himself as inconspicuous as possible. Hop off here, it could be miles to the fork and the eastbound trains, if those even exist. Gotta stay on, stick to the plan, a phrase he repeats a hundred times in the next half hour while the old dragon rattles, ripples and shakes outside its mountain cave, going exactly nowhere, while color blossoms everywhere.

And then he is off. Rolling down the gravel grading into a clump of brush, wind knocked out of his lungs by his own knees, he lies still as a dead man on his stomach, stunned by his own audacity, recovering eventually to suck in the heady perfume of the honeysuckle he's trampled. The bramble is soaking wet with dew. Coal dust streaks to ink on his arms. To his left, the black wall of the train, to his right, somebody's back-yard fence with lights on in the window just beyond. An alley of sorts between fences, just a foot path really, crammed with junk, but he lifts in terror to his hands and knees and scrambles towards it, fetching up between a washing machine and a car door, at least nominally out of sight. TV voices from the window, a snatch of old-timey song – "whachu goner dew'n I'm gone?" – heart slamming his ribs. Pale tones of morning light make the alley a tinted photograph, leaving him briefly mourning the monochrome shades and relative safety of that slow-coming dawn. Castaway in a junk pile, afraid to move a toe, but unable to stop his jaw from trembling, he flinches as brakes rattle like giant chains down the length of the train, and the hoppers nudge forward, gaining incremental speed. Stretched to his full length on the first flat surface he has known all night, seasick on a world that doesn't wobble, he comprehends that the game is over. He's lost in a watercolor blur.

THREE
CHLOE'S WORLD

AT THE END of the driveway, Chloe kicks shut the door of Joel's car without a backward glance or word. His pimped out Civic motors off, as she shoves open the wrought iron gate between its fieldstone walls and straggles up the winding graveled drive, stepping over a trio of rubber-banded newspapers scattered there. They mean the Old Man's still at work and Mom's out riding, just as she'd hoped. She trudges through dappled shadows under ginkgo trees, past mist that hunches like some kind of genie over the pool, and bends for the key in the fake rock set amidst an arranged pile of boulders that surrounds the *Venus de Milo* reproduction on its pedestal. The poolside chaises beckon. She could fall into one and drift off to an everlasting sleep.

All night as they'd trolled their club route from the *Box* and the *Silent Disco* at the *Lighthouse* downtown, to the coal tower and *Impulse,* even in Joel's cramped little car, she'd thrown out texts to the wind. Sent snapshots and voicemail. Called just to play that stupid message: "This is a digital replication of a voice from the past generated by a humanoid labeled *Lucas*. Will you please deposit an electronic replica of your voice for our collection? Snooping for you, your dear old NSA." The guy changes his message three times a day, as if anyone would even call anymore. She actually takes some delight in them, but this same rather long one has played all day and night until it had begun to tick her off. He said he would come. And then nothing.

The icy, peach-scented air of the kitchen is a hand slap as she steps indoors. She could call Ava, should try one last time for Lucas, but her phone died hours ago, Joel claimed he didn't have a cord in the car, and she doesn't dare risk the landline. Her head feels enormously swollen, a ball of yarn unraveling atop a drinking straw. She's a bedraggled doll diffracted in a fun house of gleaming cherry, marble, glass, slate and chrome, fumbling for a handful of granola from the nearest cabinet. She had thought he would come.

The climb upstairs might as well be a mountain hike. Dizzily, she falls to her knees at the throne, purging the handful of granola like thorns coming up, the jello shots, the Asian noodles, whatever is left of Joel. Menthol mouthwash completes her inner cleansing. Then the armor comes off, the heavy, clanking bling, the black work boots, the black leather shorts, at last the black t-shirt scrawled with the word *Damned,* probably some old band, in what was meant to look like pink fingernail polish across the chest. She'd gone out commando last night, had taped band aids over her nipples, but they'd still gone all perky and that's when the trouble with Joel had started. The turning point of the night, grinding in that corner at *Impulse* with her shirt up as he nibbled the band aids off while his whole lousy band of losers pinned his arms back, hooting and snapping their phones. That was when she had lost Rebecca. That's where the whole night went to hell, really, if you had to name a point.

She needs a new crew cut – it's starting to kink. One of her onyx cross earrings is missing. Perfect. The other comes off neatly, but her hands tremble almost too much to dab an alcohol-dipped *Cue Tip* on the reddened flesh beneath the silver nose-ring the parents have not yet seen. She gives up, runs steaming water to splash off what is left of the mascara and pancake. Naked before the mirror now, her image in the scalding ring of lights seems waxen, almost translucent-skinned, fairy-like. This is something she can't bear, focusing instead on the damnable freckles that spatter her cheeks. Mumbles the ritual, "my ass is so big." Then turns away to rummage for the t-shirt tucked so reverently inside her pillowcase. No big deal. Just white cotton, just a *Hanes*, a little gray under the armpits. Lucas had been gone two days before she sent him the shot of her wearing it, her trophy, and he'd texted back nothing but *gr8*. Ironic? Sincere? So what? The shirt, like Lucas, had smelled then like pumpkins and frankly is precious beyond this whole house, its humming enormity and the world surround.

A few last groaning chores before oblivion: Plug in the cell. Turn up the ringer. Lock the bedroom door. Outside her windows, the final weekend of summer explodes in all its gaudy everything, but behind black curtains and blackout blinds this suite is her cave. She has to believe he's out there, he's okay, he's on his way. It's Christmas Eve in Summer. He's on his sleigh.

FOUR

SID MOSBY – BY THE TRACKS

THE COAL TOWER has finally gone quiet, offering a few moments of peace to the man who crouches on a perch made of plywood and 2x2's laid over crossbeams at its crown. He has been there all night, bent like a Gollum beneath the concrete dome, fretting at the intruders down below. Burdened by the distractions of cell phone flashlights, boom box music, and marijuana fumes rising from the makeshift nightclub on the tower floor, it has taken him all that time to write and correct the thing that must be said. So many distractions. People down there giggling and squirming, their faces lit wanly by their phones, shuffling and flailing almost silently to their own little earbud concerts. So often he has yearned to shoo them away, claiming final ownership of this edifice they can neither appreciate nor understand. Except that would have given away his hiding place, and they probably wouldn't have listened anyway. He has a pair of rubber earplugs, a gift from Captain Steve. Good ones. They almost shut out the extraneous human chatter while at the same time opening the mind to its pulsing internal ruminations.

All night, torn by the urge to chase off the kids and the fear of discovery, he has worked desperately at the wording of his manifesto, scribbling important revelations with a fat felt tip marker on the side of a cardboard box in near darkness. Eventually, the marker had sputtered out with a last resigned squeak. The licking trick had not worked. So much more to say. A slim beam of morning light comes slanting in through a roof chink, so he can hold up the cardboard to read the night's product, pensively chewing his lip. He has worked tediously in block letters in the dark, but with care, so that every word is plain and none are crossed out. Yes, there is more to say, but this is the key, in a nutshell:

BIG GROUPS OF DEMON GENERALS SAY THAT ITS EASY TO TALK DEMONS OUT OF HELL AS LONG AS THE DEMONS THINK A MAN IS A PASTOR OR "STEVE". I'M NOT A PASTOR. AND NOT A PROPHET. AND NOT STEVE. YOU CAN GET 6 MONTHS FOR ATTACKING PASTORS AND THEY AREN'T STEVE ANYWAY.

This part of the work had come quickly, though doubts hung on each word and all of their relations to the theme had required long moments of calculation regarding their arrangement on the cardboard. He had worried mightily over the next part, fought himself for even attempting it, but finally had summoned the fortitude to write the thing that had to be said: SEE HELL IS NOT IN THE MIDDLE. NOT NOWHERE. KNOW WHERE

More to say but the ink is gone. Carefully, he tucks the raggedly torn slab of cardboard into his shirt and climbs up through the chink onto the coal tower roof, where he remembers to drag a plywood slat across the gap, weighing it down with bricks. He stands to steady himself against the base of the sculptor's dress mold, squinting up at its narrow shoulders afire with sunrise. He's been in there too long. People will see. He's miscalculated again. But he climbs down the rusted exterior ladder without incident, dropping the last ten feet to the ground onto gravel, then creeps across the four sets of railroad tracks to crawl under a gap in a chain link fence to the backyard of a bungalow that has been his only home.

Half car, half Christmas tree, a police cruiser sits dumb as an unplugged toy by the garage. Mattie's home already. Yet another misstep. Probably crashed out, but just in case he pulls himself up through the bedroom window, careful not to crease the cardboard sign tucked at his belly. He clumps down onto the floor on all fours, only to find his brother right there in the doorway, watching in disapproval from across the room, in full regalia, arms crossed and head shaking.

"Would ya use the door, Sid? I'm not gonna fix another screen."

Abashed, he scrambles to his feet, a hulking man with a thick neck and beefy hands, but can't look his slimmer, shorter brother in the eye. "Fix the screen," he mutters.

"Where've you been?" Officer Mosby demands, in his best show-me-your-license-ma'am voice.

"Where've *you* been?" Sid responds, robotically.

"You know where I've been."

"You know."

"No. Where?"

"No where."

"No, where or nowhere?" Mattie plays along, wearily.

"Nowhere," Sid replies, glancing sidelong at his brother and fingering the sign hidden under his shirt.

"That's about right. Look, Sid, I just came in here to say goodnight. I've got game duty at 1 o'clock, and all the damned UVA kids are comin' back. I'm gonna be on double shifts this whole week. So I just wanna know, are you alright?"

"Are *you* alright?"

The policeman sizes up the person he knows best in this world, looking for a clue. His big brother stands at the window in khaki shorts, filthy running shoes and a stained golf shirt, buttoned as always to the throat but never tucked in at the waist. His hair a ragged tangle about his face but sparse up top where a receding hairline almost meets the bald spot at his crown. A frat boy gone to seed. Every pocket of the cargo shorts is packed like a chipmunk's cheeks with who knows what he's found. He's one of those before and after pictures, a redo of a kid when he was five. And just as creepy as all of those pictures always are. "Look, fuck it, Sid." He turns back down the hall.

"You cussed."

"Damn, right, you old fuck."

"Don't cuss."

Sid follows Mattie down the hall to the kitchen, and they take their places at opposite ends of a dull metal table with a peeling melamine top, the table they ate at in baby chairs. Mattie's belt lies coiled between them, a lumpy snake of shiny black and gleaming silver, with red eyes and a radio hiss. They each tear into a pack of *Pop Tarts*.

Whatchu have for supper?" Mattie asks.

Chewing with a careful rhythm that seems to include a count, Sid mimics back, "What*chu* have for supper?"

"Dude, I'm tired, man, just."

Sid crumples the aluminum foil wrapper in his hand, spreads his fingers to regard its unfolding gleam. Does it again.

"Dude, I just wanna know."

"*I* just wanna know."

"Damn!" The flat of Mattie's hand slams down on the table-top, shaking the milk in his glass. Shoving himself away, he whips the police belt off the table, sweeping a stack of junk mail to the floor, and stands glaring at this man he doesn't know at all, working with all his might to reel it in, reel it in, the way they teach you in the Field. Sid has not moved, seems not to have noticed, lost in his tin foil game. It is what it is. Hefting the belt onto his shoulder, Mattie shrugs and heads off to his bedroom. Whatever it is.

Sid counts silently to six before the door slams shut, then reaches across the table to finish his brother's milk. Above the sink, a stained glass trinket hung on a string trembles with intent, splashing a dance of cheap color around the room. Red follows blue follows yellow follows blue follows red. The pattern is always the same, but you have to check. Stealthily, he pulls the cardboard sign from his shirt, lays it out on the table and tenderly fingers its words. They seem written by someone else. Make no sense at all. This is a night's work? He feels sick, and pushes the milk away. The thing about the medicine, it takes your head off, leaves you with a grain sack on your shoulders. For ages, you're just a pill in a bottle, straining to push a wad of cotton out of the top, but the cap's still on, and it's a child protection cap. The air's running out, but you can't do anything from inside, where the whole world is just more identical chalky pills and everything is a rattling jumble tinted brown. He picks up the actual pill bottle from the table. Pops it open and takes out four of the lozenges, each big enough for a horse, and dumps them in the sink. Runs warm water to dissolve them in the creeks of Virginia, go to sleep little fishies, go to sleep. Then shuffles off to the garage and his engineering books, his back hunched against the morning's rising buzz.

FIVE

DR. RAINSWORTH CANNON – INTENSIVE CARE UNIT

"MAYBE I CAN MAKE this clear to you, and maybe I can't, but hear this. I will shut this unit down in a heartbeat. Do you understand?"

Whatever the old grizzly says, even in his frequent flailing outbursts, she always thrills a little to the barrel deep voice, rich as a finger-plucked bass. "Yes sir. I do hear you. Sir."

"Then you may appreciate this fact. We have been in surgery for the past what? – nine hours – room 6 with her nasty burst aneurysm near the fornix, room 2 frankly bleeding at the eyes, this crew of residents green as grass on the hillside. I come in here, expect this ICU to be at least operative, at least viable, at least capable of some mere modicum of human life support! Do not tell me, just do not, that we are down nurses."

"We are fine. It's Labor Day weekend. Dr. Cannon."

"Labor Day – sweet irony that!"

"Sir. We have pulled in every nurse we can get, this is temporary."

"Temporary?" For a moment the booming bass line down-shifts to a rustling stage whisper that then deepens to a new rush of indignation. "So when Room 6 crumps and Room 2 goes into vasospasm and Room 4 spikes his fever? Each of which is likely within the next half hour, and when the holiday choppers stack up like Reagan National out there at the landing pad with bays full of cracked skulls?"

The charge nurse bites her lip now, calibrating a response. What went down in the operating theatre? Could this be about the stupid football game? Not her problem. She knows her best course is to ease him off the floor, get him out of his scrubs, then off premises and back in his little sports car, so that all can be right with the world. A tall order. Out of the corner of her eye, she glimpses a billing technician stifling a giggle, her two best nurses standing by the medication closet with their arms crossed, tut-tutting at the raging bull who is leaning in so close that her glasses begin to fog.

"Dr. Cannon."

"I am going to make one phone call! Do you this favor. And you can all take Labor Day and Halloween and Thanksgiving and Christmas and New Year's and all the holidays of the coming year and have your trips to Nags Head and Myrtle Beach and stuff yourselves with ribs and watermelon until you pop! I am shutting this unit down."

They have had this conversation before. Go ahead and rave, let off steam, but do not perform in this way center stage at the nursing station. The already frantic mother of a teenaged girl in a coma stands aghast at the curtain to Room 3. The automatic doors to the unit swing open, a physical therapist strolls in, stops in his tracks to catch the drift, spins on his heels and is back outside with the quick grace of a silent movie character all in about two seconds. Shift change is coming up and what her dear chief of neurosurgery does not need to know is that she will be down yet another nurse all day long. This she can handle. It is not the end of the world. He will be out basting ribs at a tailgate party at the game, half-lit on margaritas, and the rest of us will still be here, and that is the way it should be, that is fine, but this behavior has to stop, and soon, or....

"Give me the phone. Just give it to me."

"It's right here, Dr. Cannon. If you must."

"Do you give me any choice? Do you have any solution? Do you play any role around here?"

"I will fix this."

"You will fix this? How pray tell do you intend to 'fix this'?"

"Rainsworth, do this for me." Daring his given name.

"The phone."

"Before you call. One moment. Come in here, come in here to the nurse's lounge, here stop, let me get you out of these scrubs. Just come." She's an elementary school teacher now, the flat of her hand on the flat of his broad back, easing the great surgeon away from center stage.

"Do any of you people? Do any of you have one notion of duty, of responsibility, of loyalty at least to me? I don't have to tell you that I built this place. This is not just some hillbilly backwater community hospital, do you get me, and I will NOT let it fall, will NOT!"

She gets him through the door into the all but soundproofed nurse's lounge, attending to none of his rant. She is untying his gown, a huge man soaked in sweat. She has to stand on tiptoe to reach the knots of his cap. He keeps turning to face her and she keeps turning to get the knot untied at the base of his skull. They circle each other clumsily. At last he just jerks the cap off, revealing that bald and gleaming dome, and with that unleashes a primal roar, some kind of lion's call from deep in his chest, exhaling the night's exacting horrors. Then plops down in a metal frame chair, reaches for a stale donut and swallows it in two gulps.

"My cell. Get me my cell!"

"Dr. Cannon. Can we let that rest?"

"With a wave of consternation, he tosses aside everything that has just occurred, the whole little storm he has brought into her day. "Just the cell, please."

"Please now, is it? Well."

The charge nurse dares to push open the door, peeks out noting that no one has moved. They stand there, tight-lipped, their eyes meeting her scan, waiting. They all watch as she strides to the backpack left in the middle of the floor, bends to heft it with all of the chastened dignity she can muster, and hauls it back to him. The surgeon takes the bag, rummages through it to find his cellphone and taps it on, thoroughly dismissing her as if nothing at all has happened. She teeters there, absolutely ready at this moment to throw her whole career away and blast this old bear as he so richly deserves. Instead, she goes to the coffee pot, fills a Styrofoam cup and sets it near his hand, returning to the unit she knows in fact – and more than ever – that she rules.

Ten seconds later, the door flies open. It happens as if choreographed. Rainsworth Cannon, chief of neurosurgery, in the plaid Bermuda shorts and Billy Joel t-shirt, the floppy socks and scuffed Crocs he has worn all night beneath scrubs in surgery, storms out, cell phone glued to his ear, tapping the automatic door to the unit, and then gone with all his drama without even a backwards glance. Instantly back in the game, the charge nurse leans over the billing technician's shoulder to resume her discharge planning. The technician, mocking Cannon's voice, intones, "No cell phones allowed in the ICU."

She grimly whispers in his ear, "This is nothing. Have you ever worked with an orthopod?"

Storming down the long glass corridor leading to the doctor's garage, Cannon tunes his ear to the day's challenges, speed dialing the butcher at *Foods of All Nations*. "What do you mean the hams are not ready? I am getting in my car this minute, I will be there in three, so make this happen, pronto."

Then the wine store, "What do you mean you're out of Turley cab? No one got my order? I placed it personally six weeks ago with Gerard himself, where is Gerard, put him on, I don't need to hear that, I've been up to my knuckles in brain since yesterday, so excuse my lack of sympathy, I want his home phone, do you get me?"

The seafood store up Route 29: "The crabs! The crabs! Where are the crabs? Two bushels fresh-boiled for noon today, not your old stale discards, and I can tell too so don't fuck me."

The electronic Dictaphone service: "cleaned and sutured, Aimes, Donald, 32 stitches, 7-gauge silk, that intern Zhang I think, flapped and skull fragment bagged and sent to freezer, check the time, think it was 0545 or thereabouts, vitals stable on local, check Dr. Pegacci note, patient cleared to post-op 0610."

The Porsche sits poised like a frog, top down, sidewise across the first two parking spaces by the door, proud sign to all that Batman is on the job. Cannon drops his backpack onto the passenger seat and squeezes behind the wheel, punching the engine to life while firing off a voicemail to his wife: "Nothing is ready! The whole day is gone to shit! Need a quick nap before the airport, and what do you bet the plane's late and I'm stuck in game traffic and can't even get to the crabs? No delivery's going to get through after 10 with the whole state of Pennsylvania driving in! Where are you? Are you, I can't believe you're out riding – we have work to do! Why am I the only person in this backwater nowhere who even gives a shit?"

SIX
RIVER FARMS STABLES

IRIS CANNON BREAKS from a brace of trees at the ridgeline just as the sun tops the southern hills, bathing the whole field before her in brilliant glistening green. Smokey feels it too, stretching to a reeling cantor across the luxuriant lake of fescue straight down the steepest way towards the creek bottom, horse and rider devouring the landscape in a florid rush felt entirely through the knees and supple wrists and on the whip of wind and mane on her face. Coming up to the stables in brilliant form, there is one last fence, that old cross-tie laid along the creekside, yes Smokey still has the lift, even after an hour full-blown on fox trails, and he is up and over in that jaw-dropping coil and flight only a horseman ever knows, gathering himself already on landing for the two steps to the creek and one long jump across, rear hooves striking clear on the high bank with a furious snort, straight back to the broad trail now slowing just perceptibly for the cool down trot to the barn.

Tapering at last to a regal walk beneath a canopy of maples, Iris sits that last great moment of the best hour of any day. Every ride partakes of those before it, all the way back if you think of it to that first pony, her first jodhpurs, the first daunting lesson at age six, all wrapped up in a nerve-and-muscle memory borne on the air and carried on the backs of her four successive cherished steeds through all the fields and hills and glorious mornings of a lifetime. The sisterhood of equestriennes understands, dwindling minority that they are. Everyone else really is just a pedestrian, a misfortune apparent in their every chary breath. In their slouched posture, their mewly handshake, the bovine sloth of their glance. Not their fault, of course, but how really fine it is! How could her own daughter Chloe walk away from this? Think of all it was teaching her – poise, patience, responsibility, love of nature, quickness, stewardship, grace under pressure, so very many of the possible meanings of beauty and power. Such a loss, never to be regained in its entirety now after so much time, even if she could be rewon. But what can be done? Well right now, put the burden away, it will keep. Take the morning, this morning, in its glory.

It all comes together at warm down, when the grandeur of the ride, with its tip-of-the-nerve physicality, stitches itself to the mundane rest of the day. She dismounts, unstraps the saddle and lifts the lathered blanket, hanging them astride a fence post as she leads Smokey out onto the grass training track for their ritual walk. This brings a welcome relief to her knees, but each healing stride sings a rebuff to bipedalism. We are all so graceless, so civilized, so short! Then on to the barn, where she throws on a rain duster even in the heat of a summer morning to hose and sponge down her grateful gray stud. Other riders are returning now. Spindly-legged Dr. Snead – once head of the hunt, now just able to manage his enormous steed Jackson – tips his helmet as they pass. Merina Caleo – Brazilian sociologist and reputed cougar of the Lawn – chuffs her dappled pony Albion out to the track. Sarah McCutcheon and her eight year old daughter Amy laugh side-by-side on Shelby and Percy, coming down from that same trail high on the ridge, dismounting for their grooming lesson. Amy wobbles unsteadily but already knows the routine, grabbing a stool to help unsaddle her pony, murmuring sweet nothings as she sponges him down.

Bittersweet memory, as Iris nods her hello. Ten years ago, that would have been her daughter Claire, just five years ago, Chloe. But Claire – off to USC and her fanciful film career – has given up riding for cigarettes. Or whatever they call those smokeless things today. While Chloe it seems has given up everything altogether, lost in some teenaged cloister between her earbuds. Chloe, who used to idolize her sister, who in turn ignored her as some kind of outmoded toy. Do they ever talk? Has Claire ever learned to give a damn? Does anyone get through to Chloe?

Amy has splashed herself as much as her pony, her youthful skin glistening and soapy. Sarah calls over, "Y'all going to the game today?"

"Oh yes," Iris sighs.

"Well, come around if you can. We're in our new spot by the parkin' garage. David's fryin' a turkey, if you can believe it."

"Oh my, that *is* ambitious. Are you going, too, Amy?"

"No, skatin' lesson at the rink and a sleepover." Amy smiles sheepishly, still shy around adults, grateful for her mother's reply. How soon that will end! Or maybe not. Do all girls have to go bad?

"That sounds like fun! Yes, Claire will be back for one night – flying in from London on her way back to school – and Rainie has invited half of Hollywood it seems for the film festival bash."

"Oh? Anybody I've heard of?"

"Tim Drake and Roddy York. He's hoping Debra Winger will emerge from her exile."

"Excuse me? Tim Drake, the superhero, in your house? Oh my. And Debra."

"Rainsworth has this notion of featuring her films next year, something along the lines of 'Women of Courage' or 'Women on the Edge' or something. It's really just a play to bring her out really."

"Debra Winger."

"You'd have to ask him. Well, I suppose she's fine. But, I mean, Cissy lives here and they've never done anything for her."

"Isn't it always that way, though?"

"I suppose. But she's such a sweetheart. Rainsworth gets these notions."

"Don't they all. Tim Drake, though. And little Joey! Can't you just see him in his little spacesuit now?"

"You'll come by?"

"Oh yes."

It strikes her now in the long-lashed doze of Smokey's eye that the day has begun, and all this fragrant primitive glamour is done for another morning. While Smokey snarfs his Nutra-feed, she tugs off his bridle, then offers him a sugar cube and leads him out to his tail-swishing, grass-cropping laze of a day on the most gorgeous rolling pasture she has ever seen. And with that, still in her grimy jodhpurs, she pulls herself up into the cab of the Escalade, takes a moment to brush out her own long and still lustrous hair and is off down the tree-lined gravel road, the dashboard air conditioner blasting and a dust wake billowing behind as her mind almost audibly launches its calendar like the start-up whirr of a computer. First stop is *Foods*. But it turns out that Rainsworth has already stormed the place, hauling away the hams, but forgetting to pick up the cold cuts, clotted cream, and peaches on his list. She takes a moment to slip the deli man and butcher tens, the price of damage control.

At the wine store, chatting amiably with the husky teen who loads in cases of sauvignon blanc, chardonnay, red zin and Rainsworth's precious Turley cabernet, she again feels that twinge of pique at the remoteness of her younger daughter, who has spared her fewer words the whole summer than this tousle-haired boy in their three minutes at the rear hatch of her car. He's a provincial kid, public school marching band type, wearing a winsome sprinkle of freckles across his nose. She imagines him at forty – town mayor or police chief, the nose spread and the freckles faded – but this morning at this moment those cheeks wear that priceless blush of youth, and it cheers her to recognize that for him this exchange at the tailgate is something of a challenge, daring small talk with her, connecting, maybe in some callow way testing the not so easy familiarity that borders on flirtation. The way he turns suddenly serious in refusing the five she offers, as if it is an affront to chivalry, then grins in opening her car door, makes her knees go weak. She almost stumbles, and he nimbly takes her elbow. "Can I get you a bottle of water, ma'am?"

Oh this is too much. This peach-fuzzed husky kid is a born salesman, playing her like a rental clarinet. Now it is her turn to blush, though for some reason she finds herself turning abruptly curt, suddenly prom queen proper -- "Oh no, that's quite alright. Thank you." – before swinging herself up into the cab, avoiding his all-seeing, maddeningly gorgeous, jade green eyes. She fumbles for the cell phone clipped to the sun visor, dismissing him utterly, but pauses before merging onto the highway to glance back in her rearview mirror. Are his shoulders slightly stooped as he trudges back into the store? Has she burst his balloon? Will her response inform his morning's meditation on the inscrutability of the female sex? Rich bitches? Would it have killed her to pause, to accept a bottle of water, and dare one even look into those inquisitive, daunting eyes? "What is wrong with you, Iris?" she says out loud while Daughter Number One's phone – somewhere high above the Atlantic – stores her message.

Last stop is her florist shop for the centerpiece of seasonal flowers, heavy on brilliant WaHoo orange day lilies, anchored by a heavy leaden crystal bowl. Iris had come in herself to build the arrangement last night, and it sits waiting in the fridge fancy as a peacock. The shop's still closed, but the help has left it ship shape, floor swept and mopped, ahead of a busy day. Waiting for her latte at the drive-in coffee shop window next door, she flicks through messages. Rainsworth has left six in the space of a half hour. The first is a rant about the day ahead, he's headed home, so the rest she can delete. Frank her hairdresser will be out at ten, the lawn crew will finish the boxwoods by noon, and the big one – a message from the University president – "phone me."

Odd. Why would he reach out to her? Could this be it? Rainsworth's most recent greatest wish? The offer of a Pavilion on the Lawn? It's a silly thing, but ever since he has learned that this is the cherry-on-top pinnacle of success at the University, the honor of a precious key to one of Jefferson's ten Palladian pavilions, he has been relentless in its pursuit. Even the film festival is just a step towards that reward, a way of cementing his significance to the community. If President Burwell, that old buzzard, has called not the nominee but the wife, then is it possible? A surprise announcement at the game? A sly caution, be sure your husband is available at halftime, don't let him slip back out to the tailgate? Well, it could be anything, really. A VIP with an elective aneurysm, pressure to pick some favored alumna's documentary for the film festival. But why call her? There is no answer to her return call. This could be big. This is fun. It's what makes all of Rainsworth's shenanigans worthwhile.

She pulls into the driveway, angling to park under the gingkoes to protect the wines for a moment, then gently lifts the heavy cloud of lilies in widespread arms. Rounding the slate walk towards the veranda door, she first notices an oversized pink Croc sandal in her path, then the other one, then a rumpled plaid pile, the surgeon's shorts. She stoops to set the vase down on the walk, then creeps over to the pool, where her husband lies sprawled across a lawn chaise, his burnished skin decorated with glistening drops of water, his paunch rising and falling in deep sleep. He is the color of chestnuts and mahogany, its varying tones across his broad chest and shoulders, down the long stretch of his still powerful legs muscled and glowing in the dappled morning light. And, hilariously, he is turgid, pulsing, his dreaming penis tapping his belly with each heartbeat, like some dumb movie homunculus about to sprout hands and a face to speak its first words.

"Oh what shall we do?" she says aloud, fingers curling. Reflexively, she turns to Chloe's windows overlooking the pool, their black drapes pulled funereally tight. "You old pharaoh, how dare you just lay it out there for the whole world to see?" she frets. "Let others turn their heads," she imagines him mock-proclaiming. He would actually say that, too. "Well, may the hedge trimmers take off your balls, you heedless, conceited, self-involved old monster!" In answer, he begins to snore. Iris retrieves a damp towel from the poolside hamper, drapes it over and tucks in its sides, imagining the muffled cries of the struggling little man underneath. Then turns away, enlivened, to a day that grows more promising by the moment.

SEVEN

LUCAS – RICHLANDS, VIRGINIA

THE DIM SIZZLE and cidery aroma of apples frying in lard blends with the charred smell from a hot mug of instant coffee perched smoking on the windowsill. An old grandma shuffles along a track worn into the linoleum floor, humming the same tune, *Amazing Grace*, over and over, as if she has forgotten Lucas is there at all. He watches a fly as it grazes a complete circumference around the lip of a tin water bucket on the counter, then takes a right turn down the stem of a ladle hung from its side. There's a beat, a clock ticking sullenly off in another room, playing into the sizzle and shuffle and hum. He strives to sit erect in a rough-hewn chair with its comfortably sagging cane seat set near the kitchen window, which is open wide to catch a wisp of morning breeze. Turns to watch scruffy cocoa-brown hens strut and scrape in the tiny yard hard up against a neighbor's brick wall, where he had dozed for how long before she roused him? He'd come awake to the old woman standing at the end of a broom held like a rifle, poking his foot, compact as a hobbit and meaning business. "You a meth head, you a hop head? Don't you move, boy! Open up now, show me your teeth!" Weird demand, but half asleep he'd just done it, grinning like a horse, and that's all it had taken, she dropped the point of the broom and let her shoulders go round, allowing what was left of her own teeth to show in a wrinkled smile.

Flecks of undissolved coffee float on the mug's surface but the drink's bitterness washes away the coal film that has hung in his throat. Hands lined with grit, fingernails engrained with the stuff, and if anything, his bare feet in his old sandals show even worse. But the old woman hasn't even sniffed at that. Through a doorway past her tiny stove, he spies a spavined bed neatly piled with patchwork quilts, golden dust motes floating, the whole interior dim and tea-colored like an old photograph.

"You're settin' in the Sergeant's chair," she says, turning away from her cooking. Lucas startles, tries to stand. "Oh, set. I'm tickled to see it." She turns back to the stove, pouring a glistening caramel slough of melted apples onto a plate and cracking eggs back into the sizzling pan. "You in Sergeant's chair. Set there all day every day for nigh on thirty years, watchin' his chickens, just like you. Set his transistor to the Yankee game. Coughin' in a tin can." Lucas' fingers trace a pattern of crescent moon-shaped coffee stains on the sill. Unconsciously, he's been placing his own mug down in one of the plainer traces after each sip. "He's a slip of a man, like you," she clucks. "Almost skeers me to ketch you settin' there. But don't you move."

She clears a space on a table crammed with jelly jars, torn store coupons and magazines, flipping the dial on a plastic radio that once had been something like butter yellow. A wire antenna covered with crinkled aluminum foil runs up to the ceiling, where it ends in a nest of duct tape. "Kin still git the clear wave from New Orleans of a mornin'. They used to play music you could dance to, but it's jes' news and that now." A hollow citified voice, confident of its words, rattles off the sketch of a shooting in the city. "You wait now, nex' thing the mama's gonna say, 'not my baby – he wuddna done nary a thing like that.'" Indeed, the announcer does play a clip of a woman's voice, sounding bewildered and embattled, pleading her son's innocence. "It's a mother's love. They kin't help it."

Lucas smiles, catching a memory whiff of his own mother back in Columbia, probably still abed, sucking oxygen from a tube. The old lady has been watching for this, catches the flick of his eyes, but says nothing about it just now. "Son, fetch me that jar a blackberry jelly up on the shelf there will ye?" Lucas reaches on tip-toe to pull down a dusty Kerr jar from a row of them atop a plank shelf. The old lady rubs it clean with a single swipe of her apron. Everything she does is like that, automatic, something she's practiced a million times the same way in these same worn tracks in this kitchen. She owns this place and her place in it, Lucas knows, as he owns nothing he can name. "Here, pull your chair over to the table, clear off a space. Bring ye cup."

Lucas nods swooning over the plate of eggs and apples, served with a pillowy biscuit smeared with purple jelly, that she sets before him. "Jes' eat," she says, and turns away to wash a pan. It's like apple pie with the biscuit playing crust. He tries to explain how that works, but his mouth is full, the words are stupid, and he wonders if he's been misunderstood.

"Yeh want another biscuit, is it? Wisht I could do ya better but I en't got another biscuit made. Here let me make ye a foldover fir dessert." The old crone pulls a slice of store bought white bread from a pressed tin-fronted wooden cupboard, holds it flat in one hand while spreading it with blackberry jelly, then folds it neatly in half, leaving on it an impress of her doughy fingers. Lucas takes it gratefully. "The Sergeant loved them things," she sighs. Then, taking her own cup of coffee from the draining board, she lowers herself onto a chair at the other side of the cluttered table. "Good, waddn't it?"

"Yes, ma'am." He catches her watching him lick his lips and sheepishly lowers his head.

"Now, boy, you jes' set there. Matters not a hoot to me, but I wud like t'hear, just for interest's sake, how did a flatlander like you end up in my garden?"

He looks about, as if to escape, but realizes he really cannot. Is this some kind of trap, after all? He dares to look into the old woman's watery eyes, hoping for some kind of clue. She is on point now, alert in a new way, awaiting some kind of reward. "I'm sorry, ma'am, I appreciate what you've done here, but pardon me asking, are you planning to turn me in?"

Her head cocks quizzically, then she leans forward as if to see him better. "Son, you settin' in the tail-end of the known universe. There en't no 'in'. Ye gonna git out, so it'd help to learn how you got here in the first place. Ef you want me to guess, I kin do it, and leave it at that. None a my beeswax anyway."

"No, ma'am. I'm sorry. I just. I came in on a coal train."

"Well that I could guess."

"I got on last night in Columbia, down in South Carolina. I'm trying to get to a place called Charlottesville, in Virginia."

"And whut's waitin' for ye, there, kin I guess?"

"I have a friend."

"Ye do. Well John Brown." She takes a long draught from her cup, coughs a little, and waves a hand. "Jes' hang a minute, now. I do want ye to go on, but let me chew on this a sec." He understands that she's playing with him now. This is his payment for breakfast. "Kin I ask one thing?" she adds. "You ever hear tell of sump'n call a boxcar?"

Well, actually, the thinking on that had been complicated. Few of them these days, everything locked up in shipping containers, though if you could find one, they would definitely be roomier, flatter, enclosed, no coal dust, but a big draw for the bulls and they could be headed anywhere. Coal train's got one destination. Rare to do it. Maybe less scrutiny. Who knows? He says, "I have."

"They do still have the Trailways bus don't they?"

Lucas peers down into his empty cup, embarrassed and annoyed. "I've hopped trains before."

"Mm. Hobo are ye?"

"Not really. I just."

Suddenly her hands come together in a gleeful clap, ending in a gesture of mock prayer. "A romantic! I got me a full-blown, pure-D, romantic! Sweet Jesus Lord." Her look blends pity and wonder, tinged with pain. Lucas sets his cup atop his empty plate. "Oh son, ye got to understand. Boys around here, they catch the coal trains, too. Freight trucks, hide in a car trunk, jes' walk if they have te. But they don't none of 'em come back. Queer to see ye come here is all."

He skids the chair back, poised to stand.

"Ye do know it can git ye kilt."

"I'm careful."

"Ye have heard a the bulls en't ye?"

They face each other across the kitchen table's jumble, eye-to-eye now, Lucas surprised by the old woman's concern. She has not reported him, has fed him awesomely, appears to take the crazy risk of his effort at least seriously. "I en't intendin' to give ye the willies. But ye ought ter know. The Sergeant had a yeller hound. Sliced clean in half by a train wheel. He come up on the porch, draggin' on two front feet'n took his last breath at my knee. Wheel sealed him off like one of them baggies you squeeze with your fingers? Come on his back part a mile away past the switchin' yard."

Lucas clears his throat. "Whoah."

The old woman takes a last sip of coffee, then deciding something, asks, "This a good friend, I reckon. When're ye expected?"

"Whenever I get there, I guess. Last night, really."

"Ye goin' to Charlottesville, Virginny, halfway across a big state, and yer late. That's a piece. I wisht I knew a body cud take ye. I'll say it one time. Ye oughter call yer folks and git'm to take ye home."

He bites his lip and stands.

"That's what ye oughter do."

She sets her mug down. "Ye know there en't no empty trains leavin' here?

"I had thought of that."

"Had ye."

"I'm sorry."

"Well, that ye are." For a moment her eyes well, as a grim smile unfolds on her dried old apple face. She sighs, "This is whut yer gonna do. Road out front runs a mile up the hill. Past the switchin' yard. Trains headed your way come out there. They'll still be runnin' slow, pullin' up to the ridge, but the minute they get over it's hiyo silver clear to Norfolk. I 'spect you may know this, but ye want a line a hopper cars. Them gondolas that they flip? They go straight to port. If ye kin find a hopper train, the ones with the bottom chutes? Half a chance they cud stay in state, feed a power plant. Comin' off the mountain, it's a piece, first place you see of any size, big switchin' yard, that's Roanoke, yard's smack in the middle a town. You listenin'?

He is, reeling a little with a full belly and a sweet need of sleep, eyeing his filthy backpack by the door, and dreading this thing he's gotten himself into.

"Well, it's your funeral, son, but if I's you, I'd hop off there and find a highway. Stick up a thumb. They got a Interstate goin' up the valley. Ye might get lucky."

"Hitch a ride."

"Listen, Romeo, ye can be a loverboy and keep a brain, too. Whatever game ye got in yer head, like I say, that's your funeral."

She stands up to make her point, a rumpled gnome of flab and cotton at home in her shabby cottage. He thinks, if I'd had a grandma, she'd be a good one. Wiping her hands on her apron, just like a grease mechanic with a rag, she wraps up her lecture, "but a load kin sit in a switchin' yard fer days while they figure out who's gonna git it. A lotta bulls in there. They break up the trains and they head off all different ways. Ye cain't hitch here. Fools think yer a tree hugger, they'd eat ye fer breakfast. But if ye kin git out, when ye come up on Roanoke, git off. That's whut I'd do."

Lucas blinks back a spurt of tears, pockets hands that have begun to tremble. The old woman's spooky gray eyes see it all, his wavering. She nods once slowly, cocking her head towards the screen door. "Thet's all I'm gonna say. Git. And don't forgit yer pocketbook neither."

Lucas collects his backpack and turns to go. Weirdly, he wants to hug her, mumbles a thanks, stands tugging at the door, but it won't budge.

"Ye don't pull on everything, son," she chuckles, as he finally gets the door shoved open.

With that, Lucas finds himself ejected, blinking, onto the railroad track again. Inside the kitchen, eating apples and biscuits, the whole adventure had seemed cartoonish, finished. Now the hard gleam of the honed rails zoom off in both directions, taking away the strength in his legs. He has never even swapped names with that lady, but loves her dearly and irreplaceably, and already mourns her loss. Stepping just out of sight of her rear window – she has gone on about her business inside anyway – he pulls out his cellphone to snap a shot of her chickens, the back door, that bare spot where he'd fallen. Then, rounding the house to the highway at her front door, some lyrics start to come: *She was just an old hen, but she took me in, the weary old hag told me set down your bag. She was all set to die but her apples like pie.* Dude. Focus on her face, on her hands, that's what you want to keep fresh. Wish I had a picture, man. Okay, *eyes bright as marbles, skin pale as lard, she stands and she warbles songs to the Lord?*

Warbles? That line's a keeper, tapped onto a memo. A high-wheeled pickup slows and a man in a white construction helmet leans out the window, pointedly staring, reminding Lucas where he is. Probably everybody around here knows everybody else. Bedraggled stranger covered in coal dust, flashing a cellphone, backpack, that'd be a temptation on a holiday weekend. But there's nothing he can do but keep his back straight, eyes ahead and look like he's headed someplace. Rifles hung on the man's back window. Just walk. The truck tops a rise and is gone.

Lucas makes it past a one-room brick post office, where a mud-spattered jeep sits leaning on an embankment next to an oversized American flag that hangs limp from an angled pole. Everything in this town is like that, too, bending away from the railroad track and cambered on the turn. The road has no shoulder, just a sheer dropoff to the railbed. Uphill a dented mobile home has tipped off its cinder blocks as if ready to slide, its door ajar like a mouth. Behind him comes the churn of a truck engine, he doesn't dare look, a dump truck chugging past, picking up speed even as it takes the hill. A wet chaw of tobacco splats on the pavement's center line. She said a mile. He bends to his sandals, tightens the straps and picks up his pace. There is no cover, no place to hide. On his left the rails spread like fingers multiplying into the rail yard off ahead, on his right a steep hill, almost a cliff, blocks the morning sun. His only choice is the highway, straight ahead, in plain view of whoever happens along. *Not a tooth in her head, but a song on her lips, an old quilt on her bed, an old dress on her hips.* Stupid. You don't talk about an old lady's hips. Focus. Be ready to run. Deep breaths, steady, keep moving, look like you know where you're going.

Black streaks run down his arms and legs before he's cleared the town. Past the last house, the road tips up more steeply. To his right uphill, a full-blown summer forest rises almost vertical. To his left down the slope the otherwise rumpled world sits level and ruined, run full of track all loaded with coal cars. A twenty-foot chain link fence topped with coiled barbed wire rises almost to his ankles. Gray dust swirls around spidery dumping belts and the hill echoes with clanking and banging and the dim shouts of men. Like some kind of black and white movie plopped in a Technicolor world, the railyard goes on forever, one pyramid of coal after another, trains shrinking to toy size down the rails, distant workers like mice in Tonka trucks. Whatever else he's done this night, that crazy jump off the coal car was a good move, and not just for breakfast either. Never would have made it out of that place. What made him jump? Like it had to happen. Magic, a guardian angel, dumb luck. Like they say, first leap and then learn to fly.

It feels like a first spatter of rain, and bee stings on the back of his legs, then he hears the bang from downhill as he jumps. He's been shot! The legs start first, without thought, so he is off running straight up the road and away, not seeking a hiding place, just a head full of screaming. There's one more shot, but no more pellets, as the road flattens up to the railroad intersection on the downhill side ahead. A high-wheeled white truck, maybe the one that had passed him back in town, sits parked on the embankment. Trapped! There is nothing to do but scramble into the woods, climbing hand-over-hand on vines and brush up the steep hillface. A blackberry thicket, wound through with thorns, spreads like a barbed wire wall in all directions. Good for cover, maybe, but there's no way out.

He squirms desperately into the grip of the brush until he can see nothing but green, close and clinging, then collapses into its woody grip, sprawling aslant of the hill and as still as his pounding heart and bursting lungs will allow. Scratching at his neck, he pulls back a hand smeared with blood and a birdshot pellet that has lodged just under his skin. Others dot his calves. The bleeding he can see is small-scale, but he can't tell whether the little welts have shot in them or not, and he's afraid to move much to examine them more closely. Maybe no worse than all the scratches from the blackberry bushes. Dude wasn't out to kill him, but still. Did they have dogs? Why would a person shoot somebody for no good reason anyway? Can't go back down to the road, can't wend through the thicket uphill. The train track headed east had been right there ahead of him, maybe a hundred yards, but even if an engine does pull out of the switching yard, he knows those guys will be waiting. They already know the paths, the likely route he'll take. And if they have dogs.

As his panting slows, he begins to notice how the woods have hushed the noise of the railyards. Tall pines, bare for most of their length, bush out to a canopy that blocks the sky. They take the morning's first breeze, bending together in a wave. He struggles to his knees and finds that the thicket is broad but not deep, that it forms a sort of narrow girdle around the foot of the hill, which flattens out a little higher up. Squatting down again, he pulls out his cell phone and taps out a message, his plan, in case it fails: "buck^ dnt b a 8^ f I gt cot, mk it b a run." Signed with a grinning devil emoji. Which she'll only understand if he makes it. He tucks the cell back into his backpack, then begins to thread his way on hands and knees up and out of the thicket, shoving the pack ahead to block some of the briars. It's a crazy task. At some points, he has to go almost flat, half-suspended by brush, and he loses first his left sandal then his right. Minutes lost squirming back into them. The ground rumbles. Maybe a train pulling out? You'd need a machete like in those old war movies his mother so loves to cut through this stuff. It's like he's sewn into the web of a blanket, and has to break free one stitch at a time. Or he's a flea working its way through the matting of a dog's back. No sound of dogs yet. The hill seems to be humming, picking up the locomotive's vibrations. And then silence again. Damn.

But he is out, emerging on his knees onto a rusty floor of pine needles, then rolling onto his back upon that soft mattress to gaze up in salvation at the waving treetops. He takes a moment to reconnoiter. The briars seem to have taken most of their toll on his forearms and knees; somehow his t-shirt held up. The shot welts are swelling. He counts twelve of them, more or less evenly scattered across the backs of his knees and calves. Perfectly round black knobs centered in little volcanoes of angry red skin. Asshole!

Lucas scrambles to his feet on the pine needle carpeted slant and stumbles sidewise along the hillside, the thicket blocking the road from his view. And then the hill ends abruptly in a carved stone cliff and he stands looking directly down onto a line of train hoppers filled to the brim with glistening black chunks. He can see neither end of it. The line of cars snakes around the hill to his right and stretches back into the switching yard off to his left. It's just sitting there, like the old grandma had said, ready for the downhill roll, seeming to pulse with occasional brake ripples, everything black on black, those identical toylike cars, throbbing, poised.

The white truck at the crossroads has disappeared. Lucas can't believe his luck. What did the old lady say? They stop at the ridge to uncouple an engine? Don't need much to pull the train downhill? That must be this pause, happening up ahead somewhere around the curve. This is his chance. To get there, he has to somehow scale thirty feet of bare cliff, cross another bramble and the gravel grading, and that's it. He'll be home free. The easiest way would be to just work along the cliff-top back down to where it meets the road at the crossing. But that dude with the shotgun could still be hunting him, so scratch that. He pauses to tighten his pack straps and sandals, then swings down onto the cliff face, working just in control down a crack, toeing for another at least far enough down for a safe jump to the thicket. He's sprawled there, twenty feet above the railbed, when the white truck reappears. He flattens against the rock, but the game is up. His red backpack pokes out like a flag on the rock wall. Guy's getting out with something – a rifle? a bat? – in one hand. Moving deliberately but with all good speed to the tailgate, and the cage, and the dogs beginning to leap and yowl inside it.

Lucas at last finds the toehold he's been looking for, then one more, but can wait no longer, sliding down the cliff-face to a heavy landing in briars. He can't believe what happens next, leaping clear across the thicket in one bound onto the gravel railbed. The coal hopper looms, suddenly lurching with a frightening clang. The dogs pour out of the cage. It's insane, but here he goes, down on his belly, scrambling under the screeching wheels, praying the backpack won't get hung and squirming out the other side of the track just ahead of the hopper's back wheels. Gotta get on somehow. And then he sees another pickup parked at the crossing on this side, and a man in beige work clothes, wearing black boots and a yellow helmet, standing one hopper away from him, with a hand on a baton club hanging at his belt. Lucas can even read the name tag – Brian – pinned to his chest. Bland name for a goon.

You can't run on gravel in sandals. You just scramble along hoping for traction. The hounds have come up to the other side of the train, baying up a storm and seeking a way across as the train begins to roll. The goon plods patiently along, eating up the distance between them. Lucas grabs the nearest hopper ladder and climbs. At that, the guy nonchalantly swipes what looks like a cellphone at Lucas' dangling leg and a searing heat blasts his whole frame, somehow gluing his fingers to the ladder. Stun gun? It's all the goose he needs to clamor up top onto the stinking bed of coal. He scrambles across, slipping and sinking on the slaggy rock, then in the middle of the pile grabs a chunk of coal in each hand and flattens himself face down, thinking, 'Okay, come drag me off a here."

A rumbling clatter rises up through the coal load. For a minute, he fears that they are emptying the hopper right onto the track and sees himself draining through the chute to lie buried in a pile. Daring to raise his head, he feels an accelerating breeze across his face. Maybe. If the uncoupling's done, if the train can get going downhill, nobody can stop her then, right? Not a hundred cars full of coal. A firecracker pop, that shotgun again, back up the line. Lucas digs his toes into the rubble and buries his face into the choking dust with one searing image in his mind: half a dog dragging itself up to a porch stoop.

EIGHT
SID – IN THE GARAGE

A CRIPPLED GRASSHOPPER limps pathetically across the tabletop, seeking shelter behind a stack of yellowed magazines, creeping at an angle to danger as if still holding to a remnant of its former jaunty pride. Its eyes are just knobs, but could as easily be the leering cartoonish orbs of a Jiminy Cricket, spinning in horror at the butchery native to this arena. Wahoo, the last of twenty geckos, ornery old blue-and-orange monster with his swollen, pimpled tail and cold, relentless stare, goes on point, steps off Sid's wrist one delicately placed paw at a time, and positions himself athwart the grasshopper's path. The gecko stiffens, wags its tense tail like the cocking of a gun, then catapults to gobble the head and thorax in one fisted gulp. The miniature dinosaur raises its monstrous nubby head and seems to smile, his gums overflowing with the spaghetti strand legs and briefly twitching tail of his prey. The grasshopper exists, a wildly improbable and voracious yard warrior. Bam, gone. Proteins. Amino acids. Roughage.

Belly full and elbows out, the gecko tip-toes into the sunlight atop an old book to bask. Sid's gaze moves away by increments. It's a morning troubled by distractions, sharded into puzzle pieces, and every shift of attention doubles the knots in his stomach. His chafed and reddened hands clasp and unclasp. How long has it taken to clip his fingernails, to evenly pare them until they are just nubs with both forefingers bleeding? Somehow overwhelming to taste, to suck on, that salt and rust flavor spawning a toot like a train whistle and the memory of the same backyard when he was six and Daddy was showing him how. The old Adirondack glider – his father's masterpiece – sits atilt against the garage wall, gray and shaggy with rot, but light through the fence gaps throws stripes like an old movie gaining speed until an image forms, this one a bare toe that reaches to tap the swing back and in that instant for the first time ever the boy achieves a whistle blown between salty-tasting fingertips, accomplishing a sort of super power.

That's how he has organized his treasures, though the unschooled eye would only see clutter piled to the rafters. The glass box gecko terrariums are stacked against one garage wall, not as one might expect with the largest at the bottom, but in order of acquisition in four vertical columns duct taped together to keep them from falling over. He can retrieve one, set it on the table, and this is something he has never been able to explain or verify in the experience of others, the glass box switches on a memory like a tv set, replaying the little fellow inside with all his distinctive coloration, twitches and hitches, tastes, choice locations and chirps. Some of the terrariums even have special effects, telescoping outwards to envelope the whole garage. The stories they tell can alter temperature. Some hardly work at all. Those are his favorites, the weak ones, barely pulsing, staticky, their memory trace signals almost gone for good.

The opposite wall holds a similar stack of obsolete cathode ray tube televisions that his grandaddy had tried to fix, following a mail order course, in an effort to shore up his income as the stationmaster back when the railroad depot had one. Unfortunately, he had learned that vacuum tubes cost money, then transistors had made them all obsolete in a year. No one had come back to pick up their broken sets, so there they sit. Even decades later, when no one could have cared, the old man would sit with a soldering iron and the innards of an old television, working through the diagrams on a yellowed instruction sheet. Some of the televisions are shaped like teardrops, others encased in dusty maple consoles, one topped with a functional record player. Silently, like the gecko cages, they broadcast a history as real as now. Right there, Sid could reach out and grab it, a drop of the old man's sweat falls towards a Bakelite knob, suspended in the dank air of the garage as a free-floating gleaming ball.

Sid has lined the back wall with shelf after shelf of radio-controlled airplanes with broken propellers and dust-encrusted muscle cars missing a wheel or two. And the 6-foot tall Saturn V moon rocket, solid-fueled at each stage, with its shoebox holding the pristine cone-shaped command module, still hung with its three rumpled parachutes from its last glorious flight. His dad's precious moon rocket from his own childhood when people did things like that. That last time, Mattie had run across the pasture collecting rocket sections as they fell, and Sid had climbed up on their dad's shoulders to sneak onto a schoolhouse roof to recover the command module that hung swinging from an aerial there. That shoebox is the most powerful of his treasures. It harbors shape-shifting capabilities, can tip the world into instant replay.

The garage floor holds a mountain range of recent projects surrounding Sid's worktable: A stack of lawn mower engines like severed robot heads, wheelbarrow wheels, buckets and gardening tools, packets of seeds, a sack of fertilizer, a half dozen bicycle frames, rubber tubing, a camp stove, his dad's soldering tools, refrigerator compressors, a manual typewriter, computer keyboards and a half dozen junkyard CPU's. At his worktable amidst this clutter, Sid slumps on a picnic bench running his calculations for hours. This is never easy, with his whole childhood whispering from the walls. In summer, especially, outside distractions mount. By mid-morning the whole neighborhood roars with the pitchless thrum of cicadas. Mattie would say it's just noise, because like most humans he cannot distinguish among the musical voices in the din. But Sid counts seven cicadas in the backyard now, down from twenty-three at summer's height. They mostly stay put, set for life on a chosen tree limb, one perched under the eve of the garage. Sid has collected fourteen cicada shells, which are stored in individual Baggies labeled with Sharpie ink. He has given each the name of an historic hero, those that are molded in bronze at the city's parks and intersections: Stonewall, Traveller, Lewis, GR Clark, W Clark, TJ, Daedalus, and so on. And more than that, Sid has mapped the path of each insect upon leaving its shell, matching the cracked exo-skeletons to the various voices in the yard.

The twin overhead fans their father built run on belts and an old electric motor. They whine along with a whispered thrump-thrump. You can lose yourself in that music, or if you look up at them and get twirled. The rhomboid of sunlight through the garage door clamors for attention, too, fingering across the table and clocking the day until the whole room divides in two. Wahoo follows its warmth, Sid its shape, both drawn by gradations of change. Fighting all these distractions, Sid has been thumbing through a looseleaf binder bescrawled with the calculations of the past year, wherein the city's monuments point with vehemence towards a pending vortex of some kind. His measurements include a range of compass bearings at each of the statues along and near Main Street, linked by lines that make up a connect-the-dots hourglass when laid out on a map.

Imbedded in that child's game, however, lies an algorithm that can explain a lot, if it can be deciphered. The equations rest on the relative distances between the statues, correlated to the rhythm of compass point angles divided by the heights of each statue from its base measured metrically. Sid has taken the measurements many times; it has cost him the better part of two years to do so, returning again and again to each statue in order to check the accuracy of his tools. The conundrum has been maddening, requiring off-line reasoning, but all of the scribbles in his notebooks have at last reduced to one elegant equation, a matter of simple division rendering primes in all cases. But only if you eliminate all of the data from one statue, that of General Lee on Traveller in what he still calls Lee Park. So all this higher math adds up to nothing. If only there were someone he could ask, could it be, would a demon or a general, would they add in that confounder as a red herring? Could it speak to a larger theory? If they moved the statue, if forces were brought to bear to align it with the rest, then that would be the final proof. The preachers call it End Times, but little do they know.

Sid agrees with the generals about one thing: confounders aside, the world is simple, its solutions concrete. You just have to see it plainly and commit the necessary resources. A bust of Einstein -- his frazzled hair and squirrelly eyes reduced to plaster -- looked down on the UVA mathematics classroom where Sid had spent a troubling year. That head said more than the text and the professor, entrusting a larger mission. The trick is to perceive more acutely, pull back the gauze of received impressions to reveal a wound in the system so raw that most won't even look. Sid reels from the day when the revelation came and all that the professors professed turned to dust. He had walked home from campus down a Main Street swept with winter flurries never to return. Having broken through, recognizing in a flash that we walk a web patrolled by spiders, and this is possible precisely to the extent that we can measure their approach. Another thing the generals know. The pastors, in their own way, too. Why then do they endlessly debate trivialities, set up diversions, obfuscations, misdirections? Why do they string up marionettes in classrooms to jabber and jiggle? Why construct that dress frame up on the coal tower? The tower perched like Ursa Minor's North Star, the diagram's pivot point, concentrating its energies. Plain and simple, the dress frame is an antenna, and the breeze through its metal crossbars hums and whistles at calibrated frequencies. Another ignored clue, hidden in the best of all hiding places, in plain sight.

Sid cups one palm to gently lift Wahoo back onto the felted floor of his glass terrarium, smiling to watch the old lizard scurry to shelter inside a paper towel tube. The answer everybody chooses. Then, with an archeologist's care, he conducts an excavation in the freezer, stacking aside leftover steaks in decaying aluminum foil, soup in Tupperware prepared decades ago by a mother long gone, frost-burned popsicles, and a shoebox full of bugs in baggies, all in order to remove a single yogurt cup stashed at the bottom. He sets the cup on his worktable, remembering to take Wahoo's cage outside to warm in the sun before cranking the overhead fans to high and donning a paper mask. He shaves a frozen milky-white chalk from the cup with an old dinner knife and plunks it into a frying pan, then turns on a camp stove to cook it as slowly as he can. It's robot work, all larger issues held in abeyance. The ice reconfigures to sludge over time; he dials down the flame to a whisper, then plugs in his mother's ancient blow dryer to finish the task. Wrapped in wisps of vapor, raucous molecules drift up from the pan seeking nasal entry to his bloodstream and brain pan. Sid imagines them huddled against his paper mask, fiddling with a key. He turns off the dryer and goes outside for a moment, stripping off the mask to catch a decent breath in the backyard.

Mattie might wake up any minute, sleeping in fits and starts as he does, but Sid trusts a sixth sense about his brother, feels he can geo-track his position anywhere across town, but certainly within the radius of home base. His ears perk for the creak of a telltale hallway floorboard, the twist of a squeaky door knob, while at the same time the morning pops open like a cartoon in rainbowed smears of color, loud arguments among the crickets, the yodel and swoop of predatory birds, cars going whoosh on the street, and the individually distinctive hum of eleven window air conditioners along the block. He gets caught up in the transition for a moment, stepping through the door from smelly dark garage to fragrant green yard, crossing the threshold, then back inside, then through the door again, several times. It's like pulling the lid off a music box and slamming it down again.

At last the heated goo has dispersed into the air, leaving a dead gray skim of what he thinks of as demon shit. With the dinner knife, he scrapes the stuff free of the frying pan, crunching it down to rough powder through a piece of window screen, then scoops the couple spoonfuls into a hospital glove. He ties it shut like a balloon, licks the bitterness from his fingers, then licks the screen and the glove, before putting away each tool. The demons work fast, jimmying the sequence of locks to his blood brain barrier, and they now pinball around inside the bowl of his skull, pinging his sensory nodes. They shave him away to thinness and shadow, opening windows in his flesh to the dangers of the glorious day, but in all that turmoil there are hands lifting Wahoo's cage back indoors, switching on his heat lamp, scattering the telltale notebooks on the worktable, stacking televisions in their accustomed places on the freezer lid, and even pausing to smoke a cigarette stub guaranteed to mask odors while simultaneously stopping trouble in its tracks.

The demon shit wings him up, spins him into the outdoor shower stall and has him singing as it soaps him. Popping up fat and slick and soaring until his knees give way and he collapses

57

on the slick board floor, scrunched down in the rain, ass hanging out at the bottom of the stall as all matter and energy blink their separate same status. Nine times he has sung the University of Virginia's fight song, the one they call the *Good Old Song*, hugging himself and rocking while congested moments flip past in the steam. Was it nine times? He starts over and sings until the water begins to cool, then is on his feet again as an arm made of mud twists the crank to stop it. Storming hugely into the house, wet and naked, the kitchen so small it's like a snail shell and the screen slamming with a wall-shaking echo.

A disturbance in the Force. Mattie has invaded his room again, stacking clean clothes on the floor. They are all the same, uniforms. Tennis shirts. Cargo shorts. Costco briefs. That come to him now across the ragged carpet and slime onto his flesh with minds of their own. There is one more thing he has to do but it will disrupt the continuum. This act has been tempting him day after day. To wait another second would blow a hole in his head.

Sid shuffles down the hallway, reeling the storm in like some Neptune, forcing himself to focus. He avoids that saggy floor-board, lifts up on the knob as he opens the door to his parents' old bedroom to avoid its telltale creak. Everything is the same in here, down to the ragged and now almost colorless chenille bedspread and the faded roses repeating across the walls. Mattie's head is gone between pillows striped by grated light through the drawn venetian blinds. Sid's next move reflects in his mother's mirror, which has always judged and warned from its ulterior dimension. Four hands reach out to the gun holster, hold it down as if it is a living thing. Both Sid's pull out the paired handguns, Glock 9's that are sneakily heavy, seeming to hold that weight balanced at barrel and butt, but ready to shift, to challenge gravity on an impulse, as if holding their breath. Chunks of L-shaped plastic, black as black can be.

The backyard's sunshine works to erode the demon shit. Movement. A summer day, topped with cottony clouds. Sid shoves the gun into a velcroed pocket of his cargo shorts and walks out the backyard gate. Remembers and goes back to collect the hospital glove. On the second trip, he notices a human, Old Man Tillman, at his rusty mailbox and waving a desultory good morning. All down the street, sunlight piles thick as cottage cheese on a line of parked cars.

NINE

MRS. CANNON – RUGBY ROAD

NINE SHOWERHEADS OPEN up on her like fire hoses. Blasting from all angles, the lowest at her knees, the highest directly overhead, their sunflower-wide nozzles shoot pulsed needles, gentle rainfall, variously hot or cold, all computer-programmed and relentless. She stands at the center of this assault, ravished, pink and peeled, an exclamation point of sheer sensation. A Venus ten minutes a day. Iris is not even aware, really, that she shouts in here, lungs expelling a sudden joy, gasps like liberating sex rising in the steam, silly tunes from pop radio. Oh, it feels so good!

Expelled from the glass box like a butterfly from its cocoon, slick and limp, yet unfolding vivid wings before a wall of mirrors to flit across the day, she strolls nude into her closet, quickly flipping to the row of game costumery, selecting blazing orange culottes and a sleeveless blouse with swirling irises in matching orange and blue. The joke is on two levels, team colors painting the flower that is her name. The Hollywood folks in their designer black will expect a Southern belle, and that they will get. She lays out the clothes on the bed, slips into a robe and jammies and leans out the balcony window to see the yardmen finishing the hedges by the drive and the pool boy stealthily slinking a hose along the walk, trying not to waken the sleeping patriarch on the lawn chair. A hose blast up the towel would do it! She's half-tempted to run down and do exactly that, too.

Once the hairdresser arrives, the whole game board will begin to fall together in an orchestrated sequence following strict rules. Rainsworth being the wild card that makes the whole thing interesting. You have to take it like that, assured that even his shenanigans cannot disrupt the game for long. You organize expecting his behaviors, you tack and trim as needed across the day. But the board is missing a game piece.

Tying on a robe, Iris pads down the balconied hallway to Chloe's room and tries her door, though of course it is locked. She phones her cell, then clicks hers shut before the message comes on. Absurd, to stand here ten feet away from her own daughter and have to call her on the phone! Why does it make her teeth grit to hear that sullen, hollow voice on tape? Why does she choose to greet the world with all the verve of a zombie? Well, she was invited. She knows it's her one chance to see her sister before school starts. That movie stars will be here. You can hate the game, hate your parents, hate the whole world for that matter, and still enjoy the hors d'oeuvres. Her knuckles brush the door, prepared to knock. Through the rose window above the entry foyer Iris notes the hairdresser's yellow Miata with its top down crunching up the gravel drive. She turns from the locked door, sighing, "Your loss sister." We are back to the game and on our game, too. Let him ring the doorbell, let the gong ring through the house. Please do wake the dead. Down the staircase in a wink. By the time I reach the foyer, it will all be behind me, make me beautiful, dahlink. Let's play!

TEN

LUCAS – CSX TRACKS

ON THE SUNNY side of the mountain, the morning comes on hot as hell, and the coal dust has begun to stink more as it warms, but Lucas sits high on the hopper, his legs swung over the side, taking the breeze as the black train rolls relentlessly down the face of the Blue Ridge. This is what all the dark mystery of last night would have looked like in the daytime: Green hills round and nappy as sleeping bears backed by a sumptuous blue horizon fading to smoggy mists, precipitous drops down to remote trout streams under soaring trestles and the dripping welcome of tunnels, where he lies flat and dares not reach up to stroke the seeping ceilings. He finds his shades and slouch hat, improvises a collar with a red bandanna, forgets for awhile the pellets in his calves, and prays this train is on the right track.

Any minute now his cell battery will blink off with one maddening deadstop warning. But he's been checking it at every fifth mile post, hoping to pick up a signal. By the sun at least, it seems like they're headed more or less east. He's promised himself to dare the GPS only if an intersection comes up, but it's been a single track for an hour since the frenzy of Richlands. He nestles in a corner of the powdery mound, pushing stray chunks aside to make a bed in a corner of the car. Rearranging the bandanna as a mask over his mouth and nose to keep out the dust, he makes a pillow of his backpack and tries to nap, imagining himself hidden there from prying eyes at ground level. There hasn't been a shack or road to be seen for a long time anyway.

One last try on the cell, and suddenly a flood of text messages pours in, each one from Chloe, sent across a ten hour span last night: *Im so gunA e@ u! Swim? U@now? Cll me! U@now? Dis soup sux! }xx I h8 mtl b&z! B sEZhi. Wnts 2 ==}u! Its yr iyz. U@now? Or yr hnz. Meet at rvr k? Cll! UOK? ((u)) B jst brf, Gsus! 206 s so queer. Gt us cloud9. 4 u n me only ok? U@? RU here? K hrs a sng – hez a slippy slippy man w d slippy slippy hnz + she (hearts) him like a fan + she ctch him when she cn + she C hm n d**n its hm dts hu u r. K it sx. Yr turn. Goin hom. Slippy? Xxx Whr dy zzz?*

Some of the texts come with strings of her favorite emojis – an ice cream cone, a winking smiley face with a halo, a spinning star – and some are just snapshots, apparently taken indoors at a restaurant or club someplace, but it's hard to see anything in the sunlight's glare except those brilliant teeth, her crazy mouth and mirthful quarter moon eyes. Fearing a final blink out at any moment or a sudden loss of signal, Lucas dares to send one message: *mt@rvr n pm.* And that grinning purple devil.

He holds the phone at arm's length, pulls down his cowboy mask and tries to frame the coalbed in behind his selfie grin and slouch hat. Tapping send, he sighs, so I'm Slippy now. Will she be there? In that place by the river where it all started last spring? Where they'd said she would be? Or will be. *Heat and fumes, rumble and breeze. What I'd give for some shady trees.* He tightens the bandanna over his nose, pulls down the slouch hat, and squirms back into the wallow he's made, trying to imagine that this filthy slag heap really was once a tropical jungle walked by dinosaurs.

ELEVEN

SID – CAMP RIVANNA

THE HANDGUN in a side pocket pulls Sid's cargo shorts down on one side, so he has to constantly hitch them up as he walks. There's a rhythm to it, and in the long stroll down the slope of Market Street to its bedraggled dead-end at the river, he's added a half-hitch to his step, and to that a tip-toe every third stride, providing some peace from the worry that the gun may explode if not coddled according to its intricate code. The kudzu shrouded wood at road's end looks like a scribble, blocking any view of the river, but even here you can make out a musical trickle through the broken dam's sluice, leading you towards an unmarked path that veers down to the water's edge, then out around a bend thick with poison ivy to a railroad trestle and beyond that the shell of an old mill. Only two of its walls still stand, made of river stone thatched with mud, but what had been the mill floor has been swept and made again into some sort of open air room, with a sawhorse table and ragged fold-up lawn chairs, a carpet worn to thread, shipping crates and lopsided candles, and a patchwork of lawn tarps roped together and tied to the walls, providing a sort of roof over the camp. Trail fingers lead into the brush to pup tents and lean-tos scattered up the wooded hill. A dog barks viciously at a tent flap, but Sid just says, "Hey old Scruff," and the patchy mongrel trots lazily out for a scratch on the head. The place otherwise seems abandoned, maybe everybody already gone to the food line at church.

Sid unbuttons a pocket flap and pulls out the gun with both hands as if holding a living fish. He hates the thing and wants it back in his brother's holster, but lowers it to the table, where it sits throbbing like a toad, about to leap. He thinks of black holes. They can be small as dust specks, sucking in light and matter. Can be anywhere, bending space and time around them. May be the real cause of tornadoes or river whirlpools. You could have one in your stomach or your head. Pinhole highway to a backwards universe. The gun has that kind of power, or a version of it. Maybe even the real McCoy, a black hole you can trigger, a baby big bang. It's the center of wherever it is. You could have a box of donuts on the table, and all you'd see is the gun. Enough of them together, in the right place, and there's a chance. Okay, they might just cancel each other out. That's the risk. But if the magic he reads here multiplies, they might have enough pull to bend the equation, deflect the onslaught. Enough to slow the vortex, at least until another plan comes along.

Sid pulls out a Rubbermaid crate stashed under the table and removes a cellophane strip with a few Saltines stacked inside. Limp but satisfying, they taste of cardboard and salt that cuts your tongue. He presses the lid shut and remembers to burp it, as Steve insists, then sidles down the river path to the water hole. A rope swing hangs still as a pole from a craning oak, the stream beneath caught up in a just perceptible swirl down here below the caved in old dam. The long-fingered footprints of raccoons pattern the mud, along with the remains of their meals, tiny opened mussel shells scattered about. Up where the rope swing is tied, the tree house, half-built, more of a hunter's platform, balances between limbs. On the opposite bank a muddy cliff rises to mown lowland and a row of houses going up out by the highway. That'll be the end of the camp, Steve has said. But so far it hasn't been a problem.

As usual, the river acts as a sedative to slow his racing thoughts. Every time it takes hours to calm down even a little. He leans against his favorite boulder and attempts to close his eyes. But they're better off open, really. Sid's gaze pans over the slow river as his head lolls on a rubber neck, venturing the *Good Old Song*. Down here the racket of the insect world is so dense, even he cannot sort it. But it's clear that the bugs have sensed a new urgency, a worry in the trees. Maybe just autumn coming, so much to be done before frost. Or they know the real future, as farmers say animals do. It tugs at them first, borne in on antennae to whip a desperate whine from the frantic rubbing of their hollow-stemmed legs. Sid begs his own humming to pause, wowed by the anxious music. He hugs his knees and rocks.

"What the fuck is this!" The shout rings through the camp, cutting through the insect whine like a bugle. By the time Sid climbs back up to the old woolen mill, a gang of people has emerged from the tents and lean-to's, all standing around the picnic table staring at the gun. Exactly how he'd felt! Look at its gravitational pull! It's Steve who yelled, and there he stands, always the boss, glaring at the weapon. He's a huge guy, a super-hero, in his bowling shirt, baggy gym shorts and flip flops costume. A rumpled safari hat cocked atop his head slides a little as he dips his chin to tip a pair of sunglasses off his nose. It's one of his many tricks, a way for a man whose arms end at shortened wrists to get things done. His forearms stretch the shirt's fabric, making a basket to catch the sunglasses, then work together to rub them clean. It reminds Sid of a dog gripping a bone with its paws. He can never stop himself from looking.

Steve's gaze turns from the gun to Sid. A dark stubble shades the lower half of his face, his red mouth livid inside that bearded nest, his lips churning wordlessly as if he's about to spit. As if bounced on a trampoline, the sunglasses fly up to be caught in his teeth, then one arm lifts to balance them back onto his ears again. Having found the culprit, he scans the crowd as that same abbreviated arm points grandly at the object on the table. He calmly restates his question, "What. The Fuck. Is. This?"

J-Rod, an old-timer shrunken and black as a raisin inside his flannel shirt, ventures a reply. "I'd guess it's a POL-eese Glock, is what I'd say."

A heavy woman in a rumpled flowered shift who nearly fills the gap between her walker nods her chins. "That's a gun."

"That's right. POL-eese Glock 9. Fuckin' kill ya, boy."

A third onlooker, a pale teenager wearing only boxer shorts printed with hearts, leans out to touch the gun, but Steve shouts, "Boo Boo, back the fuck off!" The boy recoils as if stung.

"Bite ya," the woman at the walker warns.

"At least," Steve replies, scanning the circle of campers. "Boo Boo, where's Buster? Where's T-Bone?"

Nobody even shrugs. Then Sid steps into the clearing and everyone looks at him. Steve snorts, exhales profoundly, "Sidney, good morning. Any chance this is yours?"

"Brother is more like it," J-Rod mutters.

Mona agrees, "Boy took his own brother's gun."

"Is that right, Sid?" Steve asks, eyes narrowing. He bends over and nudges the weapon with a truncated wrist. "This your brother's weapon?"

"He call it his 'weapon,'" J-Rod mutters, and Mona frowns, shifting her weight inside the walker.

Sid absorbs the scene from two perspectives, both in the circle of campers and a hundred yards back, as a staged photograph. In this simultaneous two-camera shot, he gazes placidly at Steve's red and puffy face, tracks spit flying from broken teeth, and at the same time clocks Boo Boo moping just behind, jabbing a hand down his underpants to rearrange his crotch, catches the glint of hunger or amusement in J-Rod's yellow eyes and the stolid and weary set of Mona's jaw inside sagging cheeks. There's this guy Chollie a few steps back in the shade, at the ready with arms crossed, tipping up on his toes and heels. And framing all that the broken mill wall, the sagging tarp roof and the plastic furniture, and surrounding all that the woods spry with insect chatter and Scruffy the mutt sniffing the Saltine wrapper on the ground. As in the old slide projector in the garage, images click into place, one after the other, a sepia photograph of bedraggled troops in the Civil War or one of his dad's old album covers of some long gone hippy rock band. The whole tableau – this serves to amaze him but also grounds him in a thrilling certainty – just perceptibly beginning to whirlpool around the important black object on the table. He would not be surprised to see it all tear cleanly away from the world and disappear like a sheaf of paper into the barrel.

Steve takes a step towards Sid, waving an arm, and demands, "This your brother's handgun?"

Sid's eyes widen at the distorted image of himself doubled in the panes of the older man's sunglasses. Reaching a hand beneath his shirt, he hears everyone gasp as if on cue. Steve steps back, but Sid only pulls out a slab of cardboard with writing on it, and turns it for all to read. Steve plops down in the one lawn chair with functional arm rests, ducks his chin to again tip the shades into his lap, and reads aloud the manifesto.

"Okay, Sid, we hear you," Steve pronounces evenly. "The demons are at you again? No, you're not me, and you're not a preacher, and nobody here is a general either. And nobody's gonna fight any general or any preacher ever again, okay? Set your poem down on the table, leave the gun. Have a seat, willya?" Steve pushes a chair away from the table with one foot.

People begin to wander back to their tents or rummage in their coolers. Sid watches the mill camp rotate again, wondering if there may be a message in the spatial arrangements between the campers as they separate, if there are lines drawn between each of them and the obtuse angle made by the barrel and grip. His mouth moves as if chewing, working over the futility, that he will never be able to measure such a seemingly transient clue.

Steve says, "Sid, you know what you might want to do? I see what you're saying with that poem, I think. You're speaking truth. Not everyone can get it. But a few, the proud, so to speak, maybe they need to see this. Where can you hang this sign? Is there a good place you could post it to get the word out?"

He guesses that Sid is listening because the chewing stops. Sid takes the proffered chair. Steve doesn't really understand. The sign is an artifact of old knowledge. The situation has progressed greatly in the hours since the night's tortured transcription, all too little and too late. He tries to explain but his voice can only mumble.

Steve sits perfectly still, elbows braced on the chair arms, eyes darting from Sid to the handgun and back again. Sid follows his eyes to the gun, imagines that Steve too sees it absorbing all around it at a quickening pace. The campsite has crumpled and Steve's words have garbled in the torrent. He can make out, "hungry?" and "coffee?" but the queries are ash spun up in the wind of a fire. His hand has gone into a pocket, pulls out the almost forgotten rubber glove, and offers it to the storm. There is something calming he hopes in the way Steve cups the glove between his knobby wrists to chew its knot open without spilling the spoonful of powder inside. Like some kind of priest kissing the sacrament, Steve brings the sprinkled glove up to a tongue that obscenely licks and savors, running the powder up inside his gums. The sight allows Sid's stomach to complete the flip it's been attempting for so long, and with that the whirlpool seems to steady a little. He clearly hears, "You the man." Then something about medicine. Steve is licking his chops and asking, "You taking your meds? Fuck, why am I even asking? Sidney, look, let me tell you something. You've helped me, now let me help you. You know me. I'm Steve, your compadre. Nobody's out to fuck anybody here."

The gun has begun to swell, as if panting with exertion, but the swirl has slowed to nothing. Sid marvels at its power, beginning to regret its unleashing. Steve's arms delicately place the rubber glove on the table, then he leans over inches from Sid's face, so the brim of his safari hat taps Sid's forehead. "You in there, Sid?" Sid recoils at rancid breath like kerosene. And with that, Steve is up and dipping both arms in the cooler to pull out an unwrapped chocolate bar. "Here, man, have some. Truce." He drops the candy on the table roughly in line with the gun and the glove. Sid ponders that. Then Steve's saying, "Okay, I can see we have a lot to process here, a lot to talk about. We can take a swim. We can take a walk. Nobody's touched your shack. You can chill."

The glob of chocolate begins to sprout amoeba arms to grip the table. Steve says, "Okay, Sid. This is your brother's, right? I'm going to assume that nothing has happened. I'm going to assume that we have a little time. But we have very little time. If he comes here? If they find this here? Then our little kingdom, all of Camp Rivanna, we're fucked. Do you get that?"

Sid nods, still watching the sneaky chunk of chocolate. Steve says, "I want to thank you for this shit, we all do. Pays up your shack. But this gun, we have to get this thing out of here. Sooner rather than later, do you get me? Do this for me, Sid, please. Take your speech, this poem, what you've written. This is our plan, okay?"

There's a modulation. Sid finds he can tear his eyes away from the table and watch the man's mouth move. "Go to the place you think is right. Find a better location than this, man, and hang this poem of yours where it can be seen. The people who understand will find it, and they will know what to do. I've been saying, you don't need to take this on alone. You're a warrior, and your fight is a lonely one, but it doesn't have to be."

Sid strains to focus on the words, but the channel is breaking up again. A dance of dappled light sprinkles over the campsite, spattering everything in lurid colors that sit like mustard on the tongue. Sid stands so abruptly that his lawn chair topples over. He trembles when lifting the gun, so full of portent, yet light as a toy, slipping it gently into a pocket. Steve is speaking with dots between his words, hoping to aim true. "Exactly. Now, take it back to your brother, buddy. Put all this behind you. We don't need it here. You don't need it for nothing. We're all good. Take it back. You can come down, have a swim. But take it back now. You have to go."

Sid picks up the cardboard sign and stuffs it into his pants waist, lifting his shirt tail over to hide it against his belly. The campers have disappeared to their tents, where they may be waiting, expecting anything to happen. What happens is they see the shuffling goofus with the crazy cardboard sign turn and go out the woods path. The minute he rounds the trestle, Steve raises an arm for the all-clear, then bends into the cooler, as if he's apple bobbing, to pull out between grinning teeth for all to see the pistol's bullet clip.

TWELVE
DR. AND MRS. CANNON – RUGBY ROAD

RAINSWORTH CANNON, like many great surgeons, has an on-off switch. It is a super power, has always allowed prodigious feats of endurance, all-nighters in the lab or standing bent over an open spine. One minute he lies sprawled and drooling on a backyard chaise, the next he springs to his feet with no stretch or yawn of transition. His watch blinks awake at this sudden verticality, its numbers pulsing with the news that the morning is lost, flights from the West crossing the Blue Ridge, his daughter between planes, disembarking from the trans-Atlantic and racing for her short hop at Dulles. The night's Pavilion performers, whatever shaggy-haired posers they may be, snore away aboard a bus rocketing up the Interstate, sixty thousand football fans load their cars and their stadium seats for the drive in from all points, the second-year residents have charge of the OR and ICU for the next twelve hours, and the football teams sprawl taping their ankles and wrists, smudging their cheeks with tar, belching and farting and throwing up last night's pre-game party.

Wrapping his waist in the beach towel left by his wife, Dr.

Cannon storms into the kitchen, bellowing her name into the air-conditioned hush, the joke between them that this shout is meant to conjure a genie, Iris split by his volume into something like "I Wish". But the whispering room absorbs his roar like cotton. He then stubs a toe in his rush back to the pool for his phone. It sits crown-like atop his neatly folded shorts and t-shirt on the lounge-side table, his Crocs aligned on the slate walk beside them. One beefy paw sweeps it up, as he squints to scan for messages from the hospital. Nothing. Then his show of bluster has worked, will put them off from calling about every little hangnail for a while at least. He stabs his wife on the speed dial and as her phone rings once, twice, scans the neatly trimmed hedge, the glistening, inviting blue-black water in its slate-lined pool, each lawn chair in its designer-designated place amidst a riot of roses, not a wheel barrow or hose or pickup in sight. Just his dusty convertible, askew on the drive, and the toy-like knock-off, the hairdresser's yellow Miata, nudged up behind it.

"Rainy," she answers, in mock wonder, tongue at the roof of her mouth, waiting.

"Do you have any idea what time it is?" They say it together, he rising to exhortation, she stage-whispering. Then he is on his own. "We have no wine, we have no food, we have no plan!" He storms through the kitchen, flinging open the spare refrigerator to scan row after gleaming row of Washington pinot gris and Napa chardonnay. "The planes will be landing any minute, and there is no one to meet them! Has anyone confirmed the concert, have you heard from your daughter, we have to pack the Escalade, I don't see my Turley!" When there is no reply, he storms up the stairs, barging into the master suite, where his Navy tencel Bermuda shorts and a florid Hawaiian shirt await him on the bed, then into the sitting room, where his wife waits draped in a barber smock, while the hairdresser works at her eye lashes, her phone snarling away on the vanity top.

The hairdresser winks at his customer, turns to pack away the eyelash curling instrument, and stands to his full gangly height, meeting Dr. Cannon eye-to-eye, as few people can. With his mop of orange hair, he's a dead ringer for that poor sap comedian Carrot Top. "Why Massa Cannon, a girl might blush with you all en shabille like that. Why don't you take a seat here and let me take a snip off those bushy old eyebrows, why don't ya?" Cannon glimpses himself in the mirror, calculates the imposition, then plops down on the vanity bench. "Do it," he orders. The hairdresser bites his lip, amazed that the old bull has taken his ruse seriously. "Just wait your turn. Be right with you, sah." But if he has to wait, then screw the eyebrows. Cannon leaps up, throws off his towel and strides into the shower, still shouting garbled commands from within a rising cloud of steam.

"Oh, that will never do!" cries the hairdresser, enjoying his mammy ruse, but Iris taps his hand, pulls off the smock and leads him back into the bedroom. "We'll be fine, Jason. This little flip is perfect. I look just like the faded debutante that I am."

"Jessica Lange in *Tootsie*."

"*Horror Story*, you mean!"

"Oh, Miz Iris, do flare those nostrils for me, will you?"

"Oh, they'll flare."

"Somebody tooken his rattle." They share a wink. He gives her one last appraising scan. "You one fine lookin' white woman, Miz Iris," he mocks.

"And so are you, Jason, so are you." She pulls a pair of fifties from her purse at the bedside table, folding them lengthwise to slip on his ear inside that nest of cinnamon hair. "Don't spend that all in one place, now."

"Oh, no'am, I sah got chirren to feed." He nods towards the bathroom. "Should I get my things in there?"

"Allow me." She returns with the bag all packed and hands it over. All business now, he reminds her, "I want to know what they eat, and how they hold their forks. I want to know what shoes they wear, and their cuts, and most of all, I want to know what they say about me!"

"You will know all."

"Exactly."

"Now go, you have other old ladies to tend to, I'm sure."

"You must stop with that, Jessica."

"Git!" She waves him away with a quick hand spank, then turns back to the bedroom mirror, practicing a wry smile. "More Joanne Woodward, if I'm lucky."

Knowing that Rainsworth will be at least a half hour in his toilet, she pulls off her robe and dons her costume, selecting the most precious yet delicate gold necklace and her charm bracelet adorned with world travel trinkets, then honestly considers heels for a moment before settling on her "lucky" orange pumps. A last once over in the mirror, "Old girl, this will have to do!" And then she is off downstairs, calculating the available time to the second, allowing a moment to pour a tumblerful of Campari and soda on ice, before slipping out to the solarium for the phone call that may change everything.

The president, Professor Burwell, amazingly answers the phone himself and on the first ring. "Iris Cannon, and how are you this fine morning, young lady!" She pictures him on his hilltop balcony, fat with Jeffersonian delusions, gazing down at the domed roofs of his sprawling university nested like fat eggs in the forested landscape.

"Well, Mr. President, and you?"

"Oh, you know this is the day for us academic types. Students arriving from all points, parents discharging their precious fledglings, alumni strolling the Grounds and ripe for the plucking!"

"And to have locked up Penn State for the first game!" she schmoozes.

"That was a coup, indeed. We'll lose by a hundred points and the money will pour in," he chuckles. She imagines him training a telescope on the stadium as he does so.

Iris lets a pause occur between them, taking a measured sip of the bitter drink and fingering a staked orchid. Maddeningly, the old goat lets the pause hang there, saying nothing, no doubt enjoying the tension. At last she sets the tumbler down. "Not to keep you, Mr. President, just returning your call?"

"Oh yes, that's right," he teases. "Iris, can you keep a secret?"

This is the sort of intrigue the old buzzard lives for. Why do these games wear so well on a hairdresser and so tediously on a man with real power? "You know me, sir."

"Indeed, Iris, I do. Well, may I assume that you and hubby will be attending the game today?"

"And please do come by our spot. We'll have the boiled crabs."

"Oh, that's delightful."

"And as long as the hospital doesn't call him in."

"Of course, of course. Well, you should know that there will be an announcement at half time?"

This is it. The Pavilion. Rainsworth's dream come true. "Mm-hmm," she whispers.

"You may wish to linger in the stadium. It may be of interest. Perhaps you have a friend who can man your tailgate?"

"And what might that announcement be, Mr. President?" she asks, knowing the old trickster will never say.

"Oh, just the usual. Retiring a jersey, anointing the fencing team, you know."

"Professor Burwell."

"Have him linger, Iris. Have him linger. Oh, and save a fat she crab for me, dear, will you?"

"Oh yes, of course."

"Toodle-oo."

He's off the phone before she remembers to tell him about the Hollywood guests. Might help seal the deal. But surely he already knows all that. What doesn't he know in this little Peyton Place, after all? She turns and her husband's tent of a shirt fills her field of view like an orange danger sign, a musty after shave steaming off his damp cheeks, his eyes livid with panic.

"Chatting on the phone! A cocktail at this hour? And nothing done, nothing!"

"Rainsworth," she sighs, smiling up at his frantic mug.

He turns to dig in the coolers, rummaging recklessly through her carefully arranged covered plates of hors d'oeuvres. "Rainsworth."

Now at the wine closet, he tugs out bottles by the fistful, setting them down hard on the marble counter, grumbling to himself, his ire rising by the second.

"Rainsworth." She sets her drained tumbler in the sink.

He has begun to cram the bottles sideways into the already jam-packed coolers. She strides to the back door, opens it wide, and – imagining a matador and bull – taps her keyfob to pop open the Escalade's rear door. It rises on automatic hinges to reveal the whole day's spread: the wine cradled in bags of ice, the basket of crabs nestled in sea grass, the Tupperwared plates of ham biscuits, the folding table and chairs, even a blue and orange array of flowers, all packed in the air-conditioned cargo hold, ready to go. A tv classics channel switch from Ricky Riccardo to Ralph Kramden now, Dr. Cannon swaggers over to her, scrambling to recoup, eyes wide and unbelieving as if this has never happened before. She taps the keyfob again to lower the door, a knowing smile on her lips, as he grabs her up in a clumsy embrace, lifting her just to tip-toes, exactly as always, and bellows, "Alice, you're the greatest!"

THIRTEEN
OFFICER MOSBY – OLD BELMONT

HE KNOWS it's gone without even checking. Mosby sprawls inside twisted damp sheets, dredging himself out of a half-assed nap that has never dipped into dream, only hovering for wasted hours across the background chatter of his nerves, doing nothing to erase what seems like a lifetime of bloodshot eyes. Why hit the pills at all? It takes forever to get an eye squinted open, to squirm a leg free. Feels like a fever bed, smelly and forlorn. That parchment brown water spot next to the overhead light morphs into a target, a hand, a gaping face in profile. The whole house is falling apart, going off slab. This fuckin' ancient chenille bedspread. A woman would have to be pretty wrecked to throw down on that. It's a mausoleum. You wear the whole ragged hulk on your back like a shell.

But within the usual domestic shambles, there is something new wrong. Always, first instinct, check your gear belt. His aching eyes scan over to the bureau and he tumbles to the floor, tearing the strangling sheet off, landing sharply on one knee. Kneeling there, he drags the belt over and emits a sighing "Fuck." At eye level, the dusty surfaces of the bureau and the bedside table reveal nothing; he tips to search the floor beneath the bed. When he'd first come home, and found this job waiting, he'd slept with his belt between his legs, the way you do deployed. It was one of the things that had put off that one girl Sheila. Wasn't the only thing. So he'd taken to leaving it on the bureau, still within reach. He'd pushed her away further in the end.

It's gone. He scrambles to his feet, finally freeing himself of the bedsheet, and checks the bathroom, then throws open the back door, yelling, "Sid!" In nothing but his t-shirt, he crosses the yard and peers in the garage door – no one, just the usual pile of junk – then, discovering himself half naked, he races back into the house, pulls on a pair of shorts and wills himself to slow down, sniff for clues, use those IED eyes. In Sid's room, pulls open drawers and lifts the lids on shoe boxes packed with the sort of treasure boys collect: rusty railroad spikes, pebbles, bottle caps, Lincoln pennies, and one athletic sock stuffed with rumpled cash. Who would take the gun and not the money?

Mosby goes back to the gunbelt. Radio, mace, keys, cuffs and baton all in their slots. On the kitchen side table, the change bowl overflows. The back door left unlatched, wide open to the day. As usual. Well, fuck it, there's the one fact. Explain this one to the chief, oh shit. Forty-five minutes to road duty. Where is Sid? Probably led the actor to the belt like a dutiful puppy. Probably off tagging along for the sale. Where is he anyway? He won't have gone far, though for a walking man, that guy can lay down some miles. Maybe not on a hot day. Gotta think, gotta do this off book. Call Ronnie. He'll know. He's gotta be up by now.

"Whoah, my brotha! This is unfortunate. This is your deep doo doo."

"Ronnie."

"I'm in the saddle, dude. Gimme five."

Ronnie arrives a half hour later to find Mosby already showered and uniformed, pacing the backyard in the patchy shade of a gnarled mimosa tree, the one missing piece of his gear like a hole in his costume, all the rest of his get-up just play-acting really.

"Son, you done lost your dick, now, ain't ya?" Ronnie laughs. If the ground opened up and swallowed Albemarle County, he'd laugh. Maybe not the best person to have called after all.

Mosby sees himself doubly reflected in Ronnie's ridiculous mirrored shades. "I would gladly swap my dick for a gun right now."

"Seein' as you never used neither of 'em no ways."

"Uh huh. Look, we got duty."

Ronnie rocks back on his heels, thumbs in his gunbelt, jaw working a wad of tobacco. "Uh huh."

"Can you get me a piece?"

"Can I get you a piece?"

"Ronnie."

"Son, you cain't just be walkin' around town with a old Luger or some six shooter in your belt now. You ever hear a regulation?"

"That's what I mean, man, look I'm gonna find this thing."

Ronnie leans out to protect his uniform for a spit. "Son, that little Glock a yours is halfway to Chinatown, New York and you ain't never gonna see it again, so git used to it."

"Well, what do we do?"

"Keemo Sabe?"

"Ronnie. This is real, man."

"I know that. I do know that. Look, here, take this. Take my gun, Mattie. For these next four hours, only." He unsnaps the holster and palms it over. "I got game duty on the fifty yard line and shit my old pellet gun'll do."

"Game duty."

"It ain't who you know, buddy."

The worst of it passes as the gun slides compact and tight into his holster. "But."

"Four hours, and then you figure out what you gonna do. You got four hours on the road you see what you can think of. I ain't sayin' I'll back you up. Better be a good 'un, too."

"You want a Coke."

"I want a split-tailed cheerleader is what I want. Gonna get one, too."

"Uh huh."

"Don't doubt it."

Ronnie's paw fingers his empty holster. Maybe reconsidering, maybe making some calculation of favors owed. His eyes stray over to the shed. "How's old Sid Vicious today?"

"Your guess."

"Still the mad scientist in there?"

"I don't even go in there, man."

"You know I seen him Thursday? Had to chase him off Massa Lee again."

"Man, don't even tell...."

"He uz up on old Traveller's neck with a plastic ruler and some kinda compass, lookin' the old man eye to eye in the face."

"Shit."

"Yep."

"Any trouble?"

"Whatever. I didn't get him down. Just apprised the onlookers that I knew him and we all just stood there waitin'. I don't know how sturdy that thing is, what is it bronze or somethin'? I'm thinkin' a piece a Massa Robert breaks off, I don't wanna be up there pullin' on him.

Mosby's eyes go shut, seeing it all.

"Well, he come down on his own, like we wadn't even there, just used the stirrup like it was a real horse, and I took him by the arm and led him over to my car for a sit down. He never tol' ya?"

"No."

"He ain't the craziest loon in Charlottesville, Mattie, you know that."

"Did he say anything?"

"Oh he was talkin'! But not to me. Whatever figurin' he was doin', he had it all scribbled down on this paper bag. You seen it? Ain't a inch a that bag ain't covered in numbers.

"I don't know, Ronnie."

"Mattie, he's a grown man. He's hurtin' nobody I can see. I give him a stick a gum and sent him on his way."

"Appreciate it."

Ronnie spits another brown stream that seems to sizzle on the burnt grass. "You though. What I'm gonna do about you? Alright, it's done. You meet me back here in this yard in four hours and I'm takin' that piece back. If a bear charges you, don't you dare discharge it, don't even lay a finger on it, you hear me? We both crazier'n Sidney, you know that, right?"

"He's not crazy."

"Yeah, okay. Try to keep him off the statues will ya?"

"Ronnie."

"I'm gittin'."

Ronnie spurts on the rack lights as he pulls out, his trademark. Mosby lingers in the yard, trying to pull his thoughts together, every sense an itch. Could canvas the neighbors, ask nosy old Miss Shepherd across the street. Ask her what? Yeah, let's get her involved in this. No, Ronnie's right. Down low it. Do the job, feel it out, see if there's a rat's ass of a chance, maybe talk to Squeaky down in Orangedale. But half the cars in Cville this weekend will have out of state plates. New York, Pennsylvania, New Jersey. You just gotta hope it's gone to somebody else's jurisdiction, and think how to say it happened. Not for the first time, he imagines a grimmer future: donned in prison guard gray or trudging the rounds of a Walmart in crepe soles. And bless old Ronnie, too.

FOURTEEN

LUCAS – THE RUBBER BAND RAILROAD

Sometimes the train catches a righteous downslope and runs bracingly through miles of fuzzy hills, in and out of chilly hollers then up naked in the sky on a trestle he can't see, always picking up speed with that relentless weight and momentum that grows like a thrill to your bones. Wheels actually squeal on the wide-cut turns. But when the train slows on a flattening grade, the breeze dies and the coal almost steams, ready to burst into flames from the baking sun. Lucas figured out long ago that there's nobody out here in the boonies to bust him, even if they may have called ahead, and he's grateful for the coal-dust coating his arms and legs, knowing he'd be burned to toast without his sunshield of filth.

He has been ticking off the one-horse/no stoplight towns where the engineer blows his whistle long and lonesome, echoing up the valley, never deigning to slow. Names some trapper gave a creek fork when he put up a shack, names some pioneer learned from the Cherokee, names some settler dreamed to memorialize his Scottish home. All in peeling paint on clapboard depots abandoned since the age of steam. A few of the old buildings reclaimed as antique stores, one a barber shop, but most just sagging shells, gone gray with decades of coal dust drift. A straggle of other shacks, low brick dollar stores, a post office trailer propped on cinder blocks, but no sign ever that he is on the right track, except the ever shortening shadows showing a more or less eastward path.

As the train wends its way between mountains, the backsides lie shadowed and dewy, opening onto front faces already blasted by a hot and cloudless day. So many photographs he's missed, not daring to wear out the phone's battery. Herds of deer, a dozen or more together, grazing like slim cattle in a clearing. Flocks of turkeys striding with that funky "walk like an Egyptian" bob of the neck. A bear with a pair of cubs at play in a pebbled creek bed, sitting flat on her ass in the shallow flow with what he could swear is a smile on her face. And another stream carving an opening in deep woods, where a heavy-set woman squatted with her dress up midstream apparently taking a dump, the train passing close enough to count the dimples on her butt.

Lucas scrawls snippets on a palm-sized notebook Chloe had given him, sentence fragments that might fit in a train song someday. It's nearly full now, so he has to scribble in the margins, even across the neatly drawn heart with an arrow through it that was her signature on the first page. Nestled in the coal wallow he's made for himself in a front corner of the hopper, he's been singing whatever song he can think of, but the only ones that seem to fit where he's at and how he feels are the old church songs from when his mother could walk and she'd give him a dime to fan her, then guilt him into dropping it in the offering plate. Miserable hours in a double-wide church plopped crooked by a lazy baptizing creek that practically churned with water moccasins so they only dared the ceremony on colder winter days. Sluggish and smelly, too, so different from the rock-thrummed rush of these mountain streams that run leaping down the hills. Amazing how the songs stuck, as much as they'd bored him then. Second and third verses of weird old hymns about angel soldiers and secret gardens and bare feet on dry sand. She'd tug herself up to attention, get through the first chorus, then plop down wheezing and bug-eyed back on the rickety pew. At that little Lucas would redouble his volume, on tiptoe with his neck stretched out, trying to make up for the hole in the sound. Even here, alone on a roving coal pile years later and two states away, he squirms at the memory. Stuff like that, it was all a trap, laid square between his ears.

As the train drops down into a broad valley with a rim of low hills, it slows and groans arthritically and the towns perk up and get bigger. Now there's a crossing gate and a stoplight, and a wise guy waves at him from a waiting pickup. A place called Salem even has a wide street of old shops with light poles strung with bunting for a Labor Day parade. The problem is not so much the clamorous heat, his dried-out water bottle, the nauseating coal fumes, his pocked and aching legs or his weakly pulsing phone. These all suck in their own ways, but they pale in comparison to the real problem, and he can't pretend or make believe otherwise any longer: This train is not going to Charlottesville or anywhere near it. There had been one last chance coming into Roanoke, the place where the old lady – how had he not even asked her name? – had advised he jump off and try to hitch. But for some reason the turn-off never came, the train somehow missed the train yard she'd promised. Is it possible he'd dozed through it all? Back on top again, it's plain that the worst has happened. The train is running dead-east now and will no doubt roll all the way downhill through the Piedmont into the empty flatlands south of Richmond to the cargo ships waiting at the Chesapeake Bay. Might not even slow down again, much less pull up anywhere.

The magic rubber band between Lucas and his dear Chloe

has been shortening from its summer-long stretch all night and day, no matter what crazy other thing was going on. For a whole day it's been pulling him forward like a slow-motion slingshot up the Appalachian spine and frankly has made the whole trip a joy. For the last hour the track has followed a limpid river that swaps from side to side at trestles as if playing tag. But now for the first time his heart sinks. He knows that the rubber band is about to start stretching again, his end point swinging out east and away with every clanking mile. That wakes him up. The depot sign reads *Lynchburg*. That's scary. Daring one last look that finally kills his phone, he reads a thick red line of highway, maybe even a four-lane, running straight north to the destination he seeks: a splotch called Charlottesville. Fifty, maybe sixty miles. A long shot and one he has sniffed at in the past, but if he can gauge it right, and if the train slows down enough, then maybe that's his chance. It could be the coal fumes or just sitting and baking in the sun or even just the chunka-chunk rhythm of the rails, but whatever has spaced him out so he missed a whole city back there, he's determined to follow through this time.

Lucas rifles through his daypack, stows the phone and the map, straps the pack on and dares to climb right down the side of the hopper on its metal ladder, hanging off the train like a barnacle brazen and careless of all eyes and obstacles ahead. He hates himself for feeling so reckless, knows he's breaking a bunch of hobo rules, but just doing something, especially something so dangerous, at least clears his head a little. But you can't hang there forever with aching fingers on hot rungs, so eventually he gulps and swings back to the little cage of beams that straddles the naked wheels. It's a terrifying thing to do, and he spits as best he can down at the wheels clicking silver between his legs. Hanging inside that frame, he watches as woods and field give way in spurts to sprawling neighborhoods of monster homes scattered to the tops of hills hard up against the blank

backs of shopping malls and trailer parks that look like rows of shoe boxes.

The train has slowed immensely but in sneaky increments over the past half hour as the engineer applies a chary break from time to time down the hopper line, relying on the flat of the land to do most of the work of soaking up all that downhill momentum. Somewhere along the way a second rail line has appeared, and as the train edges past a stationary rank of chemical transport cars, fitted like fat bombs atop their flatbeds and basking to boiling point in the noonday sun, he knows that this is it.

Lucas bends precariously and holds his breath to tighten his sandal straps, then slips monkeylike back out to the side ladder, climbing down to hang just inches above the rushing gravel bed. What was it he'd read, you want to come down facing forward or was it away from a moving car? What gives you the best odds not to tumble right into the wheels? He's dangling there in space and flashing again on that old lady's toothless lips telling the tale of her bisected dog. On that first odd ride in the freight car, Jobie had made him swear never to jump a moving train, and never ever to jump off of one, and even as this baking coal train noses along, the ground rolls past at a decent clip, and seems to be picking up speed.

It isn't a decision so much as his hands eventually giving way, just at the end of the line of chemical cars. He drops with eyes squeezed shut, lands sprawled flat on his face just inches from the bladelike wheels, rolling away on the scorching gravel and coming to hands and knees, then just plopping down in the shade of the chemical car, where he crouches horrified as 30, 31, 32, 33 more coal hoppers moan their way down the slope of the state. And wham the tug and vacancy when that last car voids the space. It's like a door slam, the rattle and creak instantly gone, leaving nothing but the still and wonderless world in its place. A wash of tears welling up, whole body a map of aches, trembling for no reason at all so he hugs himself to still it, sobbing in the wavering shadow of a tank car, but who's there to see it anyway? There's a song in that, what it feels like right this scary moment in the first sea-legged grip of solid ground, the shock and loss of locomotion. Well, maybe not, but store this shiver, who knows?

Coming shakily to his feet, Lucas tries to dust himself off, but it's a joke. Dried coal dust coats his skin, highlighting every scratch, making dark circles at the pellet wounds, and layering along his arms and legs. Nobody, not even the scruffiest farm-hand in the rattiest old pickup, is gonna stop for somebody this trashed. If he could even find the highway anyway. This is a puzzle he hasn't considered. Land facts, the way things work when you're not swooping along on the back of the dragon, when the flea's on its own and the dog is gone. When you have to trudge ahead on earth's enormity one tiny step at a time. That river that has run alongside the train for most of the morning, where has that disappeared to? Maybe he could sneak down and scrub off there, at least make himself decent enough to ride in a flatbed or something?

He digs in his backpack, hoping the dust hasn't seeped into the plastic bag that holds his clean underpants and t-shirt, but the bag has come open in all the trials of the night, so the white cotton has turned dingy gray, like a monotone tie-dye in the folds. He counts on his fingers a paradise: a bottle of water, a sink, an electrical outlet, a pack of nabs, and some shade. With that handful of miracles as a starter, he could walk to Chloe if necessary. What he needs is the church of the *7-11*, the congregation of *Mickey-D*, the *Wa-Wa* cathedral. But like cops and cabs, as they say, there's never one there when you need it.

He picks his way through a barbed wire fence that separates the tracks from a farm field, for no particular reason except to get off the gravel railbed. *Just a nit that gnaws your brain. Old nip of chaw spun down the drain.* Why is it that bits come when you're ruined, when you're least ready to do anything with them? Maybe just throw-aways, fly-bys, tossed up rhymes, loops and turnarounds. You're dumped like a turd from the back of a train into Shitsville. Mouth full of coal dust and fear. But the old brain just totally thrives on all this, whips it into overdrive, spinning up cotton candy sugar wisps that can totally crash your RAM. In the field, he sticks to a cow path that runs along the inside of the fence in the occasional shade of a tree border, and gradually the train rhythms unhook, the world pretending to go still beneath his sandals.

The path leads down to a dried creek bed with one muddy pool that mocks him, moon-cratered as it is with hoof prints and cow flop land mines, one droning dragonfly hanging witless in the air. The dragonfly mesmerizes. It's the buzzing still point at the center of nowhere, radiating outwards past Lucas' dim shadow across the parched, manure dotted field, the cloudless white sky and the whatever beyond. Its dull hover whines away all the rhyming lyrics along with any sense of purpose or destination. A dimming reflexive pulse. He could just stop here, call off the game, wait until it all just eroded to bleached bones gnawed by raccoons, and that would mean as much. Then the dragonfly does this important thing. It lifts, rotates, magnifies, so that his eyes cross to keep it in focus. Zoom. Whoosh. Gone like the snap of a finger. An order. Move.

Still not a cow in sight, and the field seems to stretch out forever, but over the very next rise the fence bends to border some part of the town. Lucas drops his daypack over, then negotiates the strands of barbed wire, one hand lifting, the other pressing down to sneak first one then the other leg through. That feels significant. Maybe not train hopping but something. A narrow asphalt lane begins right at his feet, stretching into a tidy neighborhood of modest brick homes, each on its square of yellowed lawn, each with its pickup parked outside, each sealed shut behind its sucking hum of air conditioning, and no humans anywhere. Neutron bomb. Weird to walk it, sore thumb that he is, without even a tree or bush for cover. *Dumb sore thumb no gum just a bum gimme some willya son?*

He walks on, past chain link fences and rose bushes shivering weirdly under the assault of Japanese beetles in their metallic green armor, past overturned plastic tricycles and garden hoses all hooked to faucets and rolled up on little trolleys in the flat shade on the left side of every single house on the block. Man, just to get a little spray of water! The thing is, you can walk along like you're headed somewhere, eyes front and marching, but rest assured the old sentries watch from behind their drapes, and nobody will do a thing, but the minute, the very second, you veer off, turn onto a driveway, all hell will break loose. So it's just how bad you want it. It's just that he's come so far. Maybe it would be alright, but look what could happen, too. Tempting as hell, though. Well, you could ask. If you were lucky enough to pick the right door, and make just the right pitch in just the right way. But if it's the wrong door, and most of them will be.

One dead zone neighborhood leads into another, like some kind of cul de sac maze, and Lucas goes on automatic, trying to keep what there is of a shadow behind him. At the bottom of a long hill, the houses finally give over to a baking strip of bunker-like shops and offices, all shut down for the weekend. At last some action, cars passing, but it seems like each one slows down to check him out. In a storefront window, he pauses to see what's so interesting. It isn't much of a mirror, but he can make out the white tear streaks down black cheeks and pink lips like some old time clown paint. No wonder they slow down.

At the corner looms an enormous church made of limestone

blocks that runs the whole width of the street, almost glowing in the sunshine. A little campus of administrative buildings, in matching limestone, hunker around the sanctuary and steeple. Anchored in a shady square of lawn, one outrageous oak tree seems to reach out to hug the church or push it away. Church. Soup kitchen. Handout. Maybe a welcome prayer. Lucas' eyes search the perimeter for the faucet he finds in a shady corner. In a now or never moment, he dares to cross beneath the oak and kneels to gobble and spit what water really means. Gray streams run from his face and arms in what he figures may be the most religious moment of his life. He peels off the filthy t-shirt, rinses and wrings it out, uses it to scrub his arms and knees, to dab at the angry pocks along his calves, then rinses and wrings it again. He stretches the shirt out on the grass to dry, fills his water bottle and pours it down on his head. He's on all fours, shaking his hair out, still spitting gray, when the shoe appears between his hands.

Lucas squints up at a head framed in glaring sunlight, tries to squirm backwards on his knees. "Git up from there!" the head roars.

"Dude, alright." He comes up wobbly and has to brace a hand on the church wall.

"Stand up straight."

The guy's no bigger than Lucas, at least in height, but he's chunky with round shoulders that can lift. He wears glasses, a short-sleeved yellow shirt with a necktie and lime slacks. An Easter egg that has sprouted limbs.

"What you think you're doin'?"

Lucas says nothing, bends to retrieve his daypack, sidles towards his damp t-shirt.

"Can you speak, boy? You hear me?"

"Dude." That's when the guy stomps a tassled loafer right down on the t-shirt, pressing it into the damp grass.

"Sir. I'm goin'."

"That's right."

"Can you step off my shirt, please?"

Instead, the guy toes into the shirt and lifts it with one loafer, so Lucas has to bend and pull it off. "Now git."

"I'm goin'."

"I'm watchin'."

"I'm goin'. Dude."

Lucas makes it out to the sidewalk before turning back to see the guy, dim in the oak tree's shade. He's pulled a handkerchief out to turn the faucet, making sure it's all the way off. Lucas mentally flips him a bird, pulling on the wet t-shirt that stretches and sucks onto his skin. Then he remembers. "Dude. My water bottle. Sir?"

"Say what?" the other man shouts.

"Just a sip for the road."

The man frowns, looks up at the steeple, and shakes his head. Then as if laboring up a slope, he strides across the lawn and holds out his handkerchief. "You stay here. Gimme the bottle." Lucas hands it over, sips at the last drips of water running out of his hair, and when the guy returns summons his biggest thank you grin to ask, "Can you point me in the direction of a highway to Charlottesville?"

"Charlottesville? Yeah, I'd say that's about right, lookin' at you." He's standing there with his hands on his hips, picking his teeth with his tongue, King Humpty Dumpty. Says, "You're standing on it."

"Sir?"

"Route 29, you nitwit. Straight shot, if you can git there. And my advice is, go."

"Dude!" It's all he can do not to hug the man.

FIFTEEN

CHLOE – BEDROOM

OUT PAST HER tunnel of bundled down and cotton a red light blinks like Christmas. It's a beating electronic heart, a mini-lighthouse that pulls her up from drowning sleep into the gasping gift of air. Propped on elbows in her cave, Chloe grabs the phone to punch for the text and squeals in delight to see printed there a string of sweet characters: *mt@rvr n pm*. And some kind of dimmed out selfie, in a goofy hat, is he crouched under a car?

The time stamp says 9:24. What is it now? Far in the dark of the opposite wall the stupid swivel-eyed cat clock with its wagging tail shows a glowing digital 11:43 at its belly. 'Rents gone to their stupid game, maybe a free zone for now? At least prob. Who knows where he was, is, how soon he'll get here, no voice-mail, no song, *Snapchat* a void since dawn. Types back *kwhen?* She's up in the shower and out again as if ejected, at the mirror has to rub the short buzz of hair on her head to check that she's shampooed. That funhouse mirror that can play you all fat, freckled, kinked out, she hardly bothers. The kit, the black lipstick and heavy eyeliner, so last night it makes her want to hurl. Just the lightest nose ring, that silver one, still raw to slide it in, glad she's waited on the lip. The river, he would pick that. The last good place before he'd caught the bus that took him away last spring. There's an old gloss in the drawer from middle school, a total turnaround that feels like a new thrill and doing it, running it across her lips so they glisten, is the thing that wakes her up for real. Exactly as then is how it will be, only this time the new bikini with the halter tie that can unravel with a touch like porn. Expect a mess, starved, and crazy with stories to tell. Could he be there already wading around? Where was he when the text went out? No clue. So much to consider, to do fast, Mom be gone please, no time for those water-boarding eyes.

Slpy.

She grabs the phone again to re-read the cryptic text. Stabs Ava and gets nothing, stabs Izzy and is halfway through a flurry of tapping when she picks up:

"Whoah whoah whoah girl! Whaddup?"

"Izz. He's here."

"He, who he? You mean Joel?"

"Oh fuck Joel, no Izz, you know!"

"Joel is at your house?"

"Ohmigod no. Lucas, remember I told you?"

"Lucas? That guy. From last year?"

"Lucas, yes, the guitar, the train guy?"

"That guy's at your house?"

"Yeah, no, not yet but yeah soon."

"Whoah. Seriously? Are you..."

"It's just."

"Hang on."

"I gotta get downtown, to meet him."

"That a problem?"

"Mom's gone. I got nothing."

"Car still broke?"

"It's a front end job or something, could be weeks."

"Look, you don't want me to call..."

"No, totally no, do not do that!"

"Okay, chill, we're good. Maybe bike?"

"Bike, what? Really? C'mon."

"Look, I'm just."

"Okay, I'll get there, it's just."

"Yeah, um. Is this planned?"

"Look, I would a told you."

"Big secret, I get it."

"No. It's so crazy. He just left a text. But he's coming."

"And you all dizzy on it, I do hear that."

"Izzy, please."

"No, I'm in. That is so cool. Like when do I meet him?"

"Meet him? Oh, um, how 'bout."

"216, stroke of midnight. You know I'm gonna meet him!"

"Okay, def."

"Take a cab, Cee. Or Uber it."

"Yeah, right, of course."

"We prepared?"

"Three finger salute."

"That's right. You be that!"

"Oh Izzard!"

"Be yah."

It's what she needed to think. A consult. So already on the phone she's slipping into the Lair of the 'Rents to grab beach towels and sun screen. Then downstairs to make sandwiches, PB&J'll keep, grab chips, one from Mom's stash of $10 chocolate bars, a couple beers to keep the chocolate cool, *Diet Dew*, you gotta think, cloth napkins, c'mon girl, just casual. He likes apples. Banana maybe. Enough. Have card will shop. When the pack's full, stop. Stop.

Now the moment of truth, you reel it all in. Breathe on the way up the steps. Text for the ride. Don't push it, just one message for now: U cm. oxox. Okay, mirror, Frizz it up, glad it's still too short to braid. All baubles just silver. And, this makes her want to pee, a row of *Baghdad Special* mint balloons with a cammo print for her purse. Mastercard. Freedent. All she'll ever need. Now go.

During the half hour wait, she paces and squeals, remembering to scrawl a liberating fridge note: *Out with Frenz/May Sleepover*. If they get home before, if they get home before, the cab must come, right now it must come. But if they're gone, really gone, she could bring him here, whoah that's detention, girl.

The phone leaps like a frog in her hand. Unknown #. Ohmigod. She swallows hard and brings it cautiously to her ear.

"Chlo? Hey, Chlo?"

Joel. The whole past night and its disappointments run across the one and a half syllables of his name. Never texts. Loves his voice too much.

"You there? Just checkin'. You good?"

"I'm not here."

"Yo, yeah. Look."

"Don't check on me. Stop it."

"Stop what?"

"Just stop. Just go."

"Well which way you want it, girl?"

That's him right there. The way he plays it. That's like his creepy hands, a flush running up to her roots. And she knows he can tell it too.

"Look, Chlo, I was thinking."

"You think?"

"Chloe."

"Oh it's Chloe now?"

"Chlo, Chloe, whatever."

"Yeah, whatever."

"Look, I just."

"I know Joel. I get it. Now stop."

"Well, look, if it's like that."

"It is."

"I just."

"You just." The car has to come up the drive, it just has to.

"I just thought, you know, tonight."

"That is not a good plan."

"Well, what do you want to do?"

"What I want to do is nothing to do with you."

"Oh come on Chlo, like you got a big plan."

"You're a dick, you know that?"

"I got one, you know that."

"I'm out."

"Got game tix."

"Oh please." She taps him off, should have done it step one. Oh God, she thinks, I'm gonna be sick again. But grabs a stick of gum, pops a beer from the fridge and swigs the mixed flavors of toothpaste and hay. Two sips and dumps it in the sink. Leave it on the drainboard, that'll give them something to talk about. Then she walks out to the drive, shocked by the noon heat all drunk with the buzz of bumblebees and the scent of roses. That first step outside, even now today, is always a burdensome war right through her heart. The cave half of her wants back beneath the comforter in the dark. The other half, whatever that is, maybe it's the Lucas half, can sort of get a drift of the possible day. When the car comes just climb in and see.

SIXTEEN

THE CANNONS – AIRPORT

"WE SHOULD HAVE RENTED A STRETCH, not this minivan oh god, this is ludicrous, will never work! I don't believe this!" The neurosurgeon stands in the empty atrium of the glassy airport terminal spread-legged and gesturing like a ship captain agog at looming storm clouds. But there are no clouds. The tilted wall of windows frames a blank sky anchored by a foggy blue line of low mountains made to shimmer by the vaporous ghosting of noon-day heat off the runway's flat paved sea. Behind him a digital screen shows his globe-hopping daughter's prop jet from Dulles running a half hour late, while before him a gleaming spear-like Lear jet materializes to slice silently down and glide with privileged poise to a distant private terminal, far from the lumbering winged cattle cars nudged up against the window. "That's got to be them. We should be there, now!" he frets, tossing his cell phone from hand to hand.

"Rainie, let's do this," Iris says. She stands at a calculated distance, making space for his pacing, arm-waving dance.

"Any second now, I tell you, this phone will buzz, and if they end up in a cab, if they have to make their way alone...."

"Rainie, you go. Take the rental. You'll need the seats. I'll stay here and wait for Claire. Circle back around to get us. We'll follow in the Caddy."

Dr. Cannon flips the phone in the air, catching it flat in an open palm, then pockets it, saying, "I'm gone. Stay here. Let's do this." She watches him straightening his shirt buttons as he storms out the automatic sliding doors.

Iris' head swivels, seeking someone with whom to share the storied long-suffering wife grin and head bob, but the whole concourse is empty. Sad to see a single pink suitcase trundling along the luggage carousel with no one to retrieve it. Back at the window a decrepit-looking commuter plane, the compact car of air travel, feeds from a hose, a little obscenely, she thinks. It's a scorcher out there. That will help her cause at the tailgate party, drawing people in beneath the awning where proximity and gin can spur conviviality.

She imagines that movie folk view the world with simple, iconic minds. Today is a research trip, locking into their image banks the "real" way a college football game looks on that first anything-can-happen Saturday of any season. Down the road sometime in whatever they call Technicolor now she'll see it all in a swirl of camera work, the garish blue and orange striped tents, the plastic martini glasses, the ruddy crabs piled on newspaper, the straw boaters and fedoras all coded and checked and sealed forever in some set aside moment of an adventure flick.

What sort of very different person would spend her days painstakingly remaking the visual imprint of a memory? All the labor of set-building, lighting, casting, all those dozens of technicians whose names roll by at the end, just to remake an afternoon like any other at a football game. But wait, maybe it's not so foreign after all. How distant is all that industry from her own, from the beribboned and scented showplace she has made of her flower shop, from the crystal and lace of a formal dinner under the central chandelier at home, or for that matter, from all the carefully casual hoopla she has orchestrated for this afternoon at the back of an SUV? She makes, they remake, is that it?

Off at the private terminal, the Lear jet's finlike tail sticks out, as if flicking its privilege. She should be there. Rainsworth can be so clumsy in these moments, especially when he wants or needs something, big puppy dog falling all over himself to make nice. But maybe it's better this way. Let the comedy play out, the wrestle for luggage, the first sticky drips of ingratiation, all grist no doubt for the script. She turns away from the window to stroll into a pocket gift shop lined with tins of peanuts, jars of jelly, ceramic clowns and giant lollipops. She knows this shop well from travels past, holding Claire's hand or Chloe's, while they oohed and ahhed over a miniature elf, bending to warn them not to touch, with a word or two helping them develop an appraising eye.

Claire always so inquisitive, so quick to mimic, somehow even then so self-assured. Chloe always in her shadow, rebelling against what? All things bright and beautiful, it seems. It's just tragic. Or isn't that the way of sisters? Iris allows a brief flicker of her own estranged family – all the four girls named after flowers, her father's garden he had called them a thousand times. Rose married to a vintner in New Zealand, Ivy teaching school in Connecticut, now officially married to another woman with a flower name, Daisy. Tulip, poor thing, still at home in Winchester, tending to Mom in her waning days. No one phones, no one emails or texts or Facebooks. Except to plan quick visits that don't overlap. It's happening already beneath her own roof, she knows. Some seed planted at birth going to rot before her eyes.

Her phone chirps, "I've got 'em darling! We're en route to the house!"

"Um, Rainie, did you forget something?"

"No, I thought, let's not make them wait? They've had such a flight."

"They all fit?"

"These covered wagons they make, yeah, sure, not a problem."

"Rain..." He's hung up.

That steaming pile! This was probably his scheme all along, but would he admit it, not in a million years. His own daughter returning from a summer overseas. Given up for strangers! Five hundred things wrong with this behavior and so easy to climb each rung of them to a fine and long-delayed tantrum, but again, yet again, not the time or place. If she has learned anything from her two decades plus with this man, it is the virtue of patience. The ability to simmer sunnily, saving the boil over for the right impactful moment when she has his attention. The skill in caching it away, and the discipline to let most of it go, watching it evaporate, so that only the concentrated broth makes its way to the table. For this one, he will pay, if not for her sake, for Claire's.

Whose plane arrives exactly as the digital panel has predicted, just fifteen minutes after Rainsworth's departure. How difficult he would have made those minutes. And here comes Claire, early down the ramp, movie star slim, that long neck bare, those long legs in calf-length slacks, the athletic genes they share. But the glamour of youth! Can make you grit your teeth. And those eyes when they lock on you, that smile that maybe no one else receives, opening with the same warmth of gratitude, the same relief that goes back to her first scratched knee or bee sting, heart-melting and a little frightening at the same time. She was born with it, what they mean by that term *noblesse oblige*. But as they embrace, Iris knows this is what we live for. That instant when they both surrender to the game they both think of as home, when they take up the mother and daughter roles another notch, playing friends, co-conspirators, confidants. The lone porter at the gate has guessed correctly and takes Claire's luggage check to the carousel. They stand inside the surface transportation door while Claire says it all, who was in first class headed back to Capitol Hill, and the hassle at Dulles in their weird terminal-to-terminal buses on stilts, and hair problems and markers for discussion later, about galleries and cathedrals, food and vineyards and Irish horses. Fourth trip to Europe and she owns it now, citizen of the world, trilingual, holds her own at a ball or a bazaar, thank God, we did something right with this one.

It's only as they climb into the Escalade that Claire asks, "Where's the doctor?"

"Oh, he's got a special surprise for you, wanted to make sure it was ready."

"Total bullshit, Mom. He just didn't care to come."

"No, no, he came! I mean."

"What do you mean, he came? Then where is he?"

"Hmm." There is one person in the world who can fluster her, send her off her game, it's the intimate thing between them that she both loves and despises. "Oh, it's all part of the surprise, you just have to hold your horses, Dear. You'll see."

"But he was here and he left?" That brings the simmer up, almost opens the lid, but Iris holds on, bows her head, hoping that Claire hasn't read it already.

"Seriously, what's going on, Mom? What is this?"

But it is a surprise, really. It will all come off well. Maybe Rainie did the right thing despite himself. It will be better to meet them at home. "You'll see. Now let's talk. Who was that mysterious stranger you texted about?" And with that they are back at it, chattering along all the back routes she knows to avoid the building game traffic out on Highway 29. They wend through wood and pasture and rows of ranch homes set back behind fences, and yes, this is better, because we have this time, this gift – imagine a daughter who shares! And when we walk in the door all the guests will be settled, their luggage stowed away. It'll be like walking into a garden party in Hollywood. One that Claire will never forget. Oh such a day already!

SEVENTEEN

SID – IN THE LAND OF THE GENERALS

THE VAST WHITE awning of the *Intelos Wireless Pavilion* soars above its elevated stage like a cosmic maw opened wide to swallow the pedestrian mall that leads directly out from its throat. Or the mall itself is a mirage projected outward from the awning– they don't call it wireless for nothing – to fool the shoppers who go about their day as an experiment conducted by superior beings, an ant farm under central command. Radiation beams off the hot asphalt in waves, while puppet men busy themselves beneath the awning's drum-tight expanse, aligning chairs in long curving rows for the night's musical event. Drones, oblivious to the orders that drive them, tools of the coming vortex.

Standing on a brick walkway between the bus station at the top of the arena's grassy bowl and the concert stage below, Sid fights the urge to once again measure the distance from this spot to the coal tower that squats like a rusty tin can at the tree line. How many times has he triangulated the correspondence among the three structures? One time he'd even rented a laser app, the kind surveyors use, but electronics are prone to malfunction, can be hacked. The rusting protractor from his elementary school days can do the job quite well. Though the variations can be troubling. People speak of reasonable margins of error, and therein lies the problem. The sun seems to have clamped a bright hand on the day, squeezing oxygen out of the air. No breeze at all, few pedestrians, the sky like steel wool threatening sparks. As he turns slowly in place, then just a calculated step faster, Sid forces himself to repeat what he knows, that one more calculation will not change anything. You can run the numbers every day, all day, and they will still leave anxious gaps. But always pointing to a temporal certainty, a truth in a world of worry. Everyone knows after all. This coming hell on earth.

A drill-bit creature scrambles through his skull at the thought. He doubles over and pulls hard at his ears, trying to empty his head. At a garbage can rimmed with yellow jackets he vomits heavily into the void. It will be like this, he knows, until the battle is won or lost. The whole day accelerates, wobbling on its axis. He had thought that the old soldier Steve would understand, that he would pull his troops together and help somehow. But not even Steve. Why did he give back the gun? The key. He turned down the mission. Said, "This is up to you. Now make it so." But what if the calculations are mistaken? The whole scheme could be only a gambit or skirmish, a distraction from a larger catastrophe. But does it matter? You can't presume to comprehend some ultimate solution; you can only face what you see. But draining down the power, wouldn't that help? Will the little armory he's collected do the job?

And this other thing, you have to call it an antenna. When the Army Ground Command moved away from downtown to its ominous walled complex north of the city, they left this. The reason for the season, the crux of the algorithm, this signal tower awning where crowds gather as zombies. There's too much radiation here to think. The growling drillbit between his ears sits idling, guarding every impulse. You go at it aslant, pretend if you can that you're droned. The sideways walk helps confuse it. Singing helps a little, "The Good Old Song" repeated on a loop. People veer away, deflected by the shield. The gift is these sneakers, exactly 25 centimeters heel to toe by external measure. They pinch, toes squinched, but that's not what matters. You can't dead reckon, there are obstacles, but with line of sight you can adjust around them. Heel to toe, heel to toe, do the measure one more time.

Because even loaded with focusing power, the Pavilion is not the source. It's just an amplifier. The beam is forged elsewhere and he knows even as he teeters along towards it heel to toe that the old coal tower is that place. All his life, it has ruled him, looming over his backyard. It just sits there, abandoned, graffitied, camouflaged in kudzu, but other people feel it. They come from all over to camp there, they climb inside to do things they'd never do at home. It makes you wonder. That's the siren that called to the artist with his metal dress frame. He thought he was making art but served a larger purpose, shaping a weapon for demons. Or he knew, had orders from the Generals, was joining the fight. When it happens, he's dreamed it coming to life. The tower rearing up on six robotic legs, shaking off its slumber and going to work, the sculpture worn like an Easter hat.

3,210 steps to the tower. The weeds along the railroad track lie flattened, dotted with beer cans and milk crates from parties past, but in this heat even the grasshoppers avoid the place. Yet it has its own hum. He's charted this, how the structure shifts between states, phasing in and out, pulsing to a heartbeat rhythm. The handgun in his pocket will nearly complete his collection. But you can't just scale the tower in the middle of a day. Sid lets himself take a regular step, his counting finished, crosses the four rail lines and pulls himself over the backyard fence, glad to see that Mattie's cruiser is gone. If this is the day when it all comes to a head, then a nosy brother cannot be allowed to get in the way. He could help, if he would, but he's asked and he won't.

Crawling heavily in through the bedroom window, Sid crouches at the door then creeps down the hall, checking that Mattie is gone. What's needed now is more pull. Bending the future will take everything he can get. Dad's shotgun in the hall closet, but the dusty leather case is empty. He's already collected that one, weeks ago, he recalls. Sid stumbles into the kitchen and takes his chair, rummaging for a crumb in an empty *Pop Tarts* wrapper. The hanging prism above the sink has gone dead, the room itself drained of color. Something has changed, too, in the backyard whine, a shift in pitch and volume. It's definitely Stonewall, the cicada in the garage eves, he's sung his last, just bird food now. He decides to go at it with a system now, house by house, proximal to distal.

There is no time, but he has no help, and will have to do it himself, in fact is already striding around to the front gate that is never used, clanking it closed and going next door to old man Tillman's place, an identical bungalow with the same rusty chain link fence. Sid climbs up the stoop and into the front room as if he owns it. Everything is the same as at home, even the sofa opposite the front window, this one covered in dusty clear vinyl like a car seat. He could walk to the back and there would be *Pop Tarts* on the melamine table. Years ago, when grownups walked the earth, Mrs. Tillman would stand right here in the door handing out homemade cookies dusted with sugar that stained the sewn-on S at the front of his Halloween costume. Sid realizes that this is as far as he's ever gotten, has never actually stepped across the threshold into his next door neighbor's home. But the front door was unlocked, opening with the same rattling click as his own to the same doll house interior.

The place smells different and the colors are off, thick with the biting stink and resinous veneer of an eon of cigarettes, the only sound the hollow tock of a wall clock. In a corner stands the furniture he's remembered from all those many years ago, the sort of thing a boy will sock away, a glass-fronted gun cabinet that holds a double row of weapons. Shotguns, a Winchester rifle, an ancient muzzle loader. He shuffles toward the cabinet and pulls on the door, but it's locked.

"Hey, you!"

Old Man Tillman lurks in the hallway in boxer shorts and a tank top, what's left of his hair twirled out to horns above his ears. He waves a beer bottle like a hammer in one shaky fist.

"Hey Mr. Tillman."

"Sidney, boy, that you?" He points the bottle, squinting.

"Mr. Tillman, hi. I need your help." Sid reaches in his cargo pants and pulls out the pistol. "This thing."

The old man recoils. "Sid, what is that? What do you want?"

"I just need one thing. Just one."

"One what? Put that thing down now, won't you?"

Sid holds the gun flat in his palm, as if offering it for sale. "It's this. I need to borrow your guns."

"Borrow, what?"

"Just. I only need them really for one day." Talking is such a pain. Words. Why can't people just see?

"For what, take 'em where, boy?" He holds the bottle at one ear while fumbling for the glasses hanging from his shirt front. Almost aimlessly, Sid shifts the gun to his other hand, his finger slipping onto the trigger. He looks down at it, turns it in his hand.

"I would tell you. It's just..."

The old man perches the glasses on his ears. There's a wrapping of tape thick at the nose piece so they go on cock-eyed. "Sid. Son. You need to go home."

"Yes, no, see. Just one. I need one of yours, even just one."

"One what?"

"In the case. A gun. Just one."

"You need a gun? Another gun? For what?"

Sid is not so much waving the handgun as jabbing it in different directions in the air, as if targeting dust motes only he can see. "Just one."

Magnified behind his patched up glasses, the old man's eyes go round as an owl's. "Oh. You want one. Well." He lowers the beer bottle, taking a half step back to the hallway. "Well, if that's so damned important. I don't know, Sid. Is that what you want? Well, why don't you let me get the key here to open the front, let me get that, will you?"

"Alright." Suddenly embarrassed by the handgun, Sid fits it back in his pocket, forgetting for a moment why he's barged in on the old man.

"You wait." Mr. Tillman backs away down the hall out of sight. Sid follows to the door, peering into the shadows, where he sees the old man crouched over a bedside table with a phone in his hands. Everything then happens in choppy, still frame snapshots. Sid's sneaker in a jagged circle of glass. A rifle, two shotguns, a fistful of bloody shells. The bedroom door slamming shut. The barrels in his arms pointing every which way blocking his exit. Sid gets out to the stoop with his unwieldy bundle and shouts back, "I'm going now. Gotta go."

Around the corner, he stops to catch his breath at the railroad fence. He finds his spot, scrambles on his stomach under the fence, then pulls the weapons through the cracks one-by-one, clumsily cradling them back in his arms to cross the tracks to the coal tower. But there's just no way to get up there now with this haul. Maybe taking them up one at a time. But it's too much, too wide open in the daytime. They'll see and stop it all. There's nothing for it but to stash the guns in the weeds until dark, come back and take them up then. He trudges out into a strip of brush along the track and drops the guns, plopping down beside them. The weeds wave taller than his head when he sits, he could be anywhere on a farm far from town, except for the coal tower looming like a breathing thing at his back.

He sucks on a knuckle, where a glass shard has run a shallow gash, wipes off the .44 rifle shells one-by-one and methodically loads them into the Winchester. It's like a grown-up version of his old BB gun. Is that in the garage somewhere? Would it help? Only a couple buck shot shells and they only fit the 12-gauge. Who knows if the old guns will even fire, which of course is not the point. They're like copperhead snakes, dappled with rust, their fangs more dangerous in idea than in action. And the nest he's made of them up top has a swarming power, with potential to swerve off the storm. But scattered here in the weeds, even loaded, they don't seem to have any pop at all, just pipes nailed to wooden staves. Like they've shot their wad already. There has to be something, some punch left in them. For one thing, for the first time in hours, the drillbit between his ears has paused, leaving an absence so sweet he feels drowsy. That's power. That says something.

Sid lines the guns up in a row. From three feet away you can't see them at all down in the standing weeds. If it's all unreeling now. If the numbers mean what they say and this is the day. In this moment of clarity, he'll be able to explain. One more try. Steve will have to understand. If anybody else ever can. Better not to go it alone, not now. Surely Captain Steve will see that.

EIGHTEEN
LUCAS – ROUTE 29

HE'S WAITED an hour on a baking highway at the edge of town, making the age-old beggar's gesture with a thumb. Nobody even slows. Does anybody even do hitch-hiking anymore? And it's just Saturday shoppers going back and forth on short hops to the stores, moms with van loads of kids in soccer shirts, lawn care teams pulling trailers with their gear. He walks a few steps, turns at the sound of oncoming traffic and tries again, all the way over a long river bridge, where the highway cuts grandly through a cliff-face and divides out into four lanes. On the other side at a busy gas station with an unlocked outdoor men's room, he washes up a little, standing on one foot at a time to rinse some of the grunge off his feet and legs, and examining the shot pellet welts on his calves. Some look like they have pellets imbedded. His mouth fills with bile at the thought of digging them out. The toilet is disgusting, but there's a plug for his phone. The sink is too tiny to fit his head under the faucet, and handfuls of water splash coal dust mud streaks down the wall. In the cracked mirror he takes a shot at pulling strands of dirty hair into dreads of some kind, don't the rastas use mud to do that?

He's wrung out his t-shirt, but it still fits like a damp skin, and the phone's only picked up a trickle of charge before a whole van load of kids banging at the door forces him out onto the road again, where he picks up the increasingly hopeless routine of trudge, turn, thumb, trudge, turn, thumb, the service station and bridge gradually dissolving in the shimmering heat that rises off the griddle of asphalt at his feet. Cars do the zoom now, accelerating off the bridge. Eighteen wheelers groan, down-shifting up the hill with no interest in losing that momentum. Probably just a flea to them anyway, not even making their radar. No songs left, no tunes, no rhymes. The worst mistake you can make is to count. Every time you get up to a hundred, you start over, but it gets stupid, your head goes down and all your effort at trying to look spry and collegiate and cool, nursing your last sips of water, fail. In that instantaneous sizing up they do, you can't look shifty, gotta have that open look, that earnest just-need-to-get-somewhere smile, but this is why hitching sucks. You have to rely on people. The train's there, you get on it, it goes. Trusting in the good will of drivers cruising along in their giant SUVs is a whole other project.

But you only need one, and then it's done. You only need one to get some fun. It only takes one to get out of the sun. It only takes one, you better run! He's not even sure it's really happening, but a gleaming black Silverado tall as a Hummer has slammed to a stop a hundred yards up the road, and is actually backing along the shoulder towards him! As he comes up on it, the giant square thing seems to pulse with all the growling bass music straining at its blacked out windows. When the door pops open, it's four of the biggest men he's ever seen, filling their enormous seats, so that's who these monster trucks are built for! And the cabin stinks richly of reefer smoke. Lucas doesn't even pause, squirming into the third seat beside a beer cooler, and they are off with amazing, swooping speed that throws him back in his seat. A thick hand with a huge class ring swings back to slap his knee as one passenger half turns to exchange names: "Okay, I'm Al. This is Chuck, that's Truck, he's Buck and you. You Suck. Chuck, Truck, Buck and You Suck! We got ourselves another You Suck, gentlemen! You're goin' to the Game, You Suck. Let's do this thing! Yeah, grab a beer, sucker! Suck it!"

The giant turns back to his companions and the shouted conversation they've been having, while the spooky, angry music goes up to eleven and the bass woofer under Lucas' seat whomps like he's sitting on a bulldozer. But the first sip of beer does two things in rapid succession: an instant of sweet clarity that comes up to him like flute music inside the din, then an exhaustion so complete that he takes one more swig and falls dead out with the can tucked between his legs.

And then Wham that giant paw is giving him a shake. "You Suck! This is it, we're done. Haul out, end of the road, go! Don't know where you're headed, but this is where you've ended up! You Suck! C'mon!"

Lucas is up and out before he's fully awake, has to climb back up inside the suddenly silent rolling disco to claim his backpack, then stands wobbly in its shade where it sits tipped sideways on a hill behind a brick cottage surrounded by people in orange shirts. There's drool at his mouth, and as he wipes it away, he begins to realize that he's not dreaming. The back wall of a stadium looms above it all. This has got to be it – he's back, he's made it, unbelievable. Chloe. All the guys from the truck have gone deep in the crowd, all the orange backs turned in on their orange lives. He sees beer and chips and Cheez-Its and pretzels and popcorn, but don't push it, just take this gift, just live it and get the hell down the road. That old rubber band had not lost its snap after all. It's flat and slack now, she's somewhere in this town, he can see the long slope of her neck, those lovely almond sort of Oriental eyes.

He shoulders his pack and walks invisible out of the driveway, past lines of cars and people with open umbrellas and folded up stadium seats, wending against their lemming flow. The layout begins to make sense. You find the University's old Rotunda and use the shade like pointers straight down Main Street just keep going to the river on this fine afternoon. And if the message got through that's where she'll be. She'll be right there, why not? Out of all the fucked up things in his whole fucked up life, she's the one that isn't, right? The exception that proves the rule.

NINETEEN

CHLOE – THE ROPE SWING

FOR THE LAST half hour she's been firing off text messages into nowhere, pausing to type while making her way past poison ivy fronds along a narrow path downstream from the river camp, with all its shabby weirdo's, to a private place where she selects a picnic spot on a sandbank snugged in a lazy bend of the shallow river. A fisherman had been working the opposite bank, his pole propped on a stick and his line bobbing in ripples, but he's gone now, too, after taking the time to clean up his beer empties and pack them back in a plastic cooler. Chloe pops a beer herself, but only wets her lips. It's such a nothing flavor, like health food or something.

Already two scenarios do battle in her head. One is the reunion, the beach towels, the bikini, the slippy man crunching apples. The other, a long afternoon of swatting at bugs in the weeds and eventually trudging back out to the highway ashamed and defeated. The latter possibility has been gaining ground with each wasted text sent off to the cloud. She's fighting it, wanting the good thing to happen so badly, but now she's begun to see herself as the fisherman probably did, a ridiculous child out of place, mosquito harried, alone and at risk. The backpack's belongings – the apples, the mushy chocolate, the power bars, the PB&J's – all spread so tv commercial on the towels like props for the actors of this imaginary afternoon to come only play up her foolishness from this other perspective. The river glistening, rippling, so friendly and alive is also just a narrow trough, probably like totally polluted, just a shallow, rocky creek really, its banks lined with dried mud, overgrown with weeds, a joke river really.

She's been listening to Lucas' music on a single earbud, the river gurgle filling her other ear, and for the first time misgivings filter in, coloring the lines. It's that reedy voice and a sparely plunked guitar doing three songs he said were all about her, but I bet you say that to all the girls. That one song, though, was right here. It can only be about that Saturday before school let out. He mentions the trestle, her scratched up knee and - *cinnamon-sugar from a Farmer's Market doughnut on your cheek* – she could listen to that one rushed and breathy line on a loop all day.

That song is definitely them, and it's the best one, his fingers plinking like the river around the words, and every line sort of whispered like he's discovering something new that might spook if he comes on too strong. She plays it through again, thinking, if that gets ruined. You have to draw the line somewhere. But catches the devil at work, sewing a wisp of annoyance at how nasally superior, how sure of himself, how fakely real he can sound. She cuts that one off at the knees, swipes the screen off and stands up to stroll barefoot for a moment on the slimy pebbles of the river bottom. The thing is, how long do you stay? When do you stop, blow it off and just go away? They had walked here hand-in-hand. Drenched from slipping in a pool on this very bend, they had talked about this water coming out of the mountains, down from Old Rag and Stony Man and the other blue ridges to the west, running in a long, embracing curve around the edge of town and emptying on down to the James and eventually the Chesapeake Bay, *"where the whales and the manatees play"*. They had started to hum and piece together a song about that, the "Little Molecules" song, swapping lines, finishing each other's thoughts, laughing in the icy run that came in late spring to their thighs, the water so much higher and faster than today. Was that all she had to go on? A day, a million texts, three dinky mp3's?

The truth is her whole life lies collected in two piles, rumpled and wrinkled and waiting for the laundry. One pile holds all the hopeless dudgeon of another day – all the people and stuff that can make you sick just to think about, all the pukable things her Mom has bought, lurid blouses with little hand-drawn butterflies and watercolor flowers that only a dork would wear mixed up with all her stolid uniforms of black stovepipe jeans and shrunken black t-shirts sporting the names of ancient bands. The other pile just one white t-shirt, with a little rip under the left sleeve. The one she wears now.

To go out like this, in short-short cut-off jeans, in yellow low-cut Chucks, the cheapest plastic bead ankle bracelet, the thinnest gold nose ring, just a pair of ear staples, the Aviator Ray-Bans, her so-called friends would never let her live it down. The pix would hit the web in a flash, and she would forever be pinned as a loser even in the land of the lost. What are you, like five? What are you, like day camp? Excuse me, Miss Chloe, I got a boo-boo. Excuse me, Miss Chloe, I got a rash. It was just dumb to come out like this, and to be down here alone in the weeds too close to those creeps in the homeless camp on one more endless re-run afternoon.

She can head back out to the street, get a cab to come down, go home and change while her parents are at the game. Put on the uniform, head downtown again and let the same dumb night repeat. But what's happened in one day so that all of a sudden that thought is such a fail? She's absolutely decided now in this instant to chuck it all, to toss all that Goth attire with the black lipstick and face paint, the whole Kabuki joke of it, and never do it again. Leaving you with what? The Talbert's old lady silk flower look of her mom that makes her vomit? The preppy black cashmere – Miss Rich Tits – of the Sister? This hippie-dippie think global eat grass crazy costume she suddenly finds herself wearing? There's no escape. You can't be a blot, you can't not be some kind of advertisement.

For a second she flashes on that image she's had so often, herself dead in a coffin, surrounded by flowers, her face undertaker painted, maybe some pink rouge on the cheeks like a street mime or something, and of course Mom has won out this time, and her corpse has been fitted with some frilly collared chiffon floral number, the nose ring crusted with dried snot pried from her stiffening nose, some kind of peaceful fake smile massaged onto her rigor mortised cheeks, and everyone of those so-called pals in a line to sneak shots with their cellphones and plaster the web with that. It's just creepy, what they can do to you when you're dead. If you could just blow up, just fall out of the sky in a screaming death jet, just disappear in the ocean down a five-mile trench. If you could just melt or evaporate right out of your clothes.

"Why the long face, sweetie?"

She startles, almost falling backwards in the knee deep current. It's some guy. He's not wearing a shirt, and right away the first thing you notice are the stumps of his arms, each like some kind of nuzzling dog nose, gone halfway to the elbow and shiny as his bald head. A freakout. That's it. Done.

"Looking for something?"

She climbs out of the water as quickly as she can, squatting to pull her sneakers back on and gathering up the beach towels, saying nothing, acting as if she's alone, as if maybe a thunder storm just came up. He squats on the path, plainly amused, and recites, "No big deal. It's cool. No hassle," in a sort of sing-song.

She bunches the towels up, dusted as they are with the river's dank sand, and tries to cram them into her backpack.

"Look doll. Where's the fire? It's all cool." She stops, thinking no, acting hassled will just egg him on. Acting scared makes you scared. He's right at eye level, in the middle of the path, and there's something 3-D about him that gives her pause: his looming, gleaming head, the hard purple face with its lurid lips poking out of his beard. Those naked arms above the stumps all muscle and tattoo. She grabs her backpack, fingers the phone in her pocket, decides that her best bet is to bluff it through.

The guy comes out of his crouch and zooms up to full height, nearly as big as her dad, completely blocking the trail back through the woods. "Honey, look, I don't bite, y'know."

"Please go away."

"Oh, she speaks!"

"Just...."

"I know you. I know just who you are." She dares to look directly into his probing bloodshot eyes. "You're that girl – I remember. You were here, like back in the spring, right? That's right. You and that kid...that guitar kid. That was some day for y'all, wasn't it? I remember you! Well, how the hell are ya?"

"I'm...."

"Hey, look, I get it. No biggie." He waves the longer arm in the air. "I'm just here. You got your space. No biggie."

The trail ends behind her at the river bend. She could make off through the brush, but it's all mined with poison ivy. The opposite bank might work, where the fisherman had been, if she can splash across.

"Care for a smoke?"

She cocks her head to see him better, edging back toward the stream.

"Look, just a puff is all." There's a leather pouch on a string around his neck and he nudges it up to his mouth with one arm to chew the zipper open. It's fascinating and totally gross to watch him do this, like he's a giant insect worrying a meal or something. It's like his tongue is a tentacle, emerging from the little pouch with a lumpy cigarette, pulling it free with a grimace. With the nobs of his arms he holds the pouch out to her now. He's trying to grin while clenching the doobie between his teeth, but that just makes him even scarier. Nods and sort of grimaces the word, "lighter." There must be a cigarette lighter in the slobbery little pouch.

She could help, it's no big deal. But she'd have to touch it. This is weird. He's just a homeless guy, right? She would have to touch him. But she draws back, unsure, holding her backpack like a shield of some sort between them, and of course, he could care less, dropping into that crouch again, catching the pouch between his knees. He's trying to hold the cigarette between his teeth, while somehow using his lips to pull out the lighter. She can tell he's annoyed to let her see him do this, or maybe that's an act, but whatever it's kind of fascinating. The poor guy just wants a smoke. He's harmless; he's just a guy. So what? Everything is a fail anyway. Lucas isn't coming, if he ever really was. As good a time as any to let the day begin its inevitable slide. She sets the backpack down, bends to reach for the pouch, and the scary man's eyes lock with hers.

"Chloe!"

Hand poised in mid-air, her head swivels like a camera that blurs the action. On the opposite riverbank, he's halfway up a tree trunk, then launching himself on a rope swing, a gangly blur. It's not a graceful journey. A sandal falls off as his feet drag the water. He drops off midstream, landing in a splash on his knees twenty feet away, like some geek Tarzan. Then, as if on springs, she bounds off the bank into the water, tripping flat on her face in the shallows. They're on their hands and knees in the silt and the water comes up to their elbows. Like two goofy animals checking each other out.

How strange this boy looks! Gray ink streams out of some kind of stringy clotted Rasta hairdo down his face and chest. His hands reaching for hers outlined to their whorls in black smudge. Underneath all that, he's lobster pink and smells like a shaggy, wet dog. And these piercing green eyes, the only clean part of him, sparkling out of all the scraggle.

"Look, Chloe, I've been trying to call, but my battery's gone and there was just no way...."

She gets to her feet and pulls him back to the bankside, where the bagged up lunch and balled up towels wait. That guy, wherever he came from, has disappeared like he was never even there. It's horrible, that after all her plans, and all her waiting with her treats spread like a fan, it's all piled in a knot when he arrives, but the cool thing is that it doesn't even matter. She's sopping wet, her tennis shoes dripping, but then so is he. So she unfurls the towels again on the tamped down sand, and before she can unzip her backpack, he's collapsed flat on his stomach, his muddy body just ruining them.

"My god, can I ask you, I'm sorry, but what's happened to your legs?"

He lifts the hundred pound head, glances down, remembers and sits back up.

"Oh, I guess I should look at that. It's stupid. Some jerk shot me."

"Shot you? What?"

"Yeah, do you have a tweezers or something? Anything. I think some of the shot's still in some of these things, man this is disgusting, I'm sorry."

"Does it hurt?"

"I can't tell. It's like my legs have stopped sending out signals. Yeah, when you touch it, yeah that hurts!"

"Okay, look, we need to get you home and deal with these things. I can't just sit here knowing you've got bullets in your legs."

"It's just bird shot."

"They're poisoning you. They're going to get infected. We've got to cut them out, wash them."

"You just want an excuse to get the stink off me!"

"You know, I do. OMG! Okay, look, are you sure you're okay? How did this happen anyway?"

"Can I have this sandwich? I'm like beyond starving."

"No here. Take this, eat it all."

And he does. Her whole imagined extravagant lazy afternoon by the river picnic is reduced to cellophane, banana peels and crumbs in minutes, the beer drunk down like water, both apples just cores, and he's rubbing his belly, smiling, entirely drunk, and repeating, "Oh man you are so cool." He falls back laughing on the blanket, staring up through the trees, trying to pull together the last 24 hours riding the worn out rubber band that got him here. It comes out in a babble that can't be true. The coal train, the stars, some old lady, another train, the final hitchhike salvation. He's already made a song of it with a howling chorus that goes *bats and biscuits and hounds, oh my!*

Chloe sits there emptying water from a shoe and the enormity of what this boy has done suddenly hits her. She barely knows him, yet on the strength of a weekend months ago, he has journeyed to see her – did he really hitch a coal train? – five hundred miles. And all the rest of his crazy ordeal, and this is what that looks like when you're done.

TWENTY
OFFICER MOSBY – CHECKPOINT

FOR OVER AN HOUR, Officer Mosby has been playing Robin to some state trooper's Batman on a blistering hot, tar soft Interstate exit directing overstuffed Wahoo alumni in humming lines of orange flagged SUVs towards stadium parking lots. His charcoal grey city police shirt, now sweat-blackened, sticks like glue to his back, but the trooper remains starched in poise and attire, with a severely forward-cocked Smokey Bear hat – it's like he's got a hat-rack hook nailed into his forehead – shading a chin like stone. There were guys like that on deployment, stick up their ass in the kill seat but just as much Katy bar the door as everyone else when the rounds came in. You can work with them but it's hard to figure a guy who don't sweat.

The radio on Officer Mosby's belt crackles. It's Joan the dispatcher, but she's calling on a private frequency off the party line. "Mattie my friend, I need your cell number." Never good. The trooper ratchets his Terminator head a notch, seems to zoom-focus reflectored eyes on Mattie's face and the bad news to come, all without a twitch at the jaw or a shift of his Semper Fi at ease stance, still raising an arm to wave a Mickey Mouse white-gloved hand at one more in the line of steaming trucks.

This is a habit of Mattie's, before the hammer strikes, take a breath and pause, look around at the world as it is before it all dissolves to shit. And as his cell phone's tinny speaker kicks into "Sweet Home Alabama" he already knows what it is, what it always is, but chooses not to surmise what Sid may be up to this time. Lifting the phone to his ear, he matches the trooper's spread-legged stance, plainly mocking him, and stares directly into his mirrored shades at the diminished versions of himself reflected there.

Joan uses her matter-of-fact dispatcher's voice, calling him Sweetie, but making her point, while a slideshow of previous misadventures plays between Mattie's ears: Sid traipsing in sneakers and shorts through snowy woods on the flank of Monticello Mountain, astride Stonewall Jackson's monument on High Street, stretching a plumb line off the train trestle, walking in underwear backwards in Belmont, somehow sprawled high on the dome of the Rotunda at the University Lawn, then flat on his back and humming in the driving lane of Cherry Avenue. My brother, the town crazy, what now?

The trooper can smell it, he really can, which is kind of amazing. A tight grimace that probably passes for a smile among his tribe thins across his jaw. Mattie imagines Old Man Tillman leaning on the front porch, waving a pistol and a can of Miller, cussing a blue streak. Sees Sid stumbling through town wrestling with an armful of old guns, probably babbling to himself, roaming passive and relentless as a stream of water. Mattie realizes now that it's over, that this is the one that will lock him away, the one that crosses over from civic nuisance to public danger. Joan says, "Sweetie, I don't know what's gotten into the deputy chief. He knows what today is – with the game and the kids coming back – but he's puttin' out "armed and dangerous". Mattie swallows hard, his eyes still locked on the mirrored glasses of Robocop. "He won't call the chief. He's takin' this one on by himself. You're gonna get the call in about a minute, like everybody else, and then it's gonna hit the fan and splatter."

"Joan, is he there? Can I talk to him?"

"He ain't gonna talk to you, honey. He prob'ly thinks you're in on it."

"Shit."

"Look, if I were you Matthew, and I'm glad I ain't, I'd get off the highway right now, and if I had any clue where that boy might be, I'd go get him. Because Rambo here ain't kiddin'."

"Shit." The state trooper turns a smart about face, showing Mattie his gray ramrod ass.

"And Mattie. Love you Sweetie, but you never got this call."

The next thing that happens is the all points bulletin and all of a sudden the trooper is dead-stopping every car in the line and pulling everybody out of their seats. Horns blow all down the exit ramp. People in game day orange and blue are being patted down and spread-eagled, pulled off the road and cited for drunk driving. An unmarked Ford cruiser, gray and shark-like, soundlessly appears on the median strip and a second trooper goes to work seamlessly with the first. Cars back up around a curve a mile away along the Interstate. One of the Commonwealth's new helicopter drones has been unleashed, hovering briefly and annoyingly just out of reach before lifting to dragonfly elsewhere. Kick off in ten minutes, the alumni are not happy, and the mood's going sideways fast.

As if the troopers could care. They pay no attention to Mattie. He's beneath notice, an embarrassment, just in the way of the work that needs to be done. People figure that out and begin to curse him, to plead to him for mercy, they threaten his job and badge. Fuck it, he gets into his cruiser, revs the engine, pulls off the median, and hits the empty off-ramp. That's when he realizes that this is what happened to his Glock, too. No question. Sid took it. Maybe old man Tillman's guns are relics, rusty old pieces of shit, but that Glock is a loaded weapon. Mattie flares all lights as the car accelerates down the breakdown lane past the row of steaming cars. If ever there was a day to check out, this is it. Should have acted on that impulse long ago. Just drive to the bus station and park the cruiser, leave ol' Ronnie's loaner gun in the glove box, lay down cash for a ticket on the next hound out and vanish off the world.

TWENTY-ONE

THE CANNONS – HOLLYWOOD EAST

You can be ready for it, know it's going to happen, and it still knocks your socks off. That is what she'll tell the girls at lunch next Tuesday. So just think how it must strike the unsuspecting Claire. Somehow Iris has kept it a secret the whole ride home. Not that difficult really, since her daughter abounded with tales of her summer in Europe, playing Ameri-trash while interning with a German documentary film maker on a project that involved a circus of fashionistas, graphic designers, musicians and deposed royalty at play across the continent's many seasonal festivals. She had moved among them easily, developing near fluency in German and French, and dropped in phrases from each as if by accident while sharing anecdotes about shoots in Montreaux and Biarritz and Munich. Jazz puppetry, classical quartets, riverside feasts. Some kind of bull run in Provence. All unpoured in a jumble, but threaded with a message. She is aloft now, launched into the world beyond our leafy provincial village, and these tidbits, morsels of a blossoming life, are intended as markers of her escape. And doesn't she know it!

Rainsworth has at least left the driveway gate open for them, but there is no one in sight to greet them. The front entrance door stands ajar for some reason. She pulls up to it for the luggage drop, peering inside for her husband, as Claire bounds right past her with her carry-on, up the stairs and smack into the famous actor, the great heart-throb, Hollywood superhero and Broadway dancer, coming down the steps with a somewhat bow-legged gait, the way men with muscles do, and he's in a black silk blouse, like a matador, and his chestnut coif seems to swoop. He's in pointed cowboy boots and black jeans that will be hell-ishly hot at the game, poor man. Iris does not fail to note the precious moment when Claire does a double-take, gathering in a reeling instant what is going on here, who this stranger who looks just like, OMG, knees buckling that broke a high heel on Medieval cobblestone, knees buckling that drank champagne at Wimbledon, knees buckling that drove the Corniche in a rented convertible. Yes, our little old America does have its own charms, doesn't it dear?

The movie star takes Claire's hand to steady her. Their gazes lock. This charm, how dare he turn such a shtick full-blast on a helpless child! Plainly dazzled, Claire mumbles, stutters. He's releasing her hand, dipping his head politely, setting her free as a child releases a caged canary to flop and splutter about the house, and that's her dear daughter stricken on the stairs, mouth frozen in an "O" shape, staring down now at her mom, and now it's Iris' turn as the star's gaze and a smile sly as a film spy's takes her up into Hollywood, makes the day suddenly a Panavision widescreen Dolby event, "and is this your sister?" his sumptuous mouth exhales, bending to take Claire's bag. "May I help with your luggage?"

"Oh heavens please yes!" Claire sputters, the first actual words out of her mouth. And worth it too, to see that half smile crease up a dimple, before he realizes what he's done, that he's misgauged his super power, bedazzled another one, and with that same faucet-like efficiency, retreats behind sleepy eyes, sucks back the charm, relieves these poor women to breathe again, yet the loss is like a wave withdrawing. Iris glimpses her daughter up the stairs, Claire's eyes dancing now, freed of the gaze and rebounding. "I'll be right down," she laughs.

"Oh I'm sure of that," Iris smiles, and discovers she is breathing again.

"It's no trouble at all," the storied rumbling voice with its hint of the Aussie intones. He goes to the car and returns hauling Claire's three suitcases with ease, as if they are empty, his massive back in its silken shirt heading back up the stairs to her daughter's room. At that, Iris' heart, always a sucker for beauty in action, hiccups again.

Which is when she realizes that Rainsworth has been enjoying this whole exchange from the kitchen door, standing there in a halo of silent glee or gloat – it's always hard to tell which with him – actually holding himself back for once from the spotlight, saving his own welcome home for the prodigal daughter until after the star makes his entrance, and this, combined with Iris' frank embarrassment at having been caught spellbound, helps to submerge her anger over the airport abandonment. Of course, he had known it would work out like this. He always knows the angles, how to wriggle out of the tough spot, to come up smelling like a rose. Skill much needed when you're such a royal ass. Iris swallows, smoothes her skirt, and steps past him into the kitchen, smartly pinching his paunch on the way past, hard enough to win a grimace.

The childhood television star grown to celebrated movie director stands flatfooted and baldheaded at the central island, iced tea in one hand, and turns as if panning a camera, Iris thinks, to greet her. "Well, they don't make country kitchens like they used to," he grins, understanding that his hostess – like everyone else he ever meets – needs to be gently walked past the momentary, helpless reckoning with memories that place him in miniature, served by that dowdy robot maid on an ancient black and white tv screen, even now after Oscars and millions and a lifetime of power brokering. Iris sees all that, a gentlemanly graciousness long gone from the real South, strides forth to offer her hand, and realizes that the whole Southern Belle shtick will have to go after all. Everyone, she imagines, behaves like a cartoon Southerner around this man, whose entire exposure below the Mason-Dixon line must have been to simulated, backlot small towns in the dry breeze of some Los Angeles suburb. She could have some fun pretending to play cougar to the Superhero. But this balding little man disarms her, sets her feet on the ground. She meets his icy blue eyes with her own deeper blue peepers, and smiles, "Yet so little goes on in these spaces. Like airport lobbies where we pass each other sipping coffee."

Oh, that was too deep. Where did that come from? The director's eyes drop, and the dimpled smile falters. Iris realizes she may have just sketched herself indelibly as the image of a wilted flower, a Blanche Dubois, the stereotyped canary in the gilded cage type of Southern wife she most certainly is not. She rises to her full height, realizing she is actually a little taller than her guest, and asks, "Do you ride, sir? Do you ride horses?"

He nods, setting his tea down and seeming to lean just perceptibly back from her approach. "We have a lovely stables here, and it would be an honor if you would join me tomorrow morning." This is probably horribly wrong, too, Iris realizes. They haven't even exchanged names, yet here we come with all the repressed patrician passion we associate with the equestrienne. She is frightening her guest in his first tentative moments in her house. She half-steps back, resolving to play it out. She has all afternoon to override a first impression after all, but at that moment Rainsworth does this unforgivable thing, surprising her from behind and actually grabbing her in a bear hug just below her breasts, lifting her off her feet and swinging her in the air for some godforsaken reason. It is all she can do to avoid the explosion the director probably expects, the vicious kick to the shins. An elbow to the throat is not out of the question. But this is when she tips the scale back, regains her equilibrium and takes charge of the situation once and for all. Summoning the poise that can take a creek fence on a skittish steed, one toe goes en pointe, and an arm sweeps up to cradle her husband's furrowed skull while her head falls back to his shoulder in a make-believe ballerina swoon. Surprised, the oaf sets her down, yet she does not yet release his hand, spinning exactly once from his grasp, lithe and quick as a girl. Rainsworth pops his eyes wide as if startled, the director cocks his head and regains that storied smile, and applause turns all their eyes to the doorway, where the Superhero has reappeared just in time to catch the opening act.

TWENTY-TWO

SID – CAMP RIVANNA

EACH STEP of the two-mile trek back down to the river camp hurts. The drill-bit between his ears grinds away despite the shirt wrapped turban tight around his head. Sid's shadow stretches reassuringly before him, then gets swallowed with a strangled gasp in the shade of a tree or storefront before breaking free again for another few steps. Always safer to stay in the middle of the street. The few cars honk and pause, but that is not a comparable problem. By walking sideways, crab-walking, Sid can see traffic coming from both directions, keep an eye on his nurturing shadow and make a narrower solar panel of bare shoulders that charge the drill-bit's grinding. There is no hint of breeze in the baking heat of this late summer afternoon. Ghostly grasping vapors hover low on the road's soft tar. But the river will bring solace, consultation, maybe a tuna fish sandwich.

At last Sid arrives at the bottom end of town, guarded by one last house hard up against the road, its uneven porch seemingly built right out onto the pavement and heavily burdened by potted plants and a row of old Adirondack chairs. He pauses there, body weaving, longing for all that. Just to step onto the porch, to plop into that low wooden chair in an angle of delicious shade, would be to warp out of the saga once and for all. You could collapse there, switch off the remote, shut down. But he senses movement behind the screen door back in the shadows, a cat, a child? He turns away, finds his way past the house and slips down the steep path of concrete chunks that leads to the river, where the old dam's broken teeth dribble a thin gruel into the shallows.

Past the trestle, the river camp seems deserted now, except for flies and the rainforest drip. Sid goes to the nearest shanty, its pitched roof framed by sturdy two by twos covered over by vinyl sheeting from a highway sign, and pushes aside the heavy beach towel door to rummage through a jumble of blankets, fruit crates packed with magazines and wire and bent cans, and a daunting collection of foraged radios. He turns up a can of salmon, but can't find a can opener in the mess. Steps back outside to set the can on the picnic table and stares at it, as if some secret key might spring the lid open. That can, he understands, will survive the vortex. He decides to put it back, then spies a rusty bottle opener hung from a nail on the nearest birch. For the next several minutes, he repeatedly wedges its sharp edge down onto the lid, carving a circle of little triangles perfectly spaced around the rim, but he still cannot pry off the top. A swarm of yellow jackets emerges from somewhere to taunt his efforts, hovering about his hands. Finally, he sets down the bottle opener, waves the insects away and takes a swig of salmon juice, overwhelmingly salty and aromatic, the flavor of ocean condensed to soup. Tiny flecks of the pink fish make it through the holes he's carved, but the main block is still trapped behind the triangular grates, jellied and glaucous.

The vomit comes all in a rush, so he can only turn in his seat to avoid splattering the tabletop. Then comes a precious moment when the drill-bit stops, when he can unwrap his head and wipe his mouth on the rumpled tennis shirt, stand and hurl the stinking can off into the woods. Sid lurches down to the river's edge, shaking out his dripping shirt, again working the main conundrum. Figures don't lie. He has tested and retested the calculations, played the variables, accounted for every outlier he can imagine. It might happen like this: When the sun rises over Monticello Mountain, all of the shadows of all of the statues, bridges and monuments will align. The receptor proteins will leap the synapse. They will reach out like the feet of amoeba to each other, unlocking the energies lurking in the coal tower once and for all. Demons – straight out of a comic book -- unleashed. And that will be that. It might just be better not to know. *I am not a general. I am not Steve.* But he does know.

Down by the rope swing the river pools at a bend, rimmed by drying mud that marks a water mark from a storm long past. Sid stands on the bank frankly crying. Why couldn't it be someone else? Why couldn't there be one other guy at least? Well there is Steve, who at least appears to get it. Would he act, though, in the end? Sid understands at last that this is why he has trudged all the way down to the river for the second time today. Because Steve is the only one who might conceivably help. Maybe he didn't understand before, maybe the pistol scared him? He pulls off his worn sneakers, his shorts and briefs, and creeps down the bank to chill his fever in the river pool. You can almost float there, and as long as you're in the water, the drill-bit sits idle, unplugged. That tv show about a cave where sharks sleep, at rest from their lives of relentless hunting. The burrows of rabbits and frogs, the snow caves of polar bears. Each affording a warp out of this ragged world. All the internal pumping slows. Pain dissolves to distant twinges. Muscles unkink. The peace of a dozing gecko, snug in a paper towel roll.

It almost works today. He can almost go there. The water wraps his arms and legs, tinkling like piano fingers over his eyes, around his armpits, between his toes. The dribbled sound of river on stone nearly matches the thump of his heart. Only the upturned plate of his reddened face breaks the water's surface. A dragonfly alights directly on the tip of his nose. It rests there for a long moment, while he holds his breath, staring through its cellophane wings at the rope swing, tree and sky beyond. It doesn't mean anything. Not everything means something. Extraneous bytes of code. The dragonfly's flicking wings tickle his nose, but he does not flinch. One hand sneaks from the water then swats down, a hard slap to the face as the dragonfly makes good its escape.

"Almost got him, dude."

Sid doesn't have to look and says nothing. He tries to hide in the green water, rolling onto his belly in the silt, his fingers and toes digging into the bottom to pull himself under against his own buoyance. Specks float before his eyes in a golden soup that goes suddenly turbid as Steve's wrestling legs saddle his torso, push him roughly onto the bottom. Sid comes up spluttering, but Steve's legs act like pliers, flipping him onto his back, shoving him down to come up frantic, punching, gasping for air in an embrace of stunted arms. A clean punch to the reddened face, and that face head butts his chest, shoves them both underwater again, where they flail.

TWENTY-THREE

CHLOE AND LUCAS – RUGBY ROAD

EXACTLY AS SHE HAD HOPED, no one home. The house seals out the yard's noises, replacing them with its own air-conditioned hush. Only on tv, Lucas thinks, as she pulls him by the hand into an enormous gleaming kitchen horribly violated by his filth and stink. He had no idea. He had just imagined she was a normal girl who lived in a normal house, maybe a salt box like the one he shares with his mom in the flats at Fort Jackson. You could drop that house with room to spare right down into this kitchen. Weird. This calls for an adjustment and he doesn't want to make that change. One of the things it suggests being that he maybe doesn't know his little Goth so well after all. All the songs he's written for her across a blasted summer, they don't seem to fit this place.

They fit the girl all in black with pink accents who stood listening for like five songs, her head atilt, on the other side of the street, who took forever to just amble over, even after he tried out his best half smile and head toss and seemed to catch her eye, the one who bent to untie her ankle bracelet and drop it in his floppy hat while he squatted busking on the Mall. They fit the girl in the river that afternoon, the wild one who waited and waved the next morning in the shadow of Sakagawea's kneeling statue when his bus turned south out of the Greyhound terminal. But this has to be a whole different girl. A salt box won't do. This bigger box is needed. He keeps his backpack on, not wanting to set it down anywhere so clean.

Chloe hasn't noticed. She's rummaging in one of a hundred drawers that slide open almost silently for band aids, a tube of antiseptic, and tweezers. "Okay, young man," she says, "upstairs to the doctor's office". She shoos him across the kitchen with its gleaming surfaces of marble and copper out to the entry foyer, where late afternoon sunlight pours through a window as big as the one behind a church choir onto a curved and carpeted staircase like something out of Cinderella's castle. An enormous rotating fan hovers high above them. "Come on." She takes his hand and tugs him up the stairs, "Let's fix you up."

"This is where I live," she says tentatively, as they step through a corner doorway into her room. She flips a switch and it's like they're standing in a lacquered jewel box, shiny and black, a big bed with a rumpled pink comforter smack in the middle. She drops his hand to close the door behind them. "Nobody's here, and they won't be for hours. You go in there and take a shower. I'm gonna get you some things."

It's been like that since the river. He's felt floaty, sort of dreaming, while she has handled everything. Calling a cab, leading him out through the woods past the train trestle to the street, paying for the ride up into town under tree-lined winding avenues, not bothering to make small talk, just holding his dirty paw as if there was nowhere else she'd rather be. That enormous bed is crazy, decked out with a canopy and a pinned back curtain of mosquito netting. Somehow it's the strangest thing he's seen in a day of oddities, one more thing that makes him feel dirty and small. He turns to the bathroom, and at last sets his backpack down on the white tiled floor, noting the coal ash

that sifts off like pepper around it. The bathroom could be in a
tv commercial gleaming all white and chrome, or even a doctor's
office. Just the shower faucets – heavy ceramic knobs -- cost
bucks. With a twist water blasts out of a showerhead broad as a
catcher's mitt. But he does as he was told, peels off the damp and
filthy rags, folds them atop his backpack, then gasps at what he
sees in the mirror. A perfect redneck's outline of his shorts and
shirt and his torso pale, almost milky, his hair a damp tangle of
straggle dreads.

Then he steps into the shower, picks up a brown lump he
realizes must be some kind of sponge and soaps it from a plastic
bottle with girly curves. It smells like a girl, too, but it works.
The coal dust streams off of him like ink, as he scrubs his hair,
elbows, and fingernails. He can't even make out his feet in the
black water pooling around them. He just dabs the backs of his
legs, letting the soap run off the reddened welts. It's as if all the
dirt has protected him, toughening him up, but now the
perfumed soap strips away that numbness, tenderizing his skin,
so he feels vulnerable and confused. Surely at some point this
rush of steaming water will wear out the heat pump and turn
tepid then cold. But it just comes on relentlessly hot, pounding
the coal train out of his bones. Still, it's embarrassing to be in
here so long, and he doesn't know if she is out there, and he's so
skinny and so bare.

When the water at last runs clear, he turns off the faucet.
The whole room floats in a white cloud of steam. But he is
Clean. As if he'd never ridden that train at all. Except for the
welts, of course. He pulls the curtain open, and finds a plush
white towel folded on the toilet seat. On the sink, a clean t-shirt,
khaki shorts and a belt. His filthy clothes are gone, the backpack
untouched on the floor. It's a fairy tale. You take it all as magic,
don't look for explanations or try to piece it all together, just roll
with it, right?

The huge t-shirt feels softer than soft, hanging nearly to his knees. The shorts are comical, baggy as a clown's, and he has to bunch them up to cinch them at the waist. No underpants. When she knocks on the door, she finds him shaking out the pack, trying to knock the dirt off. She creeps in and says, "Slippy, just don't worry about that. Here, come with me."

She leads him back into the black bedroom. "Lie down, I'm going to fix your legs."

Lucas falls onto his face into a feather bed where no doubt you could feel a pea at any depth. Rich and warm with distant perfumes. "Cover your eyes, I'm going to crank up the lights." The world goes pink as he buries his face in the comforter and feels her sit down lightly at his side. "We're just going to do this one at a time. You tell me if it hurts, okay?"

She catches herself for a moment, sitting there. This boy's knobby legs, the pink soles of his bare feet, the pale hair across his long calves. This is not a video game. He's being so good, just patiently lying there, sunk in her comforter and lost in her dad's t-shirt. She picks up the tweezers, then puts them down. Focus. What shall we do here? Start with the easy ones first, that's a good plan. See if even that hurts too much. Because the ones up past his knees don't look so good. There could be pellets in them, and the mere thought of that makes her stomach turn. This is weird, this ministering thing, like going to a whole new place. Maybe that's what's making her head spin. Or just that here he is, flesh and blood and little wounded dots, here in her cave where no one goes. Who had just been a dream, really, from a day in the spring long ago. So she takes a determined breath, says, "Let's just start on this one," and gently dabs ointment at a nick near his ankle. He doesn't flinch. She moves on to another, and then to an angry one mid-calf. "Are you okay?"

"I'm in heaven."

"Oh My God."

"What?" He lifts his head and starts to roll over.

"No, stay there. Lucas. We're good. I'm just..."

"Are you okay?"

"Am I okay? Yes. Um, you stay there. You tell me if it hurts."

His sleepy eyes smile like some dreamy cartoon. He gets that this is something. That this is what eyes can say. "You lie down."

It's a game; he buries his face again.

Now she can work. Now she has the strength. For a fleeting second, she flashes on that tv news story, the hands of her father, gloved and quick, his instruments poised at the exposed, pulpy brain of a patient. It had not registered then, but boy now for real. This may be the first time in her life that she's ever allowed herself to visualize the work, what her father actually does for a living. How can that blustering giant, that pushy silly ogre, carve skulls and work delicately in threads of vessel and nerve? How can that be? And he does this every day. That frightening, gross and delicate thing. With exquisite attention, breathing shallowly so her hand doesn't tremble, her eyes zoom in like microscopes as the tweezer's pointed tips peel back a tiny flap of skin, probing a black dot, all time stopped on that instant and that millimeter, awaiting a flinch.

And at that moment a total surprise catches her up, so she has to pause and let the tremble pass. But the surprise grows while she works, dabbing ointment and laying on bandaids. This is it. It's as plain as anything she's ever known. This gross and scary thing. This is something she can do. Maybe for real. She moves on to another welt, and another, Lucas lying perfectly still, never flinching, neither one saying a word. She has worked her way up from his heels to the back of his knees, switching sides once to better reach his other leg, and leaving behind a ladder of mini-bandaids scattered across his calves. Now she's reached the angry welts above his knees that she's feared all along. "Okay, these are the two bad ones, are you okay?" He says nothing, but one hand trailing down to her hip gives an awkward pinch. "Okay, here goes."

She bites her lip and takes the plunge.

This is her mom with a singed needle peeling a shard of glass from her daughter's foot. Never Dad, the great neurosurgeon, with his expensively educated hands. Always Mom, even when Dad sat with his feet up reading the paper, when he could have. This is Mom, holding her hand on the grooming brush to teach her how to comb her pony, squeezing an eye dropper into the gawky beak of that orphaned baby bluebird, scrawling happy birthday in pink icing on a cake. This is me, I can do this, no prob.

There's definitely a pellet in the first one. A lump of black welt imbedded in a circle of angry red. This is something an actual doctor should do. "Okay, hang on, okay?" He doesn't move. And with a sureness that surprises her, with ferocity, she digs directly into the ugly bump and with some excruciating noodling pulls out the bloody pellet. Disgusting. It's like she can taste the pellet in her mouth. She discards it on a Kleenex and goes about cleaning the wound. This one's bleeding for real, so she rinses it with an antiseptic wash, holds a gauze compress on it with her thumb, and sits silently biting her lip.

It's Lucas. He's right here. Her eyes track up to the damp frizz of hair on his head, down to the curled toes on his feet. You can make believe all summer, but this is not a virtual experience. Guy's really here. She's hurting him, she knows, but she has to. Another few dabs, the ointment and a big bandaid on this one. "Okay, I know that was rough. Stay put and I'll show you the pellet in a minute. Let me get this last one and we're done, okay?"

Lucas hasn't even grunted. She switches sides and goes to work, and in no time it seems the second pellet is out, the wound cleaned and taped. "Let me just check," she says, and grinning now, dares to slide up the bottom edge of her dad's enormous shorts, up those skinny thighs, past the sunburn line to skin so pale it surprises her. "I think you're good," she whispers, bending to place all of her tools alongside the keepsake pellets on the floor. Then she turns and scoots up alongside him. "Slippy?" The tweezer hand, the magical one, the one with skills she didn't know she had, reaches out to tousle his hair. "Lucas?" Impossible that he's asleep! "Lucas!"

The scraggly head lifts and those droopy eyelids struggle open. Eyelashes long as Eeyore's, like a store awning shading green windows. "I guess we're done?" he asks. A smile curls up and his eyes crinkle.

"You were NOT asleep! No way!"

He rolls up on his side and scoots towards her, the down comforter bunching up between them. They're side-by-side with lolling heads pillowed on elbow crooks. "No, you were awesome. I didn't feel a thing, honest."

She half believes him. "Liar."

"No. You're good."

And then time does this rare trick where it accelerates and slows at the same time, the way you can get on a carnival ride. They wrestle in the blankets, building tunnels, cocoons, and tree houses. Skin warm here, cool there, soft or taut, all of it in flashes like a screen swipe. They giggle over the mint-flavored condom with its cammo design, tenting up the comforter for that secret procedure. There's a moment when she gets up to turn on some music. There's a moment when they both stop, breathless, listening to what seemed like a door opening downstairs, but nothing. Elbows, knees and knobby backs. The downy whiskers on his chin. Her long thin feet with toes that can spread like fingers. Gauzy light under the netting, the comforter bunched on the floor, and stuffed animals splayed everywhere.

She doesn't even know how they end up downstairs, but

there they are, in the kitchen, eating everything they can find. Cereal and apples and carrots and stinky paté. A toast over bottles of beer. She's in her dad's t-shirt that falls past her knees and he's bare-chested, holding up those huge shorts with one hand. But that happened back in the blanket tent, because the mess is all there when they come back downstairs, and somehow she had even thought to put his clothes in the dryer, or he had, because they're done. They stand barefoot on the chilly marble floor in a silent house staring out through aquarium wide windows at summer's green world, at the pool and the lawn beyond, and she realizes more than ever what a foreigner she is here and how thin are the bars of this cage. He's back in his own jean shorts, and the t-shirt he'd left for Chloe those months ago, and beneath that haze of stringy hair he's featuring this amazing grin.

"We should go."

"Okay, where?"

"Let's do what we did before?"

"Downtown? K. Let's go back and redo, but this time...."

She touches a finger to his smiling lips, shushing him. This time he has to stay.

TWENTY-FOUR

THE CANNON'S – SCOTT STADIUM

WHERE *IS* THAT GIRL? Iris stands up in the crowd, seeking one bobbed auburn hairdo in a sea of orange attire. Claire had promised to set up the tailgate. Maybe she was already out there at the Escalade, getting started? The problem is that they have to do a ju jitsu leap of some sort, two places at once, if they are to have things arranged out in the parking lot while also lingering inside the stadium for the half-time festivities. The Hollywood crowd needs tending to, but she has to be here with Rainsworth when the announcement comes. This is what daughters are for, after all, aren't they? Claire can man the tailgate, she won't even care about her father's big moment, really, but she had seemed so wrapped up in the attentions of the superhero, and now where is he, too?

The director has been exactly the boyish gentleman she had imagined, sitting loyally at her side, always wearing that cock-eyed sort of half-smile under his studio baseball cap, actually watching the game, it seems to her, though the Penn State monsters ring up three touchdowns in the first quarter and seem bent on deliberately running up the score. Down here near the sideline, when their receivers race past, their quickness astounds. These athletes accelerate with the same muscled grace of the horses she loves, so fluid and electric, thrilling. That they are boys with brains, that they can converse, that they can read and write and tell time, is almost comical.

At one point she finds herself trying to explain this to the director. The words come out in a flurry of exhalations and eye blinks, and she is not oblivious to the way he sort of shies away at the shoulders, without actually shifting in his seat, and sharpens his attention on some end zone activity while still wearing that maddening tic of a smile. He thinks I'm daft, she knows, but has already all but decided not to give a damn. After all, she will never see him again, and his films are ridiculous anyway. But he is a nice man, surprisingly, for being so high on the food chain, and doesn't really seem to mind her rattling on. Everyone nearby has recognized him, she thinks, and that is a bonus.

Rainsworth, of course, is nowhere to be found. Or you can find him, but only by seeking out his broad back in that palm-print Hawaiian shirt as he makes his way around the good seats, politicking, schmoozing, bragging about the movie stars he's snagged, glad-handing for money to enrich the town's little film festival, while blocking the view of the unfortunates he parks himself in front of. Every game is like this. On his life, he couldn't tell you the score. But this is what he loves, she knows, and today it will all pay off. She had hoped the President would drop by the tail gate before the game, provide the nod or wink that would seal the deal, because actually nothing has been confirmed, it could still all go south, but she had not seen that leonine brow making its way through the SUVs at all, and he did not seem to be in his usual box either. All a little too mysterious, at loose ends.

She starts to bring it up with the famous director. Surely he will understand. On tv, she has seen his tense freckled face at the

Oscars, nominated and waiting, the worth of his career in the hands of a gaggle of aging starlets, the decision in the envelope and cameras at the ready. Isn't this the same thing, really? But that's so presumptuous. But really winning a Pavilion on the Lawn means more, is more rare, certainly more significant in the larger scheme of things, even if not nationally televised.

It will all be a huge imposition, of course. Each semester, she will be expected to hostess a round of balls and cocktail parties and Open Houses for all the mousy Asian proto-neurosurgeons under Rainsworth's wing, the fawning nurses who act as if they know her own husband better than she does, the poorly mannered rehabilitation therapists, the unctuous neuropsychologists, the jealous heads of the other medical departments. Sort of a governor's mansion – drafty, oddly furnished, trafficked by tourists and drunken undergraduates – not a place where anyone actually lives. Though Rainsworth claims that is exactly what they will do. He and his healthy self-image striding across the Lawn, down gravel paths between Mr. Jefferson's snow-dolloped serpentine walls to his cramped and ramshackle offices in the old West Hospital. The Porsche parked under a tarp at the back door. Well, we shall see.

She comes out of her revery aghast at having lost the thread of whatever conversation she has been attempting with the famous director, but he seems perfectly at ease, lifting the brim of his cap to see past the phalanx of policemen on the sideline to the action on the field. Every few moments, the black clad and scowling girl in the Jackie O glasses at his side whispers something in his ear. She spends the rest of her time with an earphone running up into her shoulder-length mane, speed-thumbing a communication device shaped like the old powder compacts from prom days. But of course, you wouldn't want to be bothered with your own e-mail, Tweets, IM, calls, stock prices, pre-deal shenanigans, bids and counter-bids. You have a person to screen all that, your own living, breathing media filter, so you can live like the old days, in slo-mo. This is the person who knows everything. This is the person she should be talking with, who knows all the dirt, but she is probably like the Secret Service, sworn to secrecy on fear of death, though meanwhile thumbing her memoir that will bankroll that home in the hills she so covets. Oh my God, I can be so catty, she thinks. It's just the nerves, really, and where is my daughter anyway?

But there he stands, President Burwell, it has to be him. Is it the Hollywood royalty at her side that does this, making her see everything through a corny camera lens? The old buzzard down by the end zone, silhouetted in the mouth of the tunnel that leads to the team lockers. His narrow back framed by a nimbus of light. He's alone there, arms crossed, legs spread, in his summer linen suit – like a good Southern barrister wearing it right up to the last allowable day– no doubt savoring bruising memories of his own fleeting years as a wingback on yet another losing Wahoo team back when they probably wore leather helmets.

She swivels back to the scoreboard, briefly. The Cavaliers down four touchdowns and a safety, or is it three touchdowns and three field goals, or ten field goals, for all she knows, and what else is new? She has four minutes until half-time. She simply must leave now, right now, and get out to the truck to set up the tailgate. Apologizing to the director for the imposition, she rummages in her purse for her phone. Not a message or call in her own empty life. She stabs 2 and once again only gets her daughter's trilling recorded voice. No help there. Rainsworth's phone just rings. Have they grabbed him on his back-slapping rounds and pulled him down to the field, ready for the announcement? Has he rushed out to the truck to switch shirts and throw on a sports coat? Is it possible his Mistress, the Operating Room, has called him in to save some crack-skulled drunk-

ard? Of course, he'd never even think to phone. Well she hadn't
expected help from that quarter anyway. And now she's lost the
President, too, in the crowd of arthritic alumni that always
crowds the sideline. Well, there is simply no choice. She excuses
herself, with a "Duty calls. Please come out at half-time to the
truck. We'll have Mimosas," and fights her way down the row
wearing a fretful smile.

The truck sits humming, exactly as she'd left it, baking in the
shadeless parking lot with its blue-and-orange awning at the
back riffling lightly in the long day's first wisp of breeze. Other
tail-gates are already up and running, blenders at the ready,
grills afire, at each one, it seems, a high school girl on guard,
glumly thumbing away at a cellphone. Iris' breakout can happen
fast, when there's help – where is that girl? She allows herself a
fleeting thought of the other daughter, the lost one, if only she
would play nice, and come along, everything could be so simple.
But she's already opened the doors, flipped up the tailgate, and
now has the lawn chairs out, the aluminum table and its clean
half-time linen cloth, the champagne flutes, the shrimp on ice,
the phyllo canapés. The flowers – resplendent at the pre-game
festivities – have collapsed despite the truck's air conditioner, so
she starts a new garbage bag under the table and pulls out her
usual go-to half-time centerpiece, Rainsworth's helmet with its
stickman drawing of a Y from his days as a fullback at Yale. An
antique now, polished skull-white, though still scarred with the
scrapes and dents of youthful collisions.

Iris climbs into the driver's seat for one brief glance in the
visor mirror. It startles her to discover that this is not the face of
a worried and wilted flower, stern schoolmistress, which is how
she has begun to think of herself. The new yet relentless lines at
the corners of her mouth, the slightest whisper of crow's feet
despite a fortune in skin-nourishing creams, the flesh no longer
so dewy fresh, for this moment she sees past those checkpoints

and is able to take in another landscape, the yet brilliant blue eyes, the sharp nose and high cheekbones, the fetching expression that can signal curiousity and ready humor. The face of a comely woman who has lived. It's a shock, almost like running into a stranger.

But already the hordes come rushing out of the stadium gates, the circus music of the marching bands oompah, she is saved – as always – by importunity. She taps 2 on her cellphone again, where is that girl? Okay, if there will be no help, no one to hold down the fort, then so be it. She covers the iced shrimp in tacky cellophane, finds a bucket to hold the champagne flutes in a clever sort of floral array, tents the canapés in the bag they came in, and is off against the tide for her seat and the announcement that will change her life or something.

The whole walk against the exiting tide is a wrestle. James the guard waves her back in the gate with just a finger wag of admonishment. People do step aside, no doubt wondering if she has lost a small child, her upstream march so desperate and darting. But eventually she finds the seats, all but empty at the field level, abandoned by the season ticket tail-gaters. The famous director and his assistant have gone back to the car, she hopes. The superhero and her daughter still nowhere to be seen. Just a few of the old folks wilting under sunshade umbrellas. On the field, the marching band has split in two, aligned at both goal posts, tubas blaring away. At the fifty-yard line, a huddle of tiny-looking men in golf attire patiently waits, their faces pixilated and blousy-looking on the stadium's jumbotron screen. She's in time, nothing important has happened yet. But where is Rainsworth?

In a moment she knows, because for the second time that day he has crept up behind and lifted her in the air, as she stands searching on the stairs. This is his eager puppy self. His shirt damp with sweat, his arms hugging too tight, leaving a wet mark across her blouse, but he sets her down gently and actually takes her hand – when was the last time they did this? – standing with her on the stairs, winking down at her, swallowing hard in expectation.

She squeezes his mighty fingers. And at that moment sees her daughter and the superhero on the next stairway over, edging along a row of seats towards them. The director and his entourage form a silly-looking line behind them, everyone doing the crabwalk through the seats together. The guys in golf attire have left the field, having won the honor of their number being retired or something. The band stomps restlessly, its members near to fainting in their heavy uniforms. The stadium – an enormous noise machine all day – pauses as if to pounce. At last the president dodders out to midfield, trailed by deans and police officers and a cameraman. The walk takes an unseemly length of time. Crowded on the stairway now, Iris holds her husband's hand and her daughter's. The movie folk have taken seats around them. This is like the Oscars after all.

The best part is that you get the key to the Pavilion right there on the field, so that after the game, you can drive directly over, unlock the ancient door and take possession of the place. She has saved four bottles of the wine store's best small vineyard champagne, stored by the manager himself in a dry ice container of some sort guaranteed to maintain their temperature. She can hear the echo of the uncorking in the sitting room now. Her daughter leans up on tiptoe -- why so intimately? -- to the ear of the superhero, and half-shouts against the din, "Usually they make these announcements at a stuffy formal ball in the Rotunda, and nobody ever knows about it, except the attendees. It never even makes the paper. The President probably feels that, with a national audience, this is a way to tout the University's traditions or something, though the odds of showing this instead of a razor commercial...."

She releases Iris' hand, actually looping her arm on the forearm that had sprouted ugly thorns in the actor's series of summer blockbusters. What is up with those two? But now the President's throat clearing booms around the stadium bowl. Iris knows the old goat lives for the limelight, these moments of imperial glory. His stemwinders over the endowment, new construction, national rankings, can stop time itself. But today – constrained perhaps by the tv network schedule or by the restive marching bands book-ending the field – he actually gets to the point. As he goes through the Pavilion assignments, most not changing hands, simply stated for effect, she loses track of the numbers and for a moment forgets which Pavilion is at stake. The current residents -- an ancient poet who directs English studies, the burly chief of the Engineering School, and all the rest -- seem to be on the field.

The Pavilions are Roman-numbered: Is it VI or VII or VIII? That's it – she knows that's the one, VIII, right in the middle of the Lawn, the one with that lovely garden backing onto the Medical School, just uphill from Rainsworth's office. The dean of the Business School steps out of the line and shakes the old man's hand. He's in a blazer and tan slacks, the requisite college tie. She has lost track, what did he say? Was that it, was that Number VIII? On the Jumbotron the former broker accepts a velvet-lined box that cradles an old key. And then the marching bands explode into a collective honk and plow in from the end zones.

It's the strangest thing. Rainsworth, at her side, squeezes her hand too tightly, then drops it. She takes his arm as he inhales mightily, nostrils flaring exactly as her horse does when spooked. There is a shuddering while his torso absorbs the wallop of this betrayal. His head slowly rotates as his eyes behind aviator shades take in the truths of this provincial back-water where he has deigned to stake his claim, that money always wins, that life-saving hands cannot trump a vault-bursting endowment. Of course, he had known there was this possibility. Had counted his votes. For years now, he had tracked each stage of the Business School capital campaign, the new construction, the growth in applicants and national rankings, as if he himself were its dean. Against these, he had weighed his appearance on *Oprah* with the boy from the Baltics, the miracle he'd wrought on a previously thought inoperable cancer. Then there was the ghost-written book about that saga. He'd imagined, she knew, that the town's annual film festival would draw one scriptwriter, one star, who'd want to make the biopic, and that, more than anything – certainly he could care less about cinema – had driven his championing the event. Maybe this man York himself would make the movie, maybe Denzel would play the good doctor....

Against dollars he has weighed hands that wade through brains, an army of surgeons he himself has trained (now practicing in major medical centers on every populated continent), an imaging facility – yes it cost the University a princely sum – rivaling any in the South. He has served on all the President's tedious little boards, has tolerated his self-serving anecdotes, has slipped him dusty bottles of vintage Bordeaux, has even taken it on himself to personally assure a decent rehabilitation experience for the old coot's stroke-affected mother. All dust on the tongue now.

At last he lifts his hands to wipe his face, pulls off the sunglasses and turns to stare deeply for a significant instant into the eyes of the wife who knows his every achievement, ambition and vanity. This is it, all too much. "I have to go," he mumbles, and then she watches him turn and bound up the empty concrete stairway, orange shirttail flapping like a tongue of fire.

TWENTY-FIVE

SID – CAMP RIVANNA

STEVE SPRAWLS ACROSS AN AIR MATTRESS, snoring so powerfully that the tent of mosquito-netting hung from his shack's plywood ceiling trembles. It's his way, dude can go from wild boar frenzy to flat out coma in a finger snap. Sid crawls out of the netting, exhausted and aching at every joint. He collapses onto the tarp floor, staring up at shards of sunlight slanting through holes in the tenting, each pulsing a message from the onrushing Vortex. He really has to go. He digs through Steve's garbage bags for a towel to wear while retrieving his clothes from the riverbank. There's a sack full of books, another packed with cords and wire, a cardboard box stuffed with nails, plastic wrap, string ties and duct tape -- the tools of shanty building -- and somewhere a bag full of clothes. He finds it in a corner, under a fold-up card table. Sid reaches in, rummaging blindly with his fingers. Feels something hard and metallic, pulls it out. Even after he realizes what it is – a gun clip full of bullets – he sets it aside on the table for a minute while pulling on a pair of gym shorts, then realizes, wait, it has to be, it's that clip from Mattie's gun, but it can't be, Steve wouldn't do that. That would dilute the power, tip the balance, that could throw the game. And Steve has to know that. But if this is that cartridge. Then Steve – like all of the Generals and Pastors – is just one more lying fool.

Sid squats there rocking, turning the Pez dispenser cartridge in his hands. The crooked walls of Steve's plywood shed act like a vise, compressing the dank, thickening heat into a fetid cube around them, yet Steve snores on like a monster. You want this thing, you can have it, Sid thinks, dropping the cartridge back in the laundry bag. He grabs his clothes strewn on the river bank, pulls them on, then launches back up the trail at a full run.

TWENTY-SIX

OFFICER MOSBY – ON PATROL

Amazing, but on a day when the city's population seems to have tripled, Officer Mosby finds an open spot for the cruiser on a side street near the police station downtown. Engine idling with the AC cranked, he sits erect in his seat, trying to sort out a plan. The city is a beehive, abuzz with all sorts of activities at different nodes: 60,000 at the game, 20,000 returning to their dorms, another 10,000 in the malls buying notebooks for the city and county school year, the thousands headed downtown soon for tonight's concert or for post-game beers. Charlottesville has morphed into some kind of bulging shopping mall version of the small town it used to be. Almost unrecognizable. The old guys at the diner, snarfing down potato flour doughnuts, they remember. Stories his dad told of old Lane High School when the color barrier broke and the gangs chose sides, the ancient pleasure of riding the city's first escalator in the old Miller & Rhoads department store, now bank offices. Date night little square-shaped bites of pizza at Barnaby's out on the Route 29 frontier, before the road fattened to six and eight lanes lined with shopping mall acreage. Old pictures he's seen of that first

MacDonald's throwing light like a new service station in an otherwise empty asphalt desert that would sprout all the crowded shops of the Barracks Road Shopping Center.

Maybe that's what Sid has been up to all this time, he thinks, crawling around on statues, roaming the hills, scribbling on paper bags. What if it's just his way of measuring the loss? But you can't talk to the guy. You go on body language. You study the snippets of behavior, the few words he lets slip. You work on basics: how's he smell, has he bathed, what's he eating? You hope he'll come home and you sort of pray he won't. Well, that's it. Today's the day to figure it out. And there's one place to start – much as he hates the idea -- the garage.

Mattie switches off the cruiser and leaves it at the police station, then strides past the milling holiday weekend shoppers to the railroad tracks and their home down by the coal tower. This is Sid's usual path, stepping out some kind of weird rhythm as he navigates the ties. Mosby's black brogues crunch the railbed gravel, all those years of childhood rail-walking, tie-hopping, gravel-pinging wrung out and put away. What do Sid's tics say, how do you read them? Is he still just playing around? This time, at last, and it's been too long in coming, he's going to get to the bottom of it. Rather than going in the front door, where old man Tillman might see him, he slips over the back fence, using Sid's typical entranceway, and goes straight to the garage. Maybe he's there. Maybe he's stashed the old guns somewhere. If Mattie can get them back, and return them to the old man, maybe that will save his brother jail time. Sid wouldn't last a week in lockup.

The carriage door creaks open onto the tottering jumble Sid has made of their father's once pin-neat old shop. What a pack rat! There's no rhyme or reason, just piles of junk. Old pet cages and toys and broken engines and rusting tools stacked in precarious rows on every horizontal surface. The old belt fan whirrs away, stirring dust motes inside this concrete block tomb where Sid spends so much of his time, doing what? Mattie pulls the door shut, flicks on a light bulb hanging bare above the cluttered workshop table, and takes a seat on the nicked bench where their father had always done his tinkering of a Saturday afternoon. Now it's Sid's domain. What does he see from here? What does he actually do? God knows what he thinks, if he thinks at all.

You could walk around, follow the dust trail, see if he's stashed the guns somewhere obvious in the jumble. Would Sid have enough sense to even hide the guns at all? You could start in one corner and just toss it all out into the yard. Would do exactly that, if old man Tillman wasn't sniffing around outside. Just clean house, take it all to the dump, trash everything that's been cluttering up their lives forever, all the junk and all the memories that cling to it like dust. Isn't that what Sid needs? Doesn't all this mess just confuse him more? Toss it all and start over. Toss it all.

Mattie cocks his head toward the heat lamped herparium at the table's edge, peering into the paper towel tube where the old mottled blue and orange gecko sleeps. What's that guy's name, Wahoo? It makes him suddenly sick to the stomach, flashing on the day their dad had brought that creature home. Pencil thin, garishly colored, dartingly quick. They had been kids once. Gawky playmates. Sid always the ringleader with some amazing new plan, drawing up elaborate comic books with homemade superheroes, building wobbly skateboards out of scrap lumber and lawn mower wheels, digging tunnels under fences and tenting them with sheets, trying to sell lemons and gallons of water door-to-door, "Lemonade Kits" he called them.

Sid was still dressing them up in crazy fantasy costumes long after the other neighborhood kids had moved on to guitars and Pony League baseball. He remembers haunting the ruins of Main Street while they were rebricking the mall back before it caught on. They'd chunk dirt clods at workers, scampering through backhoed ditches, all that year. Guerilla fighting kids in capes. But the grown-ups kept digging, laying bricks, planting scraggly trees in the middle of the street, all the shops for blocks going out of business, even the bakery with its cream puffs baked with God's own recipe. Some kind of art gallery now.

Who knows, maybe Sid was already crazy then. But being his kid brother, how would you know? Eventually it all got to be embarrassing. You can't run the streets with your underpants on over your jeans, in galoshes and a cape, forever. Maybe that's when Sid started to crack, withdrawing to his room with his thousand notebooks, dropping out of the Royal Ambassadors at church, forgetting to talk for days so his voice creaked like an old door when he did bother to utter a word. And maybe all that was because Mama was sick, and he didn't know what to do, and nobody else did either. Dad was either at her bedside or out in the shop, building them toys they'd outgrown. Who was he really building them for anyway? Homemade kites in extravagant shapes, solid fuel rockets, a go-cart driven by a lawn mower engine. He worked so hard on those things, but in the end, some of them never even made it out of the shop.

The whole sad saga, Mattie realizes, is told right here in this little museum despite all its ragged disarray. Which is half the problem. He drags a notebook over, flipping it to a random page. A penciled scrawl of numbers and notations covers the page entirely. No way to tell where the equation begins or ends, as it snakes sideways up a margin, maybe onto the next page? Maybe some of this would make sense to a math major. Maybe Sid's a wayward Einstein. Maybe they aren't equations at all. Some kind of secret code, numbers replacing letters, like the thousand wacky codes Sid used to come up with during their secret agent days. It's a total waste of time, he knows, but for several minutes, Mattie plays with a line of numbers, trying out some of the old substitutions. Counting 1-26 backwards, skipping up one for one letter and back one for the next, then up and back two, then three. Quits at fourteen. "Snomeddnaslare." It takes ten minutes to get those clotted letters. It's a reasonable mix of vowels and consonants. Nonsense. They had so many codes, piled one on another. And Mattie sees for the first time really how deeply he'd been drawn into the compulsions snowballing inside his brother's teeming head. Giving names to ants, calculating the lengths of shadows, tape recording idling engines.

Their first run-in with the law had been another of Sid's schemes. Sid had talked him into crawling up onto one of those robot dragon yellow backhoes that had been digging up downtown, sneaking over at midnight on one of those snow days off from school. Hated taking his gloves off to do it, the backhoe radiating cold so his hands almost stuck to the frosted cowling. But he had unscrewed the cap on the diesel engine, just as he'd been directed, dipping in one knotted end of a fuse they'd fashioned by dripping hot paraffin onto string, while Sid, who'd planned the whole thing, watched from a ditch. The fuse worked, too, though the string took forever to burn. They huddled together behind a shoveled snow drift giggling. Maybe already Mattie had a clue that this was not a smart thing to do. The fuse went down into the tank, they covered their ears and ducked, scrunched down in the hard-packed snow. Nothing. No explosion. Not even a fizzle when the fuse went out.

Eventually Sid crawled forward, commando style, dragging on his belly in his bulky winter coat across ice-slicked asphalt. Curious at this hitch in his plan, he climbed up on the backhoe, switched on a flashlight and peered down into the tank, when – wham – the whole place flooded in light. Mattie screamed. He thought it was the tank going up. And that scream is what got them caught.

A police officer had seen the flashlight and collared them both, dragged them down the street to the stationhouse, and there they sat for hours, because the cops didn't want to wake up their dad. The policemen debated whether to tell the newspaper stringer. Mattie heard them discussing it, making up headlines: "Child Guerillas Declare War On the Mall!" A sentiment they all heartily cheered. Eventually, one of the officers took pity. He came over and sat beside them, offering hot chocolate in Styrofoam cups. He had kids, had been one himself, he said. Led them around the station, letting them try out the two-way, tour the holding pen, peer in at the poker game in the gear locker. To Mattie, all this grown-up behavior looked like a variation on kids' games, easy to play, and all built around one simple idea – keep the people safe. Like the police shows on tv. It made sense like nothing else he'd seen. These guys weren't forlorn and driven like his dad. They weren't in a fever like his big brother, always with a half dozen odd ideas. They were just minding their routines, doing work. In his mind at least, Mattie joined the force that night.

And the upshot? Somehow this event got Sid into the Miller School on a scholarship, got him pointed towards college. And what Mattie thought of now as the good years began. Just the two of them, Mattie and his dad, building and racing a soap box derby car, flying balsa airplanes, picking apples and making apple butter for the whole neighborhood, trying to make sense of Granddaddy's old television sets.

He stares at the corner near the door with its precarious tower of lizard cages. Every one of these pieces of junk stabs at the heart, now that he's let himself get all sentimental. But he forces himself to follow procedure, looking for clues, a footprint in the dust, a glint in the dimness, stacking and unstacking, as quietly as he can, hoping at least to stay out of sight and sound from Old Man Tillman, hoping that maybe Sid will come back, that somewhere in here lies the stolen cache of guns, and that everything once again on the verge of disaster will turn out half alright – the way it works on the cop shows – after the commercial break.

TWENTY-SEVEN

CHLOE AND LUCAS – SATURDAY ON THE MALL

THE CAB DROPS them off by the old skating rink, and they stroll hand-in-hand down the bricked walkway between the rink and the giant hotel that blocks the west end of the Mall. A pocket canyon, a little hive, where things can happen, and have. Lucas springs for a frozen latte with two straws at a hole in the wall coffee place named the *Mudhouse*. Mousy students in worn t-shirts hunch over laptops, fidgeting, caffeinated, furtively sipping at huge mugs. Chloe's relieved not to recognize any of them.

"Whooh, that was a cheerful place," Lucas sighs.

Chloe sips from her straw, "If that's what college does to you...."

"It is, right?"

She thinks of her sister, eternally perky and magnificent. The force of her personality alone would burn the place down if she ever deigned to go there. "Whatever."

She honestly hadn't planned this. She had totally forgotten the whole thing. A complete accident, embarrassing really. But there it is, and the door thrown wide open pumping out cool air in a totally not-green way, the video gallery where the school projects hang. Including the one she'd done with Ava. Okay, let's do it this way, she decides. We'll go in but saying nothing, just see.

Inside the shoebox storefront, the show looks like a cross between an art exhibit and a *Best Buy* wall, with slim flat panel tv's lined up side-by-side, each with its paired sets of head-phones hung from pegs and a card giving the name of the work and its student creators. Lucas nods at the curator, busy on her cell in a corner, and stands back to survey the whole wall, making his choice. Wouldn't you know it? He goes to the war game piece, the one work that has control paddles, the one Joel and his sidekick Lars had knocked out. They'd hacked the game, patching in headshot photos of the school faculty and adminis-tration onto robots and hulking bad guys. Lucas figures that out quickly enough, grabbing the paddles and taking his shot. It's clear, though, that he is in no way a gamer, maybe has never seen an X-Box in his life. This comes as something of a shock. Chloe files it away as one more interesting oddity about her guy, one more thing that doesn't fit with what she knows about boys. It's not off-putting, though, just weird.

"That's funny," Lucas says, as he sets down the paddles.

"The hack's just a cheat. Comes with the game. Drag and drop."

"Hmm?"

"The guys who did it got in trouble for it really. When the teacher found out they hadn't developed this amazing feat of computer wizardry, like they wanted him to believe."

Lucas then makes another typical choice – the one 3-D piece in the show. He hands her a pair of plastic glasses and slips his on. She knows what's coming, however, and opts out. The whole piece lasts five seconds and just loops. It's a dog, peering down at the screen, as if the screen is its dog bowl, in apparent discom-fort. Then it retches, projectile vomiting in color and 3-D right at you. She actually kind of likes this one. What had they done to get the poor pet to throw up on cue? Lucas chuckles, watching it loop again. "Man, your school has all this tech gear?

"I guess," she observes. "Guys who did that one, it's their video for their one song. A little screamo."

"Yeah?"

"They're okay."

"Do you know 'em?"

"Not so much. They're okay."

They pause at a couple more screens. One's a time lapse speeded-up loop of the Monticello manse, showing a whole year's change of seasons, ghost images of tourists zooming back and forth, clouds blasting past, snow falling and melting, a giant tree sprouting and dropping leaves. Lucas pauses at the title card, "Massa's House: Slave Cabin View."

"Ouch."

That one had taken some work, but Lynne and Katy already had the footage. Lynne's mom, who volunteers in the gift shop, had gotten permission to set up the time lapse camera and her photography professor dad had built the weatherproof box, long before the teacher ever assigned the project. Lynne has her whole curriculum mapped out like a military campaign, next year's projects already well underway. But it was Katy who came up with the title, and that's what makes the thing work, or so the teacher said. Both of them suck ups for real.

Past the wall of tv screens, there's a partition in one corner, forming a sort of make-shift room with a normal door and doorknob at one end. Looks like a bathroom. You can make out a plastic shower curtain with garish flowers, and the curtain seems backlit, strobed. He peeks inside. Embarrassed, she drops his hand and holds back, wincing at what he might say.

"Think I can go in there?"

"Nobody's looking."

He steps in, peers around, then gently pulls back the shower curtain. It's a clawfoot tub, filled with old computer monitors of various sizes, jumbled together, screens at odd angles, all broadcasting static, horizontal hold patterns, pixilated images of flickering websites, their buzz sort of echoing inside the porcelain tub.

"Whoah!" He steps back, closing the curtain. "Hmm." He watches the play of light on the curtain for a minute, cocks his head towards her and sort of asks, "That's wild." Then pokes his head back inside the curtain again, this time trying to close the curtain around his shoulders to get the full effect. Comes back out. "Look, you gotta try this." And then he has her sticking her head in for a few seconds. He's wondering if the artist has miked the static sounds, if the websites have been randomly chosen. Nobody else has come to the door, they've got the little partitioned room to themselves. He pulls back the curtain all the way, totally not cool, and they stand there letting the dim lightshow play around them. It's a kiss opportunity, and they take it.

Now they're actually lying down flat on their backs on the tiled floor, looking up at the way the flickering light from the monitors reflects on the ductwork of the gallery ceiling. This one she hadn't considered at all. Actually, to be honest, she hadn't considered any of this. They'd thrown the idea together in ten minutes over lattes at the school café, and Ava's dad had the tub at his restoration shop and a truck to haul it, and the monitors were just junk in a salvage shed at the landfill. The gallery already had the partition up from another show. It had been sort of a joke, a one-off, and Chloe's main contribution had been the flowery curtain from BB&B, which was cute, and maybe the way the monitors look like they were just sort of dumped into the tub, though it had taken a whole (wasted) afternoon just to make them all fit right. And the title, "Suds", which was her own secret acronym for "Suck Up Dumb Students", but which Mr. Witcover had thought was "perspicacious" when he gave them their A-plus.

Except now she's lying on the tile floor in the gallery, breaking an unwritten behavioral law of some kind, with her head propped on Lucas' arm staring up at the dappled light on the ceiling, trying to see it through his eyes, and it's not what she'd expected, he's not goofing on it. Half of her wants to tell him so bad, and the other half is completely embarrassed by the whole experience and just wants to get up and leave.

"You know what?" he whispers.

"Hm?"

His head turns, so their noses touch. "You keep trippin' me out."

"What?"

"This is yours, right?"

Her whole face flushes. She punches him in the chest and sits up.

"I'm not jerkin' your chain. I mean wow. Seriously."

She stands up, takes a moment to tuck the shower curtain back where it belongs, and storms out before he's even gotten up off the floor.

TWENTY-EIGHT

THE LAWN

DR. CANNON STANDS at the stadium mouth half-determined to just unplug all the tailgating crap and pull the Escalade right out of the lot. But even that would take too long, so he shuffles down a hill to the main road, slipping on ice dumped from some fool's cooler and crashing titanically on one hip in the slop, so a streak of grass stain and red mud runs up the whole side of his Bermuda shorts in front of a lawnful of laughing fraternity jerks. He's up again, surprisingly spry, hopping around like a trained bear as he tries to get a loafer back on. They can't get enough of it. It would be nothing to take out a row of teeth from any pencil-necked puke in the lot. Just pick one.

The rental car, that minivan. Where did Claire park the thing? At some sorority cottage? And where might that be? What he needs is the Porsche. And a backroad up the side of the mountains. Head west and just go. That's what the thing is for, after all. It's a fist you aim at the road. But it's miles away. The idea of waiting on a curb around all these jackasses for some pot-stoned cabbie to make his way through the crowd is not going to happen.

He turns up the street, headed straight for the Lawn,

despising all over again every privileged thing it stands for. He could easily follow the street off to the side, veer back towards the house and the Porsche, but instead breaks away from the sidewalk. Without even looking around, without any thought at all, he finds himself brazenly climbing a steep, vine-covered sort of cliff, two stories tall, that leads up to the old Academic Campus. His loafers toe into the ivy, his fingers grab at strands of vines to pull himself up. They come out by fistfuls. He slips, skitters sideways to gain a purchase, then goes to his knees as the knoll begins to round off towards the top. And then he's made it, on his hands and knees amidst a bed of pine needles, onto the Lawn itself. His climb has topped out behind a brick edifice of some sort. There's no one back here at all, though a couple down on the sidewalk stand agog, wondering what he will do next. He drags himself out of their sight and plops down in the threadbare shade of an ancient pine, pulling ivy out of his shoes. The effort of the climb has left his Hawaiian shirt drenched and glued to his back. Smears of mud from his fall cake at his knees and plops of moisture roll down the naked arc of his scalp, streaming right between his eyes and down his nose where they fall like raindrops to his chin.

Fuming, restless, he falls back on the pine needles and wrestles this thing that has happened. Gradually he understands that the pounding in his ears is not his pulse, but drumming from the marching bands at the stadium. Inside that pounding a cortical alphabet soup begins to sort out words sparked by fireflies up from the midbrain that trace a flickering relay race to the meaty factory above his left ear, where a sentence is hammered together, held up for examination, polished and checked for grammar, then flushed out the assembly line to the pre-frontal circuit board above his eyes, on to the motor cortex for the involuntary pre-shaping of a syllable on that wet flap of leather that is a tongue inside his copper-tasting tooth-caged mouth: "Poltroons."

The tip of that tongue now gently explores the familiar yet never mapped inward contours of molar, canine, incisor, a precious, absolutely unique part of himself, the mark of identity long after fingerprints have melted away. Yet entirely unexamined, taken for granted, given over to those technicians who call themselves doctors, dentists with their plaster imprints and x-ray guns, keeping the film negatives in a manila file down the hall from those dastardly chairs, where they await the coroner's call.

In the old days, the drivers too kind to brand would pull a front tooth to identify their property. Slave's bar mitzvah, as soon as the second teeth matured. Only a liar would say he can't feel that empty socket right now. And you can say what you want, that hole is always waiting, and with it an anger like a vise. It's why they feared a black President, it's why the bangers cap them in gold. But that's exactly as far as this line of inquiry goes. Already, it's reeling back, this movie that plays itself, as unconscious as breathing, the way the salving lies wash back of their own accord. You could go in there. You could find the circuits and pull the plug. In the same way the old lobotomists made zombies of neurotic women, you could make stone mad killers of small town accountants. You'd just have to scrape off the decency. Disconnect the wiring laid down since Mama's first kiss, the lessons taught in a million pairs of narrowed eyes and a million "uh uh's." He smells the stench of burned brain, the cautery of veins, not so different in aroma from these coppery pine needles in the heat of the sun right here on Massa Jefferson's Lawn, shorn from trees dug and planted by men the Founder owned.

He comes to his feet, a little dizzily. Fingers that can thread capillaries clumsily work the cocoanut-shell buttons of his shirt.

In this mood he would take it all the way down, ditch the soiled Bermuda shorts, walk plumb naked in loafers across this World Heritage Site Lawn. Well why not? He pulls off the baggy shorts, the sagging boxers, rolls them altogether with the sweaty rayon shirt into a bundle under one arm, then slips back into his loafers. Standing upright, a wisp of breeze plays across his massive chest, tickles hairs on a rump that once had powered runs through the line back at Yale. The liberation of that old package hanging free. He inhales a breath big as the whole city, exhales the city out like a god unfurling the world. He feels ten feet tall. Takes a few tentative steps, then stops to kick the shoes off too. Now, barefoot, that's the ticket! Regal now, strolls.

Coming onto the central Lawn, feet thrilling to the lush grass, shoulders recording the tiny shifts in temperature between shade and sunlight, all glare polarized out by his Ray-Bans, Dr. Cannon imagines himself an engineer controlling some giant robot as it takes its first experimental steps through the city it will destroy. It is a grand thing. The Lawn unfurls in incremental steps before him. Tiny families in the distance unload the belongings of the sons and daughters honored to win lodging here in the original dormitories, these drafty rooms of white-washed brick with a communal toilet around the corner. Twin colonnades held up by columned rows reach out like arms to him, framing the broad green carpet, all seamlessly converging at the storied Rotunda opposite.

Dr. Cannon decides to stride directly towards the landmark, approaching dead on, maintaining equidistance from the bordering Colonnades at every step. He must cross occasional rope fences and the little inclines up to the next plateau that the old architect had so cannily imagined. He is not immune to the visual trickery at play here, the way these ripples pleat like an accordion, so the huge Lawn seems more intimate, the Rotunda closer than it is. He appreciates the variations of style among the

Pavilions, meant to stand as teaching opportunities representing old white Europe's important architectural flourishes. He has studied it all, has heard the historians compare this much-lauded space to the human brain. What galls him now is the effort he's expended in giving a shit about any of it.

The thing he has to do now seems perfectly logical. It will solve nothing, but its importance cannot be underestimated. He is not unaware of the little knots of people that have formed, pausing even with arms full of boxes, to watch. They don't seem to know what to do. Easy to imagine their minds reeling, seeking image matches, calibrating danger, testing the truth of their eyes. He stops and turns with a military precision to face Pavilion VIII, midway down the east wing, halfway to the Rotunda, dead center in the Plan. It looks like a movie façade manse for a Regency dress drama, squat, symmetrical, down-at-the-heel under inch thick layers of whitewash, its tall windows sagging. The whole wretched thing would fit inside his house. He takes cock in hand and urinates. It's a young man's stream today, powerful and copious. Words float up from some dead white guy he can't remember, "I piss on you all from a very great height." Selfie that, mofos.

He hears a shout. "Hey, you can't do that here!"

"What do you think you're doing?"

"If you're gonna streak, you're supposed to run, dude!"

But no one takes a single step in his direction. Humored but wary of a naked man. He shakes his cock again and turns away from the Pavilion he has lost, never had, east towards the hospital he has all but built with his bare hands. Each stride now is sobering, as another thought nails its way into his fore-head. That old man with his telescope, that old ghost on the hill, had foreseen it all. That old man no one can get. You can hate on him all you want, slave-fuckin' sister-fucker that he was. But that's just one of his powers.

Dr. Cannon strides into the dank, chalky-smelling shade of an East Colonnade garden, turns down footworn slate steps to a graveled alley, and pauses to put on his clothes. He moves with languid calm, as if he has just gone for a skinny dip swim and stands back on the riverbank again. The damp rayon shirt, huge as a tent, unrolls almost unwrinkled. He tosses away the boxers. Somehow pulling on the ruined Bermuda shorts feels poignant, returns him chastened from a brink that has felt frankly delightful. And now, back in uniform, he laughs. It's hilarious. No, not what he has done. That is inconsequential. His laugh is for these ridiculous brick-thrifty serpentine walls that enclose the little gardens off the Lawn. Jefferson, what a show-off. A comedian. A canny thief. You just have to laugh about these walls. They say volumes, how they undercut and emphasize, how they bully you to reconsider givens. So you're back in conversation despite yourself, and the self-righteous old slaver never shuts up, he's always pacing that solarium on the hill, he's at the telescope peering down, clocking your labor down to the minute, ordering the whip, relentlessly probing, recording, exploring through overt action how far a brain can reach. Spraying it out across the hills, across history, across whatever little thing you want to try. Yes, you can hate on him all you want, but now try to outthink the fucker.

The damp Hawaiian shirt fits his rounded shoulders like a skin, and by the time he reaches the hospital the vacation between his ears has grown dull, as beach weeks do come a Thursday. This is his professional domain. He could stride in these wheezy automatic doors and all would await his command. At the far edge of the hospital, the blades of a rescue helicopter lazily beat to shutdown on the helipad. Ambulances idle at the ER door. There is always work to be done. But he chooses to walk on, finding his way to Main Street and heading east for no reason he can name towards downtown.

All the way back in the day, heading south from Yale, he'd understood it was a mistake. Touring the Capital-R Rotunda and the brand new gleaming white hospital, far and away the most imposing buildings in town, sharing canapés at a country club with the other candidates, of course he smelled the lie. For some reason everyone wanted to share the tale of how the head of neurosurgery had bucked the whole university in actually ordering brain surgeries for black people to be conducted in a surgical suite, rather than in the leaky basement closet where they had previously been seen. As if this were some heroic tale of leadership and human progress, but any fool could see it just lay a gloss on that larger know your place truth. So then choosing a residency here, he had to swallow that too, that his decision just polished the apple, helped them forget where they came from, made them feel all progressive and clean. And he'd fallen for the challenge, woke up before light every morning determined to show them what a good House Negro could do.

Out past the hospital, Dr. Cannon pauses atop an overpass for the train track that he has always imagined is the X-marks the spot center of this god-forsaken burg. From here he can look east to Jefferson's hill, and even spy the broad lawn spreading out from the iconic domed house that is hidden in its hilltop trees next to the bolder hill beside it, where he'd lived in a two-room cabin for four years, plotting with a general's attention what he'd imagined would be his conquest of medicine. Sitting on a sagging porch in the afternoon in his hospital scrubs, peering down with binoculars stronger than Jefferson's spyglass, he'd scanned and mapped out his plan, a life that would weave itself inextricably within the city's entrenched institutions.

In all the other cabins on the hill lived musicians and bartenders and undergraduates, dreaming out their own lives of wayward hippy passivity under the booming cumulus cupped in the enormous blue of what they all agreed was God's country.

He shared their veggie soups and songs and river pool skinny dips, their night-time raiding parties to looming Carter Mountain for bushels of windfall apples. Learned to install toilets and shower stalls, to shore up aging foundations with rock and mortar. He'd climb up there dead tired from a 36-hour shift bolting spines together and just the sweet cool air revived his burdened soul. But up there on the hill, just like down in the bedraggled offices of the West Hospital, his was the only black face.

Now the hill was shut down, just another part of the spreading Monticello empire. All the hippy kids dispersed. Dr. Cannon realizes he can't recall a single name of a single person. Not even one name of a single one of those lithe girls in flannel with their bony bare feet and stringy hair. His head swivels north along the receding train tracks. This was the path he'd taken coming down, with just two suitcases and a crate, from New Haven. Got off right here at that cartoon quaint red train station at his feet. Hailed a cab and went to work. All a blur less remembered than the hilltop hippies. How he'd zeroed in on that emerging technology, a pinpoint radiation gun called the "gamma knife" and convinced the old bull to buy one. Then became the East Coast expert, publishing amazing recoveries from inoperable sites deep between the ears, patients flying in from the Arab States and European castles to have their tumors zapped. Won an impossible coup – a co-chairmanship of the department named after his partner. Reamed the local paper for daring to headline an article on their work, "Ebony and Ivory," while privately enjoying the whole spat.

And then there was Iris, of course, dear Iris. Back during his dandy days, when he'd traded in his Jeep for a Jaguar sedan, the first of the really good money, down off the mountain now in an ascot scarf and betasseled loafers, head shaved to a gleam like Jordan's, before everyone else in the world caught on. And that was a movie, too, seeing her for the first time, one of a dozen tiny girls, erect as soldiers atop enormous steeds, their hair pinned up under helmets, the little clucks and sighs and shifts of weight they so confidently marshaled to spur and calm their mounts. He stood at the rail, champagne in hand, gawking. She was just seventeen, he always hums, "You know what I mean". It wasn't something you could explain, though the pop stars sing about nothing else. The nearest thing in his experience was that moment, the first time, back during his residency, after the surgical assistants had sawn off the skull, had peeled back the dura mater and the nurse had handed him the scalpel. God's car key. And there pulsed a glob of possibility, all hope, all disaster entirely at his disposal – a living human brain. The thing is, though, you can even get used to that.

Past the overpass, there's that little fancy converted ware-house where he always bangs his head on something, a kitchen store with a bar. They'll have Cognac, no doubt. He realizes this is the longest he's walked in ages – what, a mile or so? – and he's still in sight of the hospital, can still hear the dim boom of a cannon signaling touchdowns from the stadium. Hilarious that he'd thought to conquer this town. It's nothing. You can fit it in your vest pocket.

He pushes the kitchen store's glass door open and is met by a blast of cold air that throws his memory cascading back even further, to the walk-in refrigerator of his dad's butcher shop in Maryland, where he'd learned to chop tons of ribs, crates of chickens, sacks of barbecue, dismembering sides of beef twice his size down to segmented morsels that fed the whole neigh-borhood. As he had told the interviewer from Germany, back after he'd saved that kid with the astrocytoma, feeling a little expansive, a little nationwide, he's had his hands in meat his whole life. That quote, of course, appears to have been the one thing people took from the *60 Minutes* piece, confirming their worst fears that neurosurgeons are all Frankenstein's, saving lives but themselves callously divorced from the precious living tissue, the human beings on their tables. There was real truth in the statement on all sorts of levels, maybe even on the monster scientist level, but it was also just a fact, which is all he had meant to say.

But he'd lost patients because of it. The lily whites and yes the wealthy blacks, too, who had always had qualms anyway about black fingers cracking their skulls. Some of the Arab sheiks switched to Mayo, where their kids could play in snow. Possibly that one sentence was what had really squelched his scheme for a free-standing neurosurgical hospital, with luxury suites and a heli-pad, a glass building shaped like a brain, on that hill south of town at an elevation a little higher than Monticello. Just enough of a hit to his celebrity that the investors balked, and then the feds took their money south to the Research Triangle at Duke, leaving him stunned, stranded, wedged into that tiny office in the old West Hospital with its bathroom tile walls and window air conditioners. Maybe that one sentence had been the real misstep. Maybe everything since has just been the fall?

Ten years ago, ancient history that he's put out of his mind. But it was nearly a coup. He'd dared a plan to pull out of the school, launch his own competing venture for the super wealthy, catapult Charlottesville up a notch on the world stage, taking with him half the neurosurgeons in the hospital and all their accompanying retinue. All the negotiations had been secret, conducted in country club conference rooms out of town. But nothing can ever be secret in this little junior high school of a city. On the day the feds pulled out, he'd received a vase of roses from President Burwell with a card that read only "Welcome Back," a sly slap like the clamp of leg chains. Of course nothing else was said, no one ever mentioned it, nothing visibly changed.

Dr. Cannon eventually calculated that his near rebellion may have scared the Board of Visitors a little, nudged them towards a begrudging respect at least for his work, if not for his celebrity, convinced them to bite on that new-fangled technology, the focused ultrasound suite that cost more than a fighter jet. Well, he'd gotten their attention alright. And today on national television they'd shown the yard nigra his shovel.

Bracing himself with one hand at the zinc-topped bar, Dr. Cannon briefly swirls the fat snifter, sucks in the disinfectant vapors – why is it that every smell in the world has its partner in the hospital? – and downs a double shot of Courvoisier in one gulp. The chef-bartender-store owner stands back, warily watching, then dares to say, "That's usually a sipper not a quaffer."

"I'll quaff as I prefer," the doctor evenly replies, setting the snifter down and reaching for his wallet. But the wallet is gone. Must have dropped it on the Lawn? No big deal, but this requires a negotiation. With the guy you just scolded. Well just tell him. You see my good man, I was streaking the Lawn, an old tradition hereabouts, and it must have slipped out of my pants – such a warm day and all indications were go – wallet must have fallen out. Tut tut, run a tab for me will you? He has this at least, his reputation, his local fame. Except this storekeeper, a new arrival from Denver, has never heard of a Dr. Cannon. "Well here, phone my wife, will you?" But his cell is gone too. Of course. Well now, wouldn't you know it, I suppose this is what real nakedness means. The storekeeper eyes the other customers – a couple picking over salads, a young rake lingering a little too long at the wine rack by the door – and decides to let this one go, for the sake of decorum, for the gamble that this towering monster – maybe an old football pro? – is the surgeon he claims to be.

"No, it's on me, welcome Doctor," he smirks, and extends a pale hand in semi-serious goodwill.

"Good man, good man," the surgeon grins, drinking in this experience that, combined with the slug of cognac, provides just the boost he needs. Neglecting to shake the storekeeper's hand, he turns and lumbers towards the door, takes in the blast of summer air and its hint of wisteria scent, looks west then east, and chooses to continue his stroll away from the stadium. Except now he is not running away anymore. A new plan has begun to take shape. The Hollywood fête at the outdoor stage is just hours away. He can stop in to check on the preparations, hail a cab there over another drink, slip home, change into his evening costume and be back downtown as if it had all been planned all along. Iris will not let on. All will be right and good. Or at least provide a frame for the anger still seething, the fuse brightly running along the base of his skull.

TWENTY-NINE
LUCAS AND CHLOE – DOWNTOWN MALL

CHLOE'S EMBARRASSMENT vaporizes the minute she hits the street. She slows to a dawdle, making sure to stick to the middle of the Mall where Lucas will be able to find her. She pauses at a jewelry cart manned by a squat Latina in a tie-dyed kaftan and enormous wraparound sunglasses. No words pass between them. She lightly fingers a necklace that seems to be strung of porcelain popcorn. The saleswoman's partner, unseen until now, rises up behind the table – side-by-side they look to Chloe like the stacked kachina dolls on display – and lifts a wooden flute to his mouth. His eyes close in preparation. Chloe watches from the corner of her eye, moving on to ankle bracelets, and – this is exactly how it would happen in a movie, soundtrack soulfully swelling – a melody of gorgeous longing is suddenly sipped from the air, just as Lucas' fingers tap her elbow and she turns.

"You okay?"

"Mmhm." He's spindly armed, hair atangle, stray hairs sprouting along his sunburned cheeks, those ski slope eyelashes. It keeps surprising her. He is so here. A sudden urge to text a friend, but she turns to him instead and takes his other arm. They're up in each other's eyes, dazzled by the starbursts there, as she reaches behind and blindly lifts the first bracelet she touches. It's braided twine, white as his newly bleached t-shirt, and it goes on his narrow wrist like it's always lived there. The flutist is right behind her on the other side of the table, but his music is so achingly quiet, as if heard from a mile away. You can hear his soft sips of air punctuating long fluid lines that seem to flow with no time signature except the measured capacity of his lungs, each breath working up sorrow, memory, ages of loss from somewhere high in the mountains. A sound like planets crying. Zooming along on its orbit, spinning boldly on its axis, Chloe can actually – right now in this moment – perceive the earth's traverse – and the three of them standing abristle on its surface, turning in a vacuum towards the sun.

"Miss, you buy?"

Chloe waves a hand yes, loving the grin that spreads on Lucas' face.

"This is sweet."

"To remember me by."

"Remember you?"

"No, don't worry. To remember me today by."

"Like your ankle bracelet. I've still got it, you know."

"You better."

"Let me get you one." He digs in his shorts for the few dollars he'd stashed away. "Lame to do the same one? Or cool? Your choice."

"Okay, sure." And then she sees past Lucas' shoulder. What's he doing here? Perfect. It's her dad.

THIRTY
OFFICER MOSBY – IN THE KITCHEN

RONNIE LEANS in at the screen door and waits there pondering his partner, caught leaning over the kitchen sink rinsing his close-cropped hair under the faucet. Mattie shakes his head, spattering water on the wall, grabs a ragged towel to swab his face, and jumps back in surprise at his old friend's pink dome looming in at the door.

"Man, don't do that!"

"Like you're gonna pop me."

"Could happen."

"Which is another good reason." Ronnie lifts his heft up the step into the kitchen, pulling the screen shut but leaving one hand on the door frame. "Need my gun back, son."

Mattie slumps down onto his chair at the kitchen table, pulls the handgun from its holster and lays it down between them. "The least a my worries."

"No word, huh?"

"You?"

"Just squawk, same as you. Chief know?"

"I don't know, prob'ly. I've been workin' the old haunts as best I can, but nothin'."

"What's he thinkin'?"

"Does he?"

"Now, now, little brother. That ain't gonna help. We gotta try and think like a crazy person, you don't mind me sayin' that?"

"Call him what you want, Ronnie."

"Okay, disturbed then. Not likely he's thinkin' like anybody else. So forget him tryin' some kinda stick-up, sellin' 'em off, what have you."

"I can't go there."

"Well you know him better'n the rest of us, Matthew. You tell me."

"I don't know, man. I was just pokin' around in the garage, halfway hopin' he'd just walk in with 'em in his arms, and the more I looked the less I saw. His notebooks. All his figures. The lawn mowers and cages and shit."

"No clue?"

"I figured out a long time ago, it's no use tryin' to get inside his head, Ronnie. You just go on behavior, what he actually does, and see what you can do with that."

"Well, he's done 'er now."

"He has."

"Well, come on. Come with me. We're due up on the Mall is what I remember. He could be there like as not. No use sulkin' when there's OT to be made."

"I guess. Left the cruiser up there anyway."

"Fine. Shut her down, Matt. It's a small town. He'll turn up. Always does."

"But he might come back."

"Or not. Leave him a note."

"Yeah."

Mattie goes back down the hall and swaps out his soaked shirt and tank top for dry versions, repins his badge, and scribbles "Call Me" on the back of an envelope that he wedges into the screen door frame. Has never once worked before, and won't this time, but it's the sort of thing normal people do. Which, he knows, is the problem.

THIRTY-ONE

DR. CANNON – BUS DEPOT

ANOTHER DRINK WOULD BE JUST the thing. Anything to get off these feet gone to putty, melted down into the tassled loafers, the loafers themselves gone shapeless, flopping, slapping like sandals at every burdened step, so he finds himself mincing, his toes crabbing to keep them on. Should have left them on the Lawn. Along with everything else. Would have made an interesting sociological experiment. How far would he have gotten, stark naked on the street? Funny how on the town's most hallowed space – the plush tiered colonnade-framed carpet of Massa Jefferson's Grounds – that spontaneous exhibition made a sort of sense, fit a tradition driven by the frantic hormones of youth, a rite of passage for fraternity pledges, still followed but clichéd and barely noted in this buttoned down age of careerist children, not even worth a call to campus police. Different, though, when a middle-aged man does so. Of a certain skin tone. Ha! Perhaps today's lark will launch a new variation on the streak, call it the stroll, a more leisurely take on the nominally transgressive, essentially harmless act, necessarily punctuated by a voiding of the bladder, an old fart variation. The Boomer version. That would have them probing for tau proteins, no doubt.

Dr. Cannon pauses at a hilltop crossroads to wait at the light, chuckling again at this odd thing he's done. What would the Founding Father have made of this use of his grand phrase – the pursuit of happiness reduced to a spurting nudism, an airing of one's shaggy parts? In all the voluminous scratchings of his storied quill pen, dutifully copied by that rickety-looking duplicator contraption on display in the bedroom of the Manse on the hill, not one hint of humor, not one jot of whimsy. But wrenching irony on every page, the florid, feminine script aswirl with tangled contradictions born of reason overcome by appetite. No sign that the old slaver ever got the joke.

Cannon glances over at the modest Lewis & Clark statue planted on a concrete island in the middle of the street and shakes his head, as if tour guiding an out-of-town surgical resident. The old man's protégé, that delicate lute player standing with out-thrust breast and spread legs in front of the old soldier in buckskin pledged to get him home safe, and cowering behind them in a Hollywood travesty of female distress the one true hero of the whole expedition, the Indian Sacagawea, yet another bald-faced lie poured out in bronze to serve the prevailing fantasy. History is just marketing after all. Branding. The coining of slogans and campaign ads. Jingles. Bold colors. PR. And cash. Those who labor, who give, even those who may wield a specialized almost godly expertise, fall beneath the wheels.

Shuffling across the street, looking neither left nor right, he chooses to take the oak-shaded path down to the Mall. Where, without a wallet, might a drink be had? Who among the merchants and barkeeps might recognize him, might run a tab, offer a gimme? Bah! There is nothing for it. Without the plastic, the paper, the code, he is nobody, just that naked forked stick

Lear raged about. Mistakes were made. How is it that after three decades and more of plying a rarified trade right here in this dot on a map, he cannot think of one lowly tradesman along all the busy storefronts that he knows by name, who might recognize, acknowledge, cut him a break?

And how did he get here to the Downtown Mall anyway? What grand exhalation has propelled him to this carnival of Caucasian privilege, where the only other pigmented faces play flutes and hawk scarves at outdoor tables five thousand miles north of their mountaintop Bolivian hovels? Going back to look for the wallet is not an option. Will not trudge on tortured feet back across town to the Lawn and graze like an old bull searching for the lost phone and wallet. No, home itself is too far right now, and to straggle in the door like a wayward teen, to face the silent judgment of his guests, even the chary ministrations of his wife, all too much.

For a moment he stops, turning amidst the brick and glass, the outdoor diners and strolling shoppers, as if lost. He spies a young couple – teenagers, probably, turning down an alley – and is struck by their insouciance, by their ease with each other, by the sense of occasion surrounding them like a nimbus. *Carefree.* Like it was, in memory, with Iris in the day. Is that what all this industry has been about all along? Some contortion aimed at such a simple goal? Those teens might almost be he and Iris. The way the boy measures his step solicitously alongside hers. There was a time, yes, when he'd attended to that. And her head set erect on slim square-set shoulders, as if steering a horse. As they turn out of sight, he wonders, was that some kind of flashback? For a moment he wants to catch up with them, whoever they may be, buy *them* a drink, an ice cream cone, wish them a grand future. But, the wallet problem, and then they are gone as if imagined.

The doctor plops himself down on the lip of the Mall's dribbling fountain. He shakes his head at his own immaturity, at the rage that has driven him out and away from it all, at the tail between the legs scurry it must have seemed to Iris and the rest. No more than a baby's tantrum, but right at the edge of a breakdown, surely fatigue-driven, ridiculous, a kind of momentary hiccup, though just a crack in the wall really, easily repaired, a ribald anecdote, that thing that happened the day of the game. There's satisfaction in it. A man can't survive tied only to routine. It was the cry of a heart squeezed dry, a soul yoked, who wouldn't at last understand that? But what to do? How to bridge the yawning gap blown out of the day? Yes, of course, the party, the rooftop gala at the bus shed, must stop in to check on the preparations, put all in order, and on that mission cadge a gin and a ride back to the house!

He's up, reenergized and striding, climbing the mall's slope with lengthening steps, parting couples along his path, and in no time stands at the hilariously over-designed bus shed at the mall's edge, all sharp-angled glass and louvered walls. It's been months since he and Iris toured the roof, imagined its use as a venue overlooking the concert pavilion and its stage. A brilliant coup, really, and worth the expense despite the risk of weather and the necessity to make it pop, to make it cinematically grand. He'd envisioned it all – bandstand, pop up gourmet kitchen, flat panel screens playing closeups of the stage, a parqueed dance floor, lights strung high, crystal goblets and champagne. He'd sworn all to secrecy. It must be a surprise, eye candy, so that emerging from the bus station elevator to the roof bedazzles, an Oz moment for all.

But so many loose ends, he'd lost track of the vendors and decorators, purchase orders and invoices, licenses and due dates as the thing took on a momentum. Striding through the station's glass doors, Dr. Cannon notes the fog of smudged handprints left by the users of public transit, a wad of gum and gum wrappers littering the concrete floor, the stink of tobacco despite boldly lettered NO SMOKING signs. There is no one down here at the visitor's center level, the atrium-like space as empty as the airport terminal, he wonders if anyone even takes the bus anymore? The industrial elevator, hung with filthy quilted pads, creaks as if a hundred years old, and emerging into daylight again, what does he see? A lone workman, teetering near the roof edge, propping a string of lightbulbs onto a pole, the dance floor jagged, half-finished, a low platform that might someday be a bandstand set up sideways against a wall, and long boxes that may hold flat panel tv's stacked in the middle of it all.

A disaster! The gala just hours away! Nothing done, just as he'd feared, just as the old saw goes, if you want something done right! He shouts, "Man, what are you doing? Where is everyone?" Yet the workman goes on about his precarious business, as if deaf. Damned earbuds! Everyone and their earbuds! Dr. Cannon shouts again, then spins in place once and sets to work himself, on hands and knees tearing at the nearest cardboard box. He slides one unwieldy black slab out onto the roof, fretting at the fragile reflective glass screen, blank dumb useless. There's nowhere to hang it, no outlet to power it, no cable to take a feed. Leaving the screen upturned on the floor, he goes to a counter that may be intended as a bar and sees nothing but empty shelving. Not a bottle, no ice cooler, no wine, nothing! Just hours from now! How could this be!

Frantic, the surgeon leans out over the roof lip, looking for a delivery truck, a vendor, someone to accuse, but sees only casual strollers, oblivious and uninvolved in this higher drama. And then – the final disaster – he discovers that there is no longer any view of the stage! Somehow, since that late winter tour, the cedars planted as a decorative border that back then had just topped out at roof's edge have shouldered together, doubling in height, until they entirely block any view from the bus station roof of the Pavilion stage. But that's why he'd chosen this ridiculous location in the first place! This cannot stand. No time left. Do it. Do it now.

THIRTY-TWO

MRS. CANNON – RUGBY ROAD

THOUGH IT SEEMS to take forever for Iris' charges to make their way out of the stadium – Claire unplugging herself from the movie star's rear long enough to take the keys to the rental and lead him down the street, the director politely pausing at every step to shake a hand or pose for a selfie – their hostess has by sheer force of will somehow kept her poise. Even as they situate themselves inside the SUV that smells of old food and alcohol for the slow procession along the winding streets around the fraternity houses jammed with drunken fans leaving the game and lost families in minivans parked sideways attempting traffic blocking turns in search of dorms, she endures. At half-time amidst handing out pliers for crab cracking, pouring wine, pecking a grizzled cheek, admiring gawdy team earrings, trying to follow the wanderings of her guests, she had only been able to phone a few times, but no answer. Though he had the second pair of keys to the rental car, he hadn't used it, so where was he? When the game resumed, she had excused herself to a bathroom stall to try the hospital, but they had not seen him either, and the voice at the other end seemed to snicker, she thought, in saying so.

The director and his entourage had not returned to their seats, choosing instead to wander the stadium, scouting shooting angles or whatnot. Claire, of course, was off with the star somewhere, maybe back at a frat house party? So she sat and pondered the one word question, why? No, she could not leave. She could not strike out after her husband. But sitting in the sun-stroked end of summer crowd, pretending to follow the tedious scrum on the field, she sank into that old place that always awaits, where a haggard finger wags to moan how all of her planning, effort, and cheer amount only to maidwork, nothing but another service taken for granted, clean sheets in a hotel room. She had always imagined, in the organizational flurry that accompanies these events, that she was the central figure, the still point around which the festivals unfurled, their essential cog, but sitting alone in a stiff chair on an x-marks the spot foam pillow on the forty-five yard line, her suspicion is confirmed that to everyone else involved she exists entirely on the periphery, maybe never even seen, maybe just the help after all.

Now, back in the car, in line and waiting to exit the stadium lot, she envies her husband's recklessness. Even though the twin waifs in the back seat have not once turned off their handhelds since the airport hours ago, Iris cannot bring herself to tap the phone button on her steering wheel, it's just impolite, and if by some chance she could get ahold of her wayward husband, there's no telling what temper he might be in, and broadcasting one of his rants to her passengers would simply complete this could-have-been-magic brink-of-disaster day. Imagine. Just to bolt, to leave it all behind, to not give a hoot. Walking off the snub. Well good for him. What trouble can he get up to anyway? She aims at small talk, chattering about the ersatz Jeffersonian architecture bordering the domed prize on the Grounds, listing the smattering of new cafes that attempt a daring dish or two, even stooping to a brief homily about the charm of the local film festival, while cutting glances at her guest, unable to gauge now whether his eternal half-smile, almost stupid in its apparent contentedness, may mask boredom or frustration.

What she really needs is a good five minutes in the bathroom. A face splash, a deep breath, the phone. Every call made adds up, but you must keep on it. Will he be at home? On a head-clearing dash out the Parkway in his little pocket rocket? Setting bombs at the Pavilion, ha ha? Where? The answer is in her pocketbook, but she knows he won't answer until his pilgrimage is done, and damned if she will give those cell phone-glued bookends the satisfaction.

"Miz Cannon," the director asks, "I believe you mentioned your horse?"

"Our house? Well, it's another of those Palladian knock-offs, really, 20s vintage, at least the main wing is. And please, it's Iris."

"I'm sorry, no, Iris, I meant your horse. You ride? You're an equestrienne, I believe you said?"

Oh my god, this has been boring him to tears! Yet, yes, please, such a relief not to have to create small talk for one minute!

"Well, I don't think I'd call myself that," she smiles with what she realizes is that old cocquettish effort at a dimpling of the cheek – what must that look like these days? – "I ride to the foxes with one of the local clubs, my old stallion and I can keep up fairly well on those romps. But not dressage, not for years really, in the ring." And now she's pushing back a wisp of dry hair from her face. It's unsettling to find oneself, even for this one question, an item of interest!

"That's so cool," he says, with that boy gone to seed ease, and what seems like actual attention.

"You know," she dares, "I think I live for it. I think I still do."

"Yes."

"I just, well, do you ride?"

"Western saddle. With the kids at our ranch. That's totally it for me."

"Oh, but that's something. So few anymore even try."

She hopes this will lead to an anecdote, some tidbit along the lines of "Yeah, you'd never have thought it, but my old uncle, back on *Space Boy*, gay as a balloon but he was something of a trick rider. Taught me to rope." Or a revery over whatever Montana acreage he calls his ranch. But he doesn't go there. She fears he will take up the fox hunting thread, furrowed brow tut-tutting the inhumanity of the thing, forcing her to generate her usual rube-appropriate justification of a sport no doubt paired with dog fighting in his mind. Instead, and this really throws her off, he says, "Can you tell me, how was it to compete?"

The minivan ahead of her has stopped dead on the narrow street without signaling its intention. The Escalade's mighty yet all-but-silent air conditioner seems to have done its job too well, chilling the passenger compartment to refrigerator temps. She reaches for the dial, asking, "Am I freezing us out here?"

One of the waifs glances up long enough to shoot a dagger into the rear view mirror, aimed through the tiny gap between her graduated designer glasses and the straight-trimmed bangs at her forehead. Iris says, "You have your own controls, on the door at the top, if you can reach it?" Neither of the twins moves or acknowledges the suggestion.

"Iris. I'm sorry. Is that a prying question?" the director asks.

The minivan trolling ahead of them has begun to blink a turn signal suggesting that some decision has been made, though they edge along at a snail's pace. The driver is hidden behind a cargo bay packed to the ceiling with the essentials, no doubt, of studenthood these days. Nothing to do but tag along on this curve and see what he will do. As expected, Claire and the rental are nowhere to be seen.

"Oh, I'm sorry, Mr. York."

"If you're Iris, then I'm Rod, okay?"

"Well, Rod." She wants to say 'Roddy". When did he shorten it, maybe in the credits to that old teen show *Fun Times*? "Competing."

"Yes, what was that like for you?"

This is really uncomfortable. The great director's attitude of Howdy Doody complaisance has shifted up a gear, as if his freckled ears have perked. She turns in amazement to see his eyes alive with interest, blue spheres set inside his crinkled, thin, yet now more boyish than ever face. For the first time all day, that face fits the ragged baseball cap on his head.

"Um. Well, I suppose it's like so many things we do as children. I just grew up to it. A gymnast or a skater, or a swimmer, you know how they are up in the dark at their work, and school is just something they sandwich as best they can in between. Dressage is like that. And, well, for you it must have been acting, maybe?"

The minivan has finally backed its way up a gravel drive between hedges, and the road before them clears. The director says nothing, so she adds, just to keep the conversation going, "Mama rode, and her mother all the way back, you know."

"How far back?" He says this with a hint of expectant wonder, like a kid with a birthday package.

"Oh, we're one of those old Virginia families, FFV, fine fogies of Virginia? King's grant of land. Rode with Colonel, not yet General, Washington. A real tragedy of my great great grandmother's life, to her mind at least so they say, was that there were only sisters – six of them – of age to fight with General Lee, no boys to win honor and all that. But they all rode well and passed it down."

"Your family was here in Virginia in the Civil War?"

"Oh yes, and like all the rest, we do have stories. The old

man, my great great grandfather, I'm afraid he held slaves, shipped the women, his wife and the daughters, south to Savannah early on, but he stayed, invested everything in Confederate paper, and lost it all."

"Savannah."

"No fighting there, until the end, and that old monster Sherman."

"You know, for most of us, we hear these things, and it's like *Lord of the Rings* or something."

"Oh, it is for me, too, only we old families are the little hobbits hauling, who was it, Frodo's book around."

"And the horses."

"I suppose, yes, one of those what are they, anachronisms? Tie us back to the old days. It meant so much to my grandmother that we rode, my sisters and me. Grandpa was a small town banker – from a carpetbagger line, if you can believe that! – and he kept a fine jumper for her. They bought me my pony. Kept it on their farm."

"Pardon me saying this, I know it's a shallow thing, but may I just say wow! It's like a sequel to *Gone with the Wind*.

"Well, I think they already did that," she allows. "Maybe a rewrite? I mean, what if the little girl had lived? I always thought, *National Velvet* or something?"

"Right. With Elizabeth Taylor."

"And she looked so much like Vivienne Leigh and the daughter on the horse at the end."

"What was that girl's name. Bonnie Blue, wasn't it?"

"That was it! All of us Bonnie Blue's in our Easter dresses on our ponies in the back yard. See how the tales y'all tell in Hollywood get entangled with whatever tales *we* tell, and who knows what's true anymore?"

"Amen to that."

"But, please, Rod, please do not take back with you any

notion that I carry some torch or something for a grand lost cause or anything. There's no Confederate flag in the attic. My sisters by now would not know what a bridle is for. I do it for the morning. It's my indulgence. Some people practice yoga or take a run. I'm just one of those tiresome women who ride."

Iris, for some reason, feels tears welling in her eyes. It can't be for the commonplaces she's just shared, not one word of which is actually on point. Maybe it's just that this may be the only thoughtful thing she's said all day, and just the words, letting herself speak with some confidence about personal stuff. How tense she must be! Not just today, with so much at stake, but all the time, on the verge! And this whole conversation will circle back, as they always do, even today, even after all these years, even among friends, to the chocolate-vanilla marriage, the broken taboo or whatever it is. He'll get there. They always do. It's just too delicious a snack not to nibble.

"I was just wondering. Tomorrow, before we leave, if I could come out with you to the stables?"

"Oh, well…"

"If it's any imposition."

"Oh my no. It's not that. I did invite you! I think it's. Yes, I'd like that. Would you want to ride?"

"Uh, well, I think maybe just, well, sure if there's a horse, but I was just thinking."

"Yes, I think we can make that work. Whatever you like, yes." Now we're on familiar footing again, she thinks, something to do not feel. Whew. "Yes, let's do that. I'd be honored."

As they turn into the crunching graveled driveway, she checks off the Porsche parked in exactly the same spot Rainie had left it at dawn. So he's not out on the Parkway. One option down. But there is the rental already – how did Claire get past them? What is she up to anyway – it's like some movie groupie has replaced her daughter! But no, for this one minute all day,

Claire has truly returned. In the kitchen, with Dot and Fanny, she's laid out hors d'oeuvres, has put on music – some kind of hypnotic blippy tune – and opens the door in greeting as if she's been waiting all afternoon for their arrival.

And there stands the superhero, this time it's just weird, in that same spot almost at the top of the stairs, pausing in too-short swim trunks – are those things coming back again? – with a towel in one hand. Chiseled, hairy, coiled, and at ease. Oh it doesn't hurt to look. Claire takes her mother's arm to steer her inside, so the director and his aides can pass, a cat that ate the canary smile on her face that is impossible to process. She leans in to whisper, "Not a sign of Dad."

THIRTY-THREE

INCIDENT ON THE MALL

"You doin' alright back there, buddy?" The cabbie has taken in all the activity of the past half hour without comment, but his toothpick is now worn to shreds, and he's switched from the power pop of 106.1 *the Corner* to a gospel station on the FM dial, tuned low yet soulful. His passenger looks like a Halloween jack-o-lantern and has fretted, jabbered to himself, pounded the front headrest from time to time, pushing him on through the holiday traffic. He recognizes the face, but can't place it. Some honcho, maybe one of those car salesmen in the loud-mouthed tv ads.

The guy seems to be looking for somebody or some thing, but won't say who or what. First pointing up Pantops Mountain, through the parking lots of the shopping malls, then back down the hill and out towards McIntire Park, shouting faster no slow down now here over there, one time nearly reaching across the car seat for the wheel. Back downtown at a hardware store, not far from where this whole escapade started, he finally shouts stop, and it's all the cabbie can do to take a breath and idle the car when the man orders him to wait while he goes inside. Which is his chance to call in.

"Doris do you have a fix on me?"

"Looks like Preston, up by the pool?"

"Okay. I'm not playin' this time."

"Uh huh."

"Doris, do this. Call the police. Have 'em trail me, please, ma'am. Think I got a live one."

"You're straight up? Say the code."

"Straight up, honey. Look, I don't know the code."

"You gotta say Code Yellow or Code Red."

"Doris."

"I'll call it. But you oughtta say."

He snaps his phone shut as the guy comes tearing out of the storefront empty-handed. What is it that keeps him from flooring the gas when the man lumbers over to a work truck parked in front and lifts a chain saw out of the back? Is he straight up stealing that thing? Right out in broad daylight? But who's the crazy one here? What cowardice or confusion is it that dares to order the guy to put the saw in the trunk, but fails to just drive away before he falls back in the rear seat again?

And now this madman wants to go right back where they started for his drop off? And then, when they roll to a stop back by the old train depot on Water Street, in the shadow of the Pavilion downtown, this cinches it, dude has no cash. Things get hairy then. It's all somehow apparently the cabbie's fault. The crazy man stands at the car door, trunk still open, grungy chain saw held in one enormous hand as if it's a toy, the other balled into a pile driver fist. A vein pulses down the side of his helmet-smooth head. The guy glistens as if oiled, his frightening eyes narrowed. Demanding an IOU. No policeman anywhere. There's nothing he can do but hand over the receipt, and say a quick prayer that the vision of this orange fireball jogging up an alley to the Mall is not one he takes to his grave. He snaps a picture with his phone, but doesn't catch the face, just a half profile and the broad back, chain saw swung like a weapon in one hand.

As Dr. Cannon jogs up a side street to the Mall, he knows exactly what needs to be done. Though he has never used a chain saw, or swung an axe, for that matter. What would his mother think to see him now? Proper teacher of mathematics to public school knuckleheads. Never even let him run a lawn mower. Or hold a hammer. Not this boy. How she fought against his helping in the butcher shop. How hard can it be, though, to sweat out the dials and switches and the primitive draw-string. A child could do it, the idea surfing waves of anger that seem to roll in endlessly now across a broad and roiling ocean, a tsunami the old schoolmarm would have prayed over, knowing how it lurks unseen but deep and eventually beach bound.

And then he's got it, a bracing roar in his hands, revving the trigger, the vibration a thrill up his arms. A clotted crowd of wanderers gathered here at the Mall's east end takes a measured step back before what has to be a juggling act perhaps? Dr. Cannon pauses for a minute at full stature, the chain saw idling at his side like a lethal extension of his arm, surveys the circle of onlookers and shouts above the pulse of the engine, "Stand back. This tree is coming down!" He stoops to one knee at the base of the cedar, pushes through its annoying, prickly fronds to the trunk, fights his way closer, the tree half-swallowing him as he sidles into it, then falls as if shot onto his back, convulsing, his feet buckled under him. The saw chokes off to idle, foam gurgling at his lips.

Officer Mosby crouches in a combat pose, glaring at his partner, who everyone in the circle clearly sees did not issue the required three or even one single warning. To a man with a chain saw! His partner shrugs, "It was him or the tree, Mattie," then retrieves the barb and wire of his Taser, while Mosby goes down on a knee to check the man's pulse. He's in there, trembling, in a full body cramp. Regular heartbeat, sweat going cold on his forehead. He parts the cedar limbs to reach the idling chain saw, chokes it off, then works at prying the handle from the man's thick yet manicured fingers. Who is this guy? He's seen him. A tv newsman or something? That seems both right and impossible. If he has a wallet with ID it's buried at the bottom of this orange mountain. Mosby sets the chain saw on the ground several feet away and scans the spectators, announcing, "Evidence." His partner has already called for backup, making the scene even more of an event for the milling concert crowd that swells and presses, all of it completely at odds with every one of the chief's holiday directives to lay low, be a ghost, don't make a scene.

Rolling the stunned man up on one side for a moment is like shoving a walrus, but Mosby gets it done. His pockets are empty, except for a crumpled cab receipt. Who is this guy? He beckons and when Ronnie comes over, whispers, "We are in a world of shit." Already, he hears the whoop-whoop sound of an ambulance navigating the crowd. Ronnie whispers back, "Glad I got me some cheerleader at half time, 'cause we're done for the night."

Mosby's jaw works, but he cannot come up with a reply. No one in the crowd seems to have anywhere else to go. Everything they do is being recorded on at least a dozen camera phones. But the guy's pulse is growing stronger. He's starting to come around. At least that's a good sign. As long as he doesn't come up swinging. Because you can't Tase 'em twice. What they need more than a stun gun is some kind of cellphone signal disruptor that would block the cameras from working while a man's trying to do his job. They think they're doing the world a favor, keeping an eye on the thugs in uniform. Definitely puts a harsh on the mood. The tension, it's like the old comic book scientist Bruce Banner, it rises along his back, tightens like a yoke across his shoulders, and the world drains of color, doused in blowing sand. He needs to vacate the scene now, before he goes green, but he has to wait with this guy Ronnie has Tased. It's the triggering chain saw smell of oil and gasoline he fears the most. The crowd has to go. But anything they say now will just bring out more cameras. The chief has to see only two cops doing their job, which in this case is what, protect and defend the decorative trees of the Mall? Neutralizing a mad man with a chain saw is all.

The citizen Ronnie has Tased may be insane, but this is not going to end well or neatly. This is what he has sworn not to do. Cannot let himself get entangled in paperwork, must not get the chief involved. Because, crazy as this take down is, it's small potatoes. Somewhere out there, Sid is wandering around with guns. And if something goes south, if someone else gets the call. A drop of sweat falls from the tip of his nose and disappears into the soaked rayon of the moaning man's shirt. Like all his good intentions and all he's ever done, spinning in a whirl down the shitter.

THIRTY-FOUR
CHLOE AND LUCAS – ROOFTOP PICKUP

BECAUSE THE OLD PICKUP TRUCK – the lone vehicle on the parking garage roof – squats in a far corner on flat tires looking as though it has not moved in years, and because it has been conveniently abandoned backed up to the west wall, dropping the creaky tail gate invents a ready-made bench for watching the sunset. Nothing in the truck bed but an old car battery. If you sit on the tailgate, you're pretty much out of view of anyone driving up the ramp, at least at first, and looking back you can see that the elevator door sightline is semi-obstructed too. The parking garage is the tallest building around, with a clear view out to the embracing low hills along the town's southern rim. Is it possible that Chloe already knew all this or is it just one of those lucky miracles that seem to ring her like emoji cherubs? Lucas decides this is a question he'll save for old age. He scoots closer so she can lean into the curve of his arm, drop her ear to his shoulder and sound the depths, a shared pulse like a drumbeat quickening between them.

Then, in the half hour after the sun sinks behind the womanly recline of the Blue Ridge, the sky goes nuts with party colors. Chloe has climbed over onto his lap, wrapping herself tenderly and fiercely around him, her hands up in his shirt, doing all the wriggly work herself. He soars up into the sky with her, all Superman in his mind. It seems like the sunset tints them, her eyes flash orange and pink into his, and though his bare butt is planted squarely on a day-warmed metal tailgate, the rest of him might as well be diving in the air with the barn swallows.

The light show hasn't so much shut down as screen swiped onto duskier shades of the color wheel when they scoot up into the truck bed, lying with clothes askew somehow comfortably flat on the rusting floorboards. Chloe's close-cropped fuzzy hair hardly pillows her head in the crook of his arm. This time last night his back had lain against the similarly ungiving floor of a coal hopper. He had looked up out of that rectangular cage at the booming sky with one goal in mind. Lying together now feels like a movie lap dissolve. The whole day in between clipped out. When the first shooting star flares green then white across a sky that is still too pale for constellations, they let it go unremarked. These things just happen to people like us. Warmth radiates off the truck bed, but in no oppressive way. With twilight the stifling atmosphere that has pressed on the town like a weighted summer blanket begins to fray, giving way to a trickle of breeze up here on the roof. A hot tub on *Warm* but made of air. Her circling finger goes still on his shallow belly, her breath like a pulse at his neck. No feather bed could beat this. For long minutes, as his eyes camera shutter on the staged arrival of night, he tries to pull together some rhymes in a chain he can remember. Nothing comes. It doesn't matter. They'll be there.

THIRTY-FIVE
SID – THE COAL TOWER

WAKING up is always the worst part of any day, like waiting for a computer to reboot and you wish you hadn't even pushed the button, because you can hear the pain in its robotic ticking towards consciousness, the agony of electrons enslaved on a circuit board navigating all the grudging scripts and looping code, all the routine checklists and check-offs, the system reconfigurations and updates. The tedious orientational tracking of shadow and magnetic field. Wherever he has gone while his body was a sack wisps off irretrievably down a sneaky rent in time. The sack reanimating aches as if beaten, every joint of all four limbs and especially the throb behind his eyes the price your creaky operating system pays for daring consciousness.

Then gradually as higher algorithms kick in, the automatic functions begin their tireless sensory notations: acrid smoke, echoed laughter, a vagrant beatbox tune. His head ratchets up with a rusty creak, pivots on its tendon-driven neck to align an eye with a crack in the floorboards. People down their smoking wacky weed. Kids with contraband beer. It's that time of day, then. Check. They come in here like they own it, as if it's just a barn or something, sometimes a dozen or more, sometimes just a couple snuggling in a musty corner. All summer before the leaves start falling and the river people move in, this is the nightly parade. Peering down from his perch, Sid has witnessed fights, first kisses, sing-along choruses, crying jags and bad jokes. Sometimes somebody brings a speaker and the silo echoes with pounding bass. Once in a while, a jock will take ahold of the interior ladder's bottom rung and pull himself up, hanging one-handed for a daredevil moment in the void.

As near as Sid can tell, no one has ever attempted to go higher, testing the false roof at the top. No one has violated his attic room or even suspects there is anything beyond the board ceiling on which he lies. The sculptor came closest, when he bolted and welded his dress-frame skeleton atop the tower, running the operation from a cherry-picker crane parked outside. One day during the installation, Sid had been trapped inside, while the crew traipsed around in heavy boots atop the conical roof, at one point loudly drilling a bolt hole through it just inches from his head. He'd lain there petrified that at any moment one of them would peel back the plywood slat and find him cowering there. It had been a terrifying few hours, but thrilling, too, because even before they drove the crane away the steel-frame sculpture began to pull celestial information from the sky like the disguised antenna it really was. The cacophony made by the drills amplified whistling bytes of code as they raced through Sid like light through a prism, then slotted themselves into the tower's tubular wall as orderly as books in a library.

The damned sculpture. Now that the dress is gone and it's just a metal skeleton, some days after rain it crackles with incoming data, seemingly electrified, alive and steaming, even hot to the touch. Other days it sits forlorn as if abandoned, the whole cosmos ignoring this key slotted into a forgotten portal. If this is a portal at all. But it must be. All his calculations point here, not to the tower itself, but to one cracked corner of the floor, tiny, easily scuffed over, dime-sized. Discovered by accident during one of those early tumbles with the man with no hands, Sid's nose actually rubbed up against it. From that crack erupted reams of data, a whole other-dimensioned galaxy crammed into a slot too small to fit a finger. Every subsequent measurement drawn from all the city's monuments centered there. Though he knows that even this pinpoint is just an approximation, that the actual location must be some quark-sized dimension pulsing deep in an ancient riverbed at the floor of what must seem a Grand Canyon if he could just get there, could touch it, could shrink down small enough to put it in a bottle.

He thinks of it as a black hole, but knows that this is just a shorthand human physicists would use. Quantum physics, as he understands it, only hints at what's going on down there. The Vortex thinks time is a joke. It hangs waiting, a painting already dry and framed in God's own museum. The truth is, people kind of know, it's all in the way they behave, yet no one will own up to it. It's in their coded language shared in glances and facial tics that even children understand. Only Sid is left out of the conversation. Only Sid is doomed to wander, to fret, to calculate, dreaming of a way in. Yes, but it's only Sid who holds the key that might turn it off. And with it a message for those with ears to hear. The manifesto, left in the garage back at the house across the tracks.

The tower hums in neutral now, pulsing at a low throb. It would be better, trapped here, to just stay the night and indulge in one last round of calculations. To somehow process the data as it pours in through the roof. But the truth is it always just repeats. It's time now to get the message out, to try this one last time. The boards creak as he gets to his feet and crouches on the slatted platform. Then the crunch when he lifts the plywood flap to the roof.

Scrambling out on top, he pauses on all fours to take in the view. The sky since his nap has gone a weird green in a last color splash before the shroud of night falls again, its trembling molecules transmitting the tharump of a bullfrog in the railside creek and the first whine of that nightlong cricket symphony tuning up. From the base of the tower, the railroad track's silvered curve veers off towards the University, offering the slimmest barrier between this blasted outpost and the warren of neighborhood houses on the other side. The antenna at his back compels him forward. He imagines it melting to a witch's puddle, maybe struck by a mighty lightning bolt, at the end of this event.

Sid crawls backwards to the ladder, sends out a toe like a tentacle in search of the first rung, commits himself to the effort and scurries terrified down the rungs, seen or not seen knowing it's best to just do it and not get caught midway. Climbing up and down, he has discovered, is the sweetest of activities. It brings focus, something for all four limbs to do at once. The challenge is always the plop at the bottom in a crunch of gravel, going down hard on knees and an elbow, struggling not to gasp, then crouching, waiting to see if anyone will notice, then crablike on all fours scuttling across the quadruple set of tracks, a scurrying thing and a double take to anyone who might be watching. Like on the ladder, hands and feet is a good way to get about, gives all four limbs something useful to do, the imprint of gravel sharp to his hungry palms.

Across the tracks, back inside the yard at home, he plops down against the board fence and unzips his shorts to jerk off beneath a bent old mimosa that drips with dizzy sweet late summer perfume. Lights off, no squad car, no sign of his younger brother. He doesn't let himself spurt, relieved just to have calmed a bit, and stands up to prop his hard-on inside his waistband and rezip. The manifesto is in the garage. If he can get it without turning on lights, without making any noise at the door, and get back out again.

But something's wrong. The door's locked, for one thing, though the key hides right there under the old rusty paint can as always. Inside, old Wahoo's cage has been moved off his worktable to the floor. Notebooks lie askew. Someone took the lid off a box of current files. Demons. Generals. While he was gone. He skips in place at the doorway, then creeps over to the table, lifts Wahoo's cage back on top, and recoils at the gecko's piercing judgmental stare, the old lizard's neck ratcheting in one calibrated jerk of attention, his goose-pimpled body poised on thin-fingered paws and crooked elbows. Wahoo could tell him everything, has no doubt seen it all, but speaks in solitary squawks on rare occasions that may be just a clearing of the throat.

The weird thing, it seems that nothing is really missing. All the notebooks are there, just out of order. And the manifesto on its pasteboard rectangle lies face-down under the cricket jar. Sid dips to the floor, completing a half dozen squats, but then stops, wipes his face on his shirt, and faces facts. The only thing you can do. Play your part. He brushes himself off, tests his wits and trembling hands by pausing to feed Wahoo a couple store-bought crickets, then collects a coat hanger and the scrap of cardboard with its scrawled announcement, pockets a flashlight, and slips back out into the yard, remembering for the first time in years to lock the door against further intrusion, as if that would matter to the onrushing storm.

THIRTY-SIX
CHLOE AND LUCAS – BUSKER'S CORNER

BACK OUT ON THE MALL, Chloe and Lucas allow themselves to flow with the human tide, all pulled towards the Music Pavilion. They pass an old guitarist, squatting on a stool in a bank's entryway alcove with a lap steel guitar stretched out like a gleaming fish on his lap, his bottle slides scaling the fish so it moans and whines. Lucas cuts Chloe a sidewise grin, then tugs her into the alcove and before she can ask him what's up, he squats off to one side, and pulls a tarnished harmonica from his pocket, wagging it to get the guitarist's attention. The old man grunts, "One time, then go," and toes his top hat tip collector closer to his stool.

Lucas murmurs, "Thanks man," and hunkers down in a corner, not close enough to assume any sort of duo status, not so far as to seem competing for the alcove, then cups the harmonica to his face to suck a complementary note that Chloe hears as a half-key off, falling quickly into a one-two rhythm of flittering tweets and twips. Chloe glances around, her face flushed, but moves off to the side out of Lucas' way to scan the passing parade. The old man's shoulder twitches once, as if settling down into some new idea, then taking a cue from Lucas' respectful rhythm bed, his guitar strings erupt in a whining finger-picked flight as if electrified, even terrified, she thinks.

The sound rings inside the alcove. Leaning back just an inch changes it, so it softens and sings. No wonder the old man chose this spot, it's got concert hall acoustics! And Lucas gets that, too. Hair falling around his face, eyes squinted closed, rocking on one heel in his squat, he has evolved again, into yet some new guy that for some reason is actually not embarrassing at all. Nobody just walks up to a street musician and horns in on his show. Nobody even ever acknowledges them really. They're just homeless people with some musical training back in their blighted pasts, right? With a guitar that you hock for a ride out of town when the weather changes. Or something. Best to just slip past without a glance.

But here we have this boy, slipping characteristically, she thinks, right into that role, and his behavior – like everything else about him – a surprise. He neatly fits this minstrel hustle, this busking thing he calls it. Like some kind of street person. It's no stretch to blink and see him living that way, scrounging a week from now in some other little downtown as dirt-streaked and smelly as he'd been in the creek just this afternoon. He'd be fine with that. That's how they'd met after all, in another store-front alcove, the one down by the ice cream shop. She thinks then of how your life can turn on a whim. What if she'd not been alone for a minute, had not paused to listen to him plunking his guitar?

The guitarist lifts his slide-ringed fingers for the briefest beat, seems to cock his ear a millimeter, and Lucas – waiting for it – takes the cue. Chloe has trained on clarinet, at least up until last year when she put her foot down and refused to march like some toy soldier in the high school marching band, and she finds herself nodding along as Lucas' little strip of wood and steel unleashes a slurred but accurate variation on the old man's solo. And then Chloe surprises herself. She knows this song. It's an old Top Forty tune, it might even be country, "Walk a Mile in My Shoes," and even if she doesn't recall the exact lyrics, as she begins to shyly sway and hum, that's okay, right? She's half turned into the alcove, more an audience participant than a performer, but the guitarist perks up, actually cuts one eye at her, and as Lucas ends his loopy solo, both musicians fade back to a shared, quiet rhythm to let her do her thing. So, well, here she goes, watching Lucas' face all the while. He lowers the harmonica to smile encouragement as she tries out the lyric. For a moment, she can imagine it, the two of them on the road, wandering, busking, maybe even sleeping in doorways.

And then she hears it, "Whoah, check it out, the hippy girl!"

The worst thing that could happen. Always. She doesn't even have to look. Joel.

He's with Chip and Lars, his lackeys, the three of them dressed as if they're already college frat boys in their game day uniforms: khaki shorts, button collared dress shirts with the tails hanging out, Docksiders. He'll move into a UVA classroom next year, adding a frat tie loose around the neck, all without missing a beat.

"That you Chlo? I mean, dang!"

"Yeah, dang," the lackeys echo.

Joel takes a step closer, too close. The song has disappeared, gone on a wave of embarrassment. She says, "Go away. Just go."

"Free Mall, babe. Lovin' the rags. I mean, where's goth girl today?"

Chip simpers, "Fade to black."

Lars adds, "Tryin' on a new look."

"It suits you, Chlo, free love and all that. I like," says Joel, leaning in but pronouncing each word clearly and loudly so his cohort can hear. He's having fun now. "Why don't you come with us, huh? Come back to the garage, do some tail-gatin?"

He would say that, ass that he is!

"Yo. Have we met?"

It's Lucas. He wouldn't just stay there hunkered down, playing the street poet. He has to stand up, get into it, make everything perfect.

Joel stands a head taller than Lucas and jacks himself up to full height for this examination. It's like he's posing in his shoulder pads and helmet in those weird boxing gloves lacrosse players wear, or preening in his tennis whites, always a little too tight in the crotch. He says to Chloe, "Who's this little fella?" Chip and Lars step closer now, shoulder to shoulder, crowding the alcove.

Lucas tucks his harmonica in his cargo shorts pocket, assumes a casual we're all in this together posture and the absolutely least appropriate sort of friendly smile, and for some reason says nothing. He hasn't touched Chloe, hasn't shown any sign that they are together, yet. She notices that the crouched guitarist has set his dobro aside, reaching for his money hat, scowling. The next word spoken will give it up. In some future world, you will be able to de-materialize.

"With him?" Joel asks, not yet quite in on what will rapidly morph into the smash-up of the one sweet afternoon in her whole life.

"Name's Lucas. Yours?"

"This guy's with you, isn't he? Dudes, Chloe's got a boyfriend!"

Their snorts of privilege and ownership strike like slaps. There's nowhere to look that works, no way to get past them.

"That's right," Lucas says.

"Am I talkin' to you, Cobain?"

"I think you're bein' a little pushy here, alright?"

"Pushy. Cobain's feelin' crowded, Chlo. He with you?"

It's hard to say, but odds are if Joel's just beginning to put the two of them together, then he hasn't seen them in the garage. Or he's just playing along so he can spring it on them next.

"Look, Chip's got some weed. We got some cranberry juice and vodka in the car. Cruisin' for some mollies. You wouldn't have any on ya would ya, Cobain? Why don't you come around the corner here Chlo and take a nip, huh?"

Lucas then says this dumb thing. "Gentlemen." Which is the last thing they are. But he has their attention, briefly, leading Joel to explain, "Look, fella, this is my girl. Her name is Chlo. You're not involved. So shut the fuck up."

"That's not correct." Lucas seems confused, what a weird thing to say, but she's touched that he's not backing down.

"This guy with you?" Joel bares a head full of perfect white teeth like those of her mom's horse. He stage whispers, bending theatrically to her ear, "Please tell me this guy's with you."

"Guys." At least Lucas has ditched the gentlemen thing. "Go away, okay." It's just his everyday voice, not adding any heat or spin, a rolling serve square in the box, and it's about to be smashed back at net level with screaming velocity. Chloe flashes on Joel in that so-called friendly doubles match early in the summer when he just couldn't seem to stop himself from almost taking her head off with a lob slam. Oh, what an ass he's always been since pre-school at Molly Michie. What if this is the kind of jack-ass I end up with, she thinks. What if it's all fated, and it begins right here on this spot?

"And you are?"

"I'm a guy who can see that you're bothering my friend."

Joel's fist whizzes so closely past Chloe's nose that molecules of his florid *Axe* soap get up her nostrils. Then Lucas is sitting down with his back against the wall beside the flustered and angry guitarist, looking as if he's just fallen asleep. Joel crams his fist into his shorts pocket with a poorly hidden wince and rocks back flat-footed, stunned himself at the movie-like effect of the blow. As Chloe turns away and crouches down beside Lucas, the toe of Joel's Docksider taps her bottom and she hears him say, quite clearly, "Catch you later, at the clubs? We're gettin' mollies," before he and his chortling posse saunter off into the crowd.

"What's wrong with you kids, anyway?" the guitarist mutters, collecting his hat and guitar and stomping off. Chloe tugs on Lucas' hand and softly calls his name, but he's out cold. Through blurred tears, she watches horrified over a couple of minutes as one cheek blooms into a swollen blackened mound, shuttering the eye above it. An oblivious swarm shuffles down the Mall to the concert, but she crouches alone in a silent bubble with Lucas, who awakens slowly as if from a dream, seems to recognize her and then vomits ignobly onto his shirt the pink goop of the lunch they'd shared in another chapter of her life on a riverbank long ago.

"Oh God," he says, trying to wipe his mouth with his t-shirt. "Oh fuck."

He falls back against the brick wall, head lolling, his uninjured eye half-open, the other swelling as the flesh around it turns plum-colored. He's feeling inside his mouth with his tongue, gingerly testing his teeth.

"Chlo." It's whispered, almost a cough. His mouth doesn't even move.

"Just chill, okay," she whispers.

"No, Chlo."

"Yes?"

"Dude calls you Chlo?"

He tries to sit up away from the wall again, struggling as if tied up in rope. She helps him gather the t-shirt to pull it over his head, gasping as the collar brushes his swollen cheek. He dabs clumsily at his chest and lap with the ruined, balled-up shirt, the same one she'd hugged all summer. What was she thinking back then? Look at this rift she'd torn in her year that day when she crossed the Mall to watch a guy play guitar.

"It hurts?"

"No. Yeah. Some."

"Are you okay?"

He hums, maybe he's trying to smile or something, the good eye staring from the undamaged side of his face is almost scarier than the other side.

"Asshole," he mumbles.

"Yeah, he is that."

"You know this guy?"

"Oh, Lucas." She sits back on her heels for a moment, trying to catch a breath. There is this girl, a rebel goth, all set to abandon him here in his disgusting stink to run off without a glance behind and let another delirious evening rip. And another younger girl who really and truly must call a friend for guidance at this juncture. Both girls are with her now, but they can wait. For this other one who frowns, balls up the smelly t-shirt, and whispers, "Let's get you out of here."

THIRTY-SEVEN
MRS. CANNON – POOL PARTY

"Miz Irie."

Iris turns to the maid, already sensing trouble. They crouch side-by-side in the herb garden off the pool, where Iris' hands have grown fragrant with the mint she's snipping for mojitos and juleps, where the last of the summer's bees dip at the blossoms of neglected basil, their song and dance entirely outside the exotic drama of Hollywood energy aswim in her pool. Even the dark twins have disrobed, displaying toned to the point of anorexia six pack abs, lithe legs, pedicured toes and simple bikinis that sag from their slim rear ends. Iris cannot go there, cannot just give it up and join the party. It's a line she cannot let herself cross, a place she longs for, just once to let go, but the effort of holding back, of keeping her hair in place, of hostessing from the water, it's all outside her pay grade.

Fanny swaps the portable phone for the scissors, takes the fistful of mint, and begins to snip some more, pretending that the phone call is of no more interest than the bees. Iris turns away, though, when she hears the medical resident on the other end. For a brief instant she imagines daughter Chloe's hunched shoulders, passing wraithlike through the kitchen, and she wonders, where is that girl, still in her room? Need to check. But the resident brings her back.

"Mrs. Cannon, this is Martha Jefferson ED. It's about your husband. He's alright, for starters. A little shaken up."

"What! But his car is right here!"

"His car? No ma'am. Look, I think you need to come down. He's alright, sitting up right here next to me in a chair."

"May I speak with him?"

"He's still a little dazed, actually."

"From what?" Fanny has stopped snipping mint, but maintains the hunched pose, no doubt enjoying the half of the conversation she can hear. Iris moves off towards the driveway out of earshot.

"Um, it's a little complicated. The police are involved."

"It's what? Are you serious? I can't come down now. I've got people here."

"Well, it's like this, it's busy here, ma'am. This has already taken up a lot of our time."

"Uh huh." She changes direction and heads back to the house, neck craning for Daughter Number One, who no longer seems to be in the pool, and Hunkus Australikus has vanished, too.

"'I'd rather not get into the details over the phone, ma'am. As I said, he's okay, but the police will not release him on his own recognizance, and I can't either, so please."

"Well, may I speak with him?"

"He's a little groggy right now. Ma'am, I have to go. Please, Martha's ED. We'll have him here."

Martha's up on Pantops Mountain, clear across town on game clotted roads. But, as always, she's factored in a detour, has known this man too long, all is not yet lost, and Fanny makes a mean julep. This! This is why she'd shied from the pool! But she has to find her daughter. No one in the kitchen, the blender on the counter with bottles of whiskey, rum, and tequila. Who's started on that? Where is the other daughter? Best not to bother the recluse. But Daughter Number One? No time, will just phone her on the way.

The Escalade's tailgate gapes ajar, backed up to the garage entrance, where Fanny's middle school son – is it Charles? – has been taking his own sweet time chewing shrimp and emptying the party goods one item at a time. She'll have to take the Porsche, has not driven a stick in years, never this paddle shifter thing, but how hard can it be, get the keys and just go. She strides back to the herb garden, hands Fanny the phone and with one worried look, conveys all. Fanny has brought down the travel bag packed and ready always for just this contingency, nods, will take charge. Iris slips down into the driver's seat, stabs the ignition button, and the little space ship roars to life. Her feet are miles from the pedals, she can't figure out how to move the seat up, then does, sees the car has no Bluetooth, fumbles for her phone, aims blindly for first gear, and lurches into a stall, then another, then finally gets the thing moving and headed down the drive. They'll all just have to manage themselves for a little while. How do you text and shift one of these things at the same time?

THIRTY-EIGHT

OFFICER MOSBY – POLICE HQ

MOSBY SLUMPS almost horizontal in a desk chair, staring up at the pattern of perforated dots in the acoustical tiled ceiling of police headquarters. That briefing room in Ramadi where they had a ceiling like this and incoming would shake the place and you'd climb back to your feet to find little dirt dots all over the tables, sifted out of the ceiling holes and spaced apart exactly like the tiles above them. Amazing, the shit that stays with you. He spits sunflower seeds into a Styrofoam cup, watches the wall clock, listens fitfully to the scanner burping on the gear belt laid across his lap. He wishes he'd stayed at the hospital with Ronnie. At least there he'd felt like he was doing something purposeful, instead of this purgatory waiting for the chief.

All the paperwork has been filed, he's hidden himself from the snot-nose reporter who got wind of the Taser deployment and sits in the front room licking his chops. By now it wouldn't be a surprise if the mayor has gotten involved, working his angles with the tv station and the University to triage this downer on the city's big day. Dude was some kind of honcho, brain surgeon or something, but that doesn't qualify you to take a chain saw to a tree in a city-owned park. Came up out of his stun like a cornered bear in the ambulance, shouting "Not the University! Take me to Martha's!' They'd almost had to Tase him again when the door opened at ED. Ronnie would have gladly done it, too. Thinks the weapon is all *Tour of Duty* virtual, just so cool, and damn the consequences. As he says, "If the bad guys know you'll use it, they'll sure 'nuff git out your way." But people would rather get shot than Tased, it's the weird electricity thing, what's that doing to my heart, to my brain, to my gonads? And the paperwork's the same, really, so what the fuck? Well, numb nuts, among other things the fuck is who says a guy won't shoot you first to avoid it?

But the guy under the tree, some doctor. They own this town, probably always have, book-ended as it is by two competing hospitals and all the money that flows in and out of them. It's not what he did that matters anyway, it's the Taser. Best to tell it straight up. Just sitting here. It's the same old Army shit, except there you can snooze anytime you're off you're feet, and here if you're in uniform you're supposed to look official and on point. He pulls himself upright again, scans the empty room. Tick-tick-tick-tick. A wall clock that actually goes tick-tock. Mosby realizes he's gone an hour without thinking about Sid. But now that he's remembered, he's fretting again. Why can't his brother be like other people just enough to carry a phone or something? A wrist or ankle bracelet tracker. Oughta try to slap one of them on him sometime. But he'd go all spooky, call everybody an alien invasion, probably chew his foot off to get rid of it. If you can get up and get dressed, feed yourself, take your meds from time to time, that's all you need to have the right to walk the streets. Just don't go strolling unannounced in neighbors' houses. Don't boost some old man's precious rusty old shotgun that hasn't been fired in half a century and never will be again. Have one dot of sense enough to stay on the sidewalk.

One thing police work has taught him, every sleepy-eyed

Mommy and Daddy on the street is one heartbeat away from any damned crazy thing. Road rage. Arson. Put a chair through a window. Maybe just bitch slap the one person who gives a fuck about you. Salesmen get thrown off the plane every other day at the airport, gone red-faced over carry ons. So the hot shot doc flipped out on a tree that never meant him any harm. Coulda been worse. So Sid's crazy as a loon. You start lockin' people up and where will it end? It ends with the rich who can buy themselves out of strait jackets running the nuthouse, and everyone else in padded cells. Zombied out on prescription meds and cable tv is more like it. Or doing third shift mop-up routine.

They come with this two-step change in body temperature. First a cold sweat that feels like a roller coaster drop, then a spike that flushes toe to scalp. The whole side of the police station caves open to needles of sand on the wind. He's trying to ride them out now as if at a 3-D movie, letting it play through without any behavioral display, no sign behind the shades except the knuckles gripping his chair. His arrive with a flash of brilliance and run silent, jump-cut, with occasional jaw-dropping frame freezes. Who knows what triggers or turns them off? There isn't really a safe place. Some guys head for the woods, walk it off in the fields, lock themselves in a closet when they can get there in time, but it's a sort of seizure that takes you clean out of this world, with that hot flash preliminary aura that comes on too fast to even hunker down.

When the station house reforms, he's all the way across the room, propped against a bare wall on the floor, head down between his knees in the kiss your ass goodbye position. The wall presses the knuckles of his spine like a blade. He squirms up against it to make himself focus, grateful he hasn't soiled himself and hoping no one has seen. There's a warm weight on his neck. It's Ronnie's fat hand. "Son, we good. We chillin'. You come on back when you ready." He's sitting in a desk chair, balancing a Big Gulp-sized drink of some kind on his knee. Drops of cartoon red glisten on the Styrofoam, pulling Mattie forward and back at the same time. He notes sensory information in the room, stepping as if through a minefield, one step the tv sports announcer's droning stats, the next the dull black bulb of Ronnie's boot, the next a sickening aroma of roasted sausage and onions wafting in off the street, probably the original trigger the way smells can take you straight back to the bazaar, but pull yourself up past that now, find the path.

He wipes his mouth, discovers he can get to his feet. On a scale of one to ten maybe a four.

"You want your chair back?"

"Huh?"

"You know ain't nobody pays you no mind. You old vets go off like popcorn in here sometimes. Just have a chair, killer. We cain't go nowhere. Lockdown til the chief gets here to chew out our asses. Have a seat now." Ronnie doesn't offer him his, just takes another gulp and swivels away to face the tv screen.

THIRTY-NINE

SID, CHLOE AND LUCAS – DOWNTOWN

SID CRADLES the cardboard manifesto in a bath towel to keep it from leaking its precious message. Any number of ideal spots. His first thought had been the General Lee monument, maybe tying it around Traveller's neck. That still might work. Or on the statue of a middle-aged, trim and benign Thomas Jefferson, his back to the Rotunda that the old architect had envisioned on a corn field. Letters aren't large enough to be read if he hangs the sign from a highway bridge. You could take the serendipitous route, just affix it to a picket fence in some neighborhood, trusting that the ones who need it will happen upon it and understand.

For this undertaking, even though time is of the essence, one must observe extreme ritual. He walks the railroad track that bends through the south end of downtown, managing three steps on one rail, carefully heel-to-toe, then a single crab-step onto a tie, up onto the other rail to repeat the three steps. Any loss of balance that tips you off a rail requires a three tie retreat, stepped backwards, then a restart. Every move crucial, every mistake repaid in full, despite a world of distractions. Headlights flicker on the rails and throw hieroglyphic shadows on the bordering trees. A sewer stench rises from the rail side trenches, and when he missteps the gravel growls in reprimand. He recites the *Good Ol' Song* backwards, as he has taught himself to do in challenging circumstances, but it's as if he has four or five minds all jabbering at once.

The best place, the only place, he realizes now, is the public chalkboard at the east end of the Mall. People come there to read, to scribble, to say something. The manifesto will fit best there. It's a busy night, but busy nights can work. Everybody has somewhere to go. So much to distract them. You can walk all but invisible right through the middle if you keep your eyes down. Better odds that the right person will get the message. Plus the pedestrian Mall takes a chunk out of Main Street, a crooked road that follows an old Indian footpath clear across the state. That has to mean something. He steps off the train track, testing his footing on an alley leading up to the Mall.

"Excuse me, mister, sir?"

Sid stops. His head slowly swivels towards the voice. He feels a taste of reflux in the back of his throat. But now has paused and for some reason cannot restart.

A two-headed creature in the shadows warps into two people, a boy and a girl.

"Mister, please, do you think you can help me?" It's the girl talking.

"Could you, if I gave you some money, would you go into the drug store, it's right over there, and buy us some water, and a cup of ice?"

"Ice?"

"Yes sir. To help my friend. He doesn't feel too good."

"Feel good?" They're young, maybe high school age, one of them crumpled up against the alley wall. He smells something rotten in the alley, old food or puke.

"It would really help us if you could." She's crouched over

the other person, but stares beseechingly straight up into Sid's face. A deviation. Not good. Crab steps. He tucks the toweled bundle under one arm to make a sign of the square with four fingers, attempting to frame them out.

"I have money, sir. Just some water and ice?" She bounces up, too fast, her head ballooning towards him, waving dollar bills in the air.

"The CVS. Just right over there? Please? You can buy yourself something if you want?"

"By myself." The dollars crumple warm and soft as cotton in his hand, emitting a whiff like rusty metal. Like old guns. He totters.

"Sir, please.

No shadow in any corner of the drug store. Bright light pulsing from the electrified ceilings, walls, cosmetics displays, and glass-fronted drink coolers. That maddening fluorescent shimmering, each tube at its own strobing frequency, a visual cacophony, the sort of trap he avoids at all costs. Crab-walking helps. Follow the ticking. A person with quick fingers shifts side-to-side behind the counter, glued to one spot. Everything like one of those toy balls hung on rubber bands from paddles, zooming out and back, bam.

Sid announces, "Bag of ice." It works. The man says, "Outside. Ice box." Correct. The metal box exhales a frosty vapor, a mildewed bad breath. Sid slams shut the door. Then tries again, successfully lifting out one of the lumpy packages. Tucked under his elbow, the plastic bag comes alive, shifts clumsily as if trying to slip away. The manifesto wrapped in its towel in the crook of his other arm begins to shimmy free. The water bottles in the bag slung from his arm slap his leg as he crab walks back across the street.

Safely back in the alley, Sid unloads the bottles into the girl's hands and plops the bag of ice at her feet. Pulls the quarter and a dime in change from his pocket. And then as if viewed from far away, he sees himself unwrapping the cardboard sign, crouching down, tearing open the bag of ice and pouring fist-sized chunks into the towel. Rolls the towel neatly into an ice pack and hands it to the boy on the ground. Something's wrong with his face, but the good half of it murmurs something he can't quite get. Then the girl crouches beside them, her look curious and vibrational. "That was very nice of you, sir. Somebody hit my friend Lucas. Some jerk."

Jerks. Always. Everywhere. On one knee, Sid pulls off his tennis shirt, scrabbling to get it over his head, and offers it in a rumpled ball to the girl. Turned back to her friend, she doesn't acknowledge this gift, maybe doesn't see him drop the shirt on the ground. He hums the *Good Ol' Song*, letting the tune fill all of his sinuses so it lifts his head like a helium balloon pulling him to his feet again. He steps out of the alley onto the concrete sidewalk, still rising.

FORTY

THE CANNON'S – UP ON THE ROOF

Dr. Cannon emerges from the cramped hospital room shower feeling refreshed and squeaky clean as a beach ball. He stoops to the mirrored sink, loving the moonlike face gleaming back at him, and tells it, Yes, you have just walked buck-nekkid (as his old high school coach would have said) across the You-Vee-Aay grounds on a hot summer day, and watered it, too, from your own mighty hose. What a satisfying bit of performative derange-ment! Why not now, again? Why bother with this ridiculous attire? Just leave this pink sports coat and the little gay kerchief on the floor, the size 14-wide penny loafers, the navy slacks, the starched shirt, the baggy shorts, leave them all here. Let us be who we are for once!

A tap on the door. "Rainie?" Ah, that voice, snaps him back, like a tug on a kite string. "Yes, Mama, we on it." Alright. It's their dance, always has been, and no use in bucking it now. So he bends to the clothes she made appear, pressed and cottony soft. The bag even holds a toothbrush and pate polish. Thus turn the page, new chapter. Finger snap, come out gleaming. Though, for sure, the throb's still there. That back-handed slap in the face from an ungrateful University. Not the first time, though. He tugs on his boxer shorts and stands briefly at attention, letting himself honor this surrender to custom. He wrestles with the look of his yellow shirt, chooses to tuck, reaches for the Easter egg pink sports coat. In the mirror feels he can steel himself now. Be the don. Again his old coach: Don't get mad, get even. Play the long game. After all, when the contract on the movie story detailing his life-saving adventure with the first gamma knife gets signed later on tonight, who then will have the last chuckle?

Iris waits at the nurse's station sharp as the gal in a Viagra ad, all floral to match his jacket, back straight as a rod, and finishing up whatever tale she's sharing with a quick wink his way. As if to say, whatever you may have gotten up to this time – and we will discuss it! – we in this together, old man, and at least we ain't bored. Just a light bubble or two of perspiration across her forehead, skin yet taut across the skull after these many years, one horizontal line taking up the slack of worry all to itself. His lips taste the salt as he bends to it. No embrace. No need to signal too much. No big thing. Nobody walked on the moon. But she has clocked his wobble, sized up the dance of his eyes, made her calculations, and all in one wink has balanced the books. So he doesn't get the driver's seat, not even in his Porsche, not this evening. Just on the power of that wink he chooses not to push it, a look like that demanding in no uncertain terms the better part of valor.

It's already dark; where did the day go? He feels spacey and elevated, as if the car floats on air. What was in that shot they gave him? Coming off Pantops Mountain, sinking past all the car dealerships and stores, the city lights wash out any stars and the Blue Ridge horizon out west as they dip down to the bridge and cross that shallow excuse for a river, turning towards the night's festivities downtown. The car purrs under Iris' control, inching forward in the bunched traffic. She's figured out the gearing now and sits the engine like a new steed, feeling the thrill of its potential in her legs and up her arms, alert to anything skittish. It's slow going, with concertgoers lined up forever ahead of them, and with the top down exhaust stink hangs fetid in the air. Better that, though, then the intimacy of a closed roof. That would lead to words, and they both know it's best to keep it breezy for now. He has so many things to say, so many questions, frustration rising as he recalls all the undone tasks required of the rooftop event. He wipes his forehead with his knuckles and squirms to fit the passenger seat, knees bent up against the dashboard. Her fingers tap the gear paddles, eyes front, deliberately oblivious to his fretting.

Downtown, she finds her spot at the florist shop traffic coned like she'd left it, just three short blocks from the bus station. They leave the cartop down, as Rainsworth prefers. Take it if you can but nobody ever does. Within a block, they're holding hands, old sweethearts and good with that. Not walking too fast, no big rush, he's cool now, has shot his wad, is up for whatever goes down without much fuss, and says these things to himself, sing-songing them in his head, not an actual word spoken between them as they navigate the crowded brick-paved Mall. Loud music blares from the Pavilion stage before them. Some opening act, maybe a white boy trying to rap to a tape loop and what is that, a banjo? What the hell happened to music anyway? The bus station glows like a glass lantern, but the doorway is locked and a policeman guards the door. He lets them in at Iris' nod. In the elevator she's perfectly calm, clearly unaware of the debacle awaiting them.

He should say something, but no, seeing is believing. Let it come. Of course, it was all his idea – to throw an exclusive party on the bus station roof. Why not? Best seats in the house, up above the riff-raff, high in the bustling night. Even Hollywood visitors would be impressed. But it's been six months since the deal was inked. Since he walked the roof and pointed out where the tables, the bartender, the umbrellas, the caterers, would go. The strung lights and Hawaiian menu, the spitted hogs and cocoanut drinks. No damn cedar trees in the way then. He'd left it up to her, had gotten wrapped up in other things. The damned film festival, the suck up over the pavilions, the sycophantic Asian medical residents, plans maybe never to be realized for a new surgical suite. Bah! One man can only do so much! But then if you don't do it yourself!

He knows she's watching his face as the elevator door opens. What does she imagine? Don't blame her, he tells himself, stay chill. But then. He takes in the transformed rooftop with one ogling gaze, and damn if it isn't all that he'd imagined. Somehow a ballroom has been lifted up and set down in one piece before him. Every element in place, swirling, alive, and packed with young people, the choice few, circulating with crystal flutes upon a wooden deck built out to flatten the slanted tin roof, or leaning on railings that have picnic benches and umbrella awnings. The music from below sounding somehow sharper and less noisome, as if channeled and rebroadcast directly to the rooftop. One of those flat panel tv's hangs cantilevered over the street, projecting the show. Another plays back a roving mini-cam from backstage. And then -- this is what takes him out -- someone has looped ropes to the top fronds of the two middle cedars in that damnable row, pulled them aside like a curtain. With the trees tugged out like that, the stage down below seems cupped in upturned leafy hands, the rapping singer framed neatly between them, sawing away at his banjo. How did this happen? Somehow, in just the last few hours, a *Cat in the Hat* explosion of set up.

"You're kidding me, oh girl."

It's that storied sly wink, fast as a camera flash. One hand slips inside his jacket, takes a pinchful of love handle, and twists.

FORTY-ONE

CHLOE AND LUCAS – PAVILION

"IT'S JUST A HEADACHE."

"That's what I'm worried about."

"The ice really helps."

"It's melting all down your pants."

"Wish I could just take a bath in this stuff."

"There's a pool."

"Really?"

"City pool. You serious?"

"I'm gonna stand up. Okay, that wasn't the best idea."

"We're good. We're good."

"Let me try again."

"Whoa."

"It's kinda throbby."

"Can you see?"

"One eye. Bad?"

"Um, kinda lopsided?"

"That's what it feels like, too."

"Can you walk?"

"Let's."

"Where?"

"You lead."

"We need a car."

"I'm good, really. But you want to see."

"Yeah."

"You've been nursing me all day. You picked shot out of my butt."

"There was no shot in your butt, Slippy."

"Can you slow down a little, I'm sorry."

"I do so hate those guys."

"You know them, I guess?"

"School."

"Yeah. What is their problem?"

"They're creeps. Comes with the territory."

"Fuckin' school."

They turn past the parking garage, up towards the concert venue on a steeply sloped sidewalk that looks like it will climb right onto the top of the Pavilion awning. Lucas muses, "I'm gonna buy that pickup."

"You mean the one?"

"Yeah."

"I like it right where it is, I think."

"Mm-hmm." He reaches an arm around her waist, and she slips her arm into a loop of his jeans. It feels comfortable, fitted, exactly the right size to walk this way. And it keeps him from wobbling. Funny, how out here on the sidewalk, just steps from the stage, there's no one. But just across a chain link fence drawn across the grassy slope, it's a mob scene. Lucas gets it. They can just hang here, on the highway overpass built right up against the back of the stage and have a bird's eye view, even a backstage view, of the whole show for free. Already, a half dozen other fans have found positions there, sitting on the sidewalk, their legs dangling, arms hung across the railing, but there's room for more. Without saying anything, just in tacit agreement, and with nowhere special else to go, they find their spot, swapping cool nods with those already in place, all of them kids, high schoolers, like them.

"You good, Slippy?" Chloe pushes a drape of hair out of Lucas' eyes, careful not to touch the swollen orbit as she offers the last of the ice in the balled up towel.

"Never better," he smiles, and somehow he's just so beautiful banged up like this, like a well-worn precious toy loved more than all the gifts under the tree. Her hand drops to his lap as she takes in the milling crowd, up to the edge of the Pavilion, out to the bus station. Weird, somebody's up on the rooftop there. It looks like a restaurant or something on top of the bus station? That's the kind of thing she'd have thought of! But this, squatting out here on the overpass, it's even better. Closer to the stage, for one thing.

A kid next to Lucas has been fumbling with a baggy and some weed. Lucas notices and offers to help. The kid surrenders his papers and Chloe watches Lucas expertly roll a skinny joint, suck and twirl it tight, and hand it back to the kid. Check off another skill she hadn't known he had. At each step, he's offering instruction, and the kid tries to follow his directions, making a sloppy, torn, and bulgy-looking doobie of his own. The kid takes Lucas' perfect joint, tucks it behind his ear, and tries again with a new paper. Lucas walks him through it, and the next cigarette emerges slim and tight, much better. Lucas says, "Won't be long before old Altria will be packaging menthol reefer." The kid says, "Vape it up, too." He tucks the sandwich bag into the front of his gym shorts, and they sit awhile listening to some guy rap and play banjo onstage. There's this old-timey boombox at his feet putting out a huge bassdrop. The song's about war, and it sounds like it could be any war from the Civil on up, and what it's like to hunker in a trench.

Eventually, the kid turns back to his friends and lights up.

Lucas counts a dozen or more cops bunched around the perimeter of the arena, imagines that one or two will eventually stroll on up to their perch. Chloe says, "This is C-ville. You're white boys. They'll just take it and chase us off."

"And light up themselves when the show's over no doubt."

"I would."

The kid with the marijuana is too young and clueless to know that he's supposed to share, at least with the guy who taught him how to roll. Lucas figures he'd just fall asleep anyway, even the second-hand smoke is swelling his aching head, and he feels himself nodding a little, leaving this place on a personal song lyric that fills in the beats of the boombox. Chloe swings her feet like a little girl on a swing and replays the day they've had. Her phone burns a hole in her pocket. She so wants to tell all her friends, but where would she start now, and at the same time there's something so sneakily private about having done that impossible thing, turning it all the way off. No pings no dings no texts. She's adrift out here with this vagabond boy who has photo-bombed her thoughts all summer, disconnected from all the shared advice and nudges and emojis that by all rights should be punctuating each turn of this monumental day. This is radical. A violation of the pact, that no one makes a move off the grid. Sort of criminal. The whole day has been like that really. Like walking a tightrope that nobody sees high above the crowd. She fingers the smooth bulge of the dormant phone in her lap pocket, deciding for the hundredth time today to let it sleep. She'd promised Izzy to meet up at midnight, so all of this will keep until then, though she could use another pair of eyes to look out for Joel and his goons, keep her posted. But still.

The guy with the banjo waves at the crowd, then does this cool thing where he turns around and seems to look directly at Chloe and Lucas and the other freebie kids lined up along the walkway, points a finger and nods as if to say you're my real peeps, then leaves the stage. There's a gap in the music then, between acts, and Chloe uses it to ask a question she's been pondering all day. "Slip. Lucas. Tell me something. If you had not hopped that train, come here today, what would you be doing right now?"

"You mean at home? Seriously? I'll tell you if you tell me, alright?"

She flashes on the night before that was like so many dumb nights of the whole Summer, and she knows exactly what she'd be doing, of course, same. It all seems so – what is the word? – pointless? "Sure," she says, "deal."

Lucas works his jaw a little, testing the fat bruise at his cheek. He's hung the ice-pack towel out to dry on the railing now that the ice has melted, and it has to hurt. He presses his injured eye oh so gently onto the damp towel as if testing it. "Okay, let me see. Okay, I'm going to tell it true. I'd be walking out of the library about now with a whole notebook full of directions for how I was going to get here tomorrow."

"Good one. Charmer. But seriously, what?"

"No, that's it. Look, I saw your place. We were rolling around in your bedroom. My whole thing is so different down there."

"Okay. But like how?"

"You're right. I just." He lifts his cheek off the rail and looks into her eyes, struggling to open the bruised one. "Well it's like, Chloe, I've never been inside a house like yours. I've never seen a kitchen like that."

"What?"

"I don't know, look. Why do guys hop trains? Why do they hitch a ride? Why do you think I came here last spring?"

"Well, you had to. Or we never would have met."

"True. But before that, the reason I came up here, it's the same as anybody. I just really had to get away."

"Yeah. But from what?"

"Life. Just life is all. My mom's sick, she can't breathe without an oxygen tank, she can't hardly even move by herself."

"Your mom."

"My sister, she's older, she's with her now, this weekend. But the rest of the time, when I'm there, it's me."

"What do you do? I mean for her?"

"Oh man, Chloe. It's like everything. It's embarrassing, I mean really."

"You have to help her get dressed?"

He nods, looks away. "Everything."

She shakes her head, squeezes his hand. "Shit."

He nods again. "That too."

The loud speakers kick in again, blaring Top 40 Rock from the 1970s or something, some kind of chug-a-chug guitar band with a screechy singer. Lucas leans in close and asks, "Okay, your turn."

"No, tell me more about you."

"Okay, but your turn now, okay?"

She frowns and shakes her head, then stares out at the crowd gathered under the white wing of the Pavilion, up to the pretty pedestrian Mall with its willow oaks unfurled in all their Summer leafage. People like her are up there on top of the bus shed, of all places, doing some private party thing. Maybe even her parents. She says, "It's this, Slip. Look around, this is what I do. This is it."

"You mean you'd be sitting right here on this sidewalk breathing second hand weed with some other guy checking out the band?"

She grins, imagining that. "Funny. Uh, no. I'd be in a car. It would be my own car if I hadn't bumped that old lady a couple weeks ago. So probably my friend Izzy or this other friend Ava. The one that did the bathtub thing at the gallery? So them."

"Going where?"

"Probably anywhere but here, actually."

"This sucks?"

"No, I mean, not with you, no. But that's it. See usually."

"Yeah?"

"It's like, if something's happening, we try to do the opposite."

"Okay, but what?"

Maybe he's fishing, but she doesn't think so. He just genuinely wants to know. But no way will she tell him Joel. "I don't know. We eat pizza, we swipe a beer or two, we shop. It's bullshit, really."

"Just chill, like."

"Yeah, same old, just chill."

"It's a cool place to do it, though. I mean to grow up here."

Maybe it is, she thinks. Or maybe it's just a whole town that is only an outdoor extension of the game room at home, everything measured, shelved, portioned out, everything pastel colored and credit card available, and at least most of the time romper room safe. A town in a bubble, really. She says, "I don't know, Slip. But you know what? You did that thing. I don't even know how to think about it. You rode on a coal train, I mean, really, all the way from South Carolina."

"To see you."

"That's it. You came. You said you would and you did."

It's the right thing to say. Get back to today, not the stuff that frames it.

"I kinda can't believe it either. Scariest thing I've ever done, for real."

She reaches up to cup her palm at his purple cheek. Maybe not scary, but it's certainly the most confusing thing she's ever done.

FORTY-TWO
OFFICER MOSBY – ON PATROL

"TELL IT." That's what the chief said, with her best slit-eyed stare learned from a dozen cop shows, just like everybody plays a part they picked up from the tv and who knows what they really think? If they really think, outside of the wrap it up in twenty and put a bow on it stories we all grew up on. Which is half the problem, he knows. For one thing, you'd need smell-a-vision. Fans blowing bacon grease would help. Dropping to dank of a mountain shade. And run the story no laugh track for the rest of your life.

She heard them both out separately. Ronnie went first, Matt fretting outside her office window watching the back of his head, judging it all by the flickers of concern on the chief's face as she sat stiffly with those narrowed tv eyes, edging towards the first of many decisions this "incident" would require her to make. It could go at least a few ways that were all but entirely out of her control, now that the mayor has assured her in no uncertain terms that charges against the famous surgeon gone off his nut for a few are out of the question. The tasing would be viral already. A dozen perspectives from all the phones always at the ready, beamed out to the net by momentarily outraged attendees, who would go on to post videos of their favorite tunes, selfies with cups of local craft beer, insincere "wish you were here" calls to friends, the incident itself all but forgotten, except on the Internet where every unusual thing lasts forever. The choke point was in the mayor's hands, hers and those of the UVA president, and you could be sure that they were already working their levers to wall off the local news. Let it go viral, that cannot be helped. Out in the soup where anything goes and little makes sense. But a news producer wrapping the video with words, providing context, trying to explain, that is where it would fall apart. The University will not have it. The city will not have it. The fate of these officers – her woebegone warriors – lies in the balance.

And Ronnie, old Ronnie. Mattie shakes his head at his partner's gesticulations through the window, unable to zip his lip, expounding on the reasons, recalling the size of the man with the chain saw, the press of the crowd, the danger to children, the choice of weapon and must act now. Until the chief sees her problem is larger than she had thought and changes her mind, calls Mattie in to stand by his partner's chair for her verdict. The boss orders him to drive his buddy home and stay with him there. Call it a day, put on some shorts, fry up a dog. Keep your phone on. Stay in town. Expect nothing or anything. She can't trust that Ronnie will chill. If *Channel 29* calls or rolls up to the house. If a friend at a cookout knows somebody.

For some reason, though, this launches Ronnie onto another rant, and Mattie admires a little the way she lets that happen, gives the old blowhard a window of time to get it out, finally calming him down with a revised plan to keep him close here at headquarters with a promise of double time for every minute he's pulling guard duty in lockup, without his phone, without his walkie-talkie, without his Taser, at least until this mess of a holiday is done. Mattie fights a grimace when Ronnie hands the gunbelt over to her, heavy with the Glock he'd borrowed in it. Now he's back on the street, alone in his cruiser and unarmed. Impossible the chief didn't see that, but she hadn't brought it up. She's set him free on strict orders to stay off the Mall, but hang close, to just be a presence somewhere. No tickets, no interjections, no other instructions. Just park it and sit. But of course, that's impossible. The tasing incident just chump change. She hadn't said a word about his real concern, but she has to know what he will do.

Mosby loops around to the house again, taking the long way under the Woolen Mills railroad bridge far from the downtown crowd. Even these bedraggled streets are busy tonight, now that the sleepy backwater he grew up in has gone hip. Cars double-parked at gourmet dives. He lets it all slide, under orders and on his way. Pulling up behind his house, he checks the garage and back door, but nothing. All dark, the garage locked like he'd left it. One choice would be to sit here and wait, like the chief said. Usually the best bet any time. Bad news has a way of finding him, he knows. But the worry makes him restless. He drives on, along a loop through the townhouse apartments of Orangedale – ignoring firecrackers, teens with open beers, cars parked on sidewalks – building a slow circle around the Mall, trying to imagine which of his brother's customary routes his addled mind might have led him to now.

Of course, it's possible it wasn't Sid. It's possible some kid slipped in and relieved him of the weapon. Would have taken some ballsy banger to do that, with a cop asleep six feet away. But that's a wasted thought: It was Sid. And it sure as hell was Sid who snatched the guns from old man Tillman. That'll be jail time and who knows he might be better for it. Would he even care? That's a horrible thought. It's a bad felony, but Mattie half believes if he can get the gun back, have a sit down with the old man, that he might drop the charges. We used to mow his lawn when we were kids. His dear departed made us lemonade and cookies. Mattie had held the screws while their dad installed an old overhead fan on their porch. Long-time neighbors from the old days. The real enemies are these interlopers, the newbies in their balconied condos and BMW's. The old guard must stick together in our stucco cottages with our tomato plots. That's the bond that matters, that's the angle to work. Maybe mow his lawn or something? It's worth a shot. But only if he can bring back the guns. And Sid. Like now would be good.

FORTY-THREE

THE CANNON'S – SHOW TIME

No REST FOR THE WEARY. Over the past hour or so, Iris has gradually assured herself that her husband's constitution is yet robust enough to withstand the evening's rigors. Though he has barreled into the festivities with bull in a China shop brio, grabbing up a mojito, then a Tom Collins, then a margarita neat from passing waiters' trays – characteristically failing to remark on this detail, her attention to exquisitely crafted cocktails fashioned by fussy bartenders who charge more than chefs these days – he has seemed, as a carpenter might have said, half a bubble off. Which is all it can take with him, though half the thrill, not to mention wear-and-tear, of his company is the toeing out on that narrow ledge with him. She tucks in at his elbow, smiling with carefully calibrated self-deprecation at each sigh of wonder and enjoyment from attendees, all offered to him, universally recognized as the maestro of this event, though with a nod and wink to her, at least from those knowing spouses who play the same bolstering game with their own golf-mad husbands.

As far as she can tell, no one knows about the afternoon's escapade. She herself is in the dark, really. Where did the good doctor go at half time of the game? Why did he not answer his phone? How did he end up on the Mall? With a chain saw? Tasered? You can't hunt in a fog. She'll have to wait for the air to clear. But there is even now the chance that someone here knows, that a tweet or a post tagged here and now or there-abouts will pop up a photo or something. This is not her métier. Social media and all that. But the youngsters, thumbing their phones with one hand, while slamming cocktails with the other, they are the danger, they are the ones who will think it amazing, hilarious, worth sharing far and wide. And the President, who knows everything, always, will be judging, too. If we can get through this evening unscathed, she thinks, then there is a chance it will all blow over, that the good University will once again have performed its magic act, corralling the police and the local media and erasing the bad behavior of their – if not cherished, then necessary – stalwart. President Burwell has indeed graced them with his presence, stands dead center in the flow, stock still in his trademark orange-and-blue threaded seer-sucker suit (last day he can wear it, then on to the tweeds), martini held by the stem, eyes aprowl beneath wooly bear eyebrows.

Rainie has spied him, of course. Iris senses the prickle of recognition and the stiffening of the spine right through his pink blazer. And finds him working his way in tighter and tighter centripetally driven circles back to the old Titan, stopping at every clatch to welcome, mingle, glad hand. Gauging the crowd, building a wall of goodwill, letting the old coot see that he is loved and admired, a force to be reckoned with, even now in the humiliation of the half-time surprise. And, of course, relishing these contretemps, living for them, the President holds his ground. The old widower has come entirely alone, without an aide or any of the model-gorgeous, sleek D.C. attorneys he typically escorts to these events. You have to give him that. Whatever this disappointed prima donna brain surgeon plans, he'll take it flat-footed.

She understands, too, that Rainie is gauging the social network, sniffing out the news, even after a half dozen different alcoholic concoctions, alert to the slightest whiff of derision. Few there would be privy to the secretive dealings of the Board of Regents and the President in finagling the Pavilion out from under him. Those old lions would arrive late, if at all, and leave early. He would be lying in wait with a special message for them, wrapped in a straightforward recital that they would hear out while their bony, liver-spotted hands lay trapped in his enormous paw. Would highlight the fame, attention, and ka-ching cash his department had brought in across the years of his tenure, with a roll of the eyes as punctuation intended to convey a warning that Duke and his alma mater were calling, both appreciating the importance of modern neurosurgery to their portfolios.

Yes, the Board had grudgingly and belatedly approved the functional MRI, nodded yes at last to the new focused Ultrasound surgical suite. And no doubt will expect fawning gratitude for that. None would mention the Pavilion vote, not a word of apology or hint at next time would be exchanged. The good old boys – like some top-hatted Masonic order – would never tip their hand to a hired gun. Rainie's only recompense would come in their pained expressions, the distaste at the lined corners of their mouths, to be caught skin-to-skin for a long moment with a man whose hands routinely performed medical miracles they could only dimly imagine. When else in their cosseted lives did this occur? Because Iris knows it will not be the neurosurgery they recoil from. How often across their whole careers have they shaken an African American hand?

The party with all of its expense and grueling legwork is just a stage set after all. The action will be here with Rainie, and

TONY GENTRY

frankly anything can happen. She scans the rooftop for the Hollywood contingent, feeling a hostess' responsibility for their well-being, aware that this other game was underway that could salvage her husband's weekend, the gamma knife script and the director's interest in it. Across the floor, she spies the city's film festival board members and their spouses, decked out in expensive black fabrics, so hoping to have accurately mimicked the style of the show-biz visitors, in a mingle, necks craning for a first glimpse of a star. Why, she wonders, can't people just be themselves? Because, she knows, on brief nights like this the memorable moments of their lives are sewn, a selfie with the superhero or the aging Space Boy, and for that the plaid tie you wear to teach Film Theory 101 just won't do. She gets it, is no different, and feels gratified to have made this opportunity available to them. Really, the whole cost in worry, time and money involved in creating this fête is repaid right there. And then, a stray thought, she flashes on the freckled face of that boy at the wine shop so many long hours ago. His look of candid appraisal, the directness of his gaze, the implied question in his brilliant grin that had taken off the top of her head. That scandalous wisp of moustache at his lip. She tightens her grip on Rainie's elbow.

They have arrived at a gaggle of orthopedic surgeons in the corner nearest the stage, and Dr. Cannon expansively welcomes them with the noblesse oblige his station requires. These husky men work from the shoulder, wrestling with osteoarthritic hips like cave men breaking down an oryx, while his work these days is a delicate beveling guided by microscope. A leg is not a brain, after all, though they bring in twice the cash. At first Iris thinks everyone is watching the surgeons, their faces turned her way, but then realizes that the movie screen behind them is the draw. She cranes her neck to see, but this near the screen the images seem skewed and pixilated. She can just make out the backstage

248

scene shot by the college student with the roving camera. The film star's gleaming picket fence teeth as he gingerly lifts an acoustic guitar in the midst of a huddle on what looks like the tour bus. Well, of course, that's where they would be, with their tribe, the show-biz crew.

She leans out of Rainie's shadow to get a better look. The screen plays video from the mini-cam she'd hired, but no audio, so it's all a pantomime. The actor strums, grinning sheepishly. A long-haired boy begins to bob his head and seems to be singing. There's another kid blowing on a Coke bottle, people clap hands, slap knees, everyone silently bobbing in time. The image jumps as if even the cameraman is caught up in the little hoedown. And then she sees at the actor's elbow, well, it has to be Claire. In two dimensions, faded of color like some VHS home movie from her toddler days. She looks wan, out of her element, wavering like a ghost. Has she been crying? You can't tell, but there's something in her posture. Iris drops Rainie's arm, dabs at her eyes, finds herself mouthing to the screen, "Oh darling, after all, what have we done?"

FORTY-FOUR

SID – CHALK WALL

SID STANDS in the middle of an empty parking lot, head swiveling to track a flight of swallows as they dart for insects, criss-crossing the rising currents off the asphalt. Six swallows. Seven. Booming thumps ricochet between brick buildings, a dark one-two with a hollow middle like a cave. Can sound waves alter the flight of birds? Tugging the leashes of scurrying people, all the dogs on their evening walks look worried. He pivots, fingering the cardboard manifesto, then steels himself for the dive and steps onto the Mall. The crowd mills about the public chalkboard, but Sid must take the risk of jostling among them. It's so easy once you do it, just prop the sign on the chalk tray at knee height, amidst all the other scrawled remarks. One last time, ceremoniously, he scans down the block letter words he'd scrawled just one short night ago:

BIG GROUPS OF DEMON GENERALS SAY THAT ITS EASY TO TALK DEMONS OUT OF HELL AS LONG AS THE DEMONS THINK A MAN IS A PASTOR OR "STEVE". I'M NOT A PASTOR. AND NOT A PROPHET. AND NOT STEVE. YOU CAN GET 6 MONTHS FOR ATTACKING PASTORS AND

THEY AREN'T STEVE ANYWAY. SEE HELL IS NOT IN THE MIDDLE. NOT NOWHERE. KNOW WHERE

Is this what he'd written? What was he trying to say? But someone is speaking to him. He half turns to a slump-shouldered wisp of a guy with scrawls of hair sketched onto a pimply jaw and wincing eyes that swim up out of some haze. He's posing a question. "Are you talkin' about the new album, man?"

Sid's head pivots back to the poster, then to the talker again. "New album."

"Yeah, "*Preachers and Generals*, man. You like it?"

"Like it?"

"I don't know. I kinda miss the old stuff, back when they were raw, you know?"

"I don't know."

"Well, you know what they say, the only thing constant is change, so get on the bus, right?"

"Right."

"Get on it!" The wispy guy attempts a handshake of some sort, his elbow cocked out to one side, wrist limp and fingers dangling for the swipe. Sid looks away, mumbling, "Get on it."

"Alright, then," the guy says with what looks like a comprehending smile and a nod towards the stage.

Is it possible that this is the man? Does he know Steve? He spoke of an album. Sid paces before the chalkboard, taking small pigeon-toed steps that trace a quadrangular pattern counterpoint to the paving bricks. As he rotates, he recites just under his breath the words on the cardboard sign. He leans into a police barrier, getting as close as he can to the music funneling up from the tight little stage at the bottom of the hill. It's a muddle, but occasionally a few distinct words bubble up from the instrumental soup, repeated and delivered in a drawling sing-song. He gets it on the third go-round. They're singing to him: "My father's one lesson, don't listen to generals. And when you go seekin', be careful of preachin' in general. There's angels and demons, and fires that are steamin', and songs that will lift you up high. However it seems, you best follow your dreams, and let all of them others go by."

Of course. They know. The whole crowd. And why wouldn't they? It's the last thing. Whatever comes now has already happened and everybody is in on it. There's no big secret. They just wouldn't say. He had thought it would come as a relief. That a signal would flash. What a fool he's been! Definitely gears are turning, definitely momentum builds, maybe the time is now. Give it up. Step back. Let if flow. But what do you do when it's done? If you stop it and it doesn't happen, then would it ever have?

FORTY-FIVE

OFFICER MOSBY – OBSERVATORY HILL

You PLANT a T-Wall best you can right down the middle of your skull and crouch there hoping it holds. But the old grizzly just paces on the other side, head bobbing and throwing slobber when it turns, shaggy shoulders low, eyes glowing for prey. Sniffing your location, calculating the angles, ready to hit the concrete like a lineman at a practice sled. You can't ignore it, but there is a way. It's the other thing the desert teaches. You can hug the filthy, kerosene-stinking sand with one mind while at the same time drifting high on a California cresting wave of time, stretching it out, booming towards the surf atop brilliantly splayed toes. He's never ridden a surfboard in his life, but boy can he ride that imaginary curl, hunkered down, all reflex and cupped in a watery palm.

High atop Observatory Hill, he tries to hold it there, shirt back sweaty against the patrol car's pleather seat with the window down and the radio crackling. He gazes down on the mesh of streetlights out past the cruiser's hood. The old trees up here decked out at their furthest reach of summer foliage, but already at the brink of the sap suck reversal that will kill off every leaf in the blink of a few weeks. Capping all that, a moonless swath of stars fuzzed out by a fat smear of Milky Way that runs like a ragged bandage across the sky. So lame compared to the splattered wealth of a night sky in the Provinces, on a cold late watch along a mountain pass. You'd lie there spread-eagled, weapon in the crux of an elbow, and backstroke it all night long until you could taste the spill of stars. And then when you sat up at the kick of a boot, your ears like satellite dishes, at that moment you could hear a sparrow piss a klick away. Never before or since.

But then Sid. Always Sid. Should never have left him alone. Back from the sandbox still in cammo and the house a hoarder's hovel. And Sid himself down to flab and bones, surviving on cereal and powdered milk he wasn't even bothering to mix with water. In clothes unwashed forever. Long off his meds, the hallway wall graffitied with math equations. He'd been wearing their father's shoes and leaving them in the kitchen, in the yard, wherever they fell off of him. Shoes two sizes too small. Said they were metrically correct or something. Amazing what can happen in a year, the house abandoned, screen door slapping, heat turned off, pipes busted, the bathroom rotted out from flooding, and Sid holed up in the garage, slaving away on an ancient pc at a rickety card table with one last ornery gecko, just crashing out on the floor or in the street. Took three days of searching to find him down by the river eating out of a dinted can of tuna fish at a homeless camp under the railroad bridge. He'd been crouched down there in the mud by himself near an old rope swing, in cargo shorts and one of their dad's plaid shirts, no socks, the battered remnants of the old man's Sunday brogues full of water, his hair a knotted tangle down past his shoulders and unshaved straggles of patchy beard sprouting in a paunchy, inscrutable face. Sid did recognize him, but with eyes that were strange and cold. Like he was up in some soaring airplane vacantly scanning the ground.

He'd stepped down the bank, reached down to grip his older brother's shoulder. Said, "Sid."

And he'd repeated, "Sid."

"I'm back."

"I'm back."

"Let's go home."

"Go home."

That could have been the moment right there. Could have ended it. But with that mutual surrender they were in it all over again. Which is why it replays like a rap riff, the exact way Sid almost delicately placed the half-eaten can of tuna on a tree stump, emitted a surprising old man's creaky-legged grunt as he stood, and climbed out of the shallows, water seeping out of the holes in the brogues. Walked two miles back to the house, ruined shoes squeaking, mincing sideways up the long inclined street just humming to himself, as if Mattie had never enlisted or gone away. Mattie beside him, marching like some kind of custodian, not even trying to straighten him out, just taking a step and pausing, then another all the way home.

When you look down on it from a hill, you realize that Charlottesville proper is a compact place, a bowl really, with one old road coming in from each cardinal point to make an X. A kid's drawing of a city. And Sid has traced every inch of it over the years, no doubt, and could be anywhere down there now. Not a word on the phone or the radio. And every cop in town drawing overtime tonight. The Mounties, too, and whatever they'd been after. But nothing, no word. Who knows, he might be sitting up here on a tree limb or something right now.

Mattie opens the cruiser door and patrols around the old observatory, not expecting to find anything, just clearing his head. It's an antique, made of red brick like everything else in town, and domed, of course. In his life, he's been inside these enormous heavy doors exactly once, with his Boy Scout troop.

Big empty room with a spindly telescope that reminded him of a robot praying mantis in a cage, its one prismed eye peering up through a slit in the dome. The boys in their khaki shorts had lined up to climb a ladder and squint at Jupiter, a ribboned ball with a dot like the bruise in a peach. The planet didn't move or anything. It could have just been something an artist painted on the lens. He remembers feeling trapped under the dome, an upside down bowl that echoed like a church. It had been a creepy experience all around, frankly, and all the boys felt it. Probably why they all broke free for that famous rock throwing battle in the woods downhill that got the troop disbanded the next week.

Sid had been the leader of that little rebellion, the role he always played in the day. Even as they'd scattered in the bushes, he'd named their war, marshaled his warriors, selected a boulder to be won. He was brilliant, a champion, and more fun than anybody else. The best and truest friend he's ever had. Mattie picks his way across the dark lawn, scrunching early fallen acorns like ball bearings into the moss, and returns to the lighted room of the squad car. The river is the one place he hasn't looked, the one place nobody will look. But how could you even get down there at this hour? At least it's something to do. He doesn't report where he's going. He's off the grid anyway. Rack lights off, slow and stealthy, he noses down the hill back into the starry sprinkle.

FORTY-SIX

THE CANNON'S – UP ON THE ROOF

EVERYTHING on the screen ripples a little in the mini-cam's shimmy, limning a tribal circle down in the tour bus, where a fiddler saws, a blurry face palms a harmonica, knees slap and people bounce, but silently amidst the oldies booming from the Pavilion speakers. The young surgeons in their huddle pay it no mind. Their perfectly manicured butcher's fingers twirl martini glasses by their stems, as they calculate how best to express their alpha male status to the ingénues in their summer shifts and stilettoed sandals. Lost to all that, Dr. Cannon stands among them, counting the faces in the dancing circle onscreen. Down there on that bus stands the movie star, not here on the roof where he belongs. The famous actor's mouth opens wide to the down-searching camera's gaze, and at his side leans the director, grinning that idiotic boyish grin, that guileless mask that says nothing of what he's thinking, offering assurance of what – some general "wow" at his luck, at the world's wonders, at the arty game he plays so well?

Without them this whole rooftop extravaganza is a waste of time. It was all for them, after all, most especially for the director and his promise of the film. He has the script, owns the rights, is moving chess pieces in place to launch a production. That's why he's here, of course, to see it himself, to savor the flavor, the local color that will seal the deal. The drama of those early gamma knife experiments, the kid from Poland brought back to sight, to speech, to life itself. And the delicious hook inside the plot, the African American surgeon who developed a genius practice atop a school built by slaves and still run, it must be said, by arrogant bigots. A Denzel vehicle if he's ever seen one.

Dr. Cannon swallows his cocktail in one gulp and pawns the empty off on one of the orthopods, then turns away from their scrum without a word. Iris had been right there, at his elbow, and yes that had been annoying. Is he a Macy's balloon? Does he need a tether? But then she disappeared somewhere amidst all the rabble who will want to shake his hand. Not a person on the roof of interest. So leave. Go down there. He will storm the bus and retrieve his guests if that is what it takes.

But first, there he stands, Beelzebub himself. The Prez. Could lift his saggy old carcass in its seersucker stripes and wing him off the roof like a rag doll. How he holds court there like the hub of a wheel around which all revolves. Not a rag doll at all. He is here, Cannon imagines, for one reason. To cement his point. To rub it in good. That point being, stay on the plantation or go. Build your own clinic out on the Bypass. See what that gets you. No field hands in my Pavilions.

And seeing him there, Cannon realizes how foolish his hope had been. Despite everything he's done. Over thirty years of wrangling, grant writing, philanthropy, hundreds of callow residents gone on to their own careers cracking spines and skulls across the globe, seeing the next trend, finding a way, even striving to carve some sort of research institute out of the red dirt down in the county? To practice out of a basement office where – he knows this has been a joke all these years – his people were brought for hospital care, no black faces above ground level? All that had been a fresh memory when he arrived, and the old bird would not let him forget it. Keep him there, where he belongs, and have him buckdance.

So the humiliation at half time, the set up just to be publicly renounced, that must have been delicious. Hateful old coot. Yet there is only one thing to do.

"Mr. President."

"Professor Cannon." Always Professor, never Doctor. Even in greeting so careful to exert ownership! And with just that salutation, how diabolical, the mighty surgeon finds himself tongue-tied, glaring down at the old scholar.

"Such an evening! And how charming this notion – to throw a party at a bus stop! We missed you today!"

Clearing his throat, Cannon replies, "On call. For whom the beep tolls, you know."

"Does one ever win relief from emergency?"

"Can happen. Not my style."

"No, and I'm sure we are all grateful for that." The pitted patrician nose sniffs the air, the President stretching to see past Cannon's bulk, as if to dismiss him. He has come to the event, has deigned to speak to its host, has allowed the slightest of pleasantries and is done with him already? Perhaps things are worse than he's imagined, but how can that be?

"Well, Professor, there is one thing." Cannon attempts a last drop from his empty glass, knowing he looks buffoonish in the attempt. A couple hundred friends and acquaintances mingle on the roof, strung lights twinkling above their heads, while whiny rock tunes skronk up from the speakers onstage. All of it, he realizes, no more substantial than that molecularly small drop of vodka evaporating on his tongue, all of it just one extended expression of his mistake, of his foolishness, in thinking anything could change.

"One thing. Yes?" Cannon asks.

"Well professor, do you twitter?"

"Do I what?"

"Well, neither do I, though I suppose it is worth a look these days, but, well, have you by any chance seen the photograph?"

It is all Dr. Cannon can do to work back across the day from the moment of his half-time humiliation. That moment is the one obsessive pivot, the explosion. All the rest just a coda without import. But.... He understands now why the President has been looking around. It isn't a look of dismissal at all. He's seeking an audience, doesn't want this next precious instant to go unseen or unremarked. Who would be the best conveyor of this tidbit after all? Ah, Iris, she has found them, has come as if on a charging steed to the scene. "Why President Burwell! Have you just arrived? Such an honor! Is there anything we can do?" One hand takes the old man's elbow, the other palm presses flat against his chest. It's a gesture of maidenly supplication with a little more pressure that conveys perhaps some sort of plea or threat, so that the President's tongue, caught up halfway through his career-changing pronouncement, flicks, mouth ajar and eyes popping in surprise.

"You must have that Manhattan we asked the barman to concoct especially in your honor! Just for you! An herbal shrub, hint of mint for the whiskey, you must try one! Come. Let me take you there. Now."

Cannon notes the president's wink that says, "I shall return. We are not done here." Iris glances back, her rouged lips twisted in a quick grimace that warns him to stay put, that this one is hers to manage. He watches them go, flashing on the near future, when the old man will dodder to the toilet led by an underpaid aide with a similar grip like iron. What was the president about to say? Certainly not an apology. He pivots back to the movie screen, all a blur of movement now. The little scrum has broken up and the band is on the move, headed to the stage with the self-importance of astronauts on a launch pad. And his guests, the Hollywood celebrities? Off-screen, disappeared, who knows where?

FORTY-SEVEN

SID – THE TOWER BREACHED

SID LIES flat on his belly on the railroad embankment, propping on his elbows to peer across the four pairs of evenly spaced rails that separate him from the tower's dark outline. Shambling bodies gather at the concrete legs, phone flashlights flickering and jabbing to music that pulses from somebody's portable speaker. Too late. The kids have arrived. No way to get past them now.

The embankment's gravel stabs at his bare chest and belly. He squirms as if to burrow into it, seeking the points that fit his elbows and knees like puzzle pieces. All summer, all night, people coming and going, stirring things up, some hefting themselves into the tower's base to smoke and drink and play loud music that plonks around the inside of the concrete cylinder like a pounded gong. Others content to muster outside, lighting campfires, throwing towels down, slamming fast-food burgers and beer. Later the trains will arrive, always after midnight, sneaking their dangerous natural gas and oil-filled tanks through town while the good people sleep, or rolling an obliter-ated mountain of coal in loaded-to-the-brim black cars lined up in a clanking procession, slow as the drip of molasses, as if a train could pass on tip toe. Sid stretches forward to rest the palm of one hand on the nearest rail. No hum, no hint of an approach, the worn and silvered steel waiting like him, its nerves taut, taffy-pulled, and nailed by spikes to the earth. That all day everyday vise-grip headache urges him on. He must get up to his niche at the top of the tower or all will be lost. But if they see. Nothing to do but dig in, seek the gravel's sharp pressure, attend to that, though every cell screams to jump up and run forward across the rails.

Mosquitoes light on his bare back and moist neck. He listens for their dentist drill hum at his ears, lies patient as they sip then seal their tap with a stinging drop of coagulant and wander off sated on the air. Important to give this up, to let them feast. They are animals, too, with a reason on this earth. The distraction helps him focus, keeps him still, allows him to briefly fight the desperate urge to take a mad run at the tower. Way out in the infinity lived between clock tics everything of interest plays out. If he can go there, deep into the cogwheels, and pause along the balanced works that run on forever locked in the pause before the hand of a watch does its ponderous click. In that gap you could drive a train through that nobody sees. In that room where atoms waltz and where stuff gets made and unmade.

It would happen tonight, this getting trapped outside. An ant on a leaf in a flood and that is all he has ever been. That is all anyone ever is really, of course, in the face of the implacable. But by the same token, none of this involves choice. You go where the leaf goes. And will go or not when the waterfall breaks. Which means waiting here is just as reasonable as anything else. Not moving as useful as moving. His eyes close in surrender to the sting of gravel and the drone of mosquitoes. Anchored with shallow breaths that give way one snort at a time to a more regular beat, steady and untortured, while the summer night spins towards the sun.

FORTY-EIGHT

CHLOE AND LUCAS – BACKSTAGE

Now that the band has climbed onstage, doing their show, it looks like not a whole lot of fun. Professionals. Milking it. Hitting their marks. Maybe it's just Lucas' achy black eye or the long day catching up to him, but all that stomping effort feels sad, a little boring even. The band sings a random playlist, careening between ballad and stomp, sometimes right in the middle of the same song. It's weird how, seen from the back, it's like a puppet show or something. It's the game you choose to ignore when you pay for a ticket. Ladders and pulleys. Strobes. Cords. Fuse boxes. This is not magic, it's just gear. He thinks, yes, I could totally do this.

He says, "Let's do something."

"You sure you're okay? There's a walk-in clinic, I'm sure, we can go."

"No come on, I'm good." He stands and Chloe climbs up beside him, then gives him a clinical look, a once over. Lucas stares right back, one-eyed. Maybe it's the smoke, but it's surprising to discover that maybe this is the first time he's ever actually taken a second to observe, rather than just marvel at, her face. That's what pulled him here, got him shot at. This chance to gaze. The time will come. He'll try to sketch the flare of her nose with its little silver ring at one nostril, will sing a song about her cupped chin. At his smile she leans just an inch or two forward to tap his nose with her own. And he grasps that this tic, this little nose tap, will be their signal to each other across the years. It's how they'll reconnect in that important deep way whenever they've been apart. They'll learn not to waste it, to use it judiciously on exactly the right occasions. Their secret handshake. But thinking like this is stupid. It's like the dumb love songs he's always goofed on. A joke that she could share this wonder.

FORTY-NINE

MRS. CANNON – ROOFTOP

As Iris steers the University's president over to the corner bar, she fears that her chance may already have passed. Her hand tugs at his elbow, her fingers seeking an inkling of any sort that might provide an advantage. In seconds, they will have reached the bar, he will have his Manhattan with its curl of blood orange rind, and the world will stop. The old man turns, drink in hand, discards the stir stick, bends in for a sip, and she leaps.

"Owlsley," she leans in, affecting a flutter of the eyelashes that conveys all at once a jigger of old-school flirt, a dollop of deference, and a dash of considered desperation. This last is real enough, but she must rein it in, maintain her composure, betray no wisp of plea in what she is about to say. Two words come to her, without forethought, "We understand."

The president – tasting the astringent cocktail, and appreci-ating the expert intermingling of sweet and bitter flavors – meets Iris' gaze and chooses to linger there. What is more beautiful, after all, than a frightened woman? No need to speak. Any word might break the spell.

"That's all," she says, for the first time releasing his elbow, her hand moving to rest atop his forearm. "We do understand." My God, he thinks, this remarkable woman is not cowed in the least. He has underestimated her, so easy to do with women, after all. As he has said so often over cognacs, if ever they do take over the world, heaven help us benighted males.

But his cocktail is delightful and cold, though neat, so he allows, "Yes, well, the selection was difficult, as I'm sure I don't need to tell you."

"Yes." Now she waits, poised and at ease, it seems.

"Your turn may come, I'm sure it will, of course."

She says nothing, eyes alert, but giving nothing back.

"The thing now, however, I'm afraid, well...." He takes another languid sip, assuming this caveat will throw her offstride. But she says nothing, waiting, one hand on his sleeve. And that is all it has taken, her perfect poise, to win his surrender. The cocktail might be life itself in liquid form, oh he will have another, indeed.

He says, "I believe we have all the images. That is, we do not have them. In these days of the Facebook, no one can own these things. What I mean is, we believe we have seen them all, have examined them. We have made our overtures to the student sites, to the news organs, to the city establishment, such as it is."

"I'm sorry, what?" Iris asks. "Images?"

"I think it may attain to our good fortune, and of course, something else might turn up, but I can say with some confidence tonight. And may I add that this has occupied me – and my staff, some came back from the beach for this -- on this already challenging day for many long hours when I might have preferred any other occupation." He says this with a wry, thin-lipped smile. Well, it is funny, really the whole farce has made his day, after all. "I think you will agree, that we have dodged a bullet, so to speak. We have learned that at half time of the game a man, entirely undressed, not a stitch on, as they say, of your husband's complexion and stature indeed walked the length of the Grounds. Buck naked, as it were."

Ah, this one got her! Delightful! Is it possible, wifey didn't know? How delicious! He turns to scan the crowd, hoping again for an audience. "Yes, well, for now, as far as we can tell, and of course anything could turn up at any time, but miraculously, not one of the photos or little movies from all those many cell-phones has yet distinguished or identified the man's face! It seems that he must have caught everyone by surprise, no one dared approach, he seems to have been striding at a clip, elbows out, you know. I mean, it couldn't have been, after all!"

But Iris' eyes have strayed, seeking out her wayward spouse somewhere in the crowd. In hospital, she knows, they call it crumping. Her lips tremble. He has her now and always will, as he must have expected.

"We are concerned, of course, about the incident with the city police."

Iris' gaze rockets back to his face as she realizes that, of course, as always, he knows everything, like some aging Zeus on his bosky hill gazing down at the city's teeming mortals. "There is video of the handheld variety, some quite close-in, I'm afraid. But the gentleman seems to have fallen onto his face, and the tree limbs, cedars run close to the ground you know, again seem to block the action, well in light of our situation, and again, something of a miracle, we don't know if any shot identifies! I'd be happy to show you." With his free hand, he fumbles in his suit pocket for a phone, but Iris' grip on his elbow has tightened, and he relents, relishing the tale. "We see the ambulance arrive, but then the onlookers are pushed back, cordoned off, there's this crowd of responders who turn the man over, he begins to thrash as they cart him into the ambulance. Just amazing, when you think of it."

Her eyes frankly plead now, though still she says nothing, a hard swallow her tell. "My dear, you say that you understand. And I need you to do that for me. To appreciate our situation. What has been required. What still may be required. Whatever may have transpired this afternoon, and no doubt this is just confounding. I mean, of course, you and Dr. Cannon were quite busy entertaining your cinema people. This has nothing to do with you. Nonsense, am I right? But our portfolio. It is not all board meetings and jug wine with first years, you know. So we must remain alert. But rest at ease. I mean. I can assure you, we value our team. We protect our own." With a wink that might as well be a gavel, he concludes, "You are safe with me."

Tears well in her eyes, but she will not blink them away, as the old king takes a long draught to congratulate himself on a rubber well played. In a single day, he has held onto the chairman Wall Street had so assiduously courted by playing to the vanity of a Pavilion placement, which after all cost the school nothing, assuaging the demands of the business school donors, and – imagine that he had considered this a problem! – once and for all pinned another restless rogue under his thumb. There will be no more shenanigans from this one. Broken at last, and by his own hand. Chivalry requires, of course, that he must linger with this poor ruined woman, but another cocktail, too.

FIFTY

OFFICER MOSBY – CAMP RIVANNA

WHAT HE OUGHT to do is go home, switch out the uniform for jeans and sneakers, and proceed. Show up at the homeless camp in full battle rattle, flashlight glaring, and people will just scatter, nobody will say a word. But he's on the clock, chief's orders, and already walking that thin line. With one duty: Stay out of trouble. The chief should have sent him home. But she knew how that would go. Everybody's mama, and not a bad C.O., actually. On your ass and got your six. So he turns around at the dead end bottom of the town, parking at a mill ruin made into a shaggy monster by kudzu. He kills the cruiser and steps out of the chill A.C. into the raucous call of a bramble thicket, switching on his headlamp to scan for an opening. There it is, a silvered line of froth running across the broken dam, backwash ripe as a sewer, and a dirt track leading down the bank.

He has no plan. He's running entirely on instinct now, anticipating yet another fail derived from one sad fact. Somehow despite all the years, he knows not one important thing about the only person of interest in his life. What he does. Where he goes. What he's up to. What he may think on his rambles. That mystery gone wrong between his ears. He knows the camp squats downstream, hard up against the railroad trestle, or at least it was there last time he'd checked. Who knows where its habitants might have gone, migrating from nowhere to nowhere?

Childhood memories down here, catching crawdads, seeking out the biggest ones in their burrowing swirls of silt, some as big as their hands. Sid would tip them with their insect-like legs and draggy fan tails into an old pan to see if they'd square off and fight. Which had never felt right to Mattie. Leave them to their diminished dinosaur world, to their shallows and hunts for scraps. But it was something to do, and Sid had his reasons and always a trick up his sleeve. Would name them. In the bulging depths of his cargo pockets would dig it out, as if he'd planned it since they left the house. Dab a dot of Mama's old fingernail polish on what he called the carapace, so they could seek them out another time. Oh look, that's old Garfield! There's Woodstock! Let's see what they're up to today! All those games he made the best. That Mattie would never have thought up on his own. Who knows, even now down here among the roots – how long does a crawdad live? – there might still be an old guy scurrying around, embarrassed by that dot of pink smeared on his back?

That was then. You gotta keep the history straight. Maybe it was what the doctors call it, and it's a good description, a break. Maybe it came on slow, or was always there, and when you're young and dumb you don't see it. What's the difference, though? It's sure as hell fucked now. Mattie clicks the headlamp beam to low, hoping not to scare anybody off. The river path is surprisingly open, well-traveled, a good sign that the camp's intact. Could almost follow it with no light at all. But you don't want to get caught coming in like a sneak either. Just show up, try to downplay the badge a little, and trust in a hunch.

The trestle looms like a black machine hanging in the sky, its limestone and mortar footing shaggy with ivy. The path comes to a dead stop there, then he finds it again snaking around the river side, and there's the camp, if that's what you'd call it, a few tarps and tents scattered up the hillside in the trees. If anybody had a fire or a light on, they've snuffed it now. Maybe heard him coming. Some kind of morse code signal of warning? Do these lost souls even give a shit about such a thing?

He scans what there is of an opening in the brush, sees a picnic table somebody must have hauled out of the dump or boosted from a backyard somewhere. Would have been a project to get it down here, but there it sits. With the camp set up around it, there's nowhere you can stand with a guarded back, and anybody in any of the lean-to's or tents has line of sight. So as much as it physically pains him to do so, Mattie switches off his flashlight, waits for his eyes to acclimate to the night, then makes his way to the table, where he plants himself facing the river, his whole back exposed to most of the camp, just to see – what the hell – what may happen.

There's rustling. The inhabitants are aware. They'd likely have him clocked just from the headlamp, always in their lives a beacon of oncoming woe. So if nobody has to move, nobody will. First mole out of the hole gets whacked. Nerve-wracking, though. What the VA shrink would call an "unplanned exposure." Make yourself a target and see what happens. Even the routine patrols were ass pucker insane, though. The Spam in a can convoys worked them the worst. Mattie's squad always preferred to go on foot. At least then an illusion of control. You don't waste an RPG round or a night's work burying an IED on a line of foot soldiers. At least that was the idea. But you never went out alone like this. Which was just as stupid really, since everyone knows that you're always alone to a bullet. A truth that comes home with you, too. But nobody here will play along. All sleepwalking, all zombies, dulled out to the meat we are.

It's the smell more than anything else. You don't get it often up in the town, maybe sometimes at one of those mega-service stations, where grilled burger wafts in with the gas and diesel fumes, a specific stench every vet avoids like the plague. And down here at the river, the molecules of swamp and sweat and shit spritzing along the river current. Which until now he has also avoided. Maybe that's his mistake. Maybe it's a place like this, off the beaten track, where a guy like Sid would go. Places with people like him, who talk to themselves and walk funny, can't shake hands or look you in the eye. Places that stink. So again, it's Mattie's own walls that have blocked him. Might as well have been jabbering in Sid-speak all this time.

How in hell did this happen, he thinks with a shock. Wired to the nines, every drop of sweat like a radar, and somebody, somehow, has closed to within maybe arm's length directly at his back. Without breaking a twig.

"So what do you make me?" the guy behind him asks.

That's not a Virginia accent, sort of an Ozarks twang, those banjo vowels, little bit of educated doctoring on the edges. Mattie tenses, imagines a superheroic leap, spin and draw, but plays it like the joe he is, not even turning his head. "I'm gonna take a wild leap, so to speak, and guess like Airborne?"

"Based on?"

Guttural, smoke-clotted and whiskey-aged.

"And Nam."

"Well."

"You fucks and your fraggin' ways."

"And you must be a desert rat."

"Your turn, baby killer."

"Now, now. Wouldn't say we own the franchise. I'm gonna go with Regular Army."

"Why's that?"

"Only such a dumb fuck would come back to be a cop."

273

"Roger that."

"See how it is?"

"Takes a dumb fuck to know one." At last, Mattie turns to face the guy. Maybe too big for Airborne. Red eye of a cigarette lighting a clean-shaven face. Could be the safari hat tipped up on his forehead that stretches him. But he's got shoulders, that rangy silhouette leaning back to blow a puff to the trees.

"So, Ossifer, what brings you down to Rivanna Estates on such a fine evening?"

Mattie's sorting through the homeless bums he's seen, lined up at the church side door and the shelter, the hundred or so regulars dispersed on a normal day across the city, and he thinks he's got a match. Guy with an attitude a little different from the others, looks like he could conceivably pull it together, fill out an application, sit for an interview. But arrogant in his squalor. Like he chose it or something, could snap his fingers tomorrow and take a private jet to the coast. The kind the regulars would take down a peg in a hurry. Except there's something, and then in the wave of the cigarette, he remembers. Dude he's thinking of is missing his hands. And now, looking closer, he knows it's him. Somehow holding a cigarette, with a little style, too, in a notch of wrist bone. What'd they call 'em back then, was it Charlie? Fuckin' Charlie.

"It's a joke, right? Ossifer?"

"I get it."

The guy half turns towards the river. "Not much of a crick, is it?"

"Guess not," Mattie says.

"I seen it bone dry before." The guy's too close. Mattie can't take his eyes off the cigarette, not so much held as balanced in the wrist notch. He can't help himself, blows a puff of air at it so it tumbles off sparking to the ground.

Calmly, as if he'd expected no different, the guy whispers, "Asshole."

The cigarette glows at his feet. Would be interesting to see how he'd manage to pick it up, but he doesn't even acknowledge it there.

"I'm lookin' for somebody," Mattie says.

"No shit. Figured you were down here spotlightin' deer."

"It's not an arrest. You know a police would never come down here like this at midnight by himself if this was anything."

"True dat."

"Dude."

"I'm a dude now."

Fuck it, a waste of time. If Sid was here, he'd be stumbling around making himself known. And except for this poor guy with no handles, the place is a tomb. "Okay, I'm out. Go back to whatever you bums do down here."

"Ditto, Asshole."

Mattie steps off the table, and standing upright compares how massive the guy really is. Could kick me down in a hurry, he figures.

"So he's off the leash, huh?" the man muses, head down-tilted now at the glimmering cigarette.

"What?"

"Guy you're lookin' for. You should take better care of him, y'know that, right?"

"What?"

"C'mon man. You fuckin' Americans. I could tell you more right now about your own blood kin than you could figure out in a hundred years. Comin' down here roustin' out some folks who never caused you a day of worry, fuck with my smoke. Asshole. And the whole time blind as an old bat, too."

"You know Sid?"

"Your brother, yeah I know Sid. Question being, do you?"

"Stop it. Tell me." Always tense going Army up against a guy so big.

"Pick up my cig. Asshole."

Fuck that. Mattie grinds the butt out with his toe.

"Oh man, that was so 5-0."

Mattie squares up, ready for it. "So this is the life, huh?"

The big guy takes a half-step back, just beyond arm's reach. Darker that way, harder to read a face in the river-silvered shadow. Mattie says, "Look, if you do know my brother, then you know he ain't right."

"That a doctor's opinion?"

"He goes off his meds."

"Don't we all?"

"I gotta find him. Tonight."

"On the city's clock."

"And this is a problem for you, tax payer?"

"You sand rats, you think you're all that, bad ass door kickers."

"Who said that?"

"Who the fuck cares? I know you, man. You got the walk. Shitload in your jockeys. Then stage-whispering, as if to himself, "Figure it out in your own good time."

This is a new notion to Mattie, who prides himself across endlessly circling patrols on knowing the street and its habitants, their patterns and seasons. That a homeless bum would be doing the same thing, looking right back at him, sniffing the wind. But it makes sense. You live on the roam, you need to know the territory. If you've got the sense to give a shit. It dawns on him that this is a job, too. But what isn't? And then this sad sack may be the one guy who may actually have paid any attention to the wanderings of his brother, who may have a clue.

"Look, I don't smoke. I'd give you another cig."

"I've got cigs."

"Light you one?"

"So now you're all Help a Crip Day, huh? Fuck you, man."

The guy waves a dismissive arm and steps down to the river. Mattie sees he's barefoot, toeing into the tepid current so the black water swirls at his ankles. The river reflects light from wherever, as if it's been stored from the daytime, so he can see the guy better. Strong calves exposed by the same many-pocketed cargo shorts Sid has taken to wearing, a polo shirt with a long tail, again like Sid. Safari hat cocked back. How's he shave like that? Would be something to see. Or he has a helper, maybe a lady. Silhouetted in the dark, dude could be Sid, or Sid's brother, more than me, he thinks.

The camp lies dank beneath the crickets' airplane hum, no blink or ripple of tarp, but Mattie senses them there, the lost souls up in their tents, aware of his presence, laying low. A bat wings in clicking beneath the foliage, veers off to nothing in the dark. The man with the answer has nudged down his shorts, and stands splay-legged, dribble-pissing in the river. Zero dark fuckin' thirty right here. It's like all the other times. You know he knows what he'll never say. It's not culture, or language, or fear. It's just bein' cussed ornery, owning the thing they can't take. In his day, didn't they throw 'em out of choppers?

"So, I'm gonna go with spec 4, am I right?" the guy says.

Communication. Hang in. Don't move. "Sergeant."

"Shit. That sucks."

"It did."

"Got you clocked, now, Sarge. It's all clear as day." The guy has edged his shorts back up with a funny kind of girlish shimmy and turns to face him from the river. Could be a rumpled old bear up on its hind legs. You can almost see his jaw working, but maybe it's just river flicker in the dark.

"You know it's bullshit, right? You couldn't a changed a thing. Impossible situation. Bad luck."

"Shit happens? Is that it? You don't know shit about it, so shut the fuck up."

"Oh yeah, I do. Know shit. And you know it, too."

Mattie's eyes wince shut. He's at the VA, in a blue room, and some pretty girl is asking every stone-cold killer in the circle to take a deep breath. He never does – fuck her – but just the image can help on occasion.

"I'm not your psychotherapist, Sarge. Could care less about your personal situation. But seriously, you don't want to fuck with me."

"This is bullshit."

"Fuckin' go then. Nobody asked you down here. Get lost."

How do you do this? How do you go a life with nubs at the end of your arms and still have the spunk to hold out like this guy's holding out against every lie and handout they've got? After, what? Forty years? How old is this dude, anyway? They're calling out across the river surface now, the moist air carrying their voices with an eery tone like tin can string telephones.

"He's my brother. I'm his only family."

"That sucks."

"Can." Mattie hates this, the old bum playing him, and decides to cut to the chase. "So you know my brother."

"Sid? Oh yeah, I know Sid."

"But you won't help me find him."

"Who says he's lost?"

"Fuck you, man. I'm out."

"Because important law enforcement engagements await you in Gotham City, Ossifer."

"Fuck off you old fuck."

"Come here."

"What?"

"Do this. Take off your clodhoppers and your skinny black

socks, set 'em down. And come here. I guarantee you, you'll be glad you did."

The guy could be a driftwood lump out there, planted in the swirl a good twenty yards from the bank. His voice arrives with a half-echo, like he's in a well. Fuckin' character. Mattie looks around at the bedraggled camp. Up in the tents, they'll be snickering. But he sits down at the table, pulls off his shoes and socks, and wades out into the muddy shallows, pants legs rolled up to his knees. How many years has it been, this thrill at the soles of his feet, and as kids we used to live down here. The guy waits, watching. Mattie follows the thread of a sand bar in his general direction, never more than ankle deep. He's out past the tree canopy, in a reach of star-flecked sky.

"Feels good, right?"

"What do you want?"

"Reach in my pocket."

"What?"

"This one, by my knee."

The cigs. Okay, whatever. At this point.

"It's okay, just reach in there, Sarge, it won't bite."

Up close, the guy has a weird lady's shampoo smell, with some acrid chemical whiff blended in. He's taut as a drum, waiting. Mattie shrugs, far gone in the hopelessness of his quest, the absurdity of this whole setup, but squares his feet and does as he's told, crouching a little to reach into the cargo pants pocket for the cigarettes. Comes up against something else entirely that his fingertips instantly identify, and pulls it out, dumbfounded. A Glock clip, heavy, loaded.

The old guy doesn't so much as move, standing there with his arms crossed at his chest. It's probably a calculated pose, one that hides what's missing, and it gives him sort of a Mr. Clean posture. He's even got the earring. Mattie takes an unsteady step back. One pants leg unfolds and the cuff dips into the water. It's all he can do to keep his balance in the wavering sand.

The guy says, "Stop. Take a breath. Sarge."

Mattie has never wanted to slug someone so badly in his life. With the clip in his fist, a good shot to the face might even take the guy down. Footing's bad, though. He holds that in reserve. It'll come when it's ready, and soon.

Arms still crossed, like he fashions himself some genie oracle or something, the guy speaks in a whispered, steady, instructive tone, "You're not going to ask me any questions. I'm going to just say this one thing. Your brother Sid was here, this very day. He had a Glock. I don't think he had a clue how to use it. That's the clip. You don't have to thank me. He left, came back, maybe five o'clock, left again. That's all I'm gonna say, so don't bother goin' all Gitmo on me. Instead of pumpin' those fists, you want to get out of this river and go find him. I don't know exactly what his plan is, and I'm not sure he could tell you either. But he's got one, I do believe that. You poor lost fuck."

FIFTY-ONE

CHLOE AND LUCAS – CITY POOL

"It's not my end of town, but we used to swim against them, when I was little," Chloe says. They've turned away from the concert with no more regret than switching a tv channel, leaving the lemming crowd to their hoots and sing-along lyrics. "If you're serious about it, we could try to sneak in a swim."

The musical hubbub dims with the darkness of the adjoining street, as if all the spotlights and speakers have been zoned off by a force field. They've straggled onto a different city entirely here, strung with salt box houses framed by rose-entwined fences and overhung by shaggy mimosas ripe with headily-perfumed hairy blossoms that glisten weirdly in any stray light. The city swimming pool hides behind a chain link fence forlornly lit by a flickering streetlight near a concrete block concession stand. Lucas sizes it up, uncommitted. "If we tipped that garbage can, we could go right over, if you're up for it."

They don't speak, working with what they imagine is Seal Team stealth, both grinning hugely in the dark, as they noisily drag over a heavy industrial-strength garbage can from the curb, and first Chloe then Lucas climbs atop it. The chain link is clipped and toothy on top, but Chloe easily lifts herself over one slim leg at a time, clamoring down the backside, cat burglar style. Lucas attempts a more acrobatic crossing and has to hang there for a few fretful seconds disentangling the baggy tennis shirt the weird guy with the ice had left for him. Then he just lets go and falls back, landing square on the seat of his pants. Chloe crouches beside him, hiding a laugh with both hands. They hunker down, listening, throwing long shadows, then scurry out of the light to the pool's edge.

Here at night, the rectangle of emerald water pulses like a living thing with thoughts and feelings and a come hither look. Lucas says, "Well, we're already perps. We're on premises." But they stand at the brink for a long time, it seems, the pool's rippled reflection playing a hypnotic wash across their bodies, those fingers of tickling light enticing a mutual shiver. Chloe grins, "If there's a guard or a cop."

"Or a camera."

"Then we're already busted."

"Yep."

Neither moves. Somehow the pool's gently gurgling filter has masked the other night sounds, enveloping this space in a bubble apart. It's funny to be shy, slipping off shorts and shirts, quickly tugging down undergarments, and sliding into the water's distortions as if the other couldn't see. They hang one-handed side-by-side at the raspy concrete lip, their chins dipped and eyes locked, waiting for an alarm or floodlight to catch them out, the water warm as a bath with a chill undercurrent snaking at their ankles. Then Chloe bunches and kicks off the wall, reaching in outstretch like an arrow along the surface, leaving an explosion that wets Lucas' face. This is hands down the most beautiful thing he's ever seen her do, and the only retort is to kick off himself and follow her out to the depths, flailing. She floats there on her back, chin upstretched, eyes closed, not even breathing hard. His legs trail, resisting flotation so that he has to kick a little, but as quietly as he can, hoping not to break her trance. If they are going to get caught, it will happen now. Though, of course, there could be some leering night guard in the shadows, getting his kicks, and planning to stop them on the way out.

Mid-pool, drifting imperceptibly towards the diving tank, it's just a cavelike tinkling trickle in the ears, a sense of heartbeat. The swollen ache of his wounded cheek dulls to a stiffening throb, and the sky does that thing Lucas has always loved in night-swimming back home, merging with his stroke, so it's easy to imagine soaring. Only the brightest of stars can pierce the streetlight's bleeding glare, but that only makes the sky more inky and dreamy and near. It was just a night ago that the bed for this view was a slanted slab of steel, rumbling up through mountain gaps. His thoughts echo the pool's thrumming cardiac plumbing. So worth it. So worth it. So much.

They reach to grab the ledge near the low diving board and swing themselves down to toe the wall, imagining themselves out of sight under the board. But why hide? As near as they can tell, they are alone. "Your head okay?" Chloe asks. "Wanna race?" This is just a raucous dare to whoever may be lurking in the shadows, both of them blasting away free style across the diving tank out towards the lane line ropes. Chloe's already done and hanging on a rope by the time Lucas churns to the finish line, then she's off again for the diving board, her first stroke taking her deep and silent and far. When Lucas gets back to the wall, she's directly under the low board, hushing him to wait and see if their explosion has awakened a guard. He whispers, "You're kinda good."

"You're a little choppy."

His jaw throbs, but he's determined not to use that as any excuse for getting skunked by a girl who swims like a seal, yet another brilliant thing she can do. They cling to the wall, catching their breath, and still the world only hums around them. Then, like toy magnets, their toes touch and suck them weightlessly together, each with one hand tethered to the wall. Soon Chloe lets go, and Lucas' guitar-calloused fingers are the only thing holding them up, scraping raw on the pebbled concrete.

When she reaches again for the wall, her legs still entwined with his, he laughs, "So that's how otters do it." She tucks her glistening head to his anchoring shoulder, and they let themselves hang together there. She says, "Think we could sleep like this?"

"Just floatin'."

"Yeah, and like this, too."

"Our invention."

"We'll be rich."

"Famous."

"Stars."

For a few minutes, they actually try it, both closing their eyes, nodding together, eventually letting the slow drift of the pool's circulation tug them a little apart. But it's impossible, and that comes for them both as a disappointment of sorts. Without a word, they clamor out to sit at pool's edge, feet dragging, the summer air warm as the pool, just a thinner fabric to wear.

"I feel kinda weird."

"Same."

Shy again, they pad around to their clothes, still piled at the shallow edge, slip them on, then find a lounge chair out of the streetlight, where they fit themselves side-by-side, their shapes hammocking its rubber slats, the chair's head tilted up uncomfortably, but neither caring to reset it. They could sleep here, let the morning come, maybe even slip out with a wink when the lifeguards arrive. They both seem to think this at the same time, so that Chloe's question is the same one Lucas has begun to wonder himself: "What should we do?"

"I'm good right here."

"In Charlottesville?" she asks.

"On this spot."

"No, really."

"You mean like?"

"Yeah."

"Oh that. Biggie," he sighs. Back in the spring when they'd first met, he'd run into a college dropout drummer with a garage loft where he'd crashed while they were busking on the Corner for that one crazy week, but that guy would be gone for sure.

"Do you want to stay?"

"I want to."

"Lucas."

"We're planning now."

"No. I mean, I live here. This is where I live."

"Yeah."

"You can't just sleep outside."

Down by the tree line, a sheen appears, followed by a hollow pop that echoes. Chloe sighs, "Fireworks."

They shift slightly to better see the sky, Lucas feeling relieved by the distraction. He asks, "Why tonight?"

"Labor Day? School starting? Maybe they even won the game? Sometimes it seems like they shoot off fireworks here every week. And then all the knuckleheads with cherry bombs and sparklers come out to join in."

They wait it out, though from their spot on the lounge chair they can't make out the explosions, only a dim splash of color and distant drumming. He kisses her nose. "It's for us."

"Charmer." She reaches up to just so very gently touch his bruised cheek. "Do you really have to go?"

There isn't any way he can explain how messed up it all is.

There isn't any way to start. His sister had said two days, two days only, and she will stroll right out the door when that's done. Their mother just a lump and a hank of hair, in that frayed pajama gown, nasal cannula trailing to a tank on the floor, useless hands gone plump and freckled on armrest trays like fish on ice. The huff, huff, huff, and cough. So hard to look into those blood-shot gray eyes always straining, drowning, trying to morse code blink those desperate things her tongue can't say.

"Chloe, I want to stay, I do, really. You don't know how much."

Chloe's thoughts swim back to her own room, its black walls and curtains and shag wigs, the box of fashion dolls shoved behind sneakers and Doc Martin's in the walk-in closet. It's the room of someone else entirely. Certainly not hers. Exactly what her mother had called it, a tomb.

"You can't go, Slip."

"I didn't come here to go."

"So."

"Do you stay out this late sometimes?"

"I have, yeah."

"For stuff like this?"

"The pool? Oh no. First time, for real."

"So this late, what do you do?"

"Whatever. By now stuff's closed. There's this lake, but they patrol it. So it's kinda like here, you'd have to sneak in. And the coal tower."

"That a bar?"

"That's a funny idea. No, it's just this old thing, it's like an old barn where they used to store coal or something. It's not far from here, down by the train tracks."

"You go there?"

"Sometimes it's a party. It's a place where people end up."

"Should we go?"

"Hold on."

Chloe shifts a little to pull out her phone and her face glows in its light while she flicks down her texts for a minute. Pretty much what she'd expected, Izzie and Ava checking in at each stop on their nightly rounds, razzing her for missing out. She'd promised to meet them at midnight. A couple voice mails from Joel that she deletes instantly without playing them. That is one persistent creep, she thinks. Then she says, "You know what? Let's not do that."

"It's that guy? I'd like to see him again, actually."

"I don't think so."

"No, I would."

"Slippy. Please. He's not worth your time."

She slides the phone back into her pocket and rests her head on Lucas' slim shoulder. The old weirdo's tennis shirt smells like mothballs and smoke. She says, "I loved that t-shirt, y'know."

"It was time. Whew, barf city."

"Yeah. Hey, you know, there is a place, kinda. There's this field, it's not much, it's weeds mostly but sometimes even a deer or two, I don't know, it's close."

"You know all these places."

"It's where I live is all."

"Did you plan this stuff?"

"You mean today? Seriously?"

"No, I guess. I just, maybe for tonight, just this next little while?"

"Me too. Let's just see. If there's anything to figure out, we'll see."

"Tomorrow or something."

"Yeah, then."

FIFTY-TWO

SID – THE COAL TOWER

IT EVEN SOUNDS LIKE VELCRO, each segment of flesh unpeeling itself from the embankment one gravel imprint at a time. His head dull as stone and sore along one gravel-scored cheek. The rest of him divoted, all along his front. He gets to his hands and knees, blinking himself back online. In the dream he rode in the vest pocket of a swaggering general, whose gleaming rows of chest badges winked a Christmas tree morse code as he strode out across a blinking rainbow to do battle with the night. The digital rain from *The Matrix* films scrolled behind his eyeballs, the spinning o's and 1's pausing in the maelstrom to spit out equations that both explained and obscured all things. It was the sweetest dream, so hard to let go, but something had thrown him out of it, some noise. Maybe just one mosquito's perfectly aimed incision, perhaps the Enemy itself, having allowed a tantalizing nightmare glimpse, one more hint at the brink.

It's enough to make his empty stomach retch, hands reaching out to grab and hold the rail. He wipes his mouth, looks around at the rows of steel ribbon that seem to absorb and radiate whatever there is of light, even sparkling in places. And across the embankment, the coal tower looms atop its stolid concrete legs. It sparkles, too, lights flickering up its face, fire roiling at its base, just as he'd imagined a million times. Reeling onto his feet now he stands entranced at the physics of it, finally seeing all those notebooks scrawled with equations made real. The gravel bed begrudges his step, crunching underfoot with a hollow sound, as if the planet's crust has thinned to cave. Splintered throwaway cross-ties float like driftwood on the slippery embankment. He trips onto one knee, but scrambles up, lurching across the rails, then lands on a dirt path soft as talcum where he pauses to take it all in.

The scene could be a rocket launch in a movie, searchlights playing along the gantry's base and up its side. But it's just the usual crowd of kids bunched around a bon fire, sweeping their phone app flashlights. And there on the exterior ladder to the roof, a few have found a way to make up the distance from the ground to its first untouchable rung. Maybe they'd crawled atop each other's backs? One has already climbed high, a silhouette bobbing ahead of the others. Sid gasps as the shadowy figure reaches the slanted roof, some kind of flashlight beaming from his head like a third eye. The flash scans up the skeletal sculpture of Sally Hemings. He grabs at its base to pull himself onto the rooftop, then tries to climb the statue. Another climber has reached the top, too, now, but this one hangs back, waving a phone screen flashlight along the precariously slanted roof, laughing down at the cowards on the ground. And there is just room for the third climber, who lingers on the rungs, urging the first one on, his eyes exactly level with Sid's secret slat door.

FIFTY-THREE

DR. CANNON – ROOFTOP

YOU WOULD THINK that the end of the outdoor concert might have taken the wind out of the party overlooking the Pavilion. But instead, the action redoubles in strength, as if it has sucked in all the energy from the emptying Mall and concentrated it within the few square yards of the bus station rooftop, where people stand packed together elbow-to-elbow, jiggling with the strobing lights and the beat of the rooftop d.j. who kicks in hard, having waited and waited for the concert to end. The rooftop even trembles a little underfoot at the weight of the crowd.

Dr. Cannon finds himself conveniently penned in near a corner bar, working two-fisted cocktails and pressed on all sides by straining drunkards at last call. The music that had been all hale-fellow-well-met stomping barnyard earnestness when pumped up from the live show has gone blippy and dreamy in the hands of the d.j. Standing a head taller than the crowd, the drunken neurosurgeon scans, always scanning, but cannot find the film maker, the actor, his wife, as time ticks on towards dawn with nothing done.

He breasts out into the waves for a better vantage, rotating slowly as he pushes along both to make his way through the bobbing dancers and to continue his search, arms held high to protect his drinks. He recognizes no one anymore. This is not his party at all, if it ever was. But there, in a corner by the elevator shaft, he thinks he sees one of the film director's attendants, still wearing that black shift, still thumbing her phone, somehow having carved by force of icy hauteur a breathing space from the tumult. If she is there, the director cannot be far off. He shifts his slow planetary rotation to counter-clockwise and tacks towards her, praying she will not slip away.

It's amazing, really. He pulls out of the dancing horde into an actual cave of space around the slim girl. It's the repulsor beam energy she emits, has perfected, keeping every importunate nobody exactly at arm's length. Resisting her force field, he leans in, as if to read her text, and shouts a little too loudly, he realizes, into one ear, "Good fun?"

She ignores him, maybe shifts her feet slightly, no doubt redoubling her psychic effort to repel all comers. He doubts that she remembers who he is. He asks, "Care to dance?"

She tilts her head, silently identifying her host without deigning eye contact. Calculating the necessity of some minimal response, she shrugs a narrow shoulder. Then, having made an additional calculation, she looks directly at him, holding him in her gaze, and speaks with exactly the necessary pitch and volume needed to convey each word of her message above the din. She says, "You know there is no project."

"Excuse me?"

"You were thinking that Mr. York had an interest in your book?"

"Um, he optioned it, yes, I believe that's what you call it. There is a treatment. I approved it."

The upturned curl at the edge of her thin lips might be a smile. She whispers, "Options."

"I'm sorry, what did you say?"

"You poor old fool."

"What?" He empties the dregs of both cocktails, then leans in close to her porcelain perfect chin, as if peering into the microscope back at the office that can all but show her thoughts.

There is something of the school marm in this one. Taking satisfaction in all the knowledge she holds that he has not yet grasped. It is all he can do not to take her bony arms in his fists and shake her. But her actorly pause has been intended for maximum effect, to set the stage for the dagger to come. "Your story, well, its shelf life. It's past it's due date, so to speak."

"What?"

"Oh, Doctor, please. You can't imagine. I mean, your whole thing with the gamma knife? It's so last century. Every community hospital in SoCal has gamma knife these days. Ten years ago, maybe, it might have been..."

"But, the story. The human interest. It was a bestseller. I mean, why are you, why is York here, if not for me?"

"I, too, have wondered that."

"Look, young lady, I don't even know your name or what you do, but I know this cannot be right."

"They all say that."

"Excuse me?"

"You know." She turns back to her phone and sniffs, "The losers."

FIFTY-FOUR

CHLOE AND LUCAS – THE DEER BED

To reach the field, Chloe leads Lucas around a propane depot stacked with rows of white tanks like sleeping elephants pressed up against an enclosing mesh fence. She fears it will kill the last of her battery, but in the deep blue darkness before dawn needs her phone's flashlight to guide their way along a tangle of brush that leads down to the river where she had waited with such anticipation just hours a lifetime ago. She tugs him on with one hand, panning the phone's flashlight in front of them. No particular spot matters more, but she wants cover for later, when the sun comes up.

It's not much of a field. By now, however, realtors would have carved it into plots for a half dozen shoulder-to-shoulder craftsman cottages if they could convince anybody to live in the squeeze between a compact industrial park and a train track. No doubt on the way, but until then, the field lies tossed with litter, overgrown with tall weeds and crossed by what might be deer trails. Chloe finds the spot she had scouted before, just a shallow dip in the terrain where you can lie curtained by browning weeds, look up at the lightening sky and pretend that everything manmade is very far away.

They unfurl stolen pool towels on the ground and plop down to flatten the weeds underneath. She switches off her phone's flashlight and glances one more time at the texts that have come pouring in even in the moments since she checked them at the pool. They all seem so programmed. She knows exactly what the next post will be and the next after that. Yet in the midst of all those weekend excursions, it has always seemed so spontaneous. What a joke. Everybody operating on remote control, on a conveyer belt, pushing the same buttons at the same time and ending up right where we started all over again. Ramen...tea...the alley behind the South Street brewery where a friend's uncle smuggles out growlers of beer...the one club that still takes fake I.D.s...the library steps where the skateboard potheads hang out ...Chaps for ice cream...out to *Impulse* when the d.j. comes on...and then, maybe the coal tower out there at the edge of the field and the dregs of night when people really get stupid. That's how she'd found this spot, wandering off from the tower to pee and falling asleep until well after sunup one night back in July. And this is where she's returned occasionally to gather her thoughts, send a wistful text south, sometimes toss her cookies, at the end of one more summer weekend in the nights before junior year.

She knows it's a mistake, that it's dangerous. That no girl should ever be out alone anywhere. She never leaves the safety of her gaggle of friends without flashing on that horrific image from the news, the one of buzzards huddled in trees behind a barn, gorged on a girl's dead flesh. But she walks away all by herself anyway. And because of that knows the river trail. And because of that has this scraggly cup of weeds at the edge of a sleeping city, the only spot she claims as entirely her own in the world. Where, as she had discovered just weeks ago, if you fall back and look up and feel the spin slow beneath you, then for a minute you can let it all go.

They lie side-by-side on their towels, exhausted. The word *rendezvous*. What a cool word. This is what she has imagined. This is what she has wanted so much. One whole real day with this person Lucas. So, of course, it has to end here at her private spot, a place she could share with only one other person, the train rider guy who got shot on his way to her.

Her head leans into his pointy shoulder. She whispers, "I've seen deer in here."

"In this field?"

"Yeah, they're nocturnal animals. I think this spot right here might be a place where they bed down during the day."

"That's cool. A deer bedroom."

"Just chillin' here, sleeping, waiting for the sun to go down."

"Have you seen 'em?"

"There was one night. I spaced out a little."

"You were here?'

"Yeah. But just me. It's always just me."

"You come here."

"Weird, huh? And they were just standing all around like they owned the place. So close. I could hear them breathing. Munching grass. They do this snorty thing sort of like a horse."

"So you're Goldilocks."

"What?"

"They were coming back to crash and you were in their bed?"

"I guess. Yes. Maybe this *is* their bed."

"We should wait."

"I don't know if they'll come back."

"It'll be cool."

"Be real still."

"Okay."

He whispers, "Come home, little Bambi, come home."

295

FIFTY-FIVE

OFFICER MOSBY – BACK ON THE MALL

THE GLOCK CARTRIDGE rests warm between his thighs as the police officer drives at patrol crawl out of the river bottom. He's as confused as he's ever been, wishing he'd clocked that asshole vet. Would have helped clear his head. But no hands. Not really any kind of fair fight. That image sends his head swimming out to a bad place. How does he wake up to those stumps every morning of his life? Somehow the guy knows Sid, yet couldn't or wouldn't offer any useful help. Except this cartridge that answers one of the day's dumb questions. No one's gonna come in and take a cop's gun right out from under his nose while he's sleeping. You'd have to be crazy. Ka-ching.

He noses the car to the top of the street and eases past the old courthouse and the turn for the police station. At the edge of the Downtown Mall, he wedges the cruiser onto the brick-lined pedestrian walkway between potted plants, and switches off the engine. It's late, or early, just a straggler or two down the Mall in the distance. For some reason, he thinks again of that stupid day at the V.A., sitting on plastic chairs in a circle among fat farts from last century conflicts, while the child therapist with the curly hair, so secure in the one thing she thought she knew, encouraged them all to breathe. There's an app for that, she'd said. He taps on his phone and there it is on the second screen, a little red balloon that expands and shrinks, again and again. The app's self-assured robot voice counts 1-2-3-4-5. Like we're too stupid to breathe. With the gun cartridge in one hand and the phone in the other, he seethes quietly, just for spite refusing that breath. But even for a man who cannot rest, fatigue occasionally wins a bout. His eyelids droop. In plain sight on the empty Mall, his patrol car displayed like a show room model under the streetlamps, Officer Mosby's chin falls to his chest at last.

FIFTY-SIX

MRS. CANNON – KITCHEN

IRIS STANDS BAREFOOT at the kitchen sink, squeezing oranges with a hand crank press. This is the time of day that she most loves, when no one else is awake, when the hallway clock tick-tocks distantly and the first rays of dawn awaken the horses in the barn. She had found Daughter Number One, had made sure she stayed at the party long enough to gather up the guests and drive them home in the Escalade. Iris had slipped cash to the bar manager, assuring that the last of the drunken attendees would leave in cabs or Ubers or whatever. Had gathered her blubbering husband and wrestled him down the block to the Porsche, had strapped him in and driven home, to leave him snoring in the tiny catcher's mitt of a passenger seat, his head lolling.

The director and the actor had gone off to the pool cottage, their assistants sharing the upstairs guest room. Claire back in her bedroom, which must seem so small and ordinary these days. At least this is where everyone initially decamped. But Daughter Number Two? She has left a string of phone messages for Chloe, has even deigned to text her, without a reply. Her door was unlocked, the bed disheveled, at last she'd found the note. So she's out with the girls. Two more days of this, the hell of a Sweet Sixteen summer, and she will be back in school. But the black walls, the black clothes, the poor girl's whole bleak outlook on life. What would it take, Iris wonders, to come back? To look around at her opportunities, to take the world on her tongue? Maybe this will be the year. Just to pull the buds out of her ears, say something, return a hug?

These morning preparations before the day's ride are hers alone, as close to prayer as anything she knows. But today, despite having held herself to a single gin and tonic, switching to soda and lime across the whole enervation of the evening, her head feels dull, crowded with unsorted worries that do not seem willing to wait for sunrise. There were successes amidst the madness. The local film committee seemed to like the Debra Winger idea. The super hero actor had even suggested he might return for a panel discussion. Rainie would pout, of course, about the Pavilion. He would fret and storm, but she knows her man, that this is just a temporary setback, a move in the chess game. He will find some other windmill to tilt at, and off he will ride on his mule. The film agenda will keep him busy for a few weeks while he mulls his opportunities. At the hospital the new surgical residents are just wrapping up orientation and will want to get their hands wet. There is that film script, if there is a script?

But those photographs. It was Rainie, no doubt about it. If no one else could tell, she could. The exact sag of his once magnificent rear, the slope of those mighty shoulders eroding at midlife like old mountains. Stark naked on the Lawn. And the nervous breakdown, you'd just have to call it that, with a chain saw? Oh dear. How long will it take to know? Will someone make the match? All those viral photos out on the web. This could be rough, much worse than the slimy old President had let on. What might it take to sort it all out? But the real thing, more to the point than all that. Rainie, dear, what's wrong, my friend, what's wrong?

Behind her the patio door clicks. He must have dragged himself out of the car. But when she turns, it is not the rumpled, dome-headed bear she expects, but a t-shirted boy in pressed jeans and a baseball cap. For a second, she flashes on the kid at the wine store, feels a surge in her chest at this impossibility, as the director stands with a quizzical grin and eyes like cameras taking in the cascade of feelings that roll in rapid cross-cuts across her face. He says, "I hadn't planned, it's silly, but do you think I could ride in these?"

"Oh heavens. Yes. You will come?" She had not imagined he would remember. She offers him a glass of orange juice still slightly effervescing. "Yes, I'm sure we can borrow The General, let me just call ahead to the barn."

"If it's any trouble...."

"Let me get you a riding hat. Believe we have one that may fit in the garage."

"You know, I've been thinking," the wizened boy muses, licking pulp from his lip, "there's this script."

"The one about my husband's work with the gamma knife."

"Yeah, there's that, but no, it's this other story."

"This what?"

"The plot, well, it's hard to pitch it, and I like that, it's a day, as it's written now, sort of like a drawing room drama or something, where this stockbroker just about goes bankrupt, and he's out on his yacht, and there's a board meeting, yadda yadda."

Iris leans in from the garage, wiping cobwebs out of a pair of helmets and trying to choose between them, one a huge bowl of some early plastic composite that Rainie had worn for the week he'd tried to ride back before the kids were born, and a smaller, much lighter one that used to fit, might still fit, Chloe. "You mean how the mighty have fallen kind of thing?"

"Well, maybe." The director's eyes sparkle. He sets down the empty tumbler so he can wave his hands, his grin infectious as always, a kid with an idea. This must be how he gets his movies made, she thinks, with brio no one can resist. "It's not right, the guy's boring, nobody cares about shysters in suits anymore, it's too New York, it's just."

"You've been thinking," she says, holding a helmet in either hand, waiting.

"See, you're doing it! That thing! That you've been doing all day! After that whole day you just had, you're making orange juice. You're making it happen. You're directing me!"

"I'm just standing here."

"I love that line. That line could win somebody an Oscar."

She hands him the smaller helmet, checks the kitchen clock behind his head. She really needs to call about his horse.

"We'll talk more, but I've been on the phone, I have a pair of writers, and we want you to consult, maybe co-write if you're interested. It's not about a stockbroker. It's not about a neurosurgeon, either, though I may want that, too, if I can swing it. The thing is, I just realized, it's about you!"

"Excuse me?"

"Iris. I want to do your day again. I want to watch how you make it all happen, how you pull it all together. I'm sorry, I know this is an imposition, but we're all so sick of Masters of the Universe and all that crap. We can talk more. I know we need to get to the stables. We can talk."

"Now, Rod, did you just say I *directed* you? Is that it?" She doesn't finish her sentence aloud, smiling as she thinks, you can pretend it's about somebody like me if you want. But in the end you're like every other man I know. In the end always it's really all about you.

FIFTY-SEVEN

SID – THE COAL TOWER

"This is some crazy shit!"

The three boys atop the coal tower have torn off the plywood door to Sid's cache, tossing the flap of wood over the edge, where it sails down onto the track close to where Sid stands. Other boys hang from the ladder now, all laughing and in on the joke. Flashlights aim upwards, throwing their figures into jabbing, elongated shadows up the tower face.

"There's all kinds of shit in here!" one calls down.

"Fuck, it's an arsenal! Damn!"

A crowd grows on the domed tower top, silhouettes dancing along the edge, and someone inside passes out rifles and a shotgun.

"Anybody know how to use these things?"

"Dude, it's like a skeet gun. It's easy."

"Like I shoot skeets."

"Well, paintball, dude."

"This ain't no paintball gun."

"True dat. This shit's loaded!"

"So could you point that way, you fuck?"

They're all laughing, talking at once, it's like Christmas

morning back in the day when Mattie and Sid and the cousins from Rochester would sit on the rug in the living room and tear freestyle into their presents. But this is anti-Christmas, and Sid understands that everything now is ruined. Maybe this is it, the way it goes down and nothing left to do. But despite the commotion, he's striding down the embankment towards the tower, drawn by a stiffening anger larger than his fear.

The first shot sounds like a firecracker.

"Damn, Skip, what the fuck!"

"Shootin' skeets, dumbass. It was a bat."

"Don't be shootin' shit up here!"

But a second boy takes aim at movement along the creek. Whang. A bullet sings off the track railing, throwing up a spark.

"Awesome! Try this!"

"Throw me down one, man! A pistol or somethin'."

The boys huddled on the tower dome pass a few weapons down the ladder to the ground, keeping the shiniest for themselves up top. "Damn, it's a stash, really! What is this place?"

Sid clears the high fence bordering the tracks and lands hard in the roadway, forcing himself to conduct a necessary clockwise spin that takes him into a bath of flashlight and the gaggle of people under the ladder. He wants to shout but words fight themselves in his throat so his only noise is a long groan as he pushes a girl aside and reaches for a dangling foot.

"Shit, who is this guy? Stop that shit, man, fuck!" The dangling foot catches Sid hard under the chin. He reels backwards, grabs for shirts and stays somehow on his feet. He lunges again for the climbing boy now out of reach. The box and rope he's always used as a step to the lower rung, where is it, what did they do with it, probably burned up in the bonfire sputtering under the tower. He leaps again, misses by a good two feet, emitting a futile grunt.

"Dude's like a zombie or some shit. Watch out, man."

The crowd backs away, making a semi-circle just out of his reach. The terror is upon them all but they cannot see. Only one last hope, he realizes, born heavy in a pocket of his cargo shorts. He fumbles with wild fingers at the button, gets it open, pulls out his brother's Glock, holding it by the barrel, and waves it in offering or threat, half-spinning again, feet stomping hard, improvising. A shell wings into his open mouth, splits his tongue and drills the base of his skull, clipping his spine on its way to a ricochet against the tower's concrete wall. Strings cut, the madly dancing marionette falls, sits down hard then tips sideways onto the cinders.

"Fuck! He was gonna kill us, man! Fuck!"

"Shit – we gotta go, c'mon, we gotta go!"

In seconds the tower base is all but empty, sneakers skittering on gravel up the path back to their cars. Up top, though, the party continues, half a dozen boys with guns aiming gladly at parked coal cars, distant flagpoles, any movement along the tree line. "This fuckin' 12-gauge has a kick, man!"

"What is this like a musket or some shit?"

"That's like D-Day, man, it's a carbine or something."

They can't figure some of the weapons out. It's dark and they don't know guns. Some are unloaded. But some are simple, there's even a six-shooter like on old cowboy movies with a latch cock and safety. It flies out of one boy's hand when he fires, nearly breaking his wrist. He sits moaning in a corner, his back against the sculpture's base, watching his comrades aim and fire, and marvels at the energy of his pals, at their spontaneity and humor, at the way on any night anything can happen, can turn up crazy fun.

FIFTY-EIGHT

CHLOE AND LUCAS – IN THE FIELD

SHE AWAKENS to the first light of dawn, somehow flashing on those smelly mornings at the stables in the old days, straw on the floor and the miles of green carpet unfolding all around. The world her mom loves. Lucas lies beside her on his towel, still sleeping, his bruised eye oozing a little. She touches his face gently, not wanting to wake him. But something's not right. The wound has grown, it's like the bruise has burst somehow, and up on her knees she scrabbles at blood all around his head, soaked deep in the towel beneath him. She grabs her phone, fumbles for the flashlight and shines it on his face. A little black circle on one side of his head, the other side puckered, cracked open. Is he even breathing? She stands up in the field and screams.

FIFTY-NINE

DR. CANNON – AT HOME

HE AWAKENS TO A MOSQUITO, whining insistently at his ear. Lifts a throbbing, monstrously aching head from the hard press of the car door to find sunlight oppressively glinting on the Porsche's black hood and a hazy chorus of songbirds mad with morning's glory in the shrubs. He's trapped in the passenger seat, his legs twisted up under the diminutive glove box, so he has to dump himself out on his hands when the door opens, dragging his body ingloriously onto the driveway.

Up on his feet, he reels a bit, top heavy. His head feels stuffed with gauze to bursting. Finds the walk, the kitchen door, the sink where he pulls out the spray hose and soaks his head, water dripping onto the cold slate floor. A towel. The phone on the wall. Where is everybody? He plops down on the floor, chair's too complicated, and punches in the number. Remembers the holiday, always on holidays, the chopper busy with wrecked cars out in the Valley, dumb ass partiers who miss mountain curves.

"Doctor Cannon, it's Winkerman." Winkerman? What's he doing back. Iceland, was it? "We need you and your team. Everyone. We're readying the cardiac suites for neurosurgery, we need them, too."

"Say what?" Since when does this spine butcher give me orders?

"Multiple shooting, here in town, we've got head wounds and little time. Neuro suites already full with the usual emergencies. Wouldn't have bothered you...."

"How many?"

"Two. One's an adolescent, we think. Don't know if they'll even make it up from ED, but they're wanting you in a hurry."

"Okay, Doctor. Two is not multiple, okay? We got this. Okay, call them all, even the newbies. They might as well see. Tell them 10 minutes max, and scrub. I'm out my door."

Dr. Cannon drops the phone. It's such a long way up the wall to hang it on the hook. Shakes his head and crawls back to the sink on all fours to pull himself to his feet. He swallows hard, goes to the refrigerator and pours himself a glass of filtered water. Grabs Tylenol and Ritalin from the cabinet and swallows a few. Adrenaline flushes up through his veins, beginning to clear his head. Scrubs will be waiting. Nothing to eat. Iris no doubt at the farm. Claire's probably shacked up in her room with that actor. The Hollywood crew, fuck 'em. The kitchen hums, just the hush of the air conditioner performing its brain stem function, maintaining the pun of homeostasis.

He finds spare keys in the china bowl by the cupboard, steps back out to the buzzing day and heads for the Porsche. Bullet wounds can be the simplest of surgeries, or the messiest and most hopeless. Winkerman, typically, has provided no hint. He punches the car phone to check back in, hoping to query the ED docs as he races up the drive. The morning breeze cools his bare skull and dappled light and shade tickles the avenue as he zooms along. The old Batman line, "I have to go to work." As long as people are people, as long as their longings overshoot their capacity. As long as the machines they use run out of control. As long as movies make people think they're adventure heroes, he'll have work to do.

You don't think about that. You don't go in by the waiting room door past the frantic parents. You don't look at the face they're about to peel down from the skull. You don't ever – he teaches his callow charges – allow sentiment to enter the theatre. Your dedication is to the work, to precision, to procedure over ingenuity, ogling the microscope, swimming microfine instruments in a shattered glop, that holy information network outrageously stitched in tissue and blood. We are God's plumbers, IT engineers in the innards of some poor guy's meat computer. But you must forget that and focus. Or get out, go be a neurologist, let 'em sob on your shoulder. That hoary quote: "Life is hard. Brain surgery is easy." Well, it's clean. It makes sense. Sometimes it even works. Like his mom always said, "Do your best and leave the rest." Let the devil sort 'em out.

SIXTY

HOSPITAL WAITING ROOM

IT'S JUST an alcove off the hallway hard up against the sealed double doors to the operating suite. Nothing like the balloon tents in the mountains, with plastic walls so thin you stood outside with a chaw and hunkered against the saw's whine. Somehow these plaster walls are worse, making it all seem organized. Because it's not. He's seen the mess. How the paramedics crouched on either side of his brother, laid out like a corpse, his legs sprawled and heavy feet splayed sideways from loose ankles. They were working at his shoulders, building a brace of stiff padding around his head. It was too much to look, so he found himself staring at Sid's knobby knees, reddened and pocked, and the hair of his long calves protesting this insult, catching the little breeze that comes for an instant on Summer dawns, trembling, almost sentient, alert to all they'd lost.

The missing Glock had not been touched, of course, and it lay where it fell by his hand, the paramedics careful not to disturb the scene any more than strictly necessary. But they'd seen it. He'd fought the urge to push them aside and take it, and fingers the smooth cartridge still in his pocket. All these other weapons scattered about beneath the tower, long rifles, a shotgun, an old Luger from World War II, and spent casings like spilled coins. What the hell? The chief had been out in the weeds, in that sad strip of no man's land that he knew so well, that had been to them as boys an African savannah, a western prairie, a field to run with kites. He watched her run, her gear belt jiggling, over to the other ambulance, its tracks leading straight out from the tower. It had run over another pile of guns hidden in the weeds, pressing their bent barrels into the coal-blemished soil, an old shotgun, maybe Old Man Tillman's?

Whatever was going on over there was not his lookout; maybe this one wasn't his anymore either. What was it that made his knees sink when they tipped Sid's body sideways for the backboard? He'd seen blood like that before, the way it caked down his back, more than you could imagine a person could sack around. There isn't any sense in it, he gets that. You don't tear off a calendar page and throw it out. The truth is that all your days together make a shuffled deck. Every card's in play always. It's like that game Sid had thought such a hoot, as if he'd invented it, and maybe he did – 52 card pickup. All time tossed aflutter in the air, and landing who knows where? Sid's limp body was too tall for the backboard, his feet spilling over the end. And it took a fireman to help the three paramedics lift him. So much like pallbearers. Mattie sat down hard on the sooty ground. Somebody helped him in a cruiser and drove him in behind the ambulance to the ER. They left his Glock where it lay, a placement pin through the trigger guard.

Now he's done with sitting. He pulls back a long drape at a picture window and gazes at a silhouette of Monticello Mountain in the distance, while a long line of train cars piled high with coal stretches out below. The waiting room's a smelly mess, with magazines on the floor, spilt food or puke splattered down the side of a trash can, and sodas half-drunk on the tables. Busy holiday weekend night. First game of the season. The UVA kids back in town. Too much liquor and too much stupidity. But now there's just one other forlorn soul left in the alcove. She's wandered in alone and crouches in a corner by a wall socket charging her phones. Long limbs and fingers, that supple adolescent girl skin, her ankles, though, like Sid's, mosquito-gnawed.

Mattie turns back to the window, focusing on just standing up, on taking it without thought or expectation or plan. Was there any one thing he could have done? Sid's whole life has been a mudslide, gradually and dramatically erasing the world around it. A torrent, an avalanche, a vortex. It's just like the war. Everything that you try to do, even with death tapping at your shoulder, is a waste if you don't understand what they're thinking, if you don't know their motives, the things they love and care about, if you only have your own notions of how to live to guide you. It all happens too fast. Nobody takes the time to sit down and make the effort to communicate. What an effort that would be. One thing he does understand. When this is over, he will be free at last, whatever that may mean. Or not and it will be worse, like everything else and always out of his hands.

SHE TOLD THEM NOTHING, except his first name. She told them the truth, though, because he had never told her his last name. And she decided not to say her own either, playing shell shocked, none of their business. Somehow she'd found the wherewithal to edge his phone from his shorts pocket, but it was dead, too, and she'd crouched there stunned, bending to his chest and the faint and erratic heartbeat, afraid to pretend some kind of mouth-to-mouth, there was so much blood. Like Mattie, she too found herself focusing on the victim's bare legs, and lightly fingered the little welts dotted along his calves. She heard the ambulances, how did they know? But they couldn't get to her, all stopped instead at the old coal tower in the distance, their lights flickering on its walls competing with the dawn glow. So she stood up and waved, the way a shipwreck victim might, jumped up and down, but her shout was just a squawk, and then she just took off and ran to them, shouting and waving, begging please sir please the way they do in movies. So they came.

That one guy on the paramedic crew, the driver, had said to stick with him, but he was creepy and once in the ER waiting room, where people milled and napped and moaned, it had been easy to slip away. She tapped on the gift shop window, and the nice lady there, peering out through a frosted door, had taken a deep breath and let her in, locking the door behind. So she could buy a charging cord with the little end that seemed to fit both phones. The lady seemed so nervous for some reason, and then Chloe noticed the brown blood streaked on her arms and on her shirt.

Neurosurgery. Shit, her dad's domain. The volunteer at the help desk handed her a stick'em badge and she went there. She saw wall phones. Maybe you could call out. But realized that she didn't know any numbers, not even the one at home. Or she could walk outside and hail a cab. A line of them waiting out on the street. Just go home or go to Izzy's, but then she would have to explain and the craziness of that seemed impossible. So she took the elevator to the OR waiting room where this cop stood looking out a picture window all BA. Had he been sent to watch her? He didn't even turn around.

"YOU OKAY, YOUNG LADY?"

"Wha?" She's sitting on the floor wedged into a corner by the phones, hugging her knees, and realizes she's been tasting one knee like a kiss the way kids do. The cop crouches, a little off to the side, not blocking her, but close and with red eyes crinkled in concern.

She asks, "Do you guys. Sir, do you guys sleep?" What kind of weird question is that, of course they sleep, they're just people, they're not cyborgs or something. She pulls her knees closer if that is even possible and rests her chin on the one still wet from her kiss. He's still there. He's not saying anything. Maybe he is a cyborg. She looks at his shirt to see if it lifts with a breath. As if he knows her thought, he inhales deeply once, the air exhaling through pursed lips that seem to signal hush.

"Are you okay? Do you need a phone?" He offers her an old flip phone from his gear belt. It sits like a toy car in his open beefy palm. He just holds it there for a while even after she's sort of shaken her head a little, like he's thinking she'll change her mind. If you don't know the numbers, what's the use? "Somethin' to eat?"

Is her head moving or not? She tries again to shake it side to side and feels like she's succeeded, because the policeman sort of nods, she thinks. Then his head tips sideways towards the double doors and he whispers, "You waitin'?" Why whisper, there's nobody around at all to eavesdrop. She gives him the duh look and he sort of robotically smiles the way grownups do when it's just their mouth that bends.

"If I scrounged up a Coke would you want one?" Her stomach flips at the thought, it's like her body is checking in, confused signals blinking. She lets her head fall back against the cradling corner of the wall, with what she hopes he'll see as dismissal. He gets it, but doesn't really leave. His knees pop loudly when he stands and then he takes a seat in the chair by the door, not the closest chair but the one next to it, allowing a space to stretch out her legs in the spot where he'd crouched, but he's still there, doing that parental thing where people think they have to watch over you.

It's weird, why did she plug in Lucas' phone first? But she did and holds it in her lap like a sleeping bird. It's such a guy phone in a bulgy old cammo patterned case, and he's magic markered outlines on the patterns, made them into faces and creatures. It's pretty beat up, too, the screen criss-crossed with scratches. Every scratch a secret, a mark of something that happened somewhere else in his world that she doesn't know at all. She ought to find a way. If she walked around, there'd be a nurse and she could just say her father's name and there'd be help. She can do that. She can do that any time. Maybe if more people come.

She hears another pop, the policeman cracking his knuckles when he stretches. It's like he's forgotten her, which is a good thing. The phone in her lap beeps, and when she looks down it glows awake in her lap. The apps almost mask some kind of blurred image. It takes a minute, turning it in her hand, but then she sees it's a photo of a kid's drawing of a daisy, with a petal missing from the two o'clock position, weird, and then it comes back to her, that's *her* ankle, that's from that one time last spring at the river, he'd used that magic marker to draw it there, but she'd never seen him take the picture. So way long ago. What was it? What happened there that day? What kind of horrible mistake had they made? When he climbed on the bus that evening, why didn't he just go?

It's not really charged yet, but plugged in it will work. She glances up and the cop is watching from the corner of his eye. No privacy ever anywhere. But she knows exactly how to work the code, not even a question, it's like everything else between them. Without even really thinking about it, she taps in the letters of her name, of course, and a flood of messages appear, scrolling down the screen. That's it. That's why he came back. And now she doesn't even care that she's snooping, it's the one thing, it's like she holds his heart in her hand or something. She randomly taps a voicemail, the volume cranked up too high, so she jumps a little when it squawks. The first thing, it's just the weird accent, deeply Southern, but rushed. It sounds like a woman talking fast as if she's afraid the phone will cut off, or maybe it's just that she's so angry, and for a second Chloe recoils, thinking she's the one being yelled at, but then she stops to replay it and listen for real.

"Listen, Smarty Pants." Smarty pants? "You get your stinky ass back in this house right now, 'cause I am one foot out the door and got no time for your triflin'. You said one day and that is long past, Buster Brown!" Buster Brown? "You think I won't go and leave her be? I got my bag. My feet stand on the stoop. You can call it a mercy killin' for all I care." There's a pause with heavy breathing, maybe a drag on a cigarette. "Look, scratch that, I never said that, forget them words. But you know what I'm sayin', you sorry assed fuck, now get home and I mean lickety split!"

It's the last one. Chloe taps another and it's the same voice from an hour earlier, sometime around dawn, back when she didn't know yet, and there's more from the whole night, even deep in the night like the crazy person on the other end never slept. When they were swimming at the pool. When they were at the concert. All that time down in another world there was this woman – his sister? – screaming across the cell towers. That's his world? What kind of world is that? For a minute, her thumb rests on the call back icon, the slightest additional pressure, just a nudge and it will register, the call will go through. She will know then. But she can't go there. No more than she can stand up and go find a nurse. Because everything is on pause right now, caught between two breaths, except behind those doors.

She drops the phone to her lap, burrowing her forehead into her knees, and realizes it's the salty flavor of his blood that she's been tasting. She runs her tongue along her forearm, as if it's a drip of ice cream, and stares back at the cop like a dare.

END

ABOUT THE AUTHOR

Tony Gentry is the author of a short story collection *Last Rites* and five young adult biographies (*Paul Laurence Dunbar, Jesse Owens, Dizzy Gillespie, Alice Walker*, and *Elvis Presley*). Poems have been widely published.

Tony works as an occupational therapy professor at Virginia Commonwealth University in Richmond. He holds degrees from Harvard College (BA), New York University (MA), and The University of Virginia (PhD). He lives in Bon Air, Virginia, with his wife Christine, also an occupational therapist, their two sons and their dog Buddy.

He keeps a prose and verse blog at tonygentry.com.

facebook.com/tonygentry61

twitter.com/tony_gentry

Made in the USA
Middletown, DE
26 September 2020

20289207R00194